D0050247

"*New York Times* bestselling author Paul S Kemp has officially barreled into dark fantasy with a quick wit, incomparable style, and an unabashed desire to portray the human psyche in all of its horrific and uplifting glory."

Pat Ferrara, Mania.com

"*The Hammer and the Blade* is a gritty, rollicking yarn that captures the essence of sword & sorcery adventure. A tale of lost treasures and lusty demons that Egil and Nix are sharing right now somewhere, bellied up to a tavern bar with Fafhrd and the Gray Mouser, Conan, and, of course, Kemp's own Erevis Cale."

James Lowder, bestselling author of Prince of Lies *and* Knight of the Black Rose

"This rollicking tale hooked me from the get-go. Told with zest and humor, this is everything that is good and golden about classic old-school fantasy yarns. It joins my precious bedside shelf of favorite re-reads, 'comfort food' books I turn to again and again. Egil and Nix might not be the safest guys to go adventuring with, but they're sure good company. I'll be waiting for a sequel. Impatiently."

Ed Greenwood, bestselling creator of Forgotten Realms

"[Kemp's] voice is very engaging, the characters came across as very believable and I want to know more about the world they inhabit."

SFFWorld.com

(6) 7/14KG

The HAMMER *and the* BLA

CH

"Most heroes work up to killing demo[illegible] Nix start there and pick up the pa[illegible] enough page-turning mayhem here to sate the most avid sword & sorcery fans, but the heart and strength of this story is a friendship that goes deep and rings true."

Elaine Cunningham, author of the Thorn Trilogy

"A fast-paced sword and sorcery adventure, with some great interpretations of classic fantasy tropes and themes. Highly recommended if you like your sword and sorcery no-holds-barred, dark, action-packed and with an insouciant sense of humour."

Civilian Reader

"One of the best fantasy authors writing today."

Fantasy Book Critic

"His name should be mentioned along with not only R.A. Salvatore, but also with such luminaries as Neil Gaiman, George R.R. Martin, Terry Pratchett, and Tad Williams. I recommend all works by Paul S. Kemp. His novels are a reminder that reading can be both entertainment and thought-provoking, all in the same breath."

Grasping for the Wind

"Swords and sorcery at its best. 5*****"

Stefan's Bookshelf

DISCARD
DEC 2012
Westminster Public Library
3705 W. 112th Ave.
Westminster, CO 80031
www.westminsterlibrary.org

"*The Hammer and the Blade* provides an enjoyable afternoon of reading (with more than a few twists to keep even long term readers' predictive powers satisfied). A likeable duo, some inspired action – what more can you want from a sword and sorcery novel?"
Drying Ink

"When things heat up. Kemp gives us sequences that wouldn't look out of place in an Indiana Jones film, with the undead and vengeful wraiths only proving to be half of the fun. There is always something happening and that's just what a 'Sword & Sorcery' novel needs to be all about. Kemp really delivers the goods on that score."
Graeme's Fantasy Book Review

"A fast-paced ride full of disturbing detail, gluttonous gore and fantastic fun. Egil and Nix may not be your traditional heroes, but these two men, as close as brothers serve to check the excesses of the other's personality. The ending was both fulfilling and disturbing, and I hope we get to revisit the adventures of Egil and Nix in the near future."
Lightsaber Rattling

Also by Paul S Kemp

THE SEMBIA SERIES

The Halls of Stormweather

Shadow's Witness

THE EREVIS CALE TRILOGY

Twilight Falling

Dawn of Night

Midnight's Mask

THE TWILIGHT WAR

Shadowbred

Shadowstorm

Shadowrealm

STAR WARS

Crosscurrent

Riptide

Deceived: A novel of the Old Republic

ANTHOLOGIES & COLLECTIONS

Ephemera

Realms of Shadow

Realms of Dragons

Realms of War

Sails and Sorcery

Horrors Beyond II

Worlds of Their Own

Eldritch Horrors: Dark Tales

PAUL S KEMP

The Hammer and the Blade

A Tale of Egil & Nix

ANGRY ROBOT
A member of the Osprey Group

Lace Market House,
54-56 High Pavement,
Nottingham,
NG1 1HW, UK

www.angryrobotbooks.com
All change

An Angry Robot paperback original 2012

Copyright © 2012 by Paul S Kemp
Cover art by Richard Jones of Artist Partners

Distributed in the United States by Random House, Inc., New York.

All rights reserved.

Angry Robot is a registered trademark and the Angry Robot icon a trademark of Angry Robot Ltd.

This is a work of fiction. Names, characters, places, and incidents are the products of the author's imagination or are used fictitiously. Any resemblance to actual events, locales, organizations or persons, living or dead, is entirely coincidental.

Sales of this book without a front cover may be unauthorized. If this book is coverless, it may have been reported to the publisher as "unsold and destroyed" and neither the author nor the publisher may have received payment for it.

ISBN 978-0-85766-245-3
eBook 978-0-85766-246-0

Printed in the United States of America

9 8 7 6 5 4 3 2 1

For Jen, Roarke, Riordan, and Lady D.
My guiding stars.

PROLOGUE

Nix studied the sanctum's door, a large slab of black metal featureless save for the narrow gash of a keyhole. Intricate stone reliefs of land lampreys and sand serpents – creatures deemed holy in ancient Afirion – lunged from the door's posts and lintel, the ropes of their serpentine bodies entwined in a chaotic swirl of fangs, bulging eyes, and implied violence. Afirion pictoglyphs covered the walls, the black, gold and turquoise ink telling the tale of Abn Thahl's life.

Nix put his hands on his hips and stared at the door as if he could will it open, like one of the mindmages of Oremal.

No luck. He frowned, looked over at Egil.

"No rust on a door more than six centuries old. Odd, not so?"

Egil sat on the floor with his back against the smooth sandstone wall, his twin hammers, both gore-splattered, lying on the stone floor to either side, his legs stretched out before him. Sweat collected in the fringe of black hair that ringed his head above the ears. Blood – but not his own – speckled his thick forearms.

"Odd, aye," the priest said, worrying at a wound in the tree trunk of his leg. The tattoo inked on his bald pate – an eye looking out from the center of a starburst, the symbol of Ebenor the Momentary God – stared at Nix while Egil looked down. "Can you open it?"

The question jabbed a finger in the eye of Nix's pride. He turned to face his friend, his own finger pointed like a loaded quarrel at the top of Egil's head.

"Perhaps one of the zombies struck the sense from your head? Can I open it? *I*? You may as well ask can a whore hump, or can a wizard dissemble. These are things intrinsic to their nature. Can I open it? Hmph."

"There you are," said Egil, ignoring Nix's tirade. He brandished a sliver of bloody obsidian he'd plucked from a small gash in his left thigh and squinted up at Nix, brown eyes all innocence. "You were saying something about a wizard humping locks?"

Nix crossed his arms over his chest and glared. "You heard what I said, whoreson."

"I heard," Egil said, with a long-suffering sigh and a weary nod. He held the sliver of stone close to the lantern for a better look. "Look at this. It's a piece of one of the zombies' blades."

Nix and Egil had pulped a score of the undead creatures – onetime temple guards animated to unlife by the wizard-king's sorcerers – on their way through Abn Thahl's tomb.

"You may have heard but you didn't reply, so let

me restate. Are you acquainted with a door I couldn't open? I press the question only to illustrate your soft-headedness, as demonstrated by a faulty memory. It's important that you understand your limits."

Egil tossed the sliver to the ground, tore a strip of cloth from his shirt, and pressed it to his leg wound. "There was that time in the Well of Farrago–"

Nix shook his head emphatically. "That was not a door."

Egil looked up, thick eyebrows raised. "It had hinges, a handle. It opened and closed. How can you say–"

"It was a hatch."

"A hatch?"

"Of course it was a *hatch,* and only a fool priest of the Momentary God would confuse a door with a hatch. A hatch is a different thing from a door. A hatch can be troublesome. You see? Does having an eye inked on your head make your other two blind, or otherwise detrimentally affect your cognition?"

They stared at each other for a long moment, the lantern light flickering over their faces.

"Well enough," Egil said at last. "It was a hatch."

"Now you're mocking me? I hear mockery."

"I'm not. I'm agreeing. I said it was a hatch." Egil stood, tested the leg, and seemed satisfied.

"I heard the words," Nix said, waving a hand as if to fend off a buzzing insect. "It's the tone that bothers."

Egil opened his mouth to speak but Nix held up a hand to stop him.

"Leave off. We both know the truth."

He turned back to the door, muttering, more determined than ever to get it open. He eyed it from different angles, examined the stonework around it. There were no hinges, so he surmised it opened with hidden counterweights. Holes bored into the pale stone above the lintel caught his eye. They'd been filled with plaster long ago. Perhaps sand had been poured into the chamber beyond after the door had been sealed? He'd seen such things before.

He went down on his belly, saw that the bottom of the door sat flush on the floor, sealed with a thick layer of tar or something similar.

That he'd never seen before, and it puzzled him.

Perhaps to prevent blades from being stuck under? But why?

"Maybe try to pick the lock?" Egil offered.

Nix answered with an obscene gesture.

Egil grinned, bending his wounded leg. "Your pride is too easily tweaked. And I make that point only to illustrate the fragility of your ego. It is, after all, important to understand your limits."

Nix stood and offered the obscene gesture with both hands.

"And so my claim is validated," Egil said. The priest took his yellowed ivory dice from the pocket of his trousers, shook them in his hand.

"Must you?" Nix asked, knowing the answer.

"Yes."

Nix reached out slowly toward the door, stopping

a finger's width from its surface. He waited, waited, and after a moment, the hairs on his forearms rose. He looked knowingly at Egil.

"You see? Warded."

"Well noticed," Egil said. "Your education at the Conclave wasn't wasted. Now what?"

"Now this," Nix said, and unslung his leather satchel of needful things.

Within the satchel he carried his tools, both precise and blunt, the enchanted items he'd acquired through purchase or theft, together with sheets of parchment, sticks of chalk, a vial of ink, quills, and anything else that seemed to him likely to be of use on an expedition. It also held his collection of keys, both mundane and enspelled.

"One of your gewgaws?" Egil asked. The priest stepped to his side, eyed first the door, then the contents of the satchel.

Nix rifled through his various keys – all of them purchased in the Low Bazaar or found on expeditions – until he found the one he wanted: a small brass beauty, with a thin tube for a blade and a beaten copper coin for a bow. He held it up for Egil to see.

"My gewgaws, as you so roughly call them, have saved us more than once."

"That's truth," Egil acceded. "But the odds of that key working in an Afirion tomb are about as good as finding a virgin in the *Slick Tunnel.*"

"Or, one might say, about as likely as finding a priest possessed of wit."

Egil chuckled. "Nice."

Nix smiled in return. "And this isn't an ordinary key. I purchased it in Dur Follin's bazaar from an agent of Kerfallen the Grey Mage. It opens wards, not doors."

"Hmm," said Egil, squinting at the key. "I pray it's so, though I credit the agents of wizards not at all." He bowed his bucket-sized head reverently, putting the eye of Ebenor squarely on Nix.

"Alas, I credit your prayers still less. Ebenor isn't called the Everlasting God, my friend. The Momentary God was divine for... a moment."

Egil's eyes moved off, grew distant as they did when he discussed his faith, when his thoughts turned to the events that had brought him to a life of religion. "Lives are made of moments, Nix. You know that."

Nix heard the seriousness in his friend's tone, but the door had left him irritated, so he did not tread as lightly as he ordinarily would.

"I do, but Ebenor's dead, so there are no more moments left to him. He can't hear prayers, my friend. And you're his only worshipper as far as I know."

Egil smiled through his beard and adjusted the mail shirt he wore. "That makes me high priest, not so?"

Nix already regretted his jab. "I guess it does. Pray, then, high priest. Can't hurt."

While Egil murmured a prayer in the coarse syllables of his native tongue, Nix spoke a word in the Language of Creation to awaken the magic of the key. When it warmed in his hand, he pointed the open end of the key's tube at the door, drew his punch dagger, and lightly tapped the key's end with its point.

The key vibrated, lightly at first, then more strongly, emitting a prolonged chime that would have done credit to the Great Clock of Ool, the sound reverberating through the large underground chamber, the echo replaying itself again and again. Loose sand misted down from the ceiling blocks.

The metal warmed between his fingers, and, as the sound faded away, grew hotter. Nix held on as long as he could then dropped it with a curse. It hit the floor, flared white, and melted into slag.

A wet slithering and high-pitched shriek spiked his adrenaline and jerked his head up. He caught a flash of one of the stone lampreys carved in the door jamb, now made flesh and as thick around as his forearm, lunging at him out of the stone, the black hole of its mouth ringed by a vicious sphincter of fangs.

He stumbled back, trying to brandish the punch dagger he still held, but he was too slow, and–

Egil snatched the creature out of the air in mid-lunge and slammed it to the ground. It writhed frenetically in his grasp, hissing, attempting to twist enough of its body free to latch its teeth onto his flesh. The priest pinned it with his boot.

"Your blade, Nix!"

Nix recovered himself, jerked his falchion free of its scabbard, and cleaved the lamprey in half. Its pieces squirmed for a moment, spurting stinking black ichor, before going still and reverting back into two chunks of stone.

"Fak," Nix cursed, his heart still racing. He sheathed the punch dagger.

Egil removed his boot from the creature's body and eyed Nix.

"You see?" the priest said, kicking one of the pieces of the creature across the sand-dusted floor. "Moments, Nix. Life and death are experienced in the moments. We just had one."

Nix thumped Egil on his huge shoulder. "Point taken. Thanks."

He took a moment to let his heart still, then held his palms before the door once again. He waited, but no longer felt the tingle of an active ward.

"The key dispelled the ward," he said.

"Bah!" Egil answered. "The key activated the ward. We could've done that ourselves."

"I blame your prayers."

"And I blame your 'magical' key. Perhaps a chat with Kerfallen's agent is in order when next we see him?"

"Agreed." Nix rubbed his nose thoughtfully. "Though, in fairness, it wasn't a very expensive key."

Egil chuckled, started rattling the dice in his hand once more.

Nix kneeled before the door. "Shine the lantern's light in the keyhole for me."

Egil pocketed his dice, held both of his hammers in one hand, and with the other angled their lantern so that its light reached into the key slot.

As Nix removed his precision tools from his satchel, he realized of a sudden that he didn't particularly care if they found the serpent idol within the sanctum. He and Egil had set off from Dur Follin after a three-day drink, in the midst of which they'd bought a "treasure" map from Crustus the blind cartographer. Crustus, in turn, had received the ancient yellowed vellum from a teamster who'd taken it as payment for passage from an Afirion nobleman fleeing dervish assassins. He and Egil had followed it on a drunken whim.

He held his pick poised before the slot. The moment felt portentous. He stopped and looked over his shoulder. "Remind me again what we're doing here, Egil."

Egil's bushy eyebrows rose to a precipitous height. "I'm standing here on a wounded leg. You're picking a lock. We're both overdue for beer."

"Don't be a bunghole. I mean, what are we doing? Here. Now."

"Here? Now? Are you daft? We're retrieving a serpent idol from the tomb of the wizard-king Abn Thahl."

Nix leaned back on his haunches, tapped his lockpick on his cheek. "Right, right, but why? I remember wenches and boasts and… not much else."

The observation seemed to flummox Egil. His brow furrowed, his cheeks darkened. He shifted on his booted feet. The light from the lantern cast crazy shadows on the stone wall. He ran a hand over his tufted scalp.

"I don't recall. I think... we were quite drunk and... I remember being in the *Slick Tunnel* but... I guess coin?" He looked up as if he'd had an epiphany. "The idol must be valuable, eh?"

"We've got enough coin stashed around Dur Follin to keep us in wine and whores until we're too old to appreciate the pleasure of either. Not to mention the markers we hold."

Egil tilted his head to accede the point. "True. So?"

"So, indeed, is the question." Nix studied his wire pick, thoughtful. He did not remember what they'd been thinking exactly. They'd dodged the Demon Wastes and taken ship across many leagues of the Gogon Ocean to reach Afirion, braved the desert, thirst, the traps, and undead guardians in the tomb for... what? Coin they didn't need?

Perhaps they'd done it so often in the past that they did it now with no forethought, no real purpose, automatons who went through the motions of their lives because they didn't know what else to do or why else to do it.

"We could go back," Nix said, looking up at the towering priest. "Right now."

Egil's expression twisted uncertainly behind the nest of his beard. He chewed the hairs of his mustache. "Why would we do that?"

"Why not? If life's made of moments, here's another one. Feels important. We could use it to leave."

Egil's dice came back out of his pocket, rattled in his palm, his habit when thinking or nervous.

"We could." The priest ran a hand over his bald head, poking Ebenor in the eye, his other habit when nervous or thinking. "But... we're already here. Be a waste to just... leave, wouldn't it?"

Nix supposed that made as much sense as anything. He nodded. "I suppose. We're here. Why leave a deed half-done?" He turned back to the door. "Hold the light steady."

Peering inside the keyhole, Nix found the lock less complicated than he expected. The ancient Afirions had been expert stonemasons but inexpert locksmiths. His wire pick, sawblade, and tumbler pry would have it open in a moment. He set to work and quickly had the lock primed.

"Ready yourself," he said to Egil. The dice disappeared and Egil hung the lantern from a protuberance in the mural-splashed wall. The big priest filled each of his fists with the haft of a hammer.

Nix released the final tumbler and heard the satisfying click of an opening lock, a sound that always felt to him like... opportunity. Nothing pleased him more save the opening of a fetching girl's thighs.

He bounded back to stand beside Egil, holding his falchion and hand axe.

Somewhere within the walls, pulleys squealed, the sound like a scream. Counterweights descended and the door started to lift, metal shrieking against stone. Immediately liquid poured out from the widening crack and an acrid, eye-watering stink filled the air. All in a rush Nix knew he'd missed it.

Everything came together for him but too late – the holes in the wall where something had been poured behind the door, the unusual metal of the door itself, the tarred seal.

"Off the floor, Egil! Off!"

Nix jumped up, his boots already warming from the touch of the liquid, and grabbed hold of one of the lampreys carved into the lintel. He braced his feet on a sand serpent carved into the left post, praying to Aster that they did not animate.

Egil must have heard the alarm in Nix's tone for he responded quickly. Too big to perch on the door jamb, he put both hammers head down on the ground and, holding the hafts, went feet over head in a handstand, and just in time.

The initial slow rush of black liquid from under the door gave way to a gush of fluid as the door opened wider. The fluid bubbled as it dissolved stone, filling the air with black, stinging smoke. Nix put his face in his sleeve to shield his nose and mouth against the stench. Egil, unable to do anything but hold himself upright, had to endure it.

The acid popped as it ate at the surface of the floor and the heads of Egil's hammers. Had they been standing on the floor, the substance would already have eaten through their boots and started dissolving flesh. Tiny droplets from popping bubbles hit Egil's bare forearms, burned pink pinholes into the hairy flesh. The priest grunted at the pain, the stinging reek.

"Egil?"

The lucky dice Egil carried with him on every expedition slipped from his pocket and fell into the acid, asp eyes up. The ivory pyramids cracked, shattered, and dissolved. Egil loosed a stream of expletives cut short when he inhaled the smoke and started to splutter. The coughing upset his balance and he swayed.

"Nix!" he gasped between coughs.

Nix adjusted his weight, steadied himself on three points, and reached out and back to grab Egil by the ankle.

"Got you."

They hung there over the acid, two friends and adventurers, one balanced precariously on his melting hammers, the other hanging on the wall in a desperate three-point perch. The whole affair struck Nix as hilarious, but he swallowed his laughter lest a guffaw dislodge him from the wall and kill them both.

"Here's a moment, yeah?" Nix said through gritted teeth.

"Shut up."

"I hope you bought better hammers than usual," Nix said, watching the metal of the weapons smoke and crack.

"Do not make me laugh," Egil said. "I'll pull us both down."

"I'd let you go before that. But I'd mourn you, rest assured. For a few moments, at least."

The acid, spreading thin across the floor of the chamber, soon bubbled less, smoked less. In a few more moments the popping ceased altogether and the smoke diminished, crowding close to the high ceiling in a stinking yellow-black cloud. Nix gave it another sixty count, then said:

"That's it. It's inert."

"You're certain?"

"As certain as I was about the magic key," Nix said.

"Shite," Egil answered.

Nix chuckled as he released Egil's ankle, hopped off the wall, and landed in the thin layer of black liquid that coated the now-pitted floor.

"See?"

Egil lowered his feet to the ground and stood. "Pits, man!" He covered one nostril and blew snot from the other, each in turn, then hocked and spit.

The hallway behind the now open door was barely a hallway at all, being only a few hand spans deep and there blocked by another door, of similar make to the one they'd just opened. The walls, too, were made of the same odd metal as the doors.

"You see what they did here?" said Nix appreciatively. "They sealed this compartment and poured acid in through the holes above the door. Time spared us, I suspect. The acid must have been wizard-made to last this long. It was probably much stronger once. Your hammers probably wouldn't have lasted had we entered this tomb a century ago."

Egil eyed his hammers, the metal heads pitted and discolored, the prayers he'd engraved on the metal effaced.

"Time didn't spare us, Nix. You did."

Nix colored under his friend's praise. "You've done the same for me many times."

"Nevertheless."

Nix put a hand on Egil's shoulder, moved past him, and studied the second door. He sensed no ward, no bottom seal, no holes, no sign of any traps at all. And the lock appeared similar to the one he'd just picked.

"It's like the other. A simple lock to charm."

"Do it, then," Egil said.

Nix looked back. "You're certain? We just got a second chance. We could still walk away."

Egil shook his head, the set of his jaw hard under his thick beard. "This tomb and its idiot wizard-king owe me hammers and owe you boots." He eyed his pitted, discolored weapons and shook his head in disgust. "Give me your crowbar. These'll crack on the first skull they mean to split."

Nix took an iron crowbar from his satchel. Egil took it and tossed the hammers back into the darkness behind them. He took the lantern from its perch and aimed its light into the keyhole.

"Let's see what there's to see," Egil said.

Nix had the lock picked in under a fifty count. Counterweights descended, metal ground against stone, and the door began to rise.

The lantern light illuminated a domed, circular chamber beyond the door, the perimeter of the floor scored with deep, straight grooves. Statues of Abn Thahl stood at the compass points, the largest at due north. The statues featured the sand serpent and lamprey motifs favored by the Afirions, scaled forms coiling around the wizard-king's graven image. Painted images of still more serpents, lampreys, and even toothfish decorated the plastered walls, together with more pictoglyphs telling the story of Abn Thahl's life and rule. Fangs were everywhere in the imagery. Abn Thahl stood in the midst of the teeth and scales, unharmed, ruling not only men but the toothy creatures of the desert and sea, unleashing them on towns in great slithering waves to secure his rule. Some images had Abn Thahl with a serpent's head or a scaled body. Nix doubted the images were mere artistic license. He flashed back to his aborted education at Dur Follin's Conclave, to Professor Einz's droning voice as he lectured on magical history.

The Afirion wizard-kings were transmuters and summoners of accomplishment, routinely modifying their own forms, and commanding the spirits and creatures of the otherworld, with a particular affinity for the denizens of Hell.

"Nix?" Egil said. "You here?"

"Here," Nix said, shaking his head to dislodge the memory.

Abn Thahl's stone, gold-chased sarcophagus sat in the exact center of the chamber, the lid carved in his likeness. A large, irregular pit marred the floor before the sarcophagus, like a fanged mouth open in a scream. Atop the sarcophagus, glittering in the lantern light, stood the only treasure visible in the room: the golden, bejeweled idol of the sand serpent.

It was small enough to fit in a hand, but exquisitely made. Its ruby eyes and intricately crafted scales glittered in the lantern light. It was said to have been Abn Thahl's prized possession in life, a gift given him by his wife.

Right away Egil stepped into the room, and for the second time Nix recognized danger a moment too late. He grabbed for Egil's arm but the priest had already crossed into the chamber.

The carved lines in the floor flared orange and a flash made their shape plain, a shape Nix had recognized a moment too late – a summoning triangle.

Professor Einz would have excoriated Nix for missing so obvious a symbol.

A rumble sounded from deep under the earth, a vibration Nix felt in his bones, a shaking that put an ache in his teeth, stood the hair on the back of his neck on end.

"A summoning triangle," Nix said. "Godsdammit."

Egil hefted the crowbar and planted his feet. "Bah. It'll make things interesting."

A voice boomed in the chamber, deep and commanding, a five hundred year old echo of Abn Thahl, the words held in abeyance by the dead wizard-king's conditional magic, waiting only until tomb robbers broke the border of the summoning triangle.

"Vik-Thyss!" Abn Thahl's voice shouted in Ancient Afirion, the word profane, ominous. "Return and take those souls of these grave robbers!"

A sudden breeze gusted up from the pit near the

sarcophagus, carrying the charnel reek of a graveyard, the faint tang of dry, reptilian stink.

"Shite," said Nix, as Egil set down the lantern.

A lamprey squirmed over the edge of the pit, larger than Nix had ever seen, its body as thick around as a man's waist, its heavy form thumping wetly against the floor. Intelligent black eyes stared over the fanged sphincter of its mouth. A second lamprey appeared beside the first and then...

Nix swallowed in a throat gone dry as an enormous, scaled, misshapen form lurched up, and Nix realized with horror that the lampreys were attached to the form at the shoulders.

They were its arms.

"What devil is this?" Egil said, raising his crowbar and taking a step back despite himself.

The devil pulled the rest of its girth from the pit and stood heavily on the floor. The wrongness of its appearance put stinging bile in the back of Nix's throat. Foul fluid glistened on its scaled form. It stood on two legs as thick as temple columns. Muscles pulsed under the deep green scales of its torso. But where it should have had a neck, it instead had an enormous, tooth-lined hole that opened directly into its torso. Vertical slits in its chest, under the mouth, exhaled wetly. Its lamprey-arms writhed, the motion hypnotic, grotesque.

"It's a devil, indeed," said Nix, recovering his wits. He'd seen illustrated guides to Hell's Eleven Pits. He knew a diabolical form when he saw it. He noted the grotesque organ hanging from between the creature's thighs. "And not a she-devil, we can be sure."

The eyes of one of the lampreys focused on Nix, the others on Egil. The fang-lined mouths opened and closed, ichor dripping. The mouth in the creature's center opened in a prolonged snarl of hate.

"That idol is to be mine, fiend," said Egil, and brandished the crowbar. "Now climb back into your pit ere I and Ebenor give you this to feed on."

The creature shrieked and bounded toward Egil, its movement surprisingly rapid despite its size and shambling gait. Nix had two throwing daggers in hand and gone before the devil had taken three steps. Both hit the creature and bounced off its scales. It barely seemed to notice.

It lashed its arms at Egil, the teeth snapping. The priest held his ground and swung the crowbar two-handed at one of the onrushing arms. It connected with a dull thud across the lamprey's mouth. Teeth and dark ichor sprayed. The other arm caught Egil in the side so hard it nearly folded him in half. The impact drove the priest to the ground and sent him sliding across the floor. He dug the crowbar into the floor to stop his slide, the friction spraying sparks.

The devil lurched toward the prone priest, arms writhing, teeth snapping.

Nix rushed toward it from the side, throwing his hand axe as he did. The weapon hit the devil squarely in the midsection and again bounced off the scales. The devil roared with anger and Nix ducked under a backhand strike from the lamprey arm, darted in close, and swung his falchion two-handed at the abomination's thigh.

He might as well have struck stone. His blade rang off the creature's scales and the jarring impact numbed his arms. The devil kicked him in the chest and sent him flying across the chamber. He hit the ground in a heap, the breath knocked from him, unsure if he'd broken any ribs.

The ground vibrated with the devil's heavy tread as the creature left off Egil and charged toward Nix. Nix rode adrenaline to his feet, wincing from the pain in his sternum. He parried the attack of one of the lampreys, his arms tingling from the force of the blow. He ducked under a blow from the other lamprey and unleashed a flurry of overhand slashes and cross-strikes. His weapon struck home often, but his blade would not bite the creature's flesh. A blow to his head nearly knocked him senseless and he just ducked under the sucking fangs of the lamprey.

Egil's sharp whistle drew his attention. The priest had scaled the largest statue of Abn Thahl and stood on its shoulder, beside the wizard-king's regal visage and sand serpent headdress.

"Bring it to me!" he shouted in Urgan, his native tongue.

Nix didn't know Egil's plan and didn't need to. He feinted an overhand slash with his falchion, causing the devil to hesitate briefly, and sprinted to his left across the chamber.

"There!" Egil said, pointing with the crowbar at the ground before the statue. "Right there!"

The slurping, snapping teeth of the lampreys sounded loud in Nix's ears. The heavy stomp off the devil's pursuit was right behind him. He expected the bite of one of those arms at any moment, but he proved the faster and made it before the statue.

"Now what?" he shouted.

"Turn and face it!"

"What?"

He had no choice. The devil was upon him, arms flailing, teeth snapping. Nix ducked, spun, leaped, his blade a whistling blur as he tried to keep the devil's attacks at bay and hold his ground. His blade hit home once, twice, but did little damage. A lamprey closed on his shoulder, tore through his shirt, and seized his bicep. Only his boiled leather jack spared his arm. The bite tore loose a chunk of leather but only scraped his skin. The creature withdrew, spat the leather to the floor, and snapped at him again. He dove aside, came up swinging but missing.

"Do what you're going to do!" he shouted in Urgan.

Another rumble sounded and Nix feared a second devil emerging from the pit.

"Get clear!" he heard Egil shout, and looked up to see the large statue of Abn Thahl falling toward him and the devil. Egil was astride it, riding it down, crowbar in hand.

Nix rolled to the side as the statue toppled and Egil jumped clear just before impact. Abn Thahl fell with a wet crunch atop the devil, and the pitch and volume of its pained scream caused Nix to wince.

Egil appeared over Nix, favoring a leg, huge hand extended, and pulled him to his feet. Nix checked his shoulder – a few teeth punctures – and felt his ribs – no breaks so far as he could tell.

Egil winced with each breath and the side of his face was already swelling. He'd not be able to see out of his right eye by the end of the day. Yet he smiled anyway. Blood stained his teeth.

"I may need to keep one of these to hand from now on," he said, brandishing the crowbar. "Quite useful."

"Aye."

Behind them, the devil moaned, stirred under the crush of stone. Its large central mouth, open in a pained groan, expelled a stink that turned Nix's stomach. Its wet breathing sounded like a sodden forge bellows. Abn Thahl's stone eyes stared mournfully out of the pile at Egil and Nix.

Egil spit a mouthful of blood. "Still living, eh? Tough bastard. Help me, Nix."

The priest went to Abn Thahl's sarcophagus, took the idol from its top, and put it in his belt pouch without a second look. Nix knew they could turn that idol into thousands of gold royals back in Dur Follin.

Egil worked the crowbar under the lid of the sarcophagus and levered it loose. Plaster seals audibly snapped. The stink of rot filled the air.

Behind them, the devil exhaled a pained groan and

stirred under the ruin. A block of the statue rolled off of it and fell with a crash to the floor.

They slid the lid off to the side to reveal the corpse of Abn Thahl, his desiccated body dressed in the gold grave-goods of one of the wizard-kings of Afirion – a serpent crown, a beaten gold breastplate, a ring of turquoise, a necklace of pearl, a sea of triangular gold coins to pay his way through the afterlife. In his hand, he held an ivory wand capped with a pearl.

Nix showed the dead no more reverence than he showed the living. He snapped off two of the wizard-king's fingers as he took the turquoise ring and pried loose the wand.

"The wand for me and the ring for some lucky lass."

The priest pocketed a fistful of the gold coins, more out of principle than need. He eyed the wand skeptically. "Is it enspelled? What does it do?"

"Indeed it is enspelled. I can feel that. And I don't know yet what it does." He winked and placed the wand in his satchel. "But finding out's the fun."

"You and your gewgaws," Egil said, shaking his head. He nodded at the lid of the sarcophagus, then back at the devil. "The fiend still looks hungry, no? Let's give him a wizard-king to eat."

Sweating and grunting, the two adventurers lifted the sarcophagus's lid and carried it across the chamber. Egil positioned them a few paces from the open mouth of the still-breathing devil.

"I think it will die without aid," Nix said, noticing the shallower breathing. "Maybe we should just leave it?"

"Where's the fun in that?" Egil said. "Do you want to be able to say that we slew a devil in Abn Thahl's tomb, or that we left one to rot under a pile of stone?"

"A fair point," Nix said.

"Good. Ready? One, two, three!"

Holding the lid, they staggered as fast as they could toward the fiend. Nix released his end right before the devil's mouth, and, with a grunt and shout, Egil drove the lid half its length into the creature's gullet, shattering teeth and crushing flesh and whatever organs devils possessed.

With that, the devil moved no more.

"Done is done," Egil said.

"Truth," Nix said.

Together, the friends limped out of the tomb, out of the dark, with their prize and their lives. They passed the acid trap they'd barely escaped, the scythe blade trap they'd foiled, the stinking, now-rotting corpses of the undead guards they'd destroyed on their way in. They glanced on walls decorated with pictoglyphs. Nix couldn't read most of them but those he could were curses promising a dark death to any who dared defile the tomb of the mighty Abn Thahl.

So much for that.

To Nix, events seemed to have happened long ago, to someone else, not within the last hour to him. He felt apart from himself, oddly distant. Beside him, Egil bore the idol they'd won and eyed it from time to time as they walked.

"Now that we have it," Egil said, eyeing the exquisite figurine, "it hardly seems worth all the fuss."

Ahead, they saw the entry shaft to the tomb. Beams of light from the desert sun outside put a bright circle on the polished stone floor. An ocean of dust floated in the glow. So, too, did their rope, their way out. Before they reached it Nix turned to face his friend.

"I think maybe it's time to stop. What say you?"

"Stop what?"

"Stop this. Tomb robbing. Traipsing across Ellerth for this and that."

"You think?"

Nix nodded. "I think."

Egil stared at him for a long moment. He looked as if he might protest, but then his shoulders sagged and he relented.

"Agreed. That was close and to no good end. If we'd died here, who'd know? Who'd care?"

"Mamabird, I suppose," Nix said thoughtfully, thinking of the woman who'd fostered him as a child. "No other."

Somber, they said nothing more as they walked the rest of the way to the rope. Before climbing, Egil took one last, long look at the idol, then at Nix.

"Maybe I should toss it?"

"Maybe you should," Nix agreed.

Egil looked at the idol one last time, sighed, and reared back to throw. But before he loosed, Nix, struck with an idea, grabbed his arm.

"Wait!"

Egil kept his arm cocked. "Wait? If we're done, then let's be done with all of it."

Nix smiled. "We are done, my large friend. But we're going to need that."

"Again, why?"

"Because we're going to use it and the rest of our coin to buy the *Slick Tunnel.* We know it's burdened with several liens."

Egil looked skeptical.

"Think about it," insisted Nix. "We clear the lien, become property owners, then later, who knows? Maybe a seat on the Merchants' Council in Dur Follin? Respectability. A voice in the city. No more tombs. Lives of ease."

Egil pulled on his beard. "Respectability seems an ill fit."

"A fair point, I concede. Still..."

Slowly Egil lowered his arm. Nix could see that the priest wasn't in full agreement, but he only needed Egil to come halfway now. He'd come along fully later, as always.

"Let's get out of here," Egil said, and returned the idol to his pouch. "I need beer."

Nix nodded, and with that, they both began to climb back into the world. Nix felt lighter by half.

CHAPTER ONE

Rakon strode the halls of the manse, worry tearing a ragged edge on his emotions. The few servants who were allowed in this part of the dilapidated manse must have heard his approach and scurried out of his path, for he saw none. Floors creaked under his tread. Dust misted the air. He climbed the circular staircase of the manse's western tower until he reached the thick wooden door of his summoning chamber. He spoke the infernal words that suspended the protective wards, opened the door, and walked through into the room beyond.

The roof on the corner of the house had been removed generations ago to expose the room to the elements, lay it bare to the sky and the lines of the world's power. The bare beams looked like ribs, as if the house were decomposing, though Rakon's sorcery preserved the wood and tile and plaster from rot.

A waxing, gibbous Minnear peeked over the horizon line, casting the world in viridian. Kulven, the larger pale moon, managed only a waning crescent high above. Stars and planets winked in the vault of the sky, their relative locations a map of time and place to those, like Rakon, who knew how to read them. And they told him the Thin Veil was near. When Minnear turned full, the walls between worlds would be at their weakest.

And still no herald.

He looked to the sky-behind-the-sky and found Hell, a distant, blinking red dot in the central eye of the secret constellation, Vakros the Feeder. He stared at it in worry for a long while. The Pact would fail if not consummated during the Thin Veil. And he could not allow it to fail.

On the wood-planked floor at his feet, inlaid lines of lead formed glyphs of power, the symbols with which he did his work: a thaumaturgic triangle, a pentacle, a source-oval for elementals, a binding circle. He walked over the arcana, heedless in his worry.

In the center of the round chamber stood a stairway, supported by elaborate scaffolding. Thirteen stairs led up to a raised octagonal platform, atop which sat a simple metal lectern, rusted from exposure to the rain. He ascended the stairs, speaking in Infernal the number of each stair as he stepped over its riser. The recitation gathered energy to his locus. The wind picked up, gusted.

He stepped to the lectern, took a candle and a stick of incense from a compartment beneath it. The incense, made from the mottled brown leaves of the flesh flowers of Hell, felt greasy in his fingers.

A word of power and a minor cantrip ignited the candle, though he held the incense in reserve. He incanted the thirty-nine verses of an abjuration, a demand of the King of the Air to send him a sylph, a spirit of the air who trucked in the information carried by the winds of the world.

The wind swirled around him in response to his incantation, collecting his words and carrying them to the outer reaches of Ellerth, to the pillars that held the world aloft in the vault of night. The King of the Air would heed the call, backed as it was by the Pact with the Thyss.

He ended his incantation, waited, and soon the wind gusted more strongly, buffeted his robes, his hair. The candle flame flickered and danced, but his power kept it lit. Behind the wind's rush, he heard the faint titter of an invisible spirit.

"The King has heard your call and sent me for answer," said a high-pitched voice.

"You are fortunate, then," Rakon said, and held the flesh flower incense aloft.

The sylph gave a greedy gasp. The wind keened.

"You know what this is, then?" Rakon asked.

"Burn it," said the sylph, excitement in its tone, the winds swirling. "Let me taste its aroma."

"Only after I've had truth from you."

"Truth you shall have, Rakon Norristru. Ask! Ask!"

"The Thin Veil is upon us and no herald has arrived from Hell to prepare the way for Vik-Thyss. Why?"

The wind died to a breeze and the sylph's voice fell to a whisper.

"Vik-Thyss? Vik-Thyss is dead. His death has been in the wind for many days."

Surprise stole Rakon's speech. Finally, he stuttered, "You… you promised truth, sylph! This–"

"Is truth! I swear it! Vik-Thyss is dead, or so say the Afirion winds. Now burn it!"

"Silence," Rakon said, and tried to control his beating heart. He clutched at the lectern in a white-knuckled grasp. Vik-Thyss's death put the Pact at risk. And if the Pact failed…

In his mind's eye, he saw the family's power foundering, saw House Norristru losing what wealth it still possessed, its seat on the Merchants' Council. He saw himself losing his position as Adjunct to the Lord Mayor, saw his many enemies emboldened, coming for him. He had ordered murders over the years, many murders. He had bound spirits and elementals, destroyed some. Absent the Pact with House Thyss, he would be quickly dead and his house annihilated. His own sorcery would not be enough to preserve them.

"How did this happen?"

"I don't know," the sylph answered, and Rakon heard the truth in it.

"Find out," Rakon said. "Now."

He needed to know if one of his enemies was moving against him by trying to destroy the alliance with Hell.

The sylph keened with frustration, swirled around the incense, and was gone.

Rakon remained on the platform, the air still, but his thoughts chaotic. Vik-Thyss had sired Norristru offspring for centuries. The matings had consummated the Pact and provided heirs to both the Norristru and the Thyss. Without Vik-Thyss…

He looked off to the east, toward the city that housed his many enemies. The Norristru manse was built atop a tall escarpment, and from that lofty perch looked down on Dur Follin's crumbling walls from more than half a league away. The moonlight afforded him a clear view.

The city straddled both sides of the wide, torpid River Meander. The glowing dots of the city's street lamps blinked at him like fireflies. The temple domes of Orella, the narrow spires of the Lord Mayor's extravagant palace, and the great water clock of Mad Ool jutted into the night sky, their height unusual among the otherwise one- and two-story patchwork decrepitude of Dur Follin's urbanscape.

Minnear's light reigned viridian over the city. Barges and scows clustered along the city's countless piers, torches and lanterns glowing on their decks. Above all towered the Archbridge, an ancient stone expanse that stretched across the river, linking Dur Follin's two halves, the origin of its construction lost to the ages. Only Ool's clock compared. Master masons made pilgrimages across Ellerth to see the Archbridge.

Orange and green pyrotechnics exploded in the air off the side of the bridge, some nameless cult celebrating this or that, the whistles and pops audible even at a distance. Scores of churchless cults and apostate philosophers held worship on the Archbridge, littering its length with the detritus of belief. The monumental size of the bridge, its awe-inspiring construction, seemed to draw the faithful. Common parlance called it the Road to the Heavenly Spheres.

The pyrotechnics left a fading afterimage in the sky, a few puffs of smoke, the ghost of a celebration. A westerly wind blew, brought with it the faint stink of the Deadmire, the expansive, ruin-haunted swamp south of the city.

Rakon eyed the city for a long while, the maze of its buildings and politics a puzzle for him to solve. His mind moved through the faces of the men and women who'd kill him if they had the chance. He realized quickly that they'd become too many to count. They blurred in his thoughts into one collective countenance of hateful vengeance.

A sudden thought gave him pause. Might the Lord Mayor himself have moved against Rakon? Could Rakon's mind-numbing spells on the Mayor have weakened enough to allow the fat fool independent thought?

Before he could chase the thought further, the wind picked up and the sylph's voice gave him a start. "There are corpses in the breeze. The Deadmire is awash in bodies. Ancient bodies and old memories."

Rakon glared at the empty place in the air from which the voice had originated. "Tell me what you've learned."

"An ancient breeze in Afirion had the tale of the devil's death. Vik-Thyss was slain by Egil Verren of Ebenor and Nix Fall of no god, whose names are known on earth, in the air, and to the knowledgeable in Hell."

Rakon knew the names too, though only vaguely. He'd heard them in tavern tales and gossip, along with many other such rogues, adventurers, and tomb robbers who sometimes called Dur Follin home.

"Continue. Were they hired to kill Vik-Thyss? If so, by whom?"

"I think not. They killed Vik-Thyss while robbing the tomb of Abn Thahl. They triggered a binding even older than the Pact you hope to preserve, a binding that summoned Vik-Thyss, whom they subsequently slew."

At that Rakon felt some measure of relief. Vik-Thyss's death had been chance, not the result of the machinations of his enemies. He could still salvage the situation if he could find a way to honor the Pact before Minnear waxed to full and Kulven waned new.

"I need another true son of House Thyss," he muttered, more to himself than to the sylph.

"Indeed you do," the sylph said, tittering. "One of the half-breeds born in this house, perhaps?"

Rakon made a dismissive gesture. "A *true* son of the Thyss. Not a cambion. Name the other Thyss sons, sylph. There's where preservation lies."

A soughing wind, then, "House Thyss is empty of males."

"What? That... cannot be. You lie!"

"I spoke truth, Rakon Norristru." The spirit giggled. "The air around you stinks of terror. Do you fear for your life?"

Rakon swung his hand through the air, a futile gesture that only summoned more giggles from the sylph. He reined his emotions and replayed all he knew, considered with care the sylph's exact phrasings. The spirits of the air enjoyed toying with sorcerers.

House Thyss is empty of males.

"The incense, Rakon Norristru!" the sylph entreated.

House Thyss is empty of males.

The answer was right there.

"You said House Thyss is empty of males. But do any Thyss sons live elsewhere?"

The wind blew and the sylph giggled. "I am caught!"

Rakon glared at the empty sky. "Speak, sylph! Tell me all you know."

"Abrak-Thyss, brother to Vik-Thyss, was imprisoned on Ellerth long ago, summoned by the Great Ward. He is not dead. But neither is he free. He is the only true son of the Thyss that still lives."

Rakon grabbed at the words, his hope renewed. "Imprisoned where, precisely?"

"What matter? He knows nothing of your Pact. It was made long after his imprisonment."

"He'll honor it, sylph. His blood requires it. Now tell me, where is he?"

"Alas," the sylph sighed. "There are no winds old enough to tell the specifics of Abrak-Thyss's fate. I hear only echoes in the wind and I've told you all they say. I don't know the location of his prison."

Rakon raised a fist. "If you are lying, sylph–"

"I promised truth, Rakon Norristru, and truth you've had, though bent to my amusement for a moment. Now, burn the incense as you promised."

Rakon figured he'd learned all there was to learn from the sylph. He'd keep his bargain. He always kept his bargains.

"Very well."

Absently he put the candle's flame to the stick of incense. Foul, thick smoke spiraled into the air, collected in a cloud around the sylph. For a moment, Rakon glimpsed an outline of the sylph's current form in the smoke: a large sphere covered in hundreds of thin tendrils, flailing in the smoke.

"I may need to speak with you again, sylph," he said. "Answer when I call."

The sylph, lost in the odor of the incense, made no answer, but the breeze hummed with delight.

Rakon left the sylph to its ecstasy, turned and descended the stairway, heavier with worries than he'd been when he ascended them. He tried to focus his mind on what he must do. He would pore over the tomes in his library, consult with every spirit in the spheres, and discover the location of Abrak-Thyss's prison. Knowledge of it had to exist somewhere. He'd find it and do whatever was necessary to preserve the Pact.

He had fifteen days.

He hurried through the dusty halls of the manse, the floors creaking under his feet. Years of filth stained the faded, peeling paint and cracked plaster. Trappings of the family's once-great wealth decorated the hall, the foyer, the library – lush tapestries, sculpture, thick carpets from Vathar – but the age of it struck him now, all of it old, tattered, tarnished. The house had fallen far, its wealth spent on tithes to Hell and the exotic ingredients and creatures needed to further magical pursuits through the generations. Under Rakon's stewardship the house had finally gained the power its patriarchs had sought for generations, but in the process he'd emptied it of wealth. He'd turned it into a shell.

Portraits of previous Norristru fathers hung from the walls in the grand hall – all of them similar in appearance to Rakon: narrow faces, overlarge mouths, thin lips, and deep-set, accusatory eyes that stabbed holes of envy into whatever they looked upon.

He walked past doors behind which foul things had occurred in years past, until he reached the door to his sisters' chambers, his accursed, dangerous sisters.

He stopped, stared at the door a moment.

What was he doing there? He had work to do, knowledge to gain. His feet had carried him to his sisters unbidden.

The need to see them had crept up on him like a slow fever, but now had firm hold. He licked his lips and skulked down the hall, hoping his sisters were asleep. He hadn't the strength to fight with them again. He just wanted to make certain they were there, confirm that his grip was not slipping from everything, that he still controlled *something*.

As he neared the door he walked with a furtive tread, as if approaching a sleeping beast. He put his ear to the enspelled wooden slab but heard nothing from within. After composing his mental defenses, he took the charmed brass key from the folds of his tunic, whispered a word of awakening over it, and with it opened the lock. When he heard the soft click, when he felt the wards subside, he pulled it open.

Fetid, organic air wafted forth. He imagined it loamy with ideas, carrying thoughts on unseen currents, free-floating notions waiting for someone to bump into them and think them their own. Sometimes after leaving his sisters he wondered whether the thoughts he carried with him were his own or something they'd pushed into his mind.

Could they even do that? He didn't know for certain.

And how would he know? Did a thought of theirs in his head feel different than a thought of his own?

He shook his head to clear it of such thinking.

He leaned into the room and could have touched the back of the enormous, bald eunuch who stood guard just within. The barrel-shaped man wore tent-sized pantaloons and a shirt and leather jack stained with sweat. A wooden truncheon hung from his belt, a large curved knife, and a reel of thin line.

The eunuch did not acknowledge Rakon's presence, though he must have heard the door open. His eyes stayed on the room, as they should. He was a jailer, his sole duty to ensure that Rusilla and Merelda neither left their chamber nor harmed anyone or themselves.

A slit at the base of the eunuch's skull still seeped pink pus, the wound a consequence of Rakon's chirurgy. Perhaps it would never heal. After scalpel and spell had severed the eunuch's brain from body, Rakon had filled the fleshy shell with a memory eater. The incorporeal spirit controlled the body with intangible tendrils while it made a slow meal of the eunuch's memories. In exchange for a captive feast, the eater allowed a binding that made it a perpetual guardian for Rusilla and Merelda, its alien intelligence immune to their mind magic.

Rakon wondered in passing how much of the eunuch still existed. He hoped none, though he could not help but imagine the eunuch's consciousness caged in the cell of his own mind, railing at his captivity. He could think of few worse fates than a magical bifurcation, the slow death of a mind in a body no longer controllable by it.

"Are they asleep?" he whispered in the eunuch's ear.

The huge man did not turn. The memory eater caused the eunuch to shrug.

Embers from the large hearth cast the windowless chamber in soft light and deep shadows. Furs and polished woods abounded: twin beds, wardrobes, overstuffed chairs.

He did what he could to provide for their comfort.

The aftermath of a chess match sat on the small gaming table, the white king toppled. Rusilla always played black, and she won nine games of ten. Rakon hadn't played her in years. He'd given up trying to beat her when she'd still been a precocious adolescent.

His sisters lay in their beds, their backs to him, their forms lost in a mound of pillows and blankets. Rusilla's long hair made an auburn cloud on her bolster. He watched them for a time, noted the steady breathing that suggested they were asleep. He let himself relax, and the moment he did he tasted cinnamon and his thoughts scattered.

Why had he come to see his sisters anyway? He could not remember. In truth, he'd been unfair to them over the years and should—

His adrenaline spiked.

Those weren't his thoughts.

How long had he been standing in the doorway?

He recovered enough of his wits to recognize the velvety caress of Rusilla's mental touch in his mind.

She hadn't moved, her breathing hadn't changed, but her mental fingers were sifting through his mind, pulling on the threads of his thinking, searching his memories.

He grimaced, clutching his head, and took an involuntary step backward.

"Get... out," he said through gritted teeth, but still

she clung to his mind, a cognitive leech, violating him.

He fought for clarity, thought of arcane formulae that his sister would not be able to parse, flooded his mind with them, incanted in the Language of Creation. When he felt her recoil at the alienness of the words and formulae, he reasserted his mental defenses, strengthened them.

The cinnamon taste faded. She was out.

He winced at the headache the contact had left in her wake. Each beat of his heart put a knife stab of pain in his temple. He wiped his nose and the finger came away bloodstained.

"I will punish you if you do that again," he said, his words loud in the silence of the chamber.

Rusilla shifted her legs under the covers but still did not show him her face.

"What could you do that's worse than what you've already done? That's worse than what you already plan to do?"

He growled in response, low and menacing, massaging his temple with two fingers.

"You might be surprised," he said.

"He does, you know," Rusilla said. He still could not see her face and it discomfited him.

Rakon licked his lips and lowered his hand. "He who? Does what?"

"The eunuch, or what's left of him. He screams in his head. It's constant. He hates you for imprisoning him in his own body."

The memory eater caused the eunuch to turn his head, so Rakon could see him in profile, and smiled. The expression did not reach the empty, glazed eyes.

Rakon swallowed, looked away.

"Just as we hate you for imprisoning us in our own house," Rusilla said. "Would you like to hear them? The screams?"

Merelda giggled viciously from somewhere within her blankets.

"I don't need to hear them," Rakon said. "I did what had to be done with him and I'm content with that. I'll do what has to be done with both of you also."

"And will you be content with that, too?" Rusilla asked softly.

Concealed in the shadows and blankets, Merelda said, "We're your sisters, Rakon."

"I know that," Rakon said. He clasped his hands behind his back. "And I'm sorry. But you're Norristru. And this is the Norristru house, the Norristru line, and I can't let it fall." He put finality in his tone. "The Pact preserves us all. You'll both do what you were born to do."

"It's not what I was born to do!" Merelda said, stirring under her covers.

"It is," Rakon insisted, and tried to put brotherly affection in his voice, though even he heard the falsity in it. "It's what must be. You both know that. You've both known it for years."

"You confuse what must be with your wishes,"

Rusilla said. "You enjoy the power that comes with your position. Lord Adjunct to the Lord Mayor."

She made his title sound like an insult. How did she even know his title? He'd never told her and she hadn't left the manse in over a decade. It occurred to him that the entire exchange could have been taking place only in his head.

"Sit up," he said. "Let me see you when you speak."

They ignored him.

"I said sit up."

"We heard you," Merelda said. "But we defy you."

He stared at their beds, at their backs.

"Will you punish us now, *brother*?" Rusilla said.

He shook his head, bewildered by their intransigence. "I can't understand you, either of you. The Pact is everything. You must know that."

Rusilla's voice dripped scorn. "The Pact was made by Norristru men for Norristru men. Yet it's the women who are asked to understand."

"And made to suffer," Merelda added.

Rakon had heard it all before, sometimes filtered through tears, sometimes through anger, sometimes through threats, sometimes in his dreams. As always, he remained unmoved.

"If you force me to take harsher steps, I will. I don't want to, but if I must, I'll manacle both of you to your beds. I'll drug you. You need only be alive, nothing more. You know I'm capable of it."

"Oh, I've been in your head, brother," Rusilla said. "I know quite well what you're capable of."

The memory eater inhabiting the eunuch found Rusilla's words amusing, or perhaps it devoured something funny in the eunuch's past. The great body shook as it chuckled.

"Try what you will," Merelda said. "We'll fight."

"The first time is always the worst," Rakon said, repeating words he'd heard from someone or other since childhood. "It will go easier after that."

"How would *you* know?" Rusilla said.

Rakon'd had enough. He'd come to see them to remind himself, and them, that his grip over them was still strong. But he was leaving with it weaker than it had been before he'd opened the door. They were more dangerous than he'd realized.

"Go to sleep now. It's late."

"Yes, it is," Rusilla said.

"When you do your duty, I'll reward you. I promise."

"Words," Rusilla said, dismissively. "Mere words."

He backed out of the room, closed the door and relocked it from the outside. He spoke the words to the master charm to reactivate the wards.

His hands were shaking. The headache remained. He was sweating. He rested his brow and hands against the smooth wood, worry rooting deeply in his gut.

The sylph's words replayed in his mind, the wind articulating a problem he must solve lest all of them die.

But he didn't know how.

Or did he?

An idea bubbled to the forefront of his mind and he was taken with it immediately. He should have thought of it before.

Hope buoyed his spirit. There was much work to do, and very little time, but he could do it in fifteen days. He could.

His mind made up, he lifted his head from the door, turned, and was startled to find himself face to face with the scarred, wrinkled visage of his mother. His startled gasp embarrassed him.

"I will put a bell on you, Mother. Don't sneak around so."

The clumps of his mother's gray hair stuck out in all directions from her veined, spotted scalp. Her left eye, drooping under the weight of an old scar, fixed on him. Her nightrobe hung from her emaciated frame as it might from a bundle of sticks.

"I was looking for a servant," she said, her broken voice like grating stones.

"They're not allowed in this part of the house," Rakon reminded her.

She seemed to have little interest in his words, and looked past him to his sisters' door. "They're restful in sleep."

"They're not asleep," he said, deflecting the point of her question. With the Thin Veil so near, Rusilla and Merelda should've been experiencing nightmares.

Her rheumy eyes turned vacant, seeing not the present but something in her past.

"The dreams started for me the month I first bled

and continued through the first..." She visibly shuffled through her mind for the right euphemism. "... visitation."

She continued to stare off into space, living through her history, the wrinkles on her face a map of past pain.

"Mother," Rakon said. "Mother."

She snapped back to the present, her eyes fixing on him. "Yes, well. As I was saying, things are what they are. Norristru men sacrifice their seed, the women their wombs." She looked past him to the door, as if speaking to Rusilla and Merelda. "The first time is always the worst."

It comforted him to hear his mother echo his thinking, to hear her validate the history of their house. If she could accept the price of the Pact, why couldn't his sisters?

"I birthed six children before you and your sisters, Rakon," she said. "Did you know that?"

He hadn't known. The house bred secrets and facts unspoken. "Were they... stillborn?"

She shook her head. "They were born alive, but fiendish in appearance. The Thyss claimed them for... such ends as the Lords of Hell intend."

Over the years the Thyss had been claiming more and more of the offspring from the Pact. And yet House Thyss evidently had only one true son still living, and he was imprisoned on Ellerth. Perhaps their house was dying, too.

His mother's voice drew his thoughts back to the hall.

"The three children of human appearance that I bore are more than any women in this house has birthed in four generations. If your sisters are equally fertile, we'll soon be strong with heirs again."

Words exited Rakon's mouth as if of their own accord, his mother a magnet for his worry. "A herald has not come."

His mother's bloodshot eyes widened; her hand went to her chest. "What? A herald should have come to you days ago to prepare the way."

"Do you think I don't know?" Rakon snapped.

"What could be wrong? I don't understand, Rakon. Have you given offense to the Thyss somehow?"

"No, of course not."

"But the Thin Veil will occur later this month. If a herald hasn't come, then Vik-Thyss won't come–"

"Vik-Thyss is dead."

He might as well have slapped her. Her face paled. Her hand went to her mouth as the implications settled on her. She spoke in a small voice. "The Pact will fail, Rakon."

"I know. I–"

She lunged forward with surprising speed. Her bony hands closed on his robe and pulled him close. Her strength took him momentarily aback. Her breath, filtered through her rotting teeth, made him blanch.

"Our lives depend upon the Pact, boy! We have made too many enemies over the centuries, enemies much more dangerous than the members of the Merchants' Council – inhuman enemies. Even the spirits we use to do our bidding do so only because of the Pact."

"My binding spells also–"

"Your binding spells work on sprites and sylphs and trivial creatures! But the powerful spirits, the demons, they answer you only because of the Pact. And they are vengeful, Rakon."

"I know that, Mother!"

"You know it, you say? Then you know they will come for you, for me! They await only an opportunity! You must do something!"

"I'm going to," he said. "But right now I need to think. Go back to your quarters, Mother. Leave me be."

But she didn't go. She pointed with her chin at Rusilla and Merelda's door. "Do they know?"

"Of course not. I told them nothing."

"You don't have to *tell* them for them to know."

The accumulation of fear, frustration, and anger routed Rakon's self-control. He seized his mother by her stick-thin shoulders and shoved her against the wall.

"I know that, too! But remember that it was you who birthed them, you who brought mindmages into our house. They needn't even use the Language of Creation! Their thoughts are weapons!"

His mother sneered, her rotted teeth like old tombstones. She looked at him from under hooded eyes. "A woman's thoughts are always weapons. And all men are monsters in their hearts."

He snarled and steered her roughly down the

hallway. "Leave me, Mother. I have plans to make if I'm to save our lives."

Rusilla lay on her side, staring at Merelda's back across the gap of fur-covered wood floor that separated their beds. Her head felt muzzy, thick, her thoughts ponderous. The throbbing beat of her heart seemed intent on pushing her eyes out of her face. Merelda rolled over to face her.

Your nose, Merelda projected, the thought sweet with concern.

Rusilla dabbed her nose and the knuckle came away bloody. *It's nothing.*

"It's not nothing," Merelda said aloud, sitting up in bed.

The eunuch grunted and shifted on his feet, tense at Merelda's tone.

"Are we not allowed to speak except in the presence of my brother, eater?" Merelda snapped.

The eunuch – the memory eater – grinned stupidly. His breathing sounded heavy, wet. The consciousness of the actual eunuch continued his screams, mental wails bouncing against the walls of Rusilla's mental barricades.

Speak only through our thoughts, Rusilla projected, though the effort intensified her headache. *I don't want him to hear.*

Merelda glared at the eunuch, her eyes narrowed with anger. The firelight cast her delicate features in shadow. With her pale skin, long neck, and short dark hair, she somehow made Rusilla think of a swan.

I have learned something from Rakon, Rusilla projected.

You read him? Merelda's mental tone held admiration.

She'd done more than read him. She'd copied memories from his mind, held them even now in her own. And she'd pushed, too, inserting thoughts into her brother's head.

As best I could. And I learned…

She had difficulty forming the thought, it seemed so implausible.

The Pact is endangered. Vik-Thyss is dead.

"What?" Merelda said, sitting up in bed and shedding her blankets in a cloud of linen.

The eater grumbled and Merelda sat back, her brown eyes never leaving Rusilla's face.

How? Merelda projected, her excitement palpable. *What does this mean for us? Are we to be freed? Rakon did not–*

Rusilla shook her head. *Rakon hopes to honor the Pact another way. He plans to find another son of House Thyss.*

She spared her sister any of the details she'd learned.

The faintly hopeful tingle that flavored Merelda's thoughts melted before renewed fear, frustration, and anger.

Perhaps he won't do so in time? The Thin Veil is close. Merelda's eyes flashed to the ceiling, as if she could see Hell's dot in night's vault.

Even if he doesn't, he would still hold us, Rusilla said.

If the house survives, the Veil will thin again in another five, and another five after that. He will try again then. He will never release us, Merelda. Not unless he breaks us first.

And Rakon would never break them. Never.

Then what do we do? Merelda said. *I can't be like Mother, Rose. I can't.*

Thinking of their mother turned Rusilla's thoughts black.

"It's only a few nights each year," Mother had once said to Rusilla, as she'd winced with remembered pain. "It's not awful. We must do our duty, dear, we Norristru women. If not, the house will die."

"I don't care about the line or the house," Rusilla had said.

The words had triggered something in her mother, dredged up some emotion or memory best left in the dark mud at the bottom of her soul. Rusilla had seen it coming, had tried to run, but too late.

Mother had shrieked, a wail of rage, and beaten Rusilla unconscious. She vaguely remembered Mother weeping throughout. It was after that when Rusilla's mind magic had first manifested.

We won't be like Mother, Rusilla projected. *Don't worry.*

The words felt like fiction, like something she'd tell Rakon, or stick in his mind for her own amusement.

She'd learned many things sifting through Rakon's thoughts. And she'd taken what she'd learned and manipulated his ideas, amplified his proclivities, but she'd had to act fast, and she hadn't thought it all the way through before Rakon had sensed her intrusion and forced her out. She dared speak her hopes aloud.

I think Rakon will soon take us from the house.

Merelda sounded shocked. *What? Why? How do you know? He's never taken us from the house.*

I just know, Rusilla projected. *Be calm.*

Merelda shifted on the bed. *You pushed something into his mind, didn't you? Didn't you? How did you do it? His defenses…* She shook her head. *Reading is one thing, but to push…*

The situation was unique. He was preoccupied with thoughts of the Pact. He is very frightened.

Good, Merelda said, and pounded a fist into a pillow. *He'll drug us. Before we leave the house, he'll drug us insensate. He must.*

I know. But we'll fight through it.

How? And even if we do, then what? How can we escape drugged?

Rusilla answered honestly. *I'm not sure yet.*

Merelda's legs shifted under the covers, as if she were already readying them to run. *He's always planning, Rose. Plotting. How do we escape him?*

Rusilla smiled, looked over at the chess game, the toppled white king. She'd never lost a game of chess to Rakon, though they had not played in many years. *We plot, too. That's how. It's late, Mere. You should rest. We'll talk more tomorrow.*

Long after Merelda fell into a fitful sleep, Rusilla lay awake in her bed staring up at the ceiling, planning, plotting. In time she quietly rose and went to her chessboard. There, she played a game against herself, formulating her thoughts the while. By the time black had cornered white, she had developed her plan.

"Check," she whispered.

The memory eater grunted, shifted on his feet, causing the wood floor to creak. Rusilla eyed him sidelong. He looked upon her without seeing her, his vacant eyes staring, his mouth half-open in a distant smile. Bracing herself, she opened her mind to the fragment of the actual eunuch that still remained within the shell.

The screams, rage-filled and terrible, hit her in an onslaught of emotion, a sleet of hate and terror and madness. She winced but did not otherwise move. Blood trickled from her nose. The eater defied her magic, but the fragment of the eunuch that still existed provided her a door into the mind, a reserve unoccupied by the eater's alien intellect. Her magic wrapped her consciousness around the eunuch's screams and followed them back into the dually inhabited mind. She perceived there the vast, empty spaces left in the wake of the eater's repasts. Into those, she pushed some of her own thoughts and memories, together with the memories she'd taken from Rakon, shoved them in deep, hoping they would avoid the eater's attention long enough for her plan to unfold.

When it was done, she pulled out and once more walled off the eunuch's screams. She dabbed her nose of blood, her heart racing, her head aching, and returned to bed.

The pieces were in place. There was nothing more for her to do except play them.

CHAPTER TWO

The Warrens. The bunghole of Dur Follin.

Nix could remember the street torches in the Warrens being lit only once, years earlier when the Lord Mayor came through with his entourage of sycophants and guards to view the Heap.

Now the rusty burn cages of the lamps sat askew atop weathered, tilted posts, empty of fuel, untended, surrendered to poverty like everything else in the Warrens. Linkboys dared the narrow alleys and dilapidated shacks no more often than did the watch, and the Warrens saw a watchman about as often as it saw an honest man, which was to say almost never. The only non-residents who regularly braved the alleys were rubbish men on their way to or from the Heap, and dung collectors with their wagons of shite. Other than that, only predators, victims, and hopelessness populated the Warrens.

Here and there fire pits dug in the narrow streets burned dried dung, the smoke dark and reeking. Thin, ill-dressed people crowded like shadows around the flames, people worn down by time and the world until they looked as crumbled and dilapidated as the buildings in which they would later squat. The odor of open latrines and the stink of the Deadmire, whose waters lay just beyond the walls, polluted the air.

Ool's clock tolled eight deep notes, signifying the passage of another desperate hour for the residents of the Warrens. Nix could see the great clock in the distance, its spire a dark line silhouetted by the thin silver crescent of Kulven, Mad Ool's device looming over the filth like a doom.

The sky cleared its throat with a low, prolonged rumble of thunder. Rain was coming; it would turn the Warrens into a morass, an extension of the Deadmire.

Nix prowled the alleys and narrow roads, tense, all eyes and ears. He held his bared blade in his fist. The ubiquitous and canny rats squeaked indignantly at his approach, slunk into dens and dark hidey-holes. Urchins eyed him sidelong as they melted into shadows and alleys. The rotted body of a dead dog lay in the street, its ribs like jail bars.

The men and women of the Warrens regarded him with hooded eyes and wary glances, but kept their distance. He felt their eyes on him, whores, pimps, addicts, would-be street thugs, and the merely unfortunate, all of them evaluating him as either potential prey or possible savior. His blade and hard expression, however, pronounced him neither. He had no business with them, and only someone very stupid or more desperate than usual would dare a run at him.

He'd worn the same look once, a hard, brittle veneer of hostility that coated the terror and desperation beneath. His mind flashed back on deeds he'd rather have forgotten. Guilt dredged the depths of his past and in his mind's eye he saw the wan, sunken-eyed face of the thin old man he'd killed with a rusty piece of sharp metal. They'd fought over a chunk of bread Nix had found in a rubbish drop, the whole of it more mold than grain. Nix had killed many men since, but he regretted that one still, and probably always would. They'd both just been hungry, and Nix had been too young to stain his hands with blood and carry it well. He still saw the old man in dreams sometimes, eyes wide and fearful, mouth moving as he chewed on his last breath.

He rounded a nameless corner onto another nameless street, waving off a haggard prostitute in a tattered dress who looked like she might approach him. Two blocks ahead he saw the lesion of the Heap, a mountain of rubbish rising in a huge lumpy arc over the uneven, sagging roofs of nearby buildings. The Heap served as final resting place for most of Dur Follin's daily trash (and many of its murdered, as Nix had learned later), and each dawn and dusk brought a steady stream of rubbish men and their carts through the Warrens. The mountain grew every year, accreting waste and stink the way the Warrens accreted the hopeless. Nix figured that one day the Warrens would be nothing more than the Heap.

Though after dark, hundreds of river gulls still dotted

the Heap's surface, wheeling in the air over and around it, their calls from dawn to midnight as much a timekeeper for the Warrens as Mad Ool's clock spire. Their shite painted large swaths of the Heap white.

Shacks, makeshift tents, and lean-tos clung to the base of the Heap like malformed toadstools, a fungus of improvised homes for the urchins and other desperate residents who mined the Heap for the ore of food scraps and lost valuables. Now and again someone, usually a child, threw a stone at a gull in hopes of bringing one down to fill a stewpot, but Nix knew well the fruitlessness of the attempt. He'd managed to bring down only three in all the years he'd spent there, and he'd been a better shot than most. The birds were canny and quick.

Watching the urchins prowl the garbage, his mind drifted to his childhood. He recalled the glee he'd felt once when he'd found a piece of salted meat in a moldy sack, the excitement he'd felt when he'd discovered a finely-made lockpick – his first – in the sliding heel of an old boot. He remembered how, by sunset each day, he was always covered in stink, dirt, bird shite, and sweat, but how it would always seem worth it if the effort had landed something in his belly.

Whenever he returned to the Warrens, he made a point to see the Heap, a pilgrimage to remind himself of his former life, a reminder of who he was and would always be. He should've died many times over while living in the Warrens, but somehow the gods had overlooked him, or decided to spare him for some reason. He figured he was living on borrowed time, a divine promissory note as it were, so he lived as if he had nothing to lose.

Hence, tomb robbing.

A trio of adolescents, two girls and a boy, all too thin, dashed across the street before him, either running after something or running away from something. Rags covered them, and only the boy had shoes, mismatched. They vanished down a side alley as fast as they had appeared, ghosts of the Warrens.

He felt for them, felt for everyone who lived hungry and cold, and did what he could. Every few paces he let a silver tern or a copper common leak from a hole in his trouser pocket. If he just gave coin away, he'd have a crowd around him and maybe a riot, or some tough would have a run at him, so instead he just left dozens of terns and commons in his wake for the lucky or diligent to find. He thought of them as seeds, an attempt to grow hope from desperate soil.

Having made obeisance to his childhood at the temple of the Heap, he turned and headed for Mamabird's home, a few dilapidated blocks away. He could have walked there with his eyes closed, so well did he know the route. He dropped more coins in the road as he went.

He smiled when he saw Mamabird's house: a single-story mud-brick building with a sagging roof of wood and straw. Lean-tos were built against two sides of it, and a fire burned in a large pit near one of them. Cats, of course, seemed everywhere. Mama collected cats the way a noblewoman collected jewelry, and Nix had once seen her beat a man who'd tried to catch one for stew. Two tabbies perched on the roof of her house, a long-haired black lay near the fire pit, and a fourth orange tabby stalked something in the weeds near the fire pit. Mama kept a small vegetable garden in the small dirt plot she'd fenced off behind the house, and everyone respected its boundaries. Mamabird's house was treated by the residents of the Warrens the way other people treated temples elsewhere in the city – sacred ground.

A tentative rain started, just enough to lend humidity to the stink. Another rumble of thunder threatened a heavier downpour. The cats slunk out of sight.

Nix hustled up to the house, stood on the makeshift porch of scavenged timber, stared at the worn door a few long beats. Standing there, he transformed, reverted back to the person he'd been in boyhood, frightened, alone, desperate. He'd found a life behind that door, security, hope. And, in the end, he'd also found the man he later became and whatever conscience he carried.

He sheathed his blade, adjusted his cloak, his hair, shed the mask he wore when facing the world, and knocked his knock. The floor creaked as Mamabird came to the door. He could hear her murmuring to herself.

"It can't be, can it? Nixxy, is that you?"

"It's me, Mamabird."

She pulled open the door so hard she almost jerked

it from its rusty hinges. The smell of her onion stew – he never thought overlong about what else might be in it – wafted out, redolent with memories.

When she saw him, her pale, fat face wrinkled up in a toothless smile that reached all the way to her rheumy eyes. He could not help but answer with a face-splitting smile of his own.

He tried to take her in at a glance but she always seemed too large. He perceived her only in pieces, never in whole: the tight bun of her gray hair, the perpetually stained apron, her three chins, the immensity of her girth, the hairy mole on her right cheek, the puckered, flabby arms, the tattered dress large enough to serve as a tent.

She squealed with delight and hugged him hard enough to take his breath, enfolding him in her rolls of fat, her sour smell, her love. He returned the hug in full, losing himself for a moment. Mamabird was the sweetest person he'd ever met in this life, and sweeter than any he expected to meet in the next. He knew holy men without half her rectitude. He felt relaxed for the first time since entering the Warrens.

"My favorite chick returned to the nest!" she said.

"I always come back, Mamabird."

"But it's been so long," she said, and hugged him harder.

"Mamabird," he said into her apron, "I can't breathe."

She laughed, released the hug, and held him out at arm's length.

"Let Mama look at you."

She examined him the way she might a market chicken. Frowning at the sharp steel he carried, she turned him all the way around and tsked.

"You're not eating enough. Look how thin. You've got no backside. Come sit and eat. I've just made some stew."

"It smells delicious," he said, and meant it.

As always, she kept her damp two-room shack with its warped wood-plank floor as tidy as life in the Warrens allowed. Rain pattered softly on the roof. Blankets lay on the floor near the tiny hearth, all of them tattered but clean.

"Caring for some of the urchins, I see. Where are they?"

She tsked again. "They're not urchins, my love. They're children. As were you. And they're out doing what they do. They'll be along."

Her furniture, reclaimed from the Heap or made for her inexpertly by grateful beneficiaries of her grace, looked worn but reasonably sturdy – a few sitting chairs, a round eating table with mismatched chairs, a cabinet, the doors long removed, that held her two pots and few dishes.

"I don't have a lot of time, Mama. Egil is waiting for me back in the city."

"Time enough to eat, though," she said. Not a question.

"Of course, Mama."

She ladled her stew into a wooden bowl. "And how

is Egil? Shame about his wife and child. Such a sad man, he is."

"Aye," Nix said somberly.

"Come, sit."

They sat at the eating table: not the same one at which Nix had taken so many meals as a child, true, but Mama's presence and her stew made it feel the same. He might as well have been ten winters old. He sipped the stew, its smell and taste full of good memories, and they talked for the better part of an hour about small things. Mamabird coughed often and he noticed her rale, noticed, too, the additional wrinkles that time had added to her countenance.

"I'll send a priestess of Orella to see to you about the cough," he said.

She waved off his help. "Now, Nix, you know Mama's had the same cough for ten years. Ain't no need for a priestess. Besides–" She chuckled and the chuckle gave way to a coughing fit. She never stopped smiling throughout. "No white-robed priestess of the healing goddess will come in here. You know that."

"They will if I ask, Mama."

"I know how you ask, Nixxy."

Nix smiled to hide his concern. He tried to imagine Dur Follin without her, tried to imagine his life without her, and failed. He would've offered to move her out of the Warrens, but he knew she wouldn't abide it. She regarded the Warrens as her home and its urchins as her children. She'd die in her shack and leave only when they carried her out. He dreaded that day.

After they'd eaten and the conversation had slowed, he broached the real subject of his visit. "I have some coin for you, Mama."

She cleared his bowl. "Oh, Nix, I don't need–"

"It's just a bit."

He took a coinpurse from his cloak and dumped fifty commons and ten terns on the table. He'd included no gold because he knew she couldn't spend a royal. Merely holding gold in the Warrens could put her at risk.

Her hand went to her mouth. "Oh my, Nix! It's too much. I couldn't hope to spend it all."

He smiled but held his tongue. She always marveled at a pittance as if it were a fortune. He couldn't buy a decent blade for what he'd put on the table. But he knew she'd never take more, not all at once. He had to provide for her in dribs and drabs.

She looked up from the coin and regarded him across the table, eyes shrewd.

"How'd you come by all this coin, young man? You didn't hurt someone for it, did you? I taught you better'n that."

He felt his cheeks warm. "You did, Mama. And I earned it fair. Egil and I have had a bit of luck of late."

He and Mamabird had an unspoken agreement that he never told her about his tomb robbing explicitly and she never asked in detail.

"You two." She shook her head, chuckling, chins and breasts bouncing. "Good boys, you are."

Ool's clock sounded the hour: nine deep, discordant notes. He reached for her hand as he stood.

"So soon?" she asked.

"I know." He kissed the back of her hand. "I'm sorry, but I'll return as soon as I can."

She sighed, nodded, came around the table and embraced him. She had tears in her eyes. He had tears in his. He fell into her, memorizing her smell, the feel of her arms around him.

"Oh, I need you to keep something for me," he said, and took the rolled piece of vellum from an inner pocket. "This is a deed to some property Egil and I bought."

Mama took it, a question in her eyes. "A deed? What property?"

He nodded. "Just keep it safe for us, will you? If ever I'm... away for a long time, that deed is yours. Understand?"

"I wouldn't know what to do with such a thing. I'll just hold it 'til you come back."

She tucked it into a pocket in her apron.

"Thank you, Mama," he said.

She smiled and walked him toward the door. "You be good, Nixxy. And don't worry about your old Mamabird. I'll be fine."

Her words devolved into a fit of wet coughing that made him wince.

"I know you will," he said, and wished he believed it.

"Send my love to Egil."

"I will."

He exited her shack, the only home he'd ever had. The moment he closed the door, he donned the mask.

Nix the Quick, Nix the Lucky, a man fast with a word, faster still with a blade. He drew his falchion and pushed his past down deep.

He had to hurry. Egil would be waiting and Egil hated to be left waiting.

He picked his way back through the avenues and alleys until he reached the Poor Wall, the ancient line of crumbling stone that delimited the border of the Warrens, a binding cross that separated the Warrens' poverty and hopelessness from the rest of Dur Follin. Four lax watchmen in orange tabards manned the Slum Gate. In the torchlight, Nix saw that crossbows hung from their backs, blades and truncheons from their belts. He knew that Slum Gate duty was considered a punishment post among watchmen.

Seeing Nix approach, one of them nudged another and the second stepped forward. He was unshaven, his helm removed and his hair disheveled. "Name and business."

Nix sheathed his blade. "Nix Fall of Dur Follin, and my business is none of yours."

"Nix Fall?" The guard squinted at Nix, looked back at his fellows, back at Nix. "Nix the Quick?"

One of the other guards pushed off the wall and walked closer, attitude in his stride. "Don't you belong in there with the rest of the rubbish?"

He was tall, maybe twenty winters, barely old enough to grow a beard. He stood beside his comrade.

The insult deflected off of Nix's distraction, summoning only modest ire. "More than you know.

Better class of people living in there than I see standing before me. Now, go fak yourself and both of you get out of my way."

He knew he shouldn't cross the watch, but he was irritable, and growing moreso by the moment.

"You know what..." the tall watchman began, his hand moving for his truncheon.

The watch sergeant, a towering, fat man Nix knew by appearance from a run-in with the watch years earlier, leaned out of the guard shack to one side of the gate.

"Let him pass," he said.

The men in front of Nix glared but didn't move.

"I said let him pass," the sergeant repeated.

Reluctantly, the guards stood aside. One of them spit at Nix's feet. Nix took care to bump that one as he passed. He nodded his thanks at the sergeant.

"We should arrest that prick," the tall guard hissed to the sergeant.

"Your job ain't to pick fights, boy," the sergeant said. "It's to uphold the law of the Lord Mayor and the Merchants' Council. 'Sides, I probably saved you an unpleasant meeting with sharp steel just then."

Nix left the guards behind and stepped through the gate into Dur Follin proper. The change was almost immediate and entirely palpable. Street torches blazed at regular intervals, well tended by the city's linkboys. Carriages and wagons moved along the muddy, cobbled streets. Pedestrians walked here and there. Candlelight poured from shop windows, laughter and shouts from taverns and inns.

The first time Nix had left the Warrens, he'd felt like he'd dug himself out of a dark hole and emerged into the light. He wondered if Mamabird had ever seen the light. He suspected not. It saddened him.

He was maudlin, moreso than usual after seeing Mama, and it kept him from playing his part as well as normal. Maybe it was the rain. He consciously pushed the sentimentality aside, and with each step he fell more and more back into his normal persona. By the time he found Egil where they'd agreed, at the corner of Teamsters Avenue and Narrow Way, under the towering shadow of the Archbridge, he felt more himself.

The priest stood with his back to him, hands in his cloak pockets, staring at the huge span of the bridge. Torches and candles and even a few magic crystals lit the shrines along the length of the bridge, illuminating a swirl of colors, languages, songs, and chants. A gong rang from somewhere, the tinkle of bells.

Ebenor's tattooed eye watched Nix approach. Nix put a hand on Egil's shoulder by way of greeting. The priest whirled and had him by the wrist in a blink, the grip painful enough to make Nix wince. Seeing Nix, Egil released him.

"Apologies," Egil said absently.

"None needed," Nix said, rubbing his wrist. "I should've announced myself." He nodded at the shrines on the bridge. "Thinking of switching faiths, are you?"

Egil ignored the jibe. "Is it done?"

"It's done. I left the deed with Mama. Dram license is filed with the guild. We're good."

"So you say." Egil flipped up the hood of his cloak as rain started to fall in heavy drops. "How is Mamabird?"

"Well as can be, I suppose. She asked about you. I told her you remained as surly as ever."

Egil smiled. "Handsome as ever, too, I trust?"

"Alas, I never lie to Mamabird."

Egil chuckled. "So let's go see this thing we bought. Gettin' on to the dark part of night. The ruffians ought to be filling the place by now."

"Indeed. Two more will go unnoticed."

CHAPTER THREE

By the time Egil and Nix reached Shoddy Way, the downpour sounded like sling bullets against the cobbles. The flames of street torches sizzled, smoked, and danced in the rain.

Shoddy Way was a soup of mud and manure and the storm had mostly emptied the street. Only a donkey-pulled cart occupied the otherwise empty road, and it looked stuck in the mud.

The rain thumped like the beat of war drums off the colorful tents and canvas-covered booths of the Low Bazaar, which filled the plaza nearby. Braziers sizzled in the rain, the smoke carrying the smell of roasted mutton into the slate sky. Raucous laughter carried from one of the tents in the bazaar.

"Gods are taking a piss," Nix said.

Egil grunted agreement.

The simple wood plank sign that hung from rusted hooks over the front doors of the *Slick Tunnel* rattled in the wind. Weather and time had reduced the lettering to *The unnel,* but left intact the salaciously drawn image of a cave mouth.

"Needs a new sign," Nix said.

Egil harrumphed from the depths of his cowl. "Needs a lot of new things."

"But not new owners," Nix said, and thumped Egil on the mountain of his shoulder. "Got those, now."

"Aye," Egil said skeptically.

They eyed the building they now owned – two stories of crumbling bricks and warped wood, capped with a roof of cracked tiles. A sagging second-floor balcony overlooked Shoddy Way and would give a good view of the plaza and the Low Bazaar, but Nix wouldn't have trusted its worn brackets to hold his weight.

The building had been the home of a wealthy merchant once. But Dur Follin's rich had long ago moved across the Archbridge to the west side of the Meander, leaving the poor to the east and the very poor to the Warrens. Since then the building had changed hands many times, slowly collecting unsavory neighbors until Shoddy Way was a virtual treasure trove of drug dens, pawneries, and all manner of establishments engaged in illicit mercantilism.

A quartet of cloaked men pelted across the street from the bazaar plaza and pushed their way through Egil and Nix.

"One side, bunghole," said the tallest of the men. "It's pouring out here."

Nix resisted the urge to sink his punch dagger into a kidney. Scabbards poked out from under the hem of the men's weathered cloaks, and each wore a boiled leather jack. The mouthy one threw open the door of the *Tunnel*. Faint lantern light, laughter, conversation, and smoke leaked out onto Shoddy Way.

"I see manners haven't improved while we were away," Nix observed, his hands doing what they always did when someone bumped into him.

"Fak you," the last of the men said over his shoulder, and the door to the brothel and tavern Nix now half-owned slammed in his face. He stared after them, rubbing his nose. He turned to Egil.

"Are you as offended as I?"

Egil raised his bushy brows and his eyes went to Nix's hand.

Nix looked down and saw in his palm the small leather coin pouch he'd taken from the tall mouthy one.

"I had to lift it," Nix said. "He bumped into me. And rudely so. At that point it's a matter of principle."

"Principle?"

Nix hefted the purse and put the weight at twelve or thirteen coins. "Principle indeed. I'll say twelve. Terns and commons only. Not a royal to be seen, not from those jackanapes. Take odds?"

"From you? On that? Do I look like a fool?"

"I won't answer that so as to spare your feelings." Nix fingered open the pouch and examined the contents. "Nine terns and three commons. Scarcely worth the effort."

They had no need for more coin, so Nix sloshed through the mud over to the donkey cart and driver. The cart was sunk halfway up to the axle in mud. The donkey, ears flat, coat steaming, seemed to have given up trying to pull it, despite the entreaties of the cloaked driver, an old man with a creased face and a wispy beard. Three sacks of grain and a barrel lay in the back of the cart. The old man looked fearful as Nix approached. Nix donned his best "I'm harmless" smile.

"For your trouble, granther," Nix said, and tossed the coins onto the bench board of the wagon. Two silver terns spilled out and the old driver seemed dumbstruck.

"What is this?" the old man said, his voice cracked with age. The donkey shook the wet from his fur.

Nix winked at the man and gestured at the slate sky. "Must be raining coin. Best collect what you can before it stops."

The man looked up at the sky, then colored, perhaps realizing how silly he must have looked. He gathered the coinpurse, hands shaking. "Are you mad, goodsir?"

"I wonder sometimes," Nix answered. "The gods only know. Goodeve, granther."

"Orella keep and preserve you, goodsir."

"That's well done," Egil said, when Nix walked back to him. "I never made you one for alms, much less grace."

Nix's mind turned to the Warrens, the coin he seeded there, but he kept his thoughts from his face. "Pfft. I know nothing of alms or grace. I just know that an old peasant can use the coin better than us, and certainly better than that hiresword who bumped me."

"That's truth," Egil said, and thumped Nix on the shoulder. "I'm thinking maybe you should've joined me in a priesthood."

"I didn't want to shave my head," Nix said. "It would foul my looks."

The great water clock of Ool rang the tenth hour, the deep notes audible across the city even over the rain.

"On the hour," Nix said, and gestured at the Tunnel's door. "Shall we?"

Egil shouldered open one of the double doors and they ducked inside.

The cavernous common room, originally a dining hall no doubt, opened before them. Blue smoke fogged the air, gathered in clouds near the ceiling beams. Heads turned and looked up at their entrance, though the loud thrum of conversation and clink of tankards did not so much as pause. They stood there for a long moment, Nix expecting a raucous greeting, hearty congratulations, and instead...

Nothing.

His smile fell down to his boot heels.

"Do they not know we own it?"

"Seems not," Egil said. He crossed his arms over his chest and looked around, disapproval in his furrowed brow.

A roll of thunder shook the building, summoned a collective "ahh" from the patrons, and dislodged a rain of plaster flakes from the walls.

"It seemed nicer before we bought it," Egil said.

Nix ignored him. "How could Tesha not tell anyone? We rescued this place from the Lord Mayor's revenue men. They should be applauding or something. Don't you think?"

"Tesha's a madam, Nix, not a street crier." His nose wrinkled. "What's that smell?"

"I know what she is," Nix said in a surly tone. "Even so, she should have told someone. And it's the eel stew."

"The stew? Really? How'd I not notice it before?"

"Maybe it was nicer before we bought this place, too."

Perhaps thirty patrons sat at the sturdy, time-scarred tables that dotted the wood-planked floor of the common room, all of them hard-eyed slubbers of one ilk or other. Small lanterns hung from the cracked walls or sat on the rickety tables, lurid light for a lurid crew. The stink of stale incense, sour sweat, and hasty sex clung to the warped floorboards.

A wide, sweeping staircase, probably once grand but now decrepit, led to the second-floor pleasure rooms. Three of Tesha's girls and one of her men lingered on the stairs, their poses professional and seductive, the dim light hiding the ragged hems of their threadbare clothing. Nix could not recall their names, though he knew their faces.

Morra the serving girl danced through the crowd, her face puffed and red under the tight bun of her brown hair, the tankards she bore sloshing with Gadd's ale. Her simple dress swayed on her thick legs. She saw Egil and Nix and acknowledged them with a tilt of her chin.

"Greets, loves," she said, as she hustled past them.

"Milady," Nix said, offering a half-bow, and Morra smiled sweetly over her shoulder.

Loud laughter sounded from one of the corner tables, where a group of teamsters in tell-tale green guild armbands huddled over their beers. The fattest of them gesticulated wildly with his pipe as he made a point about this or that.

In the dim corner near the raised stage sat the four hireswords. They were just sitting down, speaking quietly among themselves, the mouthy one wearing a sour expression and patting at his cloak. Perhaps he realized he'd "dropped" his coinpurse somewhere. Morra set the ales down before them and danced away to another table.

"I need a drink," Egil said.

Nix's eyes went to the curved bar, behind which Gadd ruled. To Nix's knowledge, the willow-thin, tattooed tapkeep spoke but a few words of Realm Common, but his subjects – tankards, cups, jiggers, and hogsheads – obeyed his every command.

Two more of Tesha's girls, Lis and Kiir, leaned suggestively on the bar. Nix nodded at Kiir, a lithe, red-haired lass whose pale skin reminded him of polished ivory. Both girls smiled at Egil and Nix.

"Kiir is pleasing to view, not so?"

"Aye," Egil said. "Strong girl, to look at her."

"Indeed."

"I wager she could take you in a grapple."

Nix grinned as the thought played out in his imagination. "I think I should like to find out one day."

Morra breezed by them again, this time with an empty platter.

"But maybe not today, yeah?" Egil said. "Today we drink. Come."

Egil pulled Nix toward the bar, but Nix held his ground a moment longer. "Wait."

"Wait what? I thirst."

"Gods, man! Look about you. This place is ours now! What are your thoughts?"

The priest looked around, stroked his beard, and said, "I think we bought the worst tavern in Dur Follin."

"You what?"

"I blame you," Egil said matter-of-factly, and walked toward the bar. "Gadd, a draft! A big one!"

"Here, too!" called one of the hireswords. "And quicklike!"

"Coming, loves!" Morra called to the hireswords.

One of the teamsters spilled his beer and loosed a stream of swearing, much to the amusement of his comrades.

"For a man with a mystic eye tattooed on his scalp," Nix said, trailing Egil across the common room, "I fear you're not seeing the potential here. We can turn the place around, pretty it up."

Again Egil harrumphed. "Pretty it up? Putting a dress on an orlog, more like."

"Gods, you're in a mood tonight."

They bellied up to the bar, bookended by Kiir and Lis.

Gadd, his thin arms covered in a sleeve of patterned tattoos depicting mythological creatures from Vathar, filled a metal tankard from the tapped hogshead behind the bar and placed it before Egil.

"Make that two, yeah?" Nix said to Gadd. To Kiir, he said, "Anything for you, milady?"

She smiled shyly. "No, my lord."

Gadd grunted an acknowledgment and nodded with a vigor that made his waist-length topknot dance. The long-stemmed wood pipe he smoked, filled with fragrant leaf from the east, burned in a clay tray atop the bar. The smell of the blue smoke curling up from its bowl made Nix lightheaded. Gadd soon had a tankard of ale foaming before Nix.

"Here too, I said!" called the hiresword again, presumably to Morra. "Over here, you cow! I thirst!"

"Someone best take that slubber a beer before his voice irritates me further," Egil said.

Nix read the creases in Egil's brow the way an oracle read chicken entrails, and they told him the priest's ire was up. He really was in a mood.

Not good.

"Come now," Nix said. "Are you really that mad about buying this place? We agreed it was a good idea."

Egil merely harrumphed again.

"Something else, then?"

"A beer!" the hiresword called.

The lines in Egil's forehead deepened, Ebenor's eye in a squint.

Nix didn't see Morra so he grabbed a tankard of ale from Gadd and asked Lis, "Would you mind taking this to that oaf?"

"I'm not a serving wench," Lis said, pouting.

"I know, milady. But if I take it to him, I fear I'll stab him in the eye."

"That'd be a well-earned stab," Egil said.

"Please?" Nix asked, pleading with his eyes.

Lis sighed, shook out her long black hair, fluffed her breasts, and took the tankard in hand.

"You are the landlord, now," she said, and walked off.

Nix grinned at that. "Tesha *did* tell someone!"

"She told all of us," Kiir said. "She seemed put out by it, I'd say."

"Put out?" Nix said, frowning. "How so?"

Kiir seemed to realize she'd spoken out of turn. Her soft eyes looked everywhere but Nix's face. Her cheeks colored, visible even through her makeup. "Just that... well... I think she... There she is! Maybe you should ask her yourself."

Kiir grabbed Nix's tankard and took a long drink while Nix turned to watch Tesha descend the stairs. She wore a flowing blue dress with a tight-fitting bodice, and her dark hair hung in waves around her olive skin. Nix had heard that she'd been a harem slave once, owned by some minor sultan of Jafari, but he'd never dared ask. Her severe features did not invite familiar talk. Nix, who'd faced devils, who'd stared down three assassins hired by Kazmer the Flame to take Nix's tongue, acknowledged that Tesha intimidated him. She wasn't like most women he knew; or maybe she was, and he just didn't know women like he thought he did.

She slid down the stairway with the grace of an aristocrat. She spoke softly to the men and women in her employ who stood at the stair rail. Nix read her lips.

"Posture, ladies."

"Smile, Arno. Always smile."

Nix raised a hand to get her attention. He faltered like a boy when her eyes fell on him and her brow furrowed. He stood there like a statue, arm raised, no doubt a doltish expression on his face. He conjured the words he would speak, played them out in his mind – *Milady, Tesha. You certainly are a lovely sight.*

Shouts from the loudmouth hiresword ruined his fantasy.

"Even the whores serve tables here! Maybe it's not the shithole I took it for."

His three fellows laughed and Lis, who had just set down the tankard of ale at their table, donned a fake smile while two of the men pawed at her backside.

"Where do you think you're going?" the hiresword said loudly, jumping up from his chair and boxing in Lis against the table. He took her by the wrist, none too softly. "I might want more than a beer."

From the stairs, Tesha said, "Lis, please come see me. Goodsir, if you'd like–"

The hiresword turned and glared up at Tesha. "What? Am I not good enough for a whore's company?"

"That's not what I meant at all," said Tesha.

Nix stood up, thinking to impress Tesha by diffusing the situation.

"Here's an idea," he called. "Why don't you just take your hands off of her, retake your seat, and enjoy another drink with your crew. It's on the house."

Tesha pursed her lips and stared daggers at him. He had no idea why.

The man did not release Lis. He cocked his head, squinted his eyes. "Don't I know you? Ain't you Nix Fall?"

Nix bowed, pleased to be recognized. "Indeed, I am. I see my reputation precedes me. Now–"

"This doesn't involve you now, does it, Nix Fall? So maybe you should close your hole, shouldn't you, *Nix Fall*." He shook Lis by the arm as he spoke. "This is between her and me."

"There is no you and me unless you pay," Lis said, still playing her role. She tried to sound playful, but Nix could see the hiresword's grip caused her pain.

"We'd like to settle up here," said the fat teamster, as he and his companions rose and edged away from their table, out of the verbal line of fire.

"Friend, just let it go and go back to your tankard, yeah?" Nix said. "You don't want this to go bad, do you?"

The hiresword sneered. "Maybe I do. Would you wet your blade over a whore, Nix Fall? This whore?"

"Nix..." Kiir said behind him.

On the stairs, Tesha, still staring at him, raised her eyebrows and shook her head.

"Maybe I would," Nix said philosophically. "I've

bloodied an edge over less. But that's neither hither nor yon, since she's more than that to me. It happens she's a rent-paying tenant. *My* rent-paying tenant, since I own this place."

A few murmured comments, one soft "huzzah" from one of the teamsters.

The hiresword guffawed. "You own this place? Ha! You lose a wager or something? I heard you was called 'lucky.' This place is a shithole."

The slam of Egil's tankard on the bar, as loud as the report of a blunderbuss, cut short the chuckles of the hiresword's companions. All eyes turned to the priest. The stool groaned with relief as Egil rose.

Rakon sat his horse, blinking in the drizzle, Rusilla's slouched form before him in the saddle. The eunuch sat a horse beside him, his ham hands clutching Merelda's limp form to prevent her from falling off the mount. Rakon's men stood around an uncovered, horse-drawn wagon. All but Baras, the head of Rakon's personal guard, had cloak hoods drawn against the rain.

"That's it there, my lord?" Baras asked, pointing at the decrepit building across the street.

Rakon squinted through the drizzle at the sign that hung over the building's door. He couldn't make out the faded writing, but the image limned on the board looked like a dark tunnel.

"That's it," Rakon said.

"And they're inside, this Egil and Nix?"

"They are," Rakon said. Or so his informant had told him.

Baras nodded. His face wrinkled in a question but he did not give it voice.

"What is it, Baras?" Rakon asked.

Baras looked up at Rakon, droplets of rain adorning his beard. "My lord, why are we bothering with these two? I don't see–"

"We'll need them when we reach Afirion," Rakon said.

"Yes, but these two men are thieves by reputation. There are others–"

"No," Rakon said sharply. "It must be these two. Now do as I've said, Baras. No more questions."

Baras stiffened. "Aye, my lord."

"I need them alive. Bring them to the warehouse in the docks, the one we've used before. I'll meet you there."

"Aye, my lord."

"It may be a shithole, slubber," Egil said to the hire-sword, "but it's *our* shithole. And you and yours are no longer welcome in it."

Nix smiled, pleased to see Egil taking some pride of ownership. "I'm glad to hear you own up to–"

The hiresword let Lis go and put a hand to his blade hilt. His three companions pushed back their chairs and stood.

"Is that right?" the hiresword said to Egil. "You mean to kick us out? *Of here?*"

He chuckled darkly and his comrades echoed him. The chuckles died, however, as Egil walked toward them, shoving empty chairs out of his way as he went. Nix fell in behind him, seeing how it would go.

"This is our place," Nix hissed. "Whatever you break is our lost coin."

The priest seemed not to hear him and went nose to nose with the hiresword. "I'm not kicking you out. I'm telling you and them to leave. If I was *kicking* you out, my boot'd be in your arse."

Anger colored the man's pockmarked face. His mustache and stubble twitched. With his narrow chin and large nose, he reminded Nix of a river rat.

"Ain't you a priest or something?" the man said, his eyes flicking over the scalp tattoo.

"Or something," Egil said. "Now, get out."

The man looked over at Nix. "Is this slubber serious?"

Nix rubbed his chin and made a dramatic show of studying Egil's face, the furrowed brow, the narrowed eyes, the way his chest rose and fell. Egil's eyes never left the hiresword's face.

"Hmm. Not yet, I'd say, but–"

The man whirled back on Egil, spraying spit as he spoke. "Then tell him to stop wasting my fakkin' time, eh? And maybe get out of my face? I want to get drunk and then laid."

"Ah, don't we all," Nix said, nodding sympathetically.

"You'll do neither here," Egil said, and Nix heard

the promise of violence in his tone. The priest stood half a head taller than the man, and several stones heavier.

"Shite," Nix said, and shook his head regretfully.

"What now?" the man said.

"*Now* he's serious."

The man seemed bemused. "What are you two, a comedy troupe?"

"No, but I'm flattered you'd think–"

"Apologize," Egil said.

The hiresword blinked. "To her? For calling her a whore? Fine, apologies to milady the whore."

He made an exaggerated bow in the general direction of Lis.

"I think that resolves it, then," Tesha said from the stairs, clapping her hands once. "Let's all go back to–"

"We done?" the man said. The way he leaned in toward Egil suggested that matters had not ended.

"No," Egil said. "Now apologize to me for calling my place a shithole."

"Your place!" Nix exclaimed. "This is *our* place. And I *knew* you'd come to see the potential–"

"You're pushing now just to push," the man said.

"Isn't that what you were doing when you stood up and started shouting about whores and shitholes?" Egil said, his deep voice low and dangerous. "When you bumped into Nix and me outside? Pushing just to push, right? You and your boys used to havin' the run of places, are you?"

The man's lower lip trembled. "You know what? Fak you, Egil the Priest and Nix the Lucky. Yeah, I know your name, too." He spat on the floor. "I was trying to be cordial, but this is too much now."

"You were trying to be *cordial*?" Nix said. "Really? You need lessons."

"Too much now, is it?" Egil said.

"It is," the man said, his tone hard. "Far too much."

The man's three comrades nodded, muttering agreement.

Nix saw how things would go and sighed. To the man, he said, "Friend, I'd wish you well, but I'm not one for fruitless wishing. I think maybe those lessons I mentioned are forthcoming."

The man licked his lips. The lump in his trachea bobbed up and down as he swallowed. "And who's going to teach it? This priest?"

"Don't kill him," Nix said to Egil.

"Ha!" the man said. "There's four of us and–"

The smack of Egil's backhand across the man's cheek nearly knocked him to his knees. The onlookers gasped, even Tesha.

Snarling, red-faced from embarrassment and the blow, the man reached for the hilt of his blade as his three companions did the same.

Egil lunged forward, seized the man's wrist before his blade showed half its steel, and punched him in the jaw hard enough to mist the air with spit, blood, and at least one tooth. The man hit the floor like a poleaxed bull. Meanwhile, Nix bounded forward to the nearest of the man's companions while clearing his punch dagger of its wrist sheathe. He put its point under the man's chin before the man had cleared his own sword.

The two remaining hireswords got their weapons out and backed off a step, bumping into their table. They took half-hearted fighting crouches, looking around nervously. Sweat glistened on their foreheads.

The man at the end of Nix's dagger glared at Nix but dared not move. Nix winked at him.

"Your friend there forgot that I'm called both lucky and *quick*. But I wager you three will not soon forget that, and you can remind your loudmouthed friend of that when his senses return, yeah?"

The man bared his teeth. Nix pricked him with the blade.

"Yeah?"

"Yeah," the man agreed.

"You show respect to the workers here from now on," Egil said, loud enough to be heard by everyone. He grabbed the semi-conscious man by an ankle and dragged him toward the doors. The other two men made no move toward the priest.

The hiresword groaned, his eyes rolling, his hair collecting bits of the filth from the floor as Egil pulled him along. Bloody drool dripped from the corner of his mouth.

"Go on, now," Nix said to the other two. "Follow. And give your blades a home before I lose my smile. This is all done now, unless you're stupid. This goes any further and my friend will start plying his hammers rather than his fists."

The pair shared a glance, looked at Egil, who pulled their friend along as if he weighed no more than a child, and scabbarded their blades. As one they headed for the doors, mumbling inaudibly. Nix took his blade from under his man's chin and pushed him after them. He realized he had the man's coinpurse in his off hand. He must've lifted it. One day soon he'd have to break himself of the habit, lest it land him in trouble.

"You," he said, and the man turned. Nix tossed him the purse and the man fumbled it. "You dropped that."

The man collected the purse, what was left of his dignity, and shuffled for the door.

Egil opened the door and tossed the hiresword out onto the rain-soaked walkway, nearly hitting a group of four other men just about to enter.

"Pardon us," Egil said to them. "Rubbish drop."

The four newcomers wore mail shirts, metal caps, and long blades. They waited off to the side while the three remaining hireswords filed out.

Nix called after the three as thunder rumbled outside. "Egil and Nix own the *Tunnel* now, you hear? You three are welcome to return, but next time bring your manners. Oh, and maybe leave the loudmouth behind? Done?"

Grumbles and an obscene gesture from the one he'd pricked under the chin were the only responses. Nix figured he'd get no better.

Nix turned, grinning, and looked around the room.

Everyone save Tesha had already turned back to their drinks, conversation, stew, or work.

Again, no applause, no congratulations, no accolades, nothing.

"Come now, people," he muttered. He saw Tesha eyeing him, one hand on her hip, an irritated glint in her kohl-lined eyes. He made a "What?" gesture with his hands and immediately wished he hadn't.

Thunder boomed as she strode down the stairs. She walked up to him like she intended to put a blade in his innards. Instead, she jabbed a finger into his chest. "You won't improve my business, or yours, by bludgeoning the customers."

"What? But he said–"

"I know what he said. She *is* a whore, Nix. Hearing the truth offends neither her nor me. It goes with the work."

"True," Lis said, walking past him and up the stairs.

"But… he was disrespectful."

"So?" Tesha said. "That goes with the work, too. Do you beat everyone who's disrespectful to you?"

"Well not me, no, but Egil…"

"Don't do it again, Nix. I mean it. I can't have everyone who might be interested in one of my men or women worried about saying the wrong thing and getting crosswise of you and Egil. You want this place to make money, don't you?"

Nix found himself at a loss for words. He located some only by changing the subject. "You're quite lovely when you're angry. Did you know that?"

"And you're quite small of stature, angry or no," she said.

And with that, she turned on her heel and walked for the stairs. He stood there sputtering and she shot him a final withering glance before she ascended.

"I believe I'm in love," he said softly, watching the sway of her hips under her blue dress.

"You're always in love," Egil said, stepping beside him, and checking his fist, where he'd scraped it on the hiresword's teeth. The priest nodded surreptitiously at the four men who'd just entered. "You see those four who just came in?"

The men, all hard-eyed and armed, stood just inside the doors. They were eyeing Nix and Egil uncertainly, whispering among themselves.

"I see them," Nix said softly, then called to them, "And here are men of quality to replace the low men late of this establishment. Welcome, goodsirs."

The men pasted on fake smiles, gave half-bows, and went awkwardly for a corner table. Nix saw how they fell in behind the older, bearded man among them.

From their helmcuts and bearing, he made them as bodyguards, city watch, or soldiers. The bearded one caught Nix studying them, so Nix pasted on a fake smile of his own.

"Morra, see to those men," Nix said, waving to the serving girl.

"In a moment, luvs," Morra called to them, placing frothing tankards down at another table.

Egil took Nix by the arm and walked him toward the bar.

"Have to be watch," Egil said.

"Looks that way to me, too. We're not wanted by any authorities, though. Wait. Are we?"

Egil shrugged. "Pits if I know."

Nix wondered if his mouthiness at the Slum Gate had landed them in trouble.

"Well, even watchmen just want a drink sometimes, right?"

"Possible," Egil said. "Or maybe they're here on some other business not involving Egil and Nix."

"Are you referring to us in the third person now?"

"Shut up," the priest said, and tended to his tankard.

Kiir stood at the other end of the bar, her dress showing her curves to good effect. Nix sat and patted the stool next to him. She smiled and moved to take it, but Tesha's voice from the top of the stairs cut through the cacophony of the common room.

"Kiir, attend me here, please."

Nix tried not to look crestfallen, but doubted he succeeded. He took Kiir by the wrist as she turned to go. "Maybe we can speak later?"

"Speak?" she said, with a sweet smile and mischievous wink.

Nix chuckled and watched her as she walked off.

"Moments ago you loved Tesha," Egil said.

"I'm abundant with love," Nix answered wistfully. "A good thing, given the number of lovely women in this city."

Egil chuckled, frowned at the cut on his knuckle. "You're abundant in something, that's certain."

CHAPTER FOUR

Eating knives had scored the polished wood of the *Tunnel's* bar over the years, the lines like obscure runes, glyphs written by wastrels in the language of drunks. Nix and Egil sat there for hours, tended to by a taciturn Gadd, watching patrons enter the *Tunnel* sober and stagger out drunk, or weave up the stairs with an arm around one of Tesha's men or women.

They drank Gadd's ale under the gaze of Lord Mayor Hyram Mung, whose portrait hung from the wall behind the bar, next to the dram writ that authorized the *Tunnel's* existence. After a time, the Lord Mayor's beady eyes, doughy flesh, and double chins became too much to bear.

"Gadd, I want that portrait taken down," Nix said. "Get something more suitable."

Kiir stood beside him, sipping an apple wine. "He is ugly."

She'd come and gone several times during the night, and each time Nix felt her absence as his imagination tortured him with what she might be doing while gone.

"And fat," said Lis, sitting beside Egil and facing the common room. "I hear his adjunct is handsome, though."

Kiir giggled.

"Gadd," Nix said. "Did you hear?"

Gadd, arranging his tankards and mugs behind the bar with the same care an alchemist might show to his alembics and beakers, looked a question at him.

Nix pointed at the portrait behind the bar. "Down. I want that down."

"Drink?" Gadd said, his eastern accent as thick as his eel stew. "Ale?"

"No, no, not a drink. I have one. The painting." Nix made an expression like that of the Lord Mayor in the portrait – eliciting another giggle from Kiir – and pointed at it. He made a downward gesture. "Down. I want it down. It irks."

Gadd pointed a thumb at the portrait, eyebrows raised in a question.

"Yes, yes, the portrait," Nix said. "Down."

"Mayor," Gadd said, and mimed the Lord Mayor's expression himself. "Nice picture."

Nix cursed while Egil and the women laughed aloud.

"This seems funny to you?" Nix asked. "Our tapkeep can't speak Realm Common."

"He seems to manage well enough," Egil said. "Besides, his ale is the best thing here. This place *is* a shithole. That hiresword had the right of that, at least."

Nix sighed. "Aye. But as you said, it's our shithole."

"Hey!" Kiir said.

"Take no offense, love. You and Lis brighten it immeasurably." Nix snapped his fingers. "Egil, maybe we could convert it to a temple of Ebenor? Get the Momentary God some worshippers who aren't angry whoresons?"

Egil's expression darkened under his thick eyebrows.

Nix had meant his words as jest, but they'd gotten ahead of his sense.

"That was in poor taste. Apologies, my friend."

"But…" Lis began, and trailed off. She bit her lip, fidgeting with a question unasked.

Egil sighed. "Ask," he said.

"No, no," Lis said, obviously embarrassed. She fidgeted more. "I don't–"

"I can see you have a question." Egil sipped from his tankard, put it down. "Ask so it's out of your head. I'll not have you fidgeting with it all night."

Still she hesitated.

"He's not as mean as he looks," Nix said to her. "He won't bite… at least not more than once."

Lis smiled, turned toward Egil, and dove in. "Your tattoo?"

"Yes."

"Well, I don't understand. Why Ebenor? Why not Aster? Or Borkan? I thought Ebenor was… dead? And he was a god for only a heartbeat, wasn't he?"

"He was a god for only a moment," Egil said, staring straight ahead. "But then, we're all gods for only a moment."

"I don't... What?"

Egil said, "Why do you wear the harp of Lyyra, Lis?"

Lis looked down at the cheap charm that hung between the pale mounds of her breasts: a harp, the symbol of Lyyra, Goddess of Sensuality and Pleasure.

"Oh, I don't know. It was a gift from a regular. I'm not really religious..." She colored. "I'm just trying to make this life bearable, I suppose."

"Me, too," Egil said, and frowned. He thumped his tankard on the bar. "Discussion of this kind rarely helps in that regard. Gadd, a refill if you please."

Lis looked over at Nix and Kiir as if for help or advice, but Nix had none to give. He knew why Egil had turned to the worship of Ebenor, and he never spoke of it. Lis looked back at Egil.

"Forgive my question," she said softly. "Your beliefs are none of my concern. I shouldn't have asked. I didn't mean to... pain you."

Gadd put another tankard before Egil. Still the priest did not look at Lis, nor at any of them. He stared straight ahead, his mind in the past, on tragedy.

"Life is made up of moments, Lis," he said, his normally gruff voice turned soft. "Some good, some... bad. In these days I'm just trying to have more of the good ones. Apologies for speaking harshly just now."

Lis must have heard the hurt in Egil's voice. She

stared at him, sympathy in her eyes, then put her hand on his hairy arm. He seemed startled by her touch, but did not move his arm away. He looked down at her hand, tiny and pale on his massive, tanned forearm. After a time, he put his other hand over hers.

Nix felt as if he were seeing something private, sacred, and he found himself hoping that someone, sometime in his life, would touch him with the same sense of unabashed compassion Lis had just shown Egil.

"Yes, well," Nix said, treading lightly. "As we were discussing. Right. Well. So, do you think we should hire someone to run this place for us?"

Egil patted Lis's hand once before removing his own. "Like who?"

Nix turned around on his stool, studied the raggedy handful of men who still remained, as if one of them might be a candidate. He caught the four watchmen eyeing him as they talked softly among themselves. They hadn't touched their ales. Nix smiled falsely at them, turned back to the bar.

"I don't know."

"What about Tesha?" Kiir asked.

"She already mostly runs the place," Lis added.

Egil and Nix shared a look. Egil shrugged. The idea seemed reasonable to Nix, too.

"She is competent," Egil said.

"More than competent, from what I've seen. And she runs the… workers, so she's already halfway there. We could give her free room and board, halve the price of rent and board for her workers, and for that she runs the whole place for us. We just take the profits."

Kiir squealed, embraced Nix, her rapid motion filling the air with the scent of her perfume. "We'll go tell her."

"Wait, we're just..." Nix said, but too late. They were off.

"... talking," he finished.

"Looks like done is done," Egil said, and chewed his mustache. "Could work. Tesha, I mean. She'll need some muscle, though, else how can she deal with bungholes like that hiresword?"

"She's got her own ideas about that," Nix said, thinking of the dressing-down Tesha had given him. "Besides, we'll be here often enough, and when we're not, our names still carry weight. And if it came to it, we could hire someone."

Egil waved a hand in the air to disperse the aromatic smoke from Gadd's pipe. Nix slid the ash tray down the bar, away from them.

"It's a marvel the man can understand any Realm Common at all, inhaling all that stink."

Egil said, "I thought you wanted to be a landed gentleman, maybe get a seat on the Merchants' Council. Respectability, you said."

"Oh, I do. And we'll still be respectable. Or at least more than we are now. But... being respectable seems like a lot of work, doesn't it? Am I wrong?"

Egil laughed, raised his tankard in a toast. "You're not. It does seem like work."

"You know, maybe we should change the name from the *Slick Tunnel* to the *Shithole*? Embrace the truth, as it were. Some might find it amusing. What do you think?"

"I think my ale cup is empty again."

"That it is." Nix gestured to the tapkeep. "Ales around, Gadd."

That, Gadd understood, and they were soon staring at full tankards, listening to the sound of the common room behind them.

"Those four slubbers still watching us?" Nix asked.

"I believe they are," Egil said. "Been watching us the whole time. I guess they are here for us. What do you suppose they want?"

"The fun's in finding out, yeah?"

Egil drained his cup as he stood. "Yeah."

"Try not to throw anyone else bodily from the premises," Nix said, loosening his falchion in its scabbard. "Tesha frowns on it."

"Well enough."

They stalked across the common room. The four men saw them coming, nudged each other. Expressions tightened, and hands went low, near hilts. The men slid their chairs back from the table to give them room to stand, pushed back capes to give unfettered access to blades.

Mindful of Tesha's admonition, Nix faked a smile, an expression he'd worn both while seducing women and while putting a span of steel into a man's gut. Egil simply wore his usual surliness. False expressions weren't in the priest, no matter the circumstances. If Egil wanted someone dead, that someone would see it coming well in advance.

Out of habit, Nix and Egil spaced themselves at two paces, wide enough to ply their weapons without getting in each other's way, should it be necessary. Nix hoped it wouldn't, but it paid to be prudent.

"And how do you fare, goodsirs?" Nix asked.

"Uh, fine," said one of the younger men, and the older shot him a glance that said "shut up."

"Is the ale to your satisfaction?" Nix asked.

The three younger men, perhaps puzzled by the mundanity of the question, looked to the older bearded man, whom Nix made as their leader.

"It's quite good," said Beard. "Surprisingly so."

"Excellent," Nix said, and nothing more. He and Egil stood their ground in silence, near enough to the table to make their presence an irritant. Nix kept his smile and Egil his frown, the two of them comfortable with the other men's growing discomfort.

"Something else?" Beard finally asked.

"I don't know," Nix said pointedly. "Is there something else?"

The man seemed to take his point. He pushed his tankard away, looked to his fellows, back to Nix, then put his hands on the table where they could do nothing foolish.

"Right. So, you're Nix Fall and Egil of Ebenor?"

"And you're Dur Follin Watch, yeah? That bit at the Slum Gate–"

The man shook his head. "Isn't my concern. What makes you think we're watch?"

"If not watch then what?" Nix asked.

"Do you answer every question with a question?"

"Do I, Egil?" Nix asked the priest.

"What of it if you do?" Egil answered.

Nix looked at Beard. "Do questions bother you?"

One of the other three men smiled, probably the youngest. Beard did not. He looked from Egil to Nix and shook his head as if to clear it of confusing thoughts.

"No. Look. I mean, listen, we work for someone who's interested in your... services. We've been waiting for the right time to approach you. You were either fighting or surrounded by women 'til now."

"You speak of it as if that's a bad thing," Nix said.

More smiles from the other three.

"And I wanted to take your measure," Beard said.

"Really? And how'd you go about that?" Nix asked.

"And since when's it take four armed and armored men to make a job offer?" Egil growled. He let his hands fall to the hafts of his hammers.

"Does seem less than gentlemanly," Nix observed solemnly.

"Just tell me if you're interested," Beard said, his voice tinged with impatience. "The terms are generous."

"I'm not interested," Nix said. "Egil?"

"No."

"And there you go," Nix said.

"But–"

"See, we don't hire out," Nix said. "Not our approach, powerful patron or no."

"But–"

Egil stepped forward and put his hands on the table, nearly toppling it, staring Beard in the face. "We. Don't. Hire. Out."

To his credit, Beard looked neither frightened nor especially put out by Egil's tone and proximity. Most men would have been.

Military, Nix figured. Had to be. Or damned experienced watch.

"Offer our regrets to your employer," Nix said. "Meanwhile, enjoy the ale and the rest of your evening. Here, if you have half a mind. Elsewhere, if you have a whole."

Beard shook his head. "You're making a mistake here."

"Doubtful," Nix said.

With that, he and Egil turned and started to walk off.

"Final word, then?" Beard called after them. "You're certain?"

Nix did not like the implication dangling in the sentence. He turned around, his eyes hard.

"No, these are my final words: don't get cute with me in my own place. Oh, and *stop fakking staring holes into my back, yeah?*"

Two of the three younger men leaped to their feet, sending chairs toppling. They had hands on their sword hilts, but Beard halted them with a sharp word and a raised hand. Egil's hammers were already in his hands, a snarl on his lips.

"Barky bunch of curs, ain't they?" Nix said.

Egil grunted. "Need to be brought to heel, maybe."

"Nix!" called Tesha from her station atop the stairs.

Nix winced, and dared not turn to face her.

"We were only asking," Beard said calmly. At his gesture, his two underlings retook their seats and removed hands from hilts. "We intended no offense."

"A misunderstanding, then," Nix said, hopefully loud enough for Tesha to hear. "No harm done. As I said, enjoy your evening."

"Elsewhere's probably best though," Egil added.

As Nix and Egil walked back to the bar, Tesha descended the stairway to meet them. She smiled at a patron ascending the stairs with one of her girls, but the smile disappeared the moment the patron was out of eyeshot. Nix tried not to ogle her figure as she moved toward them.

"You can muster a fake smile as well as me," Nix said to her.

"Twice in one night you threaten–"

"Leave it be, woman, "Egil said. "They're watch or kith to watch. We only had words."

"*Heated* words," she said.

"Words, heated or no, shed no blood."

Nix cut off whatever she intended to say. "Did Kiir and Lis tell you our thinking? About this place?"

For the first time, Tesha's severe expression softened. "They did, but… did you mean it? I thought you were having a jest at their expense."

Nix shook his head. "We're earnest. Free room and board for you. As for your workers, half of what they've been paying for rent and board. Profits come to us, less ten percent as your earnings. No negotiations. That's the offer. Done?"

Her expression vacillated between surprise, hope, and skepticism. "This is business, Nix. Nothing else. You're clear on that?"

"You cut me deeply, milady. If ever I have to buy an entire tavern to procure sex, even from one as lovely as you, Egil has standing instructions to kill me."

Egil chuckled. So did Tesha, and Nix thought the sound musical.

"What about Gadd?" she asked, and looked over her shoulder at the towering tapkeep. He tended his wares, as always, working his sorcery behind the bar. Morra flew by, holding her usual platter of ales.

"He already eats and drinks free," Nix said. "His pay is your concern, but keep it reasonable. Morra's too. If you accept the offer."

She put a hand on her hip, looked around the common room.

"See how she considers?" Egil said. "A wise woman. If we'd done that, we'd never have bought the place."

"Unhelpful, priest," Nix said out of the side of his mouth. "What do you say, Tesha?"

She nodded to herself and stuck out a hand. "Done and done."

Nix shook it, feeling a charge at her touch. Egil shook her hand perfunctorily.

"We're going to drink now," Egil said. "It's your show, Tesha."

"And send Kiir down, if you would," Nix said.

"Kiir?" Tesha asked, and her lips pursed. "Oh... Fine."

As she walked away, Nix elbowed Egil. "You see how she hesitated there? She likes me."

"So you say," Egil said. "And now to the Altar of Gadd."

"For libations. Aye."

Soon thereafter the four watchmen settled their bill and left without a backward glance.

"Not sorry to see those slubbers vacate," Nix said.

"Aye. Doubtful they return."

The crowd thinned as the night got on and the water clock of Ool soon announced the small hours. Nix nursed an ale at the bar, trying to stifle yawns. Despite turning management of the place over to Tesha, he had the uncomfortable feeling that he'd bound himself to a piece of property, and that it had shrunk his world rather than expanded it.

He stuck his nose under his shirt and winced at the reek. He smelled of sweat, sour beer, and Gadd's pipesmoke. Basically, he smelled like the *Slick Tunnel*.

To Gadd, he said, "I had no idea owning a business would be so damned boring."

"One day of respectability and that about serves," Egil said.

Gadd made a non-committal grunt. His tattooed hands and arms worried at the tankards and cups. He took out a pouch of something – hops, Nix thought, or maybe some kind of snuff – crushed them in his hands, inhaled deeply.

"You don't understand anything we say, do you?" Nix said.

Gadd looked up, a dust of the snuff across his broad nose. "Drink?"

Nix smiled. "No. Still working on this one. Keep doing what you do, man."

To occupy the time, Nix examined the ivory wand he'd found in the tomb of Abn Thahl. He studied the tiny carvings on its shaft, his mind drifting back to his time in the Conclave as he tried to make sense of the characters.

The scent of perfume presaged Kiir's arrival beside him.

"You have scant idea how pleased I am to see you," he said with a smile.

She smiled shyly, sat, and nodded at the wand. "What's that?"

"'Ware my stink," Nix said. "And this? This is nothing, just one of my gewgaws, as Egil would say. I took it from the tomb of an Afirion wizard-king after defeating the devil that guarded it."

He spoke casually, but his words summoned the response he'd hoped for. Her eyes widened with wonder and she made a circle of her ring finger and thumb, a protective gesture, the symbol of Orella. She leaned in close to him, and he felt the warmth of her through his clothes. Her hair smelled of vanilla and the scent made him more lightheaded than Gadd's smoke.

"A real devil of Hell?" she asked.

"Indeed," Nix said, warming to the tale. He gestured with his hands as he spoke. "He stood twice as tall as Egil, coated in scales as large as my hand and as hard as steel. He had fanged rictuses at the ends of his arms. A terrible foe. Terrible."

"Gods preserve! How did you escape it?"

Beside Nix, Egil harrumphed. "Escape it? We slew it."

Her hand went to her heart-shaped lips. "Slew it? How?"

Nix sipped from his tankard. "Sharp steel and sharp wits, same as always."

She touched his forearm, just a brush of her fingers. "Your life sounds so interesting. It must be exciting to travel around Ellerth as you do."

"It is. We–"

Suspicion dawned. He turned on his stool, studied her face, her smile, the look of wonder. He pulled back.

"Wait. Are you Jonning me?"

Her smile widened, her brown eyes bright.

"You are!" he said. "Playing me like a Jon. Got me talking about myself while you act the innocent. I see what you're doing."

She batted her eyelashes, and damned if she didn't almost have him again.

"None of that now," he said, and she gave a genuine laugh and laid her hand on his arm. The feel of her skin on his felt warm, comforting.

"Don't take it ill," she said. "You seemed to be having fun. Besides, it's habit and hard to break. Men love to jabber on to a pretty girl."

Nix thought of the coinpurses he'd lifted earlier, both done out of habit. "Habit, I understand. And you *are* pretty. But now I feel a bit of an arse."

"Don't. And if you're not filling my ears with shite, I am interested in hearing about the wand. Is that a real pearl?"

Nix nodded. "A shaft of ivory capped with a pearl."

She leaned in close. "What does it do?"

"I don't know yet. But as I always say, the fun's in finding out."

"You don't know yet?" The surprise in her expression made her look even prettier. "Aren't you afraid to carry it around? What if it... I don't know, it went off and filled your trousers with lightning?"

Nix grinned. "Avoiding the obvious response to a pretty girl's mention of lightning in my trousers, I'll say instead that while I don't know *exactly* what it does, I have a rough idea."

"And?"

Egil looked over from his somber ruminations. "Yes, and?"

Nix leaned forward, elbows on the bar, holding the wand across his palms. "The wizard-kings of Afirion were known to practice the art of transmutation, changing things into other things, or modifying existing things to make them better. The ivory and pearl construction is consistent with a transmutational device.

The substance used to craft the wand suggests a minor transmutation."

"Continue," Kiir said.

Nix's eyebrows rose. "You understood all that?"

"I'm a prostitute, Nix, not a dolt. I know some things."

"Er… right. Well enough, then. So, now we examine the carvings that adorn the wand for some indication of function."

He turned it in the meager light, to show the many grooves and whorls that lined it. Some looked like serpents, some like abstract shapes, others like script.

"And?" Kiir said.

"And this," Nix said, pointing to a tiny image carved into the wand. "It appears right under the pearl, and also on the opposite end. It's the operating glyph."

Kiir squinted at the image. "What is it?"

"It's a bull."

She leaned forward and eyed the wand. "That's a bull?"

"Of course it's a bull." Nix eyed it more closely. "Well, I'm pretty certain it's a bull. An artist's interpretation of a bull. Maybe. What else could it be?"

"A dog." Kiir said. "A rat. A cat."

Egil guffawed.

"Pfft. No, it's a bull. I'm certain."

She leaned back. "So if it's a bull, what does that mean?"

"Not certain of that either."

"That's much uncertainty for one wand," she said.

"Well, what do think of when you think of a bull?" Nix asked her.

"Horns."

"No," Nix said. "Size, right? Strength, too. Given that, I think the wand will make its target bigger and stronger, at least for a time."

"Hmm," Kiir said. "If true, that'd be useful."

"Indeed," Nix said.

"*If* you're right," she added.

"You are possessed of little faith."

"I'm not the priest," she said.

Another guffaw from Egil. He toasted her with his ale.

"How do you make it work?" she asked.

"A word in the Language of Creation awakens the magic. That's true of all enspelled items, including and especially wands. Then… you just aim."

"You know the Mages' Tongue?" she asked, unfeigned surprise in her tone.

"I'm a tomb robber," he said with a wink. "Not a dolt. And, as it happens, my tongue knows many, many things."

She laughed, her lips parting to show perfect teeth. "You're awful."

Egil toasted her again. "The priest agrees entirely."

"I am awful," Nix acknowledged with a nod. He drained his tankard. "I really am. As it happens, I spent most of a year at the Conclave. That's where I learned the bits I know."

She looked even more surprised than when he'd

mentioned the Mages' Tongue. "I thought studies there lasted several years."

"He dropped out," Egil said.

"*No,*" Nix said irritably. "I was expelled. That's a much more honorable method to part ways with that place and its so-called instructors."

"Agreed," Egil said, and harrumphed. "Wizards."

"Third best event of my life, that expulsion," Nix said, thinking back on his younger days at the Conclave.

"So, in only a year you learned the Mages' Tongue?"

"Bits of it," Nix said, unwilling to admit that he knew some words but not their meanings. "Enough to do a few things. I wouldn't want to know much more. It's the gods' tongue, used to create Ellerth and the vault of stars. Speaking it too much is said to drive a man mad. Words not meant to be heard by mortals and so forth."

"There's truth in that," Egil said. "From what we've seen."

Now it was Nix's turn to toast his friend. He and Egil had crossed many sorcerers over the years and not one seemed to think with sense.

"They say magic's in the blood, not the tongue," Kiir said. "So I guess you're born of a sorcerer, Nix Fall."

"Ha!" Nix said. "Not likely in this blood."

Nix was born of a prostitute and a Jon and had no idea of his lineage.

"So then," Kiir said, "how'd you get into and out of a wizard-king's tomb with your lives?"

Gadd put an ale before her and she smiled her thanks at the tall easterner.

Nix just shook his head. "Tricks of the trade, love. Some secrets we must keep to ourselves. Suffice to say it was a close thing."

Egil said, "It was. But we rob tombs better than we run taverns, so here we sit."

"Here we sit," Nix said, toasting his friend a second time.

"I'm glad of it," Kiir said.

"And I," Nix said.

Tesha spoiled the moment by calling down from the stairs. "Kiir!"

"Work calls," Kiir said, standing.

Tesha stood at the top of the stairs, a young man beside her. The man eyed Kiir hopefully and Nix liked it not at all. The man shifted on his feet in his eagerness, his smile filling his whole face. He couldn't have been more than twenty winters, just some bird-witted hob with a few terns rattling around in his pocket and a prick hard for a pretty girl.

Nix said, "You know, you don't have to–"

She put a small hand to his lips. "Don't do that, Nix. This is my life. I chose it. Let's not pretend this is more than it is."

He stared into her eyes, nodded. "If it is, though?"

She smiled, patted his arm.

"I must remember never to underestimate you," he said.

"Men always underestimate women, so you're ahead on that score."

He touched her wrist, unwilling to let her go.

"Are all the women who work here as sharp as you and Tesha?"

"Every one," she said. She winked and walked away, letting her fingertips drag across Nix's forearm.

After she'd left, Nix looked to Egil. "There's no one naïve left in this town."

Egil nodded, staring into his ale cup. "Still in love?"

Nix watched Kiir walk up the staircase, the sway of her hips, the way the bodice of her dress gripped her curves. "Pits, maybe more than ever."

Egil took a slug of Gadd's ale. "I don't blame you."

CHAPTER FIVE

Baras and a dozen of his men lingered near the mouth of an alley across Shoddy Way. Drums beat in the Low Bazaar behind them, laughter. The air carried the smell of sizzling meat and exotic tobacco. The few street torches lighting the street glowed feebly in the rain-misted night air.

"What now?" Derg, one of his men, asked Baras. Both of them stared at the doors of the *Slick Tunnel*.

"We wait," Baras said. "If they come out, we take them on the street."

"And if they don't?"

"We go in when it clears out. Get some men around the back and make sure they don't sneak out that way."

"Why would they sneak? They don't know we're out here."

"Those two sneak out of habit, I expect."

"Truth," Derg said. He ordered a third of the detachment around to the rear of the *Tunnel* and the men jogged off.

"Shite night and shite street for this kind of duty," Derg said. He looked longingly back at the bazaar.

"Aye," Baras said.

A voice sounded from a shadowed alley next to the *Tunnel.*

"Baras, is that you?"

Baras and his men whirled on the speaker, hands on their hilts.

The speaker stepped out of the alley, holding his empty hands out wide.

"No threat here, lads," the man said, walking toward them, and Baras placed his voice at last.

"Jyme?"

"Aye," Jyme said, and hurried across the way. "Gods, man. What are you doing here?"

Jyme looked a bit older than the last time Baras had seen him, but he remained as thin as a willow reed. His thin mustache and beard looked like a dusting of soot on his narrow face. One eye and half his face were red and swollen, as if from a punch.

"Working."

"Working?" Jyme said, and glanced around the men. "I heard you wasn't watch anymore."

"I'm not," Baras said, and didn't bother to explain. "What happened to your face?"

Jyme's thin mouth curled in anger. He ran a hand over his swollen eye. "Big tattooed fakker got over on me in the *Tunnel.*"

"Tattooed?" Baras said. "Egil? The priest?"

Jyme spat. "He's no priest. Wait, how do you...?"

Jyme looked around at the men again, their blades, their eyes focused on the *Tunnel.* He looked at the empty horse-drawn wagon on the street before them. His eyes widened as realization set in.

"You're looking to take that one down, ain't you? The priest, I mean?"

"None of your concern," Baras said.

"He gave me this eyeshine," Jyme said. "I been waitin' on him to come out myself. Figured I'd acquaint him with my blade as answer for his punch."

Baras said nothing, but didn't figure Jyme would come out on the bloodless end of a fight with the priest.

"None of this concerns you, Jyme. Be on your way. We'll have a drink come another day."

"I ain't going nowhere," Jyme said. "Like I said. I'm waitin' on that priest to show. Maybe I'll just wait here with you, yeah?"

"I can have you moved," Baras said.

Jyme sneered. "Arrested, like? After all we saw together back in the watch? Come on, Baras. Besides, I'll make enough noise in the going that your ambush here'll go for nothing."

Baras turned to face him, irritated.

Jyme took a step back, hands raised. "Listen, I just want in. You know I can account for myself with a blade. I don't even want payment. I just want that priest to get his, see?"

Baras considered it. Jyme had been a decent watchman once, and an extra blade didn't hurt.

"If you're in, you're in," Baras said. "That work for you?"

"Yeah," Jyme said. "Works."

"Good," Baras said. "When they come out, we take them. If they don't come out, we go in and get them. But I need them both alive. And you're to do exactly as I say."

"Ah, you're no fun, Baras."

"I'll introduce you to the men."

By the time the water clock tolled three hours past deepnight, the *Tunnel* was almost empty. A few drunks slouched over tables, sleeping. Gadd and Egil escorted them out the door and Gadd made a half-hearted attempt at sweeping the floor.

Nix's eyes kept going to the stairway. No one had emerged from the upstairs pleasure rooms for hours. Nix didn't think any patrons remained up there, or at least he hoped not. In his mind's eye, he saw Kiir… servicing that country hob, and it bothered him more than he liked to admit.

Gadd's cups, tankards, and platters stood arrayed behind the bar in formation, an army of ceramic and tin. Nix put Kiir from his mind and tried to fight down yawns.

"You can go, Gadd," he said to the towering tapkeep. "We'll close up." He gestured at himself and Egil and spoke slowly. "We will close."

Gadd seemed to take his point and nodded. He gathered his cloak, smiled, showing eye teeth filed to sharp points, and took his leave.

"What do you suppose his story is?" Nix said. "Got more ink on his arms than a sorcerer's spellbook. And those teeth."

"He's from the east and brews the gods' own ale," Egil said. "That's all I know and all I need to know."

"Speaking of his ale," Nix said, and jumped over the bar. He shook the last tapped hogshead and it sloshed satisfactorily. "Still half-full."

"Let's remedy that."

"Aye."

Nix placed the sloshing barrel on the bar and drew two tankards.

"To ownership, then," Nix said, hoisting his tankard.

"Ha!" Egil said, and bumped it with his own. "To an eventful first day."

"Agreed."

They sat at the bar, *their* bar, for the next hour. They sat in comfortable silence, as only friends can do, with Ool's clock tolling the time, the Lord Mayor's portrait staring down at them, and Egil tossing his dice to no apparent purpose. Before long Egil had his head down, snoring on the bar, the eye of Ebenor tattooed on his head keeping watch on the priest's behalf.

Nix continued his war with yawns, shaking the hogshead from time to time, determined to finish it for no reason other than a sense of completion.

When the dissonant notes of Ool's clock proclaimed the fourth hour after deepnight, Kulven had set and Minnear rode high in the vault. Viridian light leaked through the *Tunnel's* windows to stain the floor, the mullions putting a crosshatch on the floor. By then, Nix was done. Fatigue and drink blurred his vision. He slid from the stool, leaned on it for a moment to steady himself. He was drunker than he'd realized. He staggered for the doors.

The common room felt enormous with no one in it. Dying embers crackled in the huge hearth. Nix stumbled, caught his balance on the hearth, and patted it appreciatively.

Made from mortared stones tossed up onto the banks of the Meander by the river's slow current, the hearth struck Nix as one of the sturdiest things he'd ever seen. He imagined all of Dur Follin could fall and the hearth and chimney of the *Slick Tunnel* would remain, keeping company with the Archbridge, jutting out of the ruins like a stone giant's erection.

The image made him chuckle, and chuckling made him lightheaded, and lightheadedness caused him to hook a foot on the leg of a chair as he walked. He stumbled and fell to the floor, cursing. Face down on the wood floor, he called for Egil. A snort and an inarticulate mumble answered him. He chuckled, rose to all fours, and the door of the *Tunnel* flew open. Through the table and chair legs he saw boots, five pairs, presumably attached to legs.

"We're closed," he said, using the end of a table to pull himself up. "Just neglected to bar the–"

Five men stood just inside the doorway, the four men Nix and Egil had made earlier as city watch, and the loudmouthed hiresword with the thin mustache whom Egil had punched in the face. Loudmouth had a shine on his right eye and a nasty grin on his thin lips. The rest had ill intent written on their faces.

"Shite," Nix said.

Beard spoke with the voice of a man used to being obeyed. "Nix Fall and Egil of Ebenor, you are both hereby detained under the authority of the Lord Mayor."

Egil groaned, lumbered up from his stool, and stood there swaying and squinting.

"What is all this now? Lord Mayor what?"

"How things looking now, slubber?" said the hiresword to Nix.

Nix didn't quite understand how the hiresword connected to the watchmen, but the threat of arrest helped clear the mold from his mind. He steadied himself on the back of a chair.

"I'm sure we can work this out," he said. "Now–"

"If you resist, we are authorized to use force," said Beard.

"Egil's voice boomed from behind Nix. "I asked: *what is this now?*"

The hiresword sneered. "This is you getting payback, priest."

The sound of opening doors carried from the second floor of the *Tunnel,* the murmur of voices.

"Stay up there," shouted Beard. "Everyone stay up there. We are on the Lord Mayor's business."

Tesha's voice carried down from the top of the stairs. "How do we know you speak truth?"

"Just do as I say, woman!" said Beard, and nodded at one of his guards, who bounded up the stairs, drawing his blade as he went.

"Back," the man at the top of the stairs said. "Stay back by authority of the Lord Mayor."

Nix heard angry grumbling from Tesha and her workers.

"It'll be fine, Tesha," Nix called, still trying to make sense of what was happening. "Egil and I will work this out."

"I know how you two work things out!" she shot back.

Nix's words seemed to relax Beard. To Nix, he said, "Now you're talking sense. So just come along and–"

"I said we'd work it out," Nix said. "But I meant with blood. Mostly yours. Maybe you understood me to mean something else?"

Beard's eyes narrowed and the tension in the room reasserted itself. He sighed and shook his head. "Bring them. Not dead, but beaten is fine."

The two watchmen and the hiresword advanced across the common room. The watchmen had fists clenched around truncheons. The hiresword had only his fists, but made up for it with the violence of his eyes.

Egil roared from behind Nix and the nearly empty hogshead arced over Nix's head as if shot out of catapult, the remaining ale misting the air in its wake. It slammed into the mouthy hiresword's chest, knocked the air from his lungs in a whoosh, and sent him sprawling. The side of his face caught a chair on the way down, no doubt aggravating his eyeshine.

The men hadn't pulled steel, so Nix didn't either. Instead he grabbed the nearest piss pot, heavy and sloshing with urine and spit – whose job was it to empty those anyway? – and flung it awkwardly at the two remaining men. They scrambled out of the way of the pot but a spray of piss caught them both.

"Ha!" Nix said, grinning, and darted back toward the bar and Egil, deliberately tipping a few tables behind him as he went.

"Does this still count as the same day?" he asked the priest. "Because if so, it's been *really* eventful."

"Same day in my view," Egil said. He picked up a barstool in each hand, holding each by a leg, and brandished them like oversized clubs. "Here's a match for the twigs you carry, whoresons!"

"What in the name of the gods is going on down there?!" Tesha shouted.

Nix wished he knew. He leaped over the bar, under the watchful gaze of the Lord Mayor's portrait – Gadd really needed to take that down – and grabbed two tankards. He hurled them at the two watchmen stumbling through the toppled tables he'd left behind him. One of the tankards clipped the taller of the two on the cheek and stunned him. The other ducked and Egil used the opportunity to charge them, roaring.

Beard, helping the hiresword to his feet, said, "I said you're under arrest by authority of the Lord Mayor!"

"That's shite!" said Nix, firing tankards as fast he could. "Where are your uniforms?"

Gadd would not be pleased with Nix's desecration of his temple. He caught one of the men upside his head with a large mug, eliciting a curse.

"Ha!"

"And your writ?" Egil said, swinging his stools like bludgeons. "Where's that?"

One of the stools caught the smaller of the two men full in his midsection. The wood snapped, but the blow sent the man reeling. In desperation, the other man went head down, charged, and grabbed Egil around the waist. The impact drove the priest back a step, but he steadied himself, dropped the stool, bent, picked the man up by his waist, and heaved him sideways. Arms careening, the man slammed into a table. The legs gave way with a snap and man and wood collapsed to the floor. For good measure, Egil stepped over and kicked him while he was down.

"Why don't you just tell us what this is *actually* about?" Nix said, pegging Beard in his mailed chest with a tankard.

"Damn it!" Beard cursed.

"Let's just kill them!" the hiresword said, and started to draw his sword. Beard halted the draw by grabbing the man's hand.

"Pull that blade and not one of you walk out of here!" Nix promised.

Beard turned and shouted through the open door. "Derg, send in the rest!"

"The rest!" Nix said, disbelieving, tankards held in each hand. "Oh, come on!"

Egil grabbed another chair with both hands, lifted it high, and charged toward Beard and the hiresword. He stopped cold when another eight men poured through the *Tunnel's* open door, all of them helmed, armed, and armored. More watch.

"Over here, Egil!" Nix said. He leaped over the bar and pulled the wand from its tube.

The priest hurled the chair he held at the men storming into the common room and retreated to Nix's side.

"Don't destroy everything!" Tesha shouted, trying to work her way around the watchman holding her and her workers at the top of the stairs.

"I think she'll work out as manager, don't you?" Nix said.

"You gonna use that wand or not?" Egil said, glaring at the men.

Beard crossed his arms over his chest. "Beat them senseless if that's what it takes. They come with us and they come with us now."

"I don't think so," Nix said, grinning.

As one, the new men and the hiresword charged the bar.

Nix spoke one of the handful of words he knew in the Language of Creation, the syllables odd on his tongue, causing a tingle in his lips. The wand answered the word, warmed in his hand, and he hurriedly touched it first to himself then to Egil, and concluded by pronouncing a second word in the language.

The pearl flashed and a sudden burst of opalescent

light staggered him, elicited surprised shouts from the onrushing men. He felt the magic take hold in him and his vision blurred for a heartbeat. His body tingled all over and started to change size, his gear and clothing, too. He knew Egil would be experiencing the same thing. He grinned and raised his fists, imagining himself and Egil wading through the men like giants, their fists like cudgels.

"Ha!" he exulted. "And now, curs, prepare..."

His voice sounded strange, higher-pitched. Instead of wonder and fear in the eyes of the men, he saw instead eagerness, mirth. They rushed forward anew.

"Nix!" Egil shouted, the priest's ordinarily deep voice also an octave higher.

The top of the bar reached Nix's eyes. The onrushing men looked like the giants.

How could that be?

"Shite," he muttered, as realization dawned.

The damned wand had shrunk them to half their normal size!

"I'm sorry, Egil. I thought–"

"Describe for me a time when one of your items worked as you thought! One time!"

Mercifully Nix had no time to reply. Nine men came at them in a rush, fists flying. Nix ducked a punch, landed an uppercut that should have floored the man he struck, but which instead barely staggered him. Someone grabbed his arm and flung him against the bar, while another dove at his legs. Nix might as well have been a child. He gave a kick, missed, and the man wrapped his legs and pulled him down. Another man jumped atop him, pummeled him with short punches to the head, again and again. Nix saw sparks, tried to squirm free, but hadn't the strength. He heard Egil roaring in anger before a final punch caused everything to go dark.

Things quieted downstairs, but Tesha could not see past the guard who barred the stairs. "I want to see whoever's in charge," she said to the guard, a young man with a lazy eye and scraggly beard. He refused to make eye contact with her.

"Sorry, but–"

Tesha stepped up close to the boy. "Don't give me 'sorry,' boy. Get me whoever's in charge."

Tesha turned to her workers, all of them in their nightclothes, frightened-looking.

"Ask them where Nix is, Tesha," Kiir said. "Please."

Tesha nodded. "I'll see to it. Now, all of you go back to your rooms. Leave this to me. Go on, now."

Reluctantly, muttering, they headed back for their rooms. As soon as they did, Tesha turned on the young guard, wearing the imperious expression that few men could long endure.

"Now," she said. "Your commander."

Without waiting for him to respond, she pushed past him and descended the stairs. He fell in behind her, a dog at heel.

"That's him," the guard said, pointing at a large, bearded man who stood near the door. Seeing her approach, the man frowned, barked an order out the door of the *Tunnel*, and walked toward her. She lost her imperiousness when she looked around at the destruction in the common room. Dozens of Gadd's tankards had been broken, a spilled piss pot stained the floor with filth, two stools were broken, a table.

"You'll be compensated for the damage," the man said. He nodded at the young guard behind Tesha and the boy scurried off.

"By whom?" she asked.

Baras licked his lips. "You'll be compensated."

"Where are Egil and Nix?" she asked. "Where's your writ?"

"Madam–"

"Do not 'madam' me," she said. "Where are they? And where are you taking them?"

He studied her face for a long beat, as if taking her measure.

"Madam, Egil and Nix are arrested. That's all you need to know. Should you insist on interfering further, I will ensure that uniformed watchman be permanently stationed outside this establishment. I imagine that will not help with patronage. I will also ensure that one of the Lord Mayor's revenue men checks and rechecks all taxes paid on this property and the goods it sells. Is that something you'd welcome?"

Tesha felt her face color. She clamped her mouth shut lest her rage spill out in a flurry of expletives. She understood well the impulse that had caused Egil to punch the loudmouth hiresword. She'd have done the same to the bearded bunghole before her if she could've.

"So I thought," Baras said. "None of this is your concern, madam. Forget you saw anything here tonight."

With that, the man turned and walked away.

Tesha stomped her foot on the wood floor. "Shite!"

CHAPTER SIX

Nix came to moments or hours later, his head covered in a sack of burlap. He was dizzy from the beating he'd taken, and the sack cocooned him with the sour, fetid stink of his own breath. He feared he might puke and make things worse.

Two men held him by his biceps, wrenching his shoulders as they dragged him. His hands were bound behind his back, going numb from blood deprivation. He was also bound at the ankles and his feet slid limply along the paving stones. The men bearing him grunted with the exertion.

He presumed he had been disarmed, though he could not verify it.

Was he still in the *Tunnel*? Maybe on the street outside?

"Quickly now," one of the men bearing him said, and Nix recognized the voice of Beard. "Get them in and get them gone."

It occurred to him that he might still be shrunken. If so, when the magic of the wand wore off, he'd return to normal size and the bindings on his wrists and ankles would cut into him. He'd be maimed or worse.

The thought of losing his hands quickened his heart. Nix the Cripple didn't sound half as appealing as Nix the Quick. He was about to confess that he was awake when the other man spoke and did him a favor.

"Whoreson couldn't do us the courtesy of staying shrunk, eh?"

Nix exhaled a stinking, relieved breath and offered a silent thanks to Aster, who watched over scoundrels.

"Just get them out of here," Beard said. "They're asking a lot of questions inside the tavern."

Inside the tavern. Then he *was* just outside the *Tunnel*. He considered raising a ruckus, but didn't see the point. It would only earn him another blow to the head. And no one in the *Tunnel* could help him. He and Egil had been arrested under the authority of the Lord Mayor, at least ostensibly. Whores, madams, and a barely literate tapkeep wouldn't know it was a sham, and even if they did, they wouldn't risk trouble with the city authorities. Nix couldn't blame them.

Not an hour ago, Nix had entertained thoughts of crawling into bed with Kiir, of sleeping with his arms around Tesha.

So much for either of those.

He really didn't understand why everyone thought him lucky.

"One, two, three," one of the men said, and his captors tossed him face first into the back of straw-lined wagon. His jaw hit the boards and the impact caused him to bite his tongue. He gritted his teeth against the flash of pain, swallowed the blood, and held his silence.

The straw smelled of goat and dung. His tongue throbbed, and his shoulders, head, and jaw all ached, but he feigned unconsciousness until the men moved off. He heard them talking some distance away from the cart, but the sack and the beat of his heart in his head allowed him to make out only useless bits of the conversation.

Tentatively, he tried the knots on his wrist – tight, skillfully tied. He could work himself free given enough time, even with his hands mostly numb, but he had no idea how much time he had or whether anyone was watching him.

"Is that you?" said Egil in a low tone.

"Aye," Nix answered softly.

"You and your damned gewgaws," Egil grumbled.

"Even bound you can't resist a jab."

"Apologies," Egil whispered. "We're not shrunk anymore."

"I know. You all right?"

"Not especially," Egil said, and shifted his weight. "I'm bloodied, hooded, and trussed like a roasting pig."

"Me, too," Nix said.

"We're outside the *Tunnel* still," Egil said. "I heard them talking."

The voices of the men grew louder, so Egil and he lapsed into silence. Nix heard a few farewells, and the wagon dipped as two or three men climbed aboard the driver's bench.

A moment later and the wagon started to move, the wheels slicing quietly through the mud of the road, the men in the front cursing at the horses and each other. Nix thought he made Beard's voice among them, and maybe the pockmarked hiresword.

Nix still couldn't understand how the hiresword fit in with the four watchmen. They must have been in it together from the outset, the events of the night one big setup.

But why?

"What's going on?" Egil whispered.

"Dunno, and don't care to find out," Nix answered. "Back to back. I undo."

"Right."

Making as though the rough ride were causing him to slide toward Egil, Nix rolled onto his side and scooted back until he could reach Egil's bonds. His blood-deprived hands, the bumpy ride, and his own bonds made things difficult, but he got his fingers on Egil's bindings and checked the knot by feel – a foursquare – and started to undo it.

"Quickly," Egil hissed.

"You sure?" Nix said over his shoulder. "Because I thought I'd go slow."

"Just do it."

Nix got half the knot undone and Egil tried to pull it loose the rest of the way, fouling Nix's progress.

"Stop!" Nix hissed. "Your movement'll retighten them."

"Hey!" shouted a voice from the front of the wagon –

the hiresword for certain. "They're trying to slip the ropes!"

Reins jangled, horses neighed, and the wagon stopped abruptly.

"Stop!" said Beard, and the wagon bobbed as men debarked.

"Come on!" Egil said. "Move!"

"Not helping."

Another of the knot's squares loosened.

"Stop!" Beard again.

"You… already… said… that," Nix said.

A thump against the side of the wagon, a curse as someone tried to climb the side and slipped off into the road. Hurried boot steps on the cobbles, coming around the back of the wagon.

"That's it!" Nix said, feeling the last of Egil's knot give way. "Go!"

Frantic motion beside him, Egil lurching up. The priest shouted a challenge and Nix imagined Egil pulling off his hood, lashing out with his fists.

"Four of them, Nix," Egil shouted, then grunted as a punch or truncheon struck him. "Whoreson!"

Another blow landed, the dull thud of wood on flesh. Another grunt of pain from Egil. Nix worried at his own knots, but was making too little progress. He cursed as more blows slammed into Egil. More grunts from the priest, a few more curses, and then it was over. Egil fell heavily back, groaning.

"Fakking bungholes!" Nix said. "My blade's soon to make a home between your ribs!"

"Can I shut him up?" the hiresword said.

"Aye," said Beard. "Knock him out and be sure of it this time."

"Right," said the hiresword.

There was a dull thunk, another groan, and Egil went still beside him.

"Shit," Nix cursed.

"Didn't have to go this way," Beard said. "All you had to do was sit still."

"Fak you," Nix said, and braced himself.

The blow to his head still summoned a grunt of pain. He saw sparks, lovely fireworks like those the cults fired from the Archbridge. They lasted only a moment, then he saw nothing at all.

Nix came to with a groan, someone shaking him hard by the shoulders. His head was still covered in the damned sack, but he wasn't in the cart anymore. Instead he sat on cold earth, the damp seeping through his trousers. He caught a whiff of fish and sewage.

That put them near the Meander, probably in the Docks.

How long had he been out this time?

"Up!" said Beard, still shaking him. "Up, man!"

The shaking made Nix's head pound. He nearly blacked out again.

"Wake up, Nix Fall," Beard said again, shaking even harder. "You're soon to be in the presence of your betters."

"That ain't saying much," Nix managed. His mouth sounded like it was filled with cloth.

"Still with the smart mouth," Beard said. He shook him again, but a bit more gently.

"Enough, man! I'm awake." Nix tried to push him away but his hands were still bound. His head started to clear a bit. "Where's Egil? Egil!"

"Here," Egil answered, from Nix's left.

Nix did not bother a go at the bonds. He'd never slip them quickly enough, and he had no desire to take another blow to the head. He resigned himself to the mercy of his captors, taking solace in the fact that if they'd wanted him dead, he'd already be dead.

Unless, of course, he'd done something to earn himself a slow, painful death.

Had he?

He didn't remember anything, but he'd had a fair number of nights recently with which his memory had only distant relations.

"Egil, we should drink less," he said.

"Bah. We should fight better. Or use fewer damned gewgaws."

"Fair point," Nix said. He turned his bagged head in the direction he'd last heard Beard speak. "So, listen, if this is about that job you mentioned back in the *Tunnel*, we've had some time to reconsider..."

Dark chuckles from before him and behind, at least four men, all of them within a few paces. No doubt several more were within earshot, as they had been back at the tavern.

"Gods, man," Beard said. "Do you ever stop blathering?"

"He fancies himself a wit," said the hiresword. "Never knowing his mouth is full of shite."

"I thought you said I was in the presence of my betters?" Nix said, blinking at a particularly painful ache behind his eye. "That hiresword with the eyeshine is two steps below the hindquarters of a horse. Hey, tell 'em how you got that eyeshine, Hindquarters."

"You shut your hole," said the hiresword, and Nix heard him take a step toward him.

"That's enough," said Beard, though Nix wasn't sure if he was talking to him or the hiresword.

"Is that the Hindquarters I backhanded at the *Tunnel*?" Egil said, joining in. "I didn't recall his voice being so girlish."

Nix chuckled, though it made his head ache worse.

"Fak you both," the hiresword said sharply.

"It *is* girlish," said Nix. "I hadn't noticed before. I suspect he was stabbed in the genitals at some point. Or perhaps was born without balls. Which is it, Hindquarters? We're all aflutter with curiosity."

A sudden cuff to the side of the head caused Nix to see sparks. He fell to his side and balled up on the floor, expecting another beat down. Hands seized him by the shirt and jerked him off the ground.

"I said that's enough," Beard said. "Enough, Jyme. And you, Nix Fall, you shut your godsdamned mouth. It runs like it has the fakkin' trots."

Jyme ignored Beard and pulled Nix close. "Let me

tell you something, Nix *the Lucky*. I knew these mates here from way back, when I was still watch. I saw them coming into the tavern while your big friend was showing me out."

"*Tossing* you out, you mean," Nix said. "And I'm surprised you could see anything through that eye-shine."

Egil chuckled. "Went down as easy as a child."

"Fak you, priest!" Jyme said. Then, to Nix, "I waited outside to get at you two, see? But then these mates came out and Baras told me they was looking to nab you two. Well, I signed up then and there for that."

Now Nix had a name for Beard – Baras.

Jyme gave Nix a rough shake. "And it was just happenstance, see? Just the gods smiling on yours truly." He cast Nix back to the ground. "So who's got the luck now, Nix? Who's got it?"

Nix sat up and his mouth kept going, as if of its own accord. "I didn't hear a word you said, distracted as I was by your breath, which, even through this sack, has stink enough to rouse the dead. You mind starting over back at the beginning?"

Jyme growled and Nix steeled himself for another blow.

"Jyme!" said Baras. "That's it. It's done. You're here on my word. You needed a job and now you have one. But you act professional, just as you did when you was watch. That, or you're out."

"If you're watch," Egil said, "then you're also liars. You denied as much back at the *Tunnel*."

"You mind your tongue, priest," Baras snapped. "Call me a liar again and I may let Jyme have his way."

"What's he going to do, kiss me?" Egil said. "You want to kiss me, Hindquarters?"

"Fak you," Jyme said.

"Your mouth keeps tolling the same time, Jyme. Fak you. Fak you. That's all it says. Are you mentally deficient?"

"Fak you! Er... Fak! Damn you!"

Nix chuckled.

"We're not watch," said Baras.

"Then what in the Eleven Pits is this about?" Egil said.

"Soon enough and you'll know," answered Baras.

"Not even a hint?" Nix prodded. "Come on. A small one? Let's make a game of it. Maybe sing a song, too."

"Shut up!" said Baras, flustered.

Moments later, Nix heard murmured voices, as if from outside a building. A bolt slid through its housing and a door creaked open. A gust of wind hit him, ripe with the odor of the river. He heard a nightgull call and thought instantly of the Heap and Mamabird. He decided that it wouldn't do for him to die with a bag over his head.

"My lord," Baras said, and Nix heard smart motion from the other men in the room, as if they were saluting.

"Baras," said a resonant male voice. Nix did not recognize it. "Who is this?"

"I'm Nix–" Nix said.

"Not you, fool," said the man.

"His name is Jyme, my lord," Baras said. "He served with me once, long ago. He was useful to us in our mission tonight. He needs employ."

"Useful how?"

"In capturing these two, my lord. He has no love for them and he's a good man."

"Agree with the former but disagree with that last," Nix said, but no one acknowledged him.

"And these are Egil of Ebenor and Nix Fall?" the man asked.

"They are, my lord," Baras answered.

"Nix is the mouthy one?"

"Aye. Mouthy like few others I've ever heard."

Nix heard the approaching tread of soft shoes. They stopped before him.

"I didn't want things to go this way," the man said. "But you left me with little choice."

Nix knew lies when he heard them. Whoever he was, the man had very much wanted things to go exactly as they had.

"What is it you want?" Nix said. He felt ridiculous speaking through a bag, looking up from the ground.

The man paced before him. "Right now, I just want you to listen. Will you do that?"

"I've been known to listen from time to time. Egil?"

"Speak, man," said the priest. "I can barely feel my hands. And this bag smells like shite."

The man affected a heavy sigh that sounded as false to Nix as a wizard's promises.

"Hear, then. I have two sisters, both young, lovely

girls. They're all that's left of my family. And both of them are very sick. I need your help to heal them."

"Lovely, you say?" Nix said.

"Dog," spat Baras.

"We're not healers," Egil said. "Talk to the priestesses of Orella."

"Or maybe we *can* offer healing," Nix said slyly. "But only if you take off–"

"Spare me such nonsense," the voice said, taking on a sharp edge before going dull once more on false sincerity. "I know quite well what you are. You're mere thieves and robbers."

Nix tried not to feel offended by the "mere."

"My sisters' sickness isn't of this world. They're cursed and it's the curse that caused me to seek you out."

"We're not wizards, either," Egil said.

"No doubt," the man said. "Further, the curse makes them... dangerous, to themselves and others."

Mention of a curse and danger piqued Nix's natural curiosity about things magical. "How'd they come to be cursed?"

Once more the sharp edge to the voice, and louder this time. Nix imagined the man standing directly over him, staring down daggers.

"*How*, you ask? You? Here is *how*: the actions of ignorant miscreants caused it. Their mess is now mine to clean."

"I have a fondness for miscreants generally," Nix said with a shrug. "Not so much for messes."

"Nix..." Egil cautioned.

"I told you, my lord," Baras said. "He never stops."

The man continued: "You may find that your fondness for low things one day puts you on the wrong end of blade or spell."

"Aye, that," Nix conceded with a tilt of his head. "Happens oft enough already. This very moment, for example."

"That's truth," Egil said.

The man inhaled deeply, as if calming himself. "The curse must be lifted before Minnear is full."

"That's not long," Nix said. "Or?"

"Or… my sisters will die."

"A sad, sad tale," Nix said. "Well, a sincere wish of good luck to you and them. There's nothing we can–"

A cuff to Nix's head from one of the guards quieted him. Probably came from Baras. Not hard enough to have been Jyme's hand.

"Even when your life hangs by a hair you jest and make light?" the man said.

"Habit," Nix explained. "One bad one of many, I admit."

"Your purpose remains unclean," Egil said. "What help can we be to your sisters? And why would we offer any, given the lumps on my skull and the bag over my head?"

"I can only lift the curse if I possess a certain item, a magical horn."

"A gewgaw," Egil sniffed.

"What horn?" Nix asked. "How can a horn lift a curse?"

The man ignored Nix's question. "My research reveals that the horn can be found in the tomb of Abn Thuset."

"Research?" Egil asked. "What are you? A sage?"

"Oh, I see now," Nix said. "You need tomb robbers to procure this horn for you." Nix shifted on his backside, feeling more in control of matters. "Abn Thuset was, of course, one of the greatest wizard-kings of ancient Afirion. But his tomb is lost to history and sand. Many have sought it, but no one knows where it is. Unless..."

"I know where it is," the man said.

"Unless *that*," Nix said, though he was still skeptical. "How do you know you've found it?"

"And if you have, then go get this horn for yourself," Egil said. "As I said to your man back at the *Tunnel*, we're not hirelings."

"I'm not offering you employment," the man said, his tone cool. "I could, however, order you to do it."

"Order us?" Egil said with a chuckle. "And just who in the Pits are you to order us?"

A long pause, then a hand seized the burlap sack around Nix's head and tore it off, taking a few hairs with it. Nix blinked in the lantern light. Jyme held the bag and leered at him, all pockmarks, bad breath, and poorly groomed facial hair.

"Bottom rung on top now, eh?" Jyme said.

"Maybe for now," Nix answered.

They were in a dirt-floored warehouse filled with barrels, amphorae, sacks, and crates. A block and tackle, and a net for loading transport carts hung from the ceiling. Nix looked for any trading coster marks, but saw none. It was probably a rented warehouse used to move illicit goods.

Egil was on the ground near Nix, and Baras pulled the bag from his head. Like Nix, the priest blinked in the lantern light. Nix eyed the man who'd been speaking, the man who purported to have authority to issue them orders.

He wore a tailored shirt of silk and trousers of velvet, with a high-collared fur-ruffed wool cape thrown over the whole. A thin sword – a nobleman's blade, not a warrior's – hung from a wide belt with a silver buckle. His narrow face, combined with his sharp nose and the widely spaced, deep-set eyes, gave him a reptilian cast. His short brown hair had a part in it as sharp and straight as a plumb line. Dark circles stained the skin under his bloodshot eyes. He looked like he hadn't slept in days.

"You're the Lord Mayor's sorcerer," Nix said, recognizing the man's face. He searched his mind for a name, couldn't quite find it.

"I'm the Lord Mayor's Adjunct," the man corrected, and then Nix had the name.

"Rakon Norristru."

Rakon held the ivory and pearl wand Nix had taken from the tomb of Abn Thahl, the wand with which he'd accidentally shrunk himself and Egil.

Seeing it, Nix winced with embarrassment. Rakon pointed the wand at Nix.

"My men say you know a bit about sorcery. History, too, I gather, from your knowledge of Abn Thuset."

"I had a year at the Conclave."

Rakon's thin eyebrows went up. "Really? And how might you have afforded such an education?"

Nix did not bother with the sordid story that ended with him stealing an education from a dead man. "Well, that's a tale long in telling. I managed, let's say."

"Hmm. And you dropped out after a year?"

"No!" Nix said, trying to stand and nearly toppling himself sidewise in his irritation. "Dammit! Why does everyone assume I dropped out? I was expelled after a year. *Expelled.*"

Rakon nodded, not really listening. He tapped the wand on his palm. His hands were small, the fingers long.

"Well, in that year you seem to have learned only enough to endanger yourself. I looked through your satchel. It's filled with magical trinkets you're probably too stupid or undereducated to use properly."

"Listen, if you're trying to charm me with kind words..." Nix said.

"A bag of gewgaws," Egil breathed contemptuously.

"Unhelpful," Nix snapped at him.

"Perhaps you should stick to plying the many blades my men removed from your person?" Rakon said.

"Perhaps," Nix grumbled. "I'd give much to have one in hand right now."

"I'd wager you would," Rakon said. He bent down and held the wand before Nix's eyes. He tapped the pearl tip on the end of Nix's nose. "You see that?"

Nix went cross-eyed. "Well, no, not really."

"That's an inversion notation, written in the Mages' Tongue. You missed it, I assume, unless you *intended* to shrink and weaken yourself and the priest?"

The guards chuckled.

"Probably you thought it would make you stronger, larger?"

Nix felt himself color. Egil had the good grace not to mock him.

"Leave off, Adjunct," Egil said.

"*Lord* Adjunct," Baras corrected.

"Adjunct is what he gets from me," Egil said again, and stuck out his jaw.

Rakon did not look at Egil. He stood up straight, looming over Nix. A dark look came into his reptilian eyes.

"The wand is Afirion, is it not? How did you come to possess it?"

"As you'd expect," Nix said.

"You stole it?"

"'Stole' is a strong word. We *took* it, and other things, from a tomb in Afirion."

"The tomb of Abn Thahl," Rakon said softly. His knuckles were white around the wand.

"Aye. How would you know that? Abn Thahl is an obscure, minor wizard-king of the nineteenth dynasty who ruled only three years."

"There are many things I know," Rakon said, his jaw clenching, as if he were biting down on more words he'd like to say. "Were there... guardians in the tomb?"

Nix had no idea where the questioning was going. He looked to Egil but the priest shrugged, his expression puzzled.

"Were there?" Rakon pressed.

"Answer him," Baras said.

"Of course there were. There always are with Afirion tombs. There were walking dead, deadfalls, an acid trap, a devil."

Some of the guards smirked with disbelief, others went wide-eyed.

Rakon kneeled, jabbed at Nix's cheek with the wand as if he would stab him through the eye with it. "Killed devils, have you? *Have you*?"

Nix leaned back, bewildered. Anger brewed behind Rakon's eyes, and Nix had no idea what had put it there. Whatever control he thought he'd had over the discussion had just been lost. At the moment Rakon looked capable of anything.

"I... don't know what to say."

He could not bring himself to call Rakon "my lord."

Rakon inhaled and stood. Staring down at Nix, he snapped the wand between his fingers. It died in a puff of smoke and green sparks.

"Say nothing, Nix Fall. I've heard all I need to hear. You two are the men I want for this task. So you're the men I'll have."

"Is that so?" Egil said, his tone threatening. "I guess we'll see about that."

"Egil..." Nix began.

"Oh, I know threats would be idle," Rakon said.

"Depends on the threat, I suppose," Nix said thoughtfully. "Egil is terrified of–"

"So I'll make none. But you'll do what I wish nevertheless. You know I'm the Lord Mayor's personal sorcerer, yes?"

Nix nodded.

Rakon smiled at him, took a step back, and looked to Baras. "The priest first. Then the talker."

"My lord," Baras said, and he, Jyme, and a third guard took station around Egil.

A vein rose in Egil's brow, thick and pulsing, but he did not gratify them with fear or a pointless struggle. Instead, he stared straight at Rakon, his eyes holding a promise of eventual violence, as he awaited whatever was coming.

"None of this is necessary," Nix said. "Whatever *this* is. You want our help. We'll give it. Egil, tell him you're reasonable."

Egil spit a glob of phlegm at Rakon's shoes.

"Among the hill people that's a sign of friendship," Nix tried.

"Shut up," Jyme said.

"This will be uncomfortable," Rakon said to Egil, and began a recitation in the Mages' Tongue, the language sharp-edged, ragged.

"Shite," Nix muttered, squirming against his bonds to no avail.

The magical words seemed to have a physical existence as they exited Rakon's mouth, the syllables pelting Nix like hail. He could not follow the incantation, could only blink against the growing magical energy. Even Rakon's guards – even Jyme – looked uneasy in the presence of the sorcery.

The energy in the room gradually intensified, manifesting as a distortion in the air that snaked behind the sorcerer's gesturing hands. When Nix finally recognized the nature of the spell, the hairs on his neck rose.

"There's no need for this," Nix said, struggling with his bonds to no avail. "Shite, shite."

"Nix?" Egil asked, looking at him sidelong.

"A compulsion," Nix said. "A spellworm."

Egil cursed, kicked at the guards around him with his bound legs. The men, cursing, pushed him flat onto his back.

Jyme secured his legs, Baras held him down at the shoulders, and the third guard lay across his chest. Rakon stepped over to Egil, still incanting, the energy trailing his gestures in a finger-thick rope of reified magic.

Nix shouted to Egil in Urgan, Egil's native tongue, the language of the hill folk of the north. He hoped no one else in the room understood him.

"Focus on Ebenor, Egil! Look to your faith! You have to preserve a piece of your will. Your life depends on it! Focus on Ebenor!"

The energy in Rakon's hands solidified into a wriggling worm of power. Still chanting, he took the worm in his hands and crouched over the prone priest.

Baras drew a dagger and stuck its tip into Egil's

mouth, scraping teeth, forcing the priest's jaws apart. The moment it was open, Rakon loosed the spellworm headfirst into Egil's mouth.

The priest gagged as the worm wriggled down his throat. Egil thrashed his head from side to side, nicking his cheek on Baras's dagger, a froth of spit and blood foaming his mouth. The spellworm squirmed in further, finally disappeared down his throat.

Egil went still, his eyes wide. The men holding him looked at one another, nodded, and released him. Egil only lay flat on the ground, chest heaving, staring up at the rafters.

"Whoresons!" Nix said, straining against his bonds. "Fakking whoresons!"

Rakon turned to Nix, his expression fixed and hard.

"Get him ready," the lord Adjunct said, and began to incant anew.

Nix's mouth went dry; sweat poured down his back. The three guards left off Egil and seized Nix by the arms and around the legs. He could barely move. He might as well have been in a vise. Baras brought his dagger toward Nix's cheek.

"Not necessary," Nix said. "But I meant it sincerely when I called you whoresons."

"Let me," said Jyme, brandishing a dagger of his own.

"Shut up, Jyme," said Baras, then to Nix, "Sorry it went this way."

Rakon moved toward Nix, incanting, a second spellworm forming in the air between his gesturing hands.

Nix took a deep breath and ignored the chant and focused his mind inward. He had to preserve a mental refuge within himself, isolate a bit of him from the magic of the compulsion.

I am Nix Fall of Dur Follin, he told himself, attempting to counter Rakon's chant with a chant of his own. He pictured the Heap, the cawing gulls, the layer of shite. *I am Nix Fall of Dur Follin. Nix Fall of Dur Follin.*

The spellworm solidified in Rakon's hands.

Baras tapped Nix's cheek with his blade. "Make it easy, eh?"

Nix closed his eyes and opened his mouth.

The spellworm slipped into his mouth, as slick as a string of mucus. It slithered down his throat and wriggled into his guts. He gagged, spat, and heaved, but the worm went deeper, sinking into his guts and diffusing through his body, sorcerous tendrils wrapping themselves around his will, rooting in his mind. He resisted, teeth gritted, but still it expanded in him, trying to fill him up, conquer his mind.

I am Nix Fall of Dur Follin.

He thought of Mamabird, the smell of her onion stew. He thought of the mask he wore to cover the frightened boy at his core, the pith of him a secret even from Egil.

I'm Nix Fall of Dur Follin. Of Dur Follin.

The muscles in his body, head to toe, seized all at once. He bit his tongue again and blood filled his mouth. The men lowered him to the ground while spit and blood ran down his cheeks. He lay there, staring up at the ceiling, breathing, breathing, as sorcery stole his will.

Nix Fall of…

"Sit them up," Rakon said after a time, and rough hands sat Nix up. His head lolled on his neck, a marionette without strings. His eyes wouldn't focus. Rakon was a blur before him.

Nix Fall. Nix Fall.

It seemed insufficient. Rakon's spell bent him, twisted his will, made it the sorcerer's own, and when Rakon spoke, his voice, redolent with power, echoed in Nix's braincase like the words of a god.

"Nix Fall and Egil of Ebenor, you will travel with me and my men to the tomb of Abn Thuset, enter it when I say, take the Horn of Alyyk from within, return, and give it to me. Do you understand?"

The words pulled a response from Nix the way a fisherman pulled a hooked fish from the Meander. Egil echoed him.

"I understand."

Rakon crossed his arms over his chest, satisfied. "Bring them, Baras. We leave with the dawn."

"Yes, my lord," Baras said. "But…"

"But?"

"I think they may have helped without use of a spell. Is this the best way to secure their aid? I wonder if this was necessary."

Rakon stared at him. "You wonder, do you?"

Baras lowered his head. "I'm sorry, my lord."

"Do you think they wouldn't have run the moment opportunity presented itself?"

Baras looked from Nix to Egil, back to Rakon. "I… don't know. Probably."

"Almost certainly. Now that's no longer a risk. I can't take a chance with my sisters' lives, Baras. The compulsion is a distasteful necessity."

That convinced Baras. "Yes, my lord."

Jyme pulled Nix to his feet. Nix wobbled. Jyme's breath was hot against Nix's ear.

"Say again who's got the luck, now?"

Jyme's tone sounded far less prickish than his words. The sorcery had unnerved him, too.

Nix shook off Jyme's grip, stood on shaky legs, and adjusted his shirt. He licked his lips and said, "The spellworm in my gut doesn't stop me from sticking a blade in your belly, Jyme. You remember that when smart words knock against your crooked teeth, wanting out."

The words came out partly slurred, but he'd made his point.

Jyme frowned, swallowed, and backed off.

"Jyme, you will accompany us, of course," Rakon said. "To Afirion."

"What? Afirion? No, my lord. I just wanted to see these two get what they had coming. And even then I didn't know they'd get this or…"

He caught himself and stopped talking.

"Jyme, you *will* accompany us," Rakon said. "That's an order."

"My lord?"

"Whatever business you may have, it'll keep," Baras said.

"This wasn't the deal," Jyme said to Baras. "You didn't say anything about this."

"You didn't ask," Baras said with a shrug. "You wanted in. Now you're in."

"Or if that's not enough to convince you," Rakon said, "perhaps another compulsion is in order?"

Jyme held up his hands. "Not necessary, my lord. I'm happy to come to... Afirion. But I have no kit. I'd need–"

"We have everything you'll need. The supply wagon and carriage are already loaded. You're not to leave Baras's sight. If you attempt to, my men are authorized to use force. I am understood, I trust?"

Jyme swallowed his anger. He looked at Nix, back at Baras, to Rakon. "You are, my lord."

Rakon pointed at Egil and Nix. "The compulsion is a blade at your throat. Do other than I've instructed and it will kill you." He sneered at Nix. "But maybe you already knew that from your year at the Conclave?"

Egil swayed on his thick legs, his clenched fists held clumsily before his face. Even the eye of Ebenor on his head looked disconcerted. He spoke in a voice more slurred than Nix's.

"I'm going to kill you, all of you. I'm looking at dead men."

No sooner had he uttered the words than he puked all over the ground.

"Bring their weapons," Rakon said, eyeing the vomit with a pinched expression. "And the small one's bag of tricks. They'll need them when we reach the Wastes."

"The Wastes?" Nix said. "What?"

He must have misheard.

"Yes, my lord," Baras answered. "Awake or not?"

Rakon eyed Nix and Egil. "I don't care. Just don't kill them."

"Understood, my lord."

"Shite," Nix said, a moment before the painful blow of a sword pommel sent him once more into oblivion.

CHAPTER SEVEN

Nix awakened with a groan, flat on his back, thrown once more into the back of a cart. He blinked, staring up at the canvas-covered ribs of the wagon. The gray light of dawn trickled in through the loose flap at the back. Rain tapped lightly on the canvas, and even that soft drumbeat made Nix wince. His head hurt worse than his worst hangover, and his tongue tasted like he had taken a lascivious lick of Shoddy Way.

At least he was no longer bound. He ran a hand over his skull, felt the tender, painful lumps under his hair. He seemed to be collecting them. He massaged the pink furrows the rope had left on his wrists. He was disarmed and his satchel was gone. He tried to sit up but dizziness and a flash of nausea put him back down.

Egil lay on his side beside him, still unconscious, snoring, drool collecting in his beard. The priest had a discolored lump as large as a gull's egg on the top of his head, the tattooed Eye of Ebenor with an eyeshine.

Nix swallowed down his dry throat, found it as coarse as sand. He flashed on the spellworm, Rakon's manic gaze, the slippery, squirming thing wriggling down his throat, expanding in him, stealing his will.

He thought of the mental space within himself that he'd tried to reserve. If he'd done as he intended, he could use that mental space as a starting point from which to try to slip the compulsion.

"I am Nix Fall," he said tentatively, the words little more than a harsh mumble. But even that small bit of resistance caused him a bout of nausea as the worm squirmed. The magic had rooted deeply.

He left off, in no condition at the moment to try to slip a compulsion. Instead, he sat up on an elbow and looked around.

Supplies filled the wagon: barrels of beer and skins of water, wheels of cheese, salted meat, sacks leaking onions and potatoes, rolled tents, straw and oats for draft animals, even a few stacks of firewood bound in cord. The abundance of supplies put him in mind of Rakon's mention of the Wastes. He'd hoped he'd misheard.

"Shite," he said.

Beside him, Egil groaned.

"Egil," Nix said softly, and shook the priest by the shoulder. "Egil."

The priest opened a bloodshot eye, blinked blearily, squinted at Nix, finally cocked an eyebrow.

"Nix?"

"Yeah. You all right?"

The priest lifted himself up, groaning and wobbly, and sat cross-legged. "Muzzy, but all right. You?"

"As well as I might." He touched the lumps on his head. "A bit tired of getting knocked unconscious, though. Let's avoid that in the future, yeah?"

"Agreed," Egil said, rubbing his head, the back of his neck. "Where are we?"

"I fear to guess."

"The last thing I remember clearly is that sorcerer's spell," Egil said, grimacing at the recollection.

Nix leaned forward, earnest. "Did you do as I said? When the spellworm went down? I told you to focus on Ebenor. Tell me you did that, Egil."

Egil's brow furrowed with thought and he nodded, but not convincingly. "I… tried. I thought of Ebenor, my faith, as you said. A lot of good it did, though."

"You may be surprised," Nix said.

Egil pinched his nose between his fingers. "How do you mean? Gods, my head. Not sure if it's a hangover or the blows."

"Both, I'm sure. Get it cleared. If we're where I think we are, we're going to need our wits."

"Aye. Gods, I'm thirsty." Egil eyed the barrels hopefully, but before he could grab one, the flap at the back of the wagon parted and a pockmarked, mustached face appeared, the hiresword Jyme, now helmed. He must have heard them talking.

"They're up!" he shouted over his shoulder.

"Not so damned loud," Nix said with a wince.

Baras soon appeared, also helmed. He looked grim behind his beard. "Welcome back."

"Uh, thanks?" Nix said.

Baras nodded at a blanket-covered pile in the far corner of the wagon. "Your weapons are there. You carry a lot of blades. Your bag with all the… things in it is there, too."

"Gewgaws," Egil said.

"As you say. The priest's hammers are there also." Baras leaned into the wagon and spoke in a lower tone. "Listen, don't get stupid because you're armed, eh? Stupid will mean you ride in the wagon unconscious. The lord Adjunct doesn't need you until we reach the tomb in Afirion, but I'd rather you awake and walking on your own feet, since I'm not sure your heads, hard as they are, can take another meeting with a sword pommel."

"Yeah," Nix said, massaging the lumps on his scalp. "We were just talking about that. Walking sounds right to me."

Nix crawled to the corner of the wagon and unrolled the oilcloth to reveal his blades, sling, pouch of lead bullets, his satchel of equipment and magical items, and Egil's hammers. He handed the priest his weapons and the crowbar he'd taken to carrying.

"I don't know how you survive with just hammers," Nix said to his friend, while repositioning sharp things all about his person.

"Crowbar, too," Egil said, as he slipped his hammers into loops on his belt. To Baras, he said, "You said Afirion, but we're not on a boat."

"I was going to mention that," Nix said.

"Mention what?" Egil said.

"We're not on a boat," Baras said, "because we're cutting through the Wastes."

"The Demon Wastes?" Egil asked.

"You know of others?"

Egil sniffed, cleared his throat, and said matter-of-factly, "Then we're all going to die."

Nix just shook his head. "Traveling the Wastes is madness, Baras. Everyone knows that."

"My Lord Norristru–"

"Is mad," Nix finished. "No one gets through the Wastes."

Baras's face remained blank, the vacant look of a soldier falling back on a sense of duty to get him through. "We do and we will. My lord has his reasons for the route he's chosen."

"Then his reasons must be to get us all killed," Nix said. "Egil has the right of it."

"Give us his reasons," Egil said. "I'd hear them."

Baras shook his head. "His reasons are his own. Now, get up and get out. You walk like the rest of us."

He turned on his heel and left them, the flap closing in his wake.

The moment he disappeared, Egil scooted to the back of the wagon, stuck a hand between the flaps, and looked out. He hefted his hammers and closed his eyes in a silent prayer.

"What are you doing?" Nix asked.

"I'm getting out of the wagon," Egil said. "Isn't that what Baras said to do?"

"He did."

"I'm also causing a ruckus with these slubbers."

"You're what?"

"Meet you out there," Egil said, and bounded out the back of the wagon.

"Egil, wait," Nix said, but the priest was already gone. "He didn't say to cause a ruckus, dammit."

Outside, the priest shouted his usual challenges. A driver shouted at the horses and the wagon lurched to a stop. Horses neighed, men cursed, hurried footsteps trod on coarse ground. More shouts, curses.

Nix knew Egil wouldn't get far, but he didn't want his friend to get hurt. He put his falchion in his fist and slid out through the flap. He blinked in the drizzle and gray light of dawn.

He and Egil must have been unconscious several hours, for they were already in the Wastes, on the scree-covered plains east of Dur Follin. The jagged, broken boulders and rust-colored rockscape stretched around them, the land devoid of everything but the toughest scrub and an occasional malformed tree.

Seven of Rakon's guards, including Baras and Jyme, stood in a loose circle around Egil. The men had swords drawn, though they made no move to attack. An eighth had a cocked crossbow leveled at the priest.

Nix caught a glimpse of Dur Follin in the distance behind them, its crumbling gray walls and the monumental span of the Archbridge ghostly and faded in the dim light and rain.

Egil, hammers in hand, lunged first at one guard,

then at another. The men backed off, positioned their blades defensively, but didn't engage.

"Come on, slubbers!" Egil shouted.

"I can order him to shoot," Baras said to Egil, nodding at the guard with the crossbow.

Nix filled his off hand with a throwing dagger. "He'll die before he fires. I don't miss at this range."

Eyes turned to Nix. The guards shifted on their feet. The crossbowman, a young man of perhaps twenty-five winters, licked his lips, backed off, and moved his crossbow from Nix to Egil, from Egil to Nix.

"Take your finger off that pull, boy," Nix said to the crossbowman, his dagger ready for a rapid throw. "Ere I put this dagger in your eye."

Egil lunged at one of the guards and he backpedaled so fast he slipped and fell down. Egil stomped on his wrist. He squawked with pain and released his sword.

"Could have broke it, but I didn't," Egil said to the downed man, and backed off. To Baras, he said, "We just want to walk away, yeah?"

"We can't allow that," Baras said.

"Then we've got a problem," Egil said.

Rakon's voice sounded from a nobleman's lacquered carriage, one of the two horse-drawn vehicles, along with the supply wagon, that made up the caravan. "Let them go, Baras."

Baras looked over his shoulder. "My lord?"

Rakon slid aside the window slat on the carriage and leaned out, looking back. He wore a skullcap and a scowl.

"I said let them go."

Baras's expression remained puzzled, but he said to his men, "You heard."

All of them backed away from Egil. The priest backed off a few steps in the direction of Dur Follin. He grinned.

"Let's go, Nix. Now."

Nix nodded and headed after his friend.

They wouldn't make it far, he knew, but at least he could evaluate the power of the spellworm.

As he passed Baras, Nix said, "We'll be right back, I think."

Baras's puzzled expression deepened.

By the time Nix reached Egil's side, he felt the compulsion working against him. At first he felt only mild resistance, like muscle fatigue and a pit in his stomach, but both grew stronger with each step.

As he and Egil started to back away farther, he felt as if he were yoked to the wagon. His stomach twisted into a knot. Bile crawled up his throat. He found it hard to lift his legs. His falchion and dagger felt like hundredweights in his hands.

Egil, too, had slowed, one thick leg thudding into the rocky ground, then a long pause, then another step.

"What... is... this?" the priest said.

The guards trailed after them, uncertain, weapons held loosely.

Egil began to curse, his arms fell to his sides, as if unable to bear the weight of his hammers. The priest lifted a leg, took another step, one more, then fell to his knees and violently vomited.

"What sorcery is this?" Egil said, down on all fours, spitting the last of his vomit onto the ground.

"The spellworm," Nix said, and fell to all fours. "We have to stop."

"My very teeth ache," Egil said.

"A few more steps and they might have cracked," Nix said. "Or your heart might have exploded. It's a strong worm."

The guards circled them at a distance. Nix felt like a fool down on all fours before them, bent by Rakon's sorcery.

"You two make everything difficult," Baras said.

"It's... a character flaw," Nix said, and hissed at a sudden flash of pain.

"My lord," Baras called back to the carriage. "What should we do with them?"

Nix lifted his head, looked back, and saw the carriage door open. An enormous man in a sweat-stained shirt and pantaloons emerged first, the carriage bouncing on its suspension as he debarked. He stood a hand shorter than Egil, but much wider at the shoulder and middle. His misshapen bald head wouldn't have fit in a well-bucket. Small unblinking eyes floated in shallow sockets, giving him a wide-eyed, wild look. His gaze flitted over Egil and Nix, the guards, and seemed to deflect off without seeing them. His mouth hung partially open, frozen in a vacant smile. His appearance struck Nix as... bulging, overstuffed, as if there were too much of him packed into the bag of his skin.

Probably a eunuch. Definitely a servant of Rakon's.

A large, curved knife hung from the broad sash that circumnavigated the eunuch's waist. He lifted the thick trunk of an arm to assist Rakon out of the carriage.

Rakon stepped onto the scree and eyed Egil and Nix's suffering with a smug smile on his thin lips.

Nix would've given much to punch him hard in the balls. The thought, however, caused the spellworm to twist his stomach yet again and he groaned, holding down the vomit through sheer force of will. He *hated* vomiting.

"I trust this will prevent any further attempts at escape," Rakon said. "Had you gotten much farther, the spellworm would have maimed or killed you. Did you learn nothing in your year at the Conclave?"

"Fak you," Nix tried to say, but instead the vomit finally won the war with his will and rushed out between his teeth in a flood. Nix coughed, eyes watering, and spit puke onto the rocks, cursing through the chunks.

"Did I not say they would try to run, Baras?" Rakon asked the guardsman. "At first opportunity, I said."

"You did, my lord," Baras answered.

To Egil and Nix, Rakon said, "You must do exactly what I say, when I say, or you'll suffer. The worm feeds on your resistance, whether in thought or deeds. Do you understand?"

"Fak you," Egil grunted.

"Seconded," said Nix, and felt the worm squirm.

"My sisters' lives are far more important to me than yours," Rakon said. "Help me and you help yourselves. Get me the horn and the compulsion will be satisfied. Get them up, Baras."

"Yes, my lord," Baras said, and walked toward Nix. "Jyme, a hand."

"We don't need help to stand, bungholes," Nix said. "Get up, Egil."

Nix rose to his knees, then slowly to his feet, grunting with the effort, his body screaming with pain. He endured and stood, swaying. Egil did the same, pulling his arms off the soil one at a time and climbing to his feet.

Rakon looked on with annoyance. "We don't have much time before Minnear is full," he said tightly, "so no more of this. Defy me, and the worm does its work."

An intense itch behind his left eye caused Nix to blink and set his eye to watering. He wondered for a moment if Rakon was using some kind of eyebite on him; he'd heard of such things from sorcerers.

"They can stand, so they can walk," Rakon said to Baras. "The pain from the worm is temporary, lasting only as long as their defiance. Let's get moving again."

"Yes, my lord," Baras said.

Rakon walked back to the carriage.

The pain from the spellworm abated almost immediately, but the itch behind Nix's eye remained. A thought seized him, blossomed fully into an idea. His mouth formed words, though he didn't remember thinking them.

"Rakon," he called, and started walking toward the carriage.

"*Lord* Norristru," Baras corrected. He stepped in front of Nix and put a hand on his chest.

"Show me your sisters," Nix called. "Let me see them. You said you're doing this for them. You stole our wills for them. Show them to me."

"Shut your mouth," Baras said, giving him a shove, but Nix didn't stop. He wanted to see Rakon's sisters, *needed* to see them. He thought much depended on it, though he had no idea why.

Rakon stopped on the footstep to the carriage, looked over at Nix and Baras.

"They walk, Baras."

With that, Rakon disappeared into the black, lacquered box of the carriage. The eunuch followed, vacant-eyed and smiling, but Nix did not relent.

"I call you a liar until my eyes see these so-called sisters! Rakon!"

"That's enough!" Baras said to Nix. "What's into you, man?"

Nix ignored Baras. He stared after Rakon, breathing hard, convinced the inside of the carriage held an answer to a question he could not articulate but needed to hear. The itch behind his eye would not relent.

Baras took him by the bicep and steered him away from the carriage. Jyme tried to do the same for Egil but a glare from the priest put an end to that.

"Suit yourself," Jyme said.

"I'm sorry it went this way," said Baras. "It's not personal. My lord is honorable. Help him and I have no doubt he'll reward you."

"Not personal," echoed Nix, turning his head to stare at the carriage, still blinking at the irritation behind his eye.

"You don't seem stupid," Baras said. "And yet..."

"Never underestimate my ability for stupidity."

Egil snickered. Baras almost smiled.

"This isn't personal either, Baras," Nix said.

"What's that?"

"This," Nix said, and snapped a reverse elbow into Baras's jaw, sending him careening backward, cursing and bleeding.

Jyme reached for his blade, but before he could draw it, Egil tackled him. Priest and hiresword fell to the ground in a tumble, the priest's fists thudding against Jyme's midsection, chiming the links of his mail shirt.

The other guards shouted and drew blades while Nix sprinted for the carriage. He wanted to see the sisters, had to see them. He grabbed the handle, threw open the door, parted the shade curtain and...

"You dare!" Rakon said, wide-eyed with shock and anger. He held a small metal vial in one hand, perhaps an elixir to give to one of his sisters, who slouched in the coach seats across from him.

Blankets wrapped the women's slim forms and their skin, pale and nearly translucent, looked as delicate and colorless as ice. Glassy eyes looked in Nix's direction, bright in the ovals of their faces, but their blank expressions told him that they didn't see him. Long auburn hair fell in waves from the head of the older. Short, almost boyishly cut dark hair crowned the smaller and younger. They looked like beautiful corpses.

"What's wrong with them?" he said, and the itch behind his eyes grew painful. His vision swam, blurred. He dug a knuckle into his eye, groaning.

Rakon half-rose from his seat, careful of his vial, but not before the huge eunuch grunted and lurched toward the door, toward Nix, still wearing the same vacant smile. He pulled his knife free as he advanced.

"Help us!" a woman cried, and a stabbing pain exploded in Nix's temples. He screamed, recoiled as the eunuch reached for him. He stumbled backward, spitting a shout of pain between gritted teeth, his head feeling as if would split asunder. He tripped on a rock, fell backward into the scree, and hit the ground hard enough to drive the air from his lungs.

The eunuch leaped awkwardly from the carriage, knife raised, still smiling stupidly. Nix heard the tread of feet on the rocks as the other guards closed on him, too.

"Nix!" Egil shouted.

Nix raised his hands defensively as the hulking form of the eunuch loomed over him, all dumb smile and sharp edge.

Rakon appeared in the carriage doorway. "No!" he

shouted, and at his utterance the eunuch froze, the huge chest rising and falling like a bellows, the light rain glistening on his face and bald head, and those eyes, those vacant, unblinking eyes. He lowered the knife to his side.

The pain in Nix's head subsided, leaving only the ghost of agony to haunt him. He lay flat on his back, the rain falling softly on his face, the hard earth of the Demon Wastes digging into his skin.

Some of the other guards came around him, blades bare. One of them pulled him to his feet.

Rakon stood on the rail of the carriage door, his face floating above the head of the eunuch and the guards.

"I just wanted to see them," Nix said, his words inexplicably slurred. His head felt thick, sluggish, stuffed with cloth. "Your sisters. I needed to see them."

Rakon stepped down and picked his way past the eunuch and guards. He stared at Nix as if he were a pile of dung. "I told you they were dangerous."

"Needed... to see them," Nix muttered.

Rakon looked back into the carriage, then took Nix's face in his hand. "You needed to see them why?"

Nix's tongue seemed made of sand, which was just as well. He could not have answered. He had no idea why. A compulsion had driven him, as strong as Rakon's spellworm. It had come from nowhere. He uttered the first lie that popped into his head.

"Thought you were lying."

Rakon sniffed and pushed him back into the arms of the guards. "Now you know better. Let's get moving."

While Rakon and the eunuch boarded the carriage, the hands gripping Nix turned him around.

Baras glared at him, eyes hard, bleeding from the mouth.

"Sorry," Nix said. "I don't know what happened."

"Apology accepted," Baras said, and punched him in the jaw.

Nix went down in a heap, sparks exploding before his eyes. He heard Egil shout in anger but couldn't make out the words. Baras's face appeared over him, a grizzled moon against the gray of the sky.

Nix blinked in the rain, winced in anticipation of another blow. Instead, Baras took him under the armpits and lifted him to his feet.

"I give as good as I get," Baras said. "Fair is fair."

"Well enough," Nix muttered, swinging his jaw from side to side on loose hinges, tasting blood. Without warning, he vomited again, directly onto Baras's boots.

"Sorry," Nix said, wiping his mouth. "Came on of a sudden. You're not going to pay that one back, are you?"

Baras shook the vomit from his boots and handed Nix off to Egil. The priest had a red mark on his left cheek.

"Jyme catch you?" Nix asked.

"Pfft. One of the others joined in mid-scrum."

"Ah."

Egil kept Nix upright until he'd recovered enough to handle his own locomotion. Soon, the caravan was moving once more, cutting through the Wastes.

"Seems silly to have brought the wagon and carriage," Egil said.

Both vehicles struggled over the terrain.

Nix grunted agreement.

"What was that all about?" Egil asked. "With the sisters?"

Nix shook his head. He rubbed his jaw, his head, his backside, and stared at the carriage, wondering the same thing. "I'm... not sure. It was odd, Egil."

"Odd, aye," Egil said. "And stupid. You saw them, though, eh?"

Nix nodded slowly, seeing the older sister's green eyes so clearly in his mind's eye they might as well have been graven into his brain. "They're sick. Rakon spoke truth about that. Beautiful, too, as much as I could see."

"Well, there's that, then."

"But..."

"But?" Egil prompted.

"Did you... hear something when I cracked the carriage?"

"Something like what?"

"Like a shout for help. A woman's shout."

Egil shook his head. "Not that I heard. You heard it?"

"I thought. But maybe not."

Egil eyed the carriage. "One of the sisters crying out in a fever dream?"

Nix shook his head. "I don't think they can speak. They look very near death."

Egil grunted.

"Rusilla and Merelda," Nix said. "That's their names."

"Had time for introductions, did you?"

Nix shook his head. His thoughts were muddled. "Wait... no."

How did he know their names? *Were* those their names?

"What?" Egil asked.

"Nothing. I'm... still a bit muzzyheaded, is all."

Egil eyed him. "You're bleeding."

"I know," Nix said, massaging his jaw. Baras had caught him clean. He'd be feeling it for days.

"No. Your nose."

"Huh?" Nix put a knuckle to his nose and it came away bloody. "Shite."

Egil chuckled. "You're slowing down, Nix."

"Must be," Nix agreed, though he didn't remember taking a blow to his nose.

How odd. He stared at the carriage.

"I think Rakon said something else truthful, too."

"And what's that?" Egil asked.

"His sisters *are* dangerous."

CHAPTER EIGHT

Within an hour, Dur Follin had vanished from sight behind them. Broken, rust-red earth extended as far as Nix could see in all directions. The ground became more broken as they advanced. It looked shattered, as if the world had bucked, the lower strata trying to shed the disease of the upper. Deep valleys and cuts scarred the terrain, steep rock walls, sheer chasms, hills of jagged rocks, fields of large boulders.

Bits of tenacious scrub, the fronds thin and sickly, grew here and there. Lichen the color of mellowed piss clung on the shade-side of many of the boulders. Low mountains rose in the east. The air carried an acrid stink that made Nix's throat raw and eyes water. When the wind gusted, it threw up clouds of red dust and wailed over the shattered terrain, as if grieving.

"Wounded earth," Egil said to Nix.

"Aye."

By late morning, they reached Deadman's Way, a wide, incongruously smooth stretch of ancient road that stretched across the otherwise blasted terrain.

Nix had heard of the road, but had never expected to lay eyes on it.

Inexplicably, the road had been spared the ruin of the surrounding terrain. It was not paved with stones, but rather looked as if the gods had driven a chisel across the terrain, leaving the unmarred ribbon of the road in their wake.

Deadman's Way showed no cracks, and no scrub or weeds grew on its surface. To Nix it called to mind the same precise, flawless, uncanny construction that marked the Archbridge.

"This pristine after so long?" Nix asked.

"Now we know why he brought the carriage and wagon," Egil observed.

"Aye."

Rakon emerged from the carriage long enough to study the terrain ahead, and then the caravan headed out, following the road and making good speed.

Two guards paced the carriage to either side, which was driven by another guard and pulled by a pair of shaggy draft horses. The supply wagon followed, likewise driven by a guard and pulled by two horses. The rest of the group walked or jogged on foot behind and around the wagons, though from time to time one or another guard would ride on the wagon to rest his feet.

As they put more and more distance behind them, Nix felt as though he were swimming in ever-deeper water. Dur Follin was lost to the distance behind them. They were deep in the Wastes, the broken, red earth roofed with a cloudy, slate-gray sky. At least the rain had relented.

The others seemed to share his growing sense of ominousness. Now and again the horses tossed their heads and stomped at nothing in particular. The drivers kept cocked crossbows on the benches beside them, and the guards afoot held bare blades in hand. Egil shook his dice as they walked. The sky pressed down on them, a gray, miasmic blanket.

Nix worked at the compulsion as he walked, seeking a place within himself that the spellworm had not reached.

I am Nix Fall of Dur Follin.

But the effort itself – contrary as it was to Rakon's wishes – nauseated him, and he found it hard to keep pace with a roiling stomach. He resolved to work at slipping the spellworm during the night, when they camped. They had three, maybe four days' travel through the Wastes before they reached the Afirion Desert.

Assuming they lived that long.

He took a headcount. Including the eunuch and Rakon, they totaled eleven men and the sisters.

Eleven men.

He would have laughed if his jaw and head didn't hurt so much. Phrases moved through his mind, foreboding words he'd heard used to describe the Demon Wastes.

Cursed earth.

Ruined ground.

At the Conclave, Nix had read a few treatises containing theories about the Demon Wastes' origin. All agreed that the Wastes had once been fertile ground, part of a now-lost and forgotten civilization, probably the same one responsible for building the Archbridge.

Some held that a sorcerer had accidentally created a doorway to Hell and an army of devils had destroyed the realm and left the land barren. Others said a curse infected the ground, spreading incrementally closer to Dur Follin each year. Others said wrathful gods had reached down from the vault of night and smashed an arrogant people.

Nix had thought all the theories nonsense, but now, walking the Wastes, treading an ancient road that shouldn't exist, he wasn't as sure. The land was forsaken, a wasteland. Theories Nix had thought outlandish now seemed quaint seen in the light of the actual desolation.

"This road's better than even the Promenade in Dur Follin," Egil said.

"Makes no sense," Nix said, and then an idea struck him.

He fell to his knees and held the palms of his hands a finger's width over the surface of the road. He closed his eyes, concentrated on the skin of his palms, his fingertips.

"What are you doing?" Baras called from his right. "Keep moving."

"Hsst," Egil said to the guardsman.

The drivers halted the wagons. Rakon shouted from the carriage.

"What is going on? We are not to stop moving."

Nix's palms and fingertips tingled. The hairs on his knuckles rose and stood on end. He smiled, nodded, stood.

"It's enspelled," he said to everyone "The road. That's why it's remained intact. Powerful magic. Wearing thin now, but in its day it must have been powerful."

Egil eyed the blasted terrain all around them. "They might have used it to preserve more than just the roads."

Nix chuckled. "Aye."

"Why would anyone enspell a road?" Baras asked.

Nix shook his head. It made little sense.

"Get us moving again, Baras," Rakon said from the carriage.

"Yes, my lord. You heard him," Baras said. "Leg it."

Reins cracked and the caravan started again.

"I'm half-tempted to move at a dilatory pace," Egil said. "Slow these bastards down."

The moment he said the words, the priest burped loudly, put a hand on his stomach. His face greened behind his beard.

"You can't," Nix said. "And your body's telling you why. The spellworm's rooted deep and it responds to your intent. Just *thinking* something at odds with Rakon will make you sick at the least. Actually acting at cross-purposes will bring pain, just as it did before. Even death, if we push too hard."

They walked on for a short while before Nix said, "Did you say 'dilatory' a moment ago?"

"I did."

"Aren't I supposed to be the educated one in this pairing?"

"Maybe. But that'd make me the good-looking one then."

"Ha!"

Egil hung onto his own smile for only a moment. "Gonna be hard to get over on this sorcerer with this worm in our guts." He winced, probably as the worm did its work in response to his thoughts of getting over on Rakon. "I've no desire to be in his thrall or puking for the rest of my days."

"You won't. Retrieving the horn he seeks is one way to end the compulsion."

"What's the other way?"

"We slip it sooner," Nix said.

Egil looked intrigued. He glanced around to make certain none of the guards were listening. "Slip it how? Argh. Even asking the question upsets my stomach."

Nix spoke in a low tone. "When the worm first infected you, I told you to focus on your faith, yeah?"

Egil nodded. His hand went to the tattoo on his head.

Nausea rose in Nix – the spellworm exerting itself in response to his thoughts – but he endured it. He tried to explain things in a way that would make sense to Egil. "The purpose of that was to wall off a bit of your will from the worm before it expanded in you. Think of the compulsion as a net around your will. You think or do something at odds with the compulsion and it draws tight, making your own mind and body an enemy of itself."

"Thrice-damned sorcery," Egil said.

"Quite. But if you did as I said, you may have kept the worm's net loose or absent around your core. In your case, that's your faith."

"You think faith is my core?"

"You know better than to have to ask that. I mock your beliefs only because we've been blooded together. Anyway, you focus inwardly and find that place. You focus on it to the exclusion of everything else. You worry at it as you might an itchy scab or pained tooth. Gradually that'll open it up, expand it. Open it enough and you'll have enough space to slip the compulsion's net entirely."

"So you've done this before?" Egil asked.

"Of course not."

Egil stopped and glared at him.

"Keep moving!" Baras called.

They gave Baras an obscene gesture but started walking again.

"You're guessing then?" Egil said. "How do you know it'll work?"

"Guessing yes, but it's an informed guess."

"Informed by what? Your year at the Conclave?"

"Well, yes."

The priest shook his head. "Gods, man, that's a thin

thread on which to hang hope. How will I know if I've slipped it? I don't feel that different except when I think about dropping a hammer on Rakon's head."

He groaned, the thought, no doubt, twisting up the worm.

"And that's how you'll know," Nix said. "If you can think about killing Rakon or running back to Dur Follin without puking, without your bones and teeth aching, then you've slipped it. Or think of it this way: working at slipping it will make you sick. That's why you don't do it except after camp. When you finally find yourself worrying at it and it *doesn't* make you sick, then you're free of it."

"You mean whenever I think about slipping it, I'll be nauseous?"

"Of course."

More cursing. "And if we don't slip it?"

"Then Rakon owns us until we get him that horn."

A final, inspired round of cursing that drew Baras's skeptical eyes, then, "So where'd you keep it loose?"

The question cut a little too deep for Nix to answer honestly, even to Egil. For a moment he considered confessing the mask he wore around his true self, exposing for his friend the boy of the Warrens who lived in his core, but he had no easy words to express it. He wasn't sure Egil would believe him anyway.

"I focused on my arrogance, of course. I don't want for that."

Egil looked skeptical, but let it pass. "As you say. Anyway, you're the better of us with knots and nets, so get to it."

"You work at it, too."

"Aye." Egil took out his dice, shook them as he walked.

For a time they said nothing, then Nix said, "Egil, I think… the sisters did something to me."

"How do you mean?"

"I mean, my eye pained me and I ran for the carriage and I still don't know why. And then my head felt like it was going to burst and I heard a voice, a woman's voice telling me to help her."

Egil considered Nix's confession for several beats. "You think the sisters are sorcerers, too?"

"I think maybe."

Egil eyed the carriage. "That makes us caught between witches and a warlock. All the more reason to slip this spellworm and get clear, I suppose."

"Aye."

Hours passed. The cloud cover blocked the sun so they trekked under a gray roof. The ground grew still more blasted as they advanced deeper into the Wastes, all but the magically protected road. Cracks and wide chasms bisected the parched ground here and there. Jagged rock formations jutted from the earth, carved by wind, dirt, and rain into thin, unsettling alien towers. Sharp stones poked up from the soil, as if the flesh had been stripped from the earth, exposing the bones of the world.

The road cut through it all, through gulleys and deep,

barren valleys, leading them on, guiding them toward whatever doom awaited them. A tumble of rocky hills to their left cast them in late afternoon shadows. Caves opened here and there in the hills, open mouths hissing profane conspiracies into the wind.

Nix felt his eyes drawn to the carriage throughout the day. He replayed in his mind the events from earlier, the vacant expressions on the faces of the sisters, the nosebleed, the fact that he *somehow knew their names*.

How? None of it made sense.

Help us, he thought he'd heard, but that too made no sense.

Sorcery, he concluded. Had to be.

Rakon's sisters might be cursed, but they were also sorceresses.

They'd enspelled Nix somehow, forced him to open the door to the carriage, put thoughts in his mind. But why? He winced when he recalled the painful itch behind his eye, the agonizing feeling that his head would burst.

He worked at the spellworm with ever more urgency.

"I am Nix Fall of Dur Follin," he whispered as he walked, and thought of his childhood, the Heap, Mamabird, the old man he'd murdered over bread. "I'm Nix Fall of Dur Follin."

The exercise unsettled his stomach and weakened his legs, but he told himself that he felt some slack in the worm's grip. Bile crept up his throat, stinging and foul, but he kept at it as long as he could, hoping his efforts would wear down the compulsion. Taken with his task, he didn't notice Baras approach until the guardsmen stood at his side.

"You talking to yourself now?"

Nix swallowed the bile, cleared his throat. "No one else in this motley crew is half as interesting. Have to avoid boredom somehow."

Baras nodded, glanced around at the ruined land. Worry reached his eyes. "I suspect we'll have excitement enough at some point."

Seeing the worry, Nix dared a hard question. "What in the Pits are you doing here, Baras? You don't seem the kind to work for Rakon Norristru."

The guardsmen stiffened, looked straight ahead. "The lord Adjunct is my superior. It's my duty to serve. And I take my duty very seriously."

"See if that doesn't land you in a pile of shite one day," Nix said.

"Your jaw seems all right, given how well it's flapping at the moment."

"I've been hit by worse."

"I don't doubt it."

"You carry a decent punch, though."

"As I said, if I can help it, I don't take one without giving one back. That elbow caught me flat."

"Yeah," Nix said, grinning. "It did. Uh, sorry."

Baras cleared his throat. "Listen, you see that you're in this now, right? You and the priest? Whether you like it or not. I don't want to have to hawk over you. Got enough to worry my mind."

Nix looked over at him. For the first time, he noticed

the dark circles under Baras's eyes, the worry wrinkles in his brow and around his eyes. He looked worn. "Whether I like it or not? Seems to me that goes for both of us, yeah? What with your duty and all."

Baras said nothing for a long moment. "We've a few more hours of travel left in the day. Keep legging it, Nix."

Nix stared at Baras's back as he walked away. He couldn't even work up the will to curse him. The man was just doing his duty as he saw it. He might be a fool, but he was a noble fool.

At Rakon's order, the drivers of the carriage and wagon drove the horses at a faster pace as twilight came on. The men afoot jogged to keep up. Rakon leaned out the carriage door from time to time and studied the sky for long stretches, his gaze intense, irritable. At first Nix assumed he was worried about a storm slowing them, but it seemed something more than that. Rakon seemed to see through the roof of clouds, to something beyond them, something that had him worried.

Before sunset, they reached an intersection. The new road was as pristine and well preserved as the old, and they took it, heading more or less due east. As dusk deepened, the wind picked up, howling over the jagged stonescape. The guards lapsed into silence, somber, huddled into their cloaks, alone with their thoughts. Baras did what he could for their morale but it helped little. Darkness threatened, darkness in the Wastes, far from Dur Follin, far from anything.

"What is that?" one of the guards called. He pointed off to the south.

There, black against the darkening sky, a cloud whirled and jerked wildly above the ruined earth.

"What in the Pits is that?" Nix asked, peering through the failing light. "Some kind of fog?"

Egil, with his better vision, said, "It's a flock of something. Doesn't move like birds, though."

"Then what?"

Egil shrugged.

"There's nothing for it," Baras said. "It's nothing to fear. Keep moving."

And they did keep moving, but all of them kept their eyes on the flock. For a time it flew in their direction and Nix got a sense of its huge size. There must have been thousands of… creatures in it.

The horses whinnied nervously. Out came Egil's dice. Nix, too, felt exposed under the bleak sky, but in time the flock turned away from them and they lost sight of it behind low hills.

Presently the setting sun slipped out from beneath the clouds just long enough to stain the western sky orange and red. The rocky terrain looked like a sea of blood in the dying light. The drivers of the wagon and carriage pulled the horses to a stop.

Ahead, the terrain fell away and the road descended through a deep cut. The fading sunlight did not reach very far into the declivity, leaving the bottom a lightless gash in the earth. A few crooked trees clung to the top of the cut, rattling in the gusts. While Baras conferred with Rakon, the rest of the group had a quick drink or sank to the ground with fatigue.

Presently a shout sounded from the right, Jyme's voice. "Here! Over here!"

Heads turned. Egil and Nix, seated on the road to rest, rose. The other guards did the same.

"Found his balls, maybe?" Nix said to Egil.

"Those are as lost as Abn Thuset's tomb," Egil said.

"What is it?" Baras called.

"Come over and see for yourself," Jyme said.

He stood twenty paces off the road, on a low rise, amid a tumble of oddly shaped rocks, wind-stripped scrub, and a few large boulders. He was looking at something on the ground, the wind whipping his cloak and hair. He didn't have his blade drawn, so Nix figured whatever he saw couldn't be too dangerous.

Baras and the other guards hurried over. Egil and Nix shared a glance, shrugged, and headed over, too.

"What is it?" Rakon called, leaning out of the carriage.

"I'm... unsure, my lord," Baras called back over his shoulder.

When they reached the top of the rise, they found Jyme standing at the edge of a deep hole. The coarse ground around it, littered with queerly shaped stones and sticks, crunched underfoot. The wind blew dust everywhere.

The hole was circular, about two paces in diameter, and it fell away into the earth at a steep angle. The dying light of the setting sun did not reach down it very far.

"You called out for this?" Baras said, frowning. "It's just a hole."

"No it's not. Smell that." Jyme leaned over the hole and sniffed. "It smells like a bunghole down there."

"Familiar with that smell, are you?" Nix said, eliciting chuckles from two of the other guards.

Jyme ignored him and pointed. "There are more holes just like this one over there and there. I came over to piss and noticed them. One might be natural, like a cave, right? But lots of them? That ain't natural. Something dug them."

Baras rubbed the back of his neck, eyeing the hole. Two of the younger guards coughed in the blowing dust. The setting sun stretched their shadows over the ground.

Egil reached into his beltpouch, removed his dice, and rattled them in his right hand. Nix pulled his cloak over his mouth and nose and walked the area around the first hole, found the others that Jyme had mentioned. He counted five, all of them perfectly circular, all of them descending away into darkness under the Wastes, all of them stinking like a latrine.

"I count five more," he said, upon returning. "And as much as it irks me, I agree with Jyme. Something dug them somehow. I don't see any tracks so I don't think they've been used in a long while."

"Used?" Baras asked. "Used by what?"

Nix shrugged, though his mind turned to the flock of creatures they'd seen earlier.

The wind gusted and whistled over the holes,

which keened eerily. One of the guards looped finger and thumb in the protective gesture of Orella.

Egil edged closer, crouched at the edge of the hole, and looked down. "It's like a bug hole or a worm's boring. Looks to go deep."

"No such thing as bugs or worms that big," Baras said.

"Shouldn't be any such thing as the Demon Wastes, either," Egil said. "Yet here we stand."

The other guards shifted uncomfortable on their feet, passed worried glances.

Nix imagined a honeycombed earth under his boots, crawling with horrors. There were many stories about the Wastes.

"What could be down there?" one of the young guards said.

"Go see," another of the guards said, and gave him a fake shove, creating a shortlived panic in the first, and laughter or a smile from everyone else except Baras.

"Bunghole!" the first said. "I piss in your soup for that."

"Enough," Baras said. "They're just holes in the ground. Dug or natural doesn't matter. There's nothing down there." He looked at the darkening sky, the setting sun. "Lord Norristru wants to press on into the declivity before nightfall. We've got another half-hour or more of light. Let's get into that cut and find a likely spot. Leg it, men."

Sighs and groans answered Baras's command, but everyone turned to go. As they did, Nix spotted a thin cylindrical stone sticking out of the scree at an odd angle. He stepped over to it, nudged it with his boot to free it, and saw it for what it was: not a stone, but a bone. He glanced around at the ground under his feet and realization dawned.

"Wait," he said, and the guards and Egil turned back.

Nix fell to all fours and scraped the soil all around the hole with his punch dagger. His work made the dust worse, and loose dirt, caught by the gusting wind, stung eyes and drew curses.

"What are you doing, man?" Baras asked, shielding his mouth with his cloak.

Nix stopped in his work long enough to toss the bone at him. "That's a bone." His digging revealed another, another. As he found them, he tossed them toward Egil and Baras, one after another.

"It's all bones," Nix said, looked up at them. "This whole hill. Bones and dirt."

The young guards cursed nervously. They all looked under their feet, wide-eyed, as if fearful the hill of remains would soon vomit up an army of animated dead.

Egil picked up the bone and examined it. Jyme and Baras looked over his shoulder.

"Are they… human?" Jyme asked.

Egil shrugged. "Could be, but I can't say for certain. Any skulls, Nix?"

"Gods," Baras said. "You talk of this as if they were melons at market."

Egil shrugged again, handed the bone to Baras. "We're tomb robbers. The dead hold no fear for either of us."

Nix worried at the heap a bit longer, looking for a skull, darkening the sky with powdered death. He found shards of bone with every dug furrow, but no skulls.

"Maybe it's a burial mound of some kind," Baras said.

"Not likely," Egil said to Baras. He took the bone from Baras and pointed at various features. "See that? Cracked open for marrow. And those grooves there, those are from teeth."

"Gods," one of the guards said.

All of them made the protective gesture of Orella, even Jyme.

"Maybe we should just leave them be," said Jyme, his voice quaking. "Show some respect for the dead."

Nix left off his digging and stood, his clothes and face coated in the dust of the dead. "The dead need respect no more than they need air or food. Didn't have you as the superstitious sort, Jyme."

"I should be back in Dur Follin in my damned bed," Jyme said.

"Shouldn't we all," Nix said, and wiped his face with his gloved hand. He glanced around. "Bodies, carcasses, whatever these are, they must have been stacked here waist deep. This was the scene of a slaughter."

All eyes went to the hole. The wind gusted, whistled over the opening, the sound like a prolonged scream.

"I ain't camping near this hole," one of the young guards said.

Nods around.

"We could still go back to Dur Follin," said another.

Baras cleared his throat. "No, we can't. And what happened here happened long ago. There's nothing to fear. Let's move, men. Nix, we go. Egil. Now."

When they returned to the caravan, they found Rakon standing near the carriage, looking up at the sky, muttering as if he could speak to wind. When he saw them approach, he made a sharp, dismissive gesture with one hand and turned to face them, hands on his hips.

"What was it?" he asked.

"Holes, my lord," Baras answered.

"Holes?"

The guards around Egil and Nix muttered.

"Unusual holes," Egil said. "Dug by something. With the bones of many old kills near them."

Rakon stared at them, his thin face unreadable. He checked the sky a final time, looked to the west, at the fading light. "We press on a bit more today. Into the cut so we're out of the wind."

With that, he vanished into the carriage.

As the wagon and carriage started to move, Egil sidled up to Nix.

"I'm disquieted by those bones."

"First 'dilatory' and now 'disquieted'? My priest has been replaced by a scholar."

"The bones weren't that old."

"I know," Nix said.

"I think if we don't get clear of this soon, we're going to die here. All of us."

Nix nodded. "We can't go anywhere unless we slip the spellworm. We're in it, Egil. Us and them."

Egil looked at the darkness creeping into the sky, infecting the air. "No one has ever gotten through the Wastes that I've heard."

"Fatalism ill suits you. Recall that you and I have done many things most said couldn't be done. We'll add traversing the Wastes to that list."

"Well enough," Egil finally conceded. "Nix, you see the way Rakon's been watching the sky? He's watching more than the Mages' Moon. There's more afoot here."

"Agreed," Nix said.

Before descending into the cut, the guards took a moment to take torches from the supply wagon and fire them. Nix declined to take one. Instead, he rifled through his satchel until he found what he sought: a fist-sized black globe of polished volcanic glass scribed with the symbol of a closed eye.

"Another gewgaw," Egil said.

"Indeed." Nix held the globe in his palm, spoke a word in the Language of Creation to awaken the magic, and poked the scribed eye with his forefinger. It opened as if alive, squinted at him in anger.

"Come on," Nix said, and poked it again, harder. "Come on."

That did it. The eye closed tightly for a moment, as if charging itself, then opened, emitting a glow as bright as a lantern. The guards looked on with wonder. Baras came over, looked at the globe, looked at Nix, and walked away.

"We could have used that a number of times previous," Egil said. "Where'd you get it?"

"Where else?" Nix said, shining the light around at the red, cracked walls. "The Low Bazaar."

Egil's eyeroll was audible in his tone. "Not a servant of Kerfallen the Grey Mage again?"

"No," Nix said. "I learned my lesson there. This came from a Narascene fortune teller. A pretty one, too."

Egil eyed the bauble skeptically. "Well, if it explodes, at least we'll know who to blame."

"*Whom,*" Nix corrected, and couldn't resist a jibe. "Now leave me alone and go be disquieted or dilatory or something."

CHAPTER NINE

The caravan descended into the cut, leaving even the fading light of sunset behind. The torchlight flickered on the cracked walls of reddish stone that rose to either side and hemmed them in. The meager light provided by the torches and Nix's magic crystal put tall shadows on the wall, but did only a little to dispel the black. The darkness in the cut seemed to have weight, growing heavier as they descended, a blanket of ink that threatened to blot them out.

"Like walking into Hell," Egil said, his voice bouncing loudly off the walls.

"At least we're out of the wind," said one of the guards.

The steep slope carried them down a hundred paces or so to the bottom, where the cut flattened and widened. Boulders and piles of scree flanked the road, but the way ahead looked clear.

A sliver of sky was visible above, through the gash of cut, and the dying light of the day colored it the purple of an old bruise. Looking up, Nix glimpsed a flock of creatures they'd seen earlier, the roiling, spinning cloud of them black against the purple sky. They looked about as big as ducks and flew with the jerky changes of direction typical of bats.

"There," he said, pointing, but they were already gone.

Tense hands went to blade hilts.

"What?" Baras asked, looking around in alarm. "What?"

"That flock of creatures," Nix said. "I just saw them above."

Baras opened his mouth to speak but before he did a high-pitched, uncanny shriek sounded from above. The sound spooked the mounts and those pulling the wagon reared, jolting the cart and spilling two bags of grain. The guards jerked blades from scabbards.

"Crossbows, you dolts," Baras hissed, unslinging his crossbow and readying a quarrel.

While the other guards sheathed blades and readied quarrels, Egil filled his fists with the hafts of his hammers. Nix drew his falchion and shined the light from his magic eye up the irregular face of the cliff. Cracks lined it, veins in the earth.

Another shriek sounded from above, inhuman and savage, but this time from the other side of the cut. The pitch of it put Nix's hairs on end. He thought of the holes they'd found, the heap of bones. He spun around, aiming the crystal eye's beam at the top of the cut. For a moment he thought he caught a flash of movement, but couldn't be sure.

It occurred to him of a sudden that the crystal would make him an easy target from a foe above, so he covered it with his palm and hid under his cloak. The etching of the scribed eye squirmed irritably against his grip. He poked it in the eye with his thumb.

"What in the Pits was that?" Jyme said softly. He scanned the top of the cut behind the aim of his crossbow.

"I thought I saw something move up there," one of the young guards said, pointing up to the right. "Over there."

"Calm heads, men," Baras said, backing toward Rakon's carriage. "No one saw anything moving. You're imagining things."

Rakon's head emerged from the carriage window. "Baras?"

The moment Nix saw Rakon, a sharp pain rooted behind his eye and for a fleeting moment he had an overpowering impulse to charge the carriage, slay the eunuch and the driver, and flee with Rusilla and Merelda. The impulse was so strong that he actually took a step toward the carriage.

Of course, the thought and the step agitated the spellworm, sent vomit up his throat and caused his chest to ache. He groaned, staggered a step. Egil's hand closed on his bicep, steadied him.

"You all right?" Egil whispered.

Nix shook his head. "No. They're trying to do something to me."

"Who? The sisters?"

Nix nodded.

"Rakon," Egil called, apparently intent on confronting the sorcerer about his sister.

"No!" Nix hissed. "No, leave it. Leave it."

Rakon looked at Egil, eyebrows raised, but Baras stepped between them.

"Did you hear that sound just now, my lord?" Baras asked.

Rakon looked up at the slit of dark sky visible between the cliff walls.

"The wind, maybe," he said. "Or an animal."

For a moment, Baras said nothing, then, "Probably we should camp soon, my lord. The light is soon to fail entirely. We should set up before that."

"Find a spot of your choosing, Baras."

"Very good, my lord."

Once more Rakon disappeared into the carriage and they started moving. The caravan traveled only a short distance more, everyone wary and with weapons to hand, before Baras called a halt for the night. The shriek did not recur, though the tension lingered.

Even with only torchlight by which to see, the guards set up the campsite with impressive efficiency. In under a half-hour, they'd pitched six tents, kindled a fire, distributed dried meat and cheese from the supply wagon, put feedbags on the horses, and started a large pot of water for coffee. Egil and Nix had little to do but watch. Even Jyme was of more use than them.

They ate with the guards, Egil with his usual volume

of gustatory noise, Nix nibbling and still trying to figure out what to do about the sisters. He began to doubt his thinking. He'd seen them, and they did not look capable of working witchery. Perhaps it was the Wastes that was making him feel so off?

But that thinking fled before the fact that he knew their names.

"What's in your mind?" Egil asked.

"The Hells if I know," Nix said.

Rakon emerged from the carriage only once, to tell them to keep the fire low.

"My lord?" Baras asked.

"We don't want to be seen," Rakon explained.

"By what?" Egil asked.

Rakon considered his answer a long time. "By anything," he said, and returned to the carriage.

Later, the eunuch emerged from the carriage to retrieve food for his master. Nix stood, hurried over, and tried to engage the plodding giant in conversation.

"How fare your master's sisters?" he asked. He wanted to see them again, to look them in the eyes, to see if they were the cause of his discomfiture. "I can help you bear this food–"

The eunuch, arms laden with a wheel of cheese and two loaves of flatbread, responded with only a vacant stare so otherworldly that Nix, for once, found himself at a loss for words. He stepped aside so the giant wouldn't walk over him.

"He's a mute," Baras called from around the crackling fire. "And he'll welcome no help."

Nix nodded, eyeing the eunuch as the man walked back toward the carriage. A scar made a pink line above the fold of skin on the back of the eunuch's neck, a scar too clean to have been caused by a weapon. Nix had heard of such scars before, though he could not quite remember where – something about magical chirurgy.

"There's something off in that eunuch," Nix said, when he returned to Egil's side.

"Everything about this is off," the priest answered, shoveling a chunk of cheese into his mouth. "The people and the place. Still need to eat, though."

"Aye," Nix said, and did just that, though he found his eyes returning frequently to the carriage.

After the meal, Baras posted guards and set the watch schedule for the night. The men not on duty lingered around the low flames of the fire, saying little, watching smoke rise into the air. Egil shook his dice and Nix endured nausea to work at the spellworm. He needed to get himself free, now more than ever.

Everyone sat with weapons near to hand but the night got on peacefully.

Above them, the cloud cover broke, revealing a wedge of sky between the cliff walls of the cut. They could not see the skeletal trees standing watch on the cliff tops above, but the branches rattled in the wind like dry bones. As the hours passed, the darkness grew predatory. The wind howled above them, whistling dark promises.

"Heard lots of stories about you two," one of the young guards said to Nix. "Are they true?"

"Lies, all," Nix said, stretching out his legs.

"Can't all be lies," pressed the guard. "Tell us about one of these adventures you been on."

"Very well," Nix said. "Once, Egil and I were forced to travel the Demon Wastes with some guards of a doltish cast. One of these, a young whoreson who couldn't grow a respectable beard, insisted on hearing stories from me. I strangled him while he slept."

Uncertain laughter from one guard, silence from the rest, a frown from Baras.

"Did I give away the ending?" Nix asked Egil.

"I believe you did, yes."

"He was just asking, is all," said another guard, perturbed. "To pass the time. No need to be a prick."

"No need?" Nix said. "Really?"

"Nix," Egil said, but Nix ignored him.

"We're not here for your entertainment, boy, and we're not friends. Egil and I are prisoners. You're our keepers. Do I not speak the plain truth?"

"It ain't like that," one of the young guards protested.

Nix scoffed. "Can we just get up and walk home, then? We're a long day out of Dur Follin. Can we return if we wish?"

Baras frowned in his beard, sipped his coffee. "It isn't personal."

"So you say," Egil said.

"The lumps on my head feel personal," Nix added.

Baras shrugged, scratched his beard. "Have it as you will." He topped his tin cup with more coffee from the pot. "I offer no apologies. Duty is duty, and done is done."

"Duty," Nix said, shaking his head, and Baras said nothing.

"I think you've ruined the mood," Egil said to Nix.

Nix waved a hand derisively. "Bah. What mood?"

For a time, silence, then Jyme spoke, his tone incongruously light.

"It was for me," he said.

"Was what?" Nix asked, leaning back, his hands behind his head, staring up at the clearing sky, the stars. Minnear would rise soon. He did not relish sitting in the dark of the Demon Wastes under the Mages' Moon.

"Personal," Jyme said. "It was personal for me."

Nix smiled darkly. "Of course it was. Egil *personally* knocked the sense from you. Wait..." He sat up and looked across the fire at Jyme. "Did you mean that as a *jest*?"

Jyme was smiling, and Nix's frustration went out of him in a rush.

"Egil, is it possible that Jyme, *Jyme*, has a sense of humor?"

"Come now, no need for insults..." Jyme began.

"I've seen demons and devils," Egil said. "More than a man should. Even bloodied a few, so I know much is possible in this world. But this notion of Jyme having a sense of humor strikes me as preposterous."

Chuckles around the fire, certain this time, and including Jyme.

"I was just pissed, see?" Jyme said, setting down his tin cup. "You beat me down in front of my men. I didn't know you was all right, then. I just wanted to get even."

Nix toasted him with his coffee. "And instead of getting even you got a trip into the Wastes. Well played, Jyme."

More chuckles, except from Jyme, who looked sheepish. He nudged a log with his boot. "Who's got the luck, right? I suppose I'm as much a prisoner here as you two. They made me come, too."

"True enough," Egil said philosophically, then, "Listen, you caught me in a foul mood right then, back in the *Tunnel*. I had other things on my mind. We'd just bought a shithole, after all. Apologies for the punch."

"None needed," Jyme said, waving it away. "I was owed it. I was rude to that girl and for no reason."

The current of the priest's more forgiving nature caught Nix up in its wake. To the young guard he'd embarrassed, he said, "And a foul mood infected me as well, just now. With that story, I mean. Apologies. I vow not to strangle you."

The young guard inclined his head and Jyme raised his cup. "Well, done is done, as Baras said."

Nix shook his head. "Gods, I was quite happy disliking all of you, *you in particular, Jyme,* and now you've gone and fouled that up. One day in the Wastes and I don't know who to despise. I almost wish I'd never taken your coinpurse."

Jyme's mouth fell open. "Back at the tavern? That was you what took my coinpurse? I wondered where that went."

Nix nodded absently, eyed his hands, which so

often worked of their own accord. "When you bumped me outside of the *Tunnel*. I put it into the hands of an old man I saw on the street."

"Alms," Egil said.

"Pshaw," Nix answered. To Jyme he said, "I'll repay you when we return to Dur Follin."

"Well enough," Jyme said. "There were, uh, fifteen terns and two royals in there."

"Ha!" Nix said. "There were exactly nine terns and three commons and you haven't seen a gold royal since the Year of the Jackal."

More laughter around.

Despite the situation, Nix found himself warming to the men. The Wastes had birthed quick camaraderie from shared menace. Before long, he'd find himself liking Rakon and his sisters.

Or perhaps not.

"Well," Jyme said, looking up at sky. "You won't have to repay if we don't get back to Dur Follin. And right now, I don't see how that happens."

"There is that," Egil said. The priest stretched his long legs out before him and crossed his hands behind his head.

"There is that," Nix agreed.

"None of that now," Baras said, though the words sang a false note. "We'll be fine."

Egil tipped back the rest of his coffee, shook out the cup, and nodded at the supply wagon. "Here's what I say. Women and fine ale seem much more than only a day gone, the night is cold, the fire feeble, and we're all going to die out here in the Wastes. Before we do, I say we make the best of it. Since this coffee tastes like piss, I offer we look to the beer in that wagon."

"The priest speaks with wisdom," Jyme said. "How about some beer, Baras?"

Baras considered, nodded, and two of the younger guards quickly rose, smiling, and made for the supply wagon.

"Meanwhile," Egil said, "why not tell them of that time in the Well of Farrago, Nix, when that door defied your talents?"

"It was a *hatch*, whoreson, which you well know."

The guards returned with two small beer barrels, cracked them, and started to pour.

"But well enough," Nix said, his cup sloshing with beer. "I'll tell them about that hatch, *and* about how you nearly pissed yourself when..."

Hours later, their bellies full of beer, Egil and Nix sat around the glowing embers of the small fire. Nix's storytelling had put everyone at ease for a time, but the moment he stopped, the sense of foreboding crept back into camp and took a seat at the fire.

The guards without watch duty had either gone to their tents to sleep or snored on their bedrolls near the embers. Above them the wind howled, and Nix swore he heard voices in the gusts, a mad muttering that made his skin crawl.

"This is an unholy place," Egil said. The priest stared into the fire, dice in hand but idle.

"No argument from me. Shake those dice, will you?"

"Eh? Oh." Egil shook the dice, his habit when tense, but he kept at it only a short time. As he put them away, he said, "I've been thinking about what you said. The woman's voice you heard?"

"And?"

"We've both heard of Oremal and the mindmages, Nix."

"We're far from Oremal."

"Yes, but what's to say such magic is limited only to Oremal?"

"They're not even conscious."

"And yet they seem to be affecting you somehow. To what purpose we don't know, but it seems reasonable to assume a sinister intention."

Nix could only shrug. He could not disagree.

"We have to do something," Egil said.

"Like what?" Nix said. "Even if I could harm a woman – which I can't – the spellworm would prevent it. His sisters are the very point of Rakon's charge to us."

"Maybe we tell him what they're doing. Maybe he can stop it."

"I don't trust him any farther than I can spit," Nix said. "He'd turn it further to his advantage somehow."

Egil toed the embers with his boot. "So, what then?"

"We get the horn for Rakon or we slip the compulsion."

"I've had no luck on that last," Egil said. "I've just made myself sick."

"Likewise. But either way, we get clear of this and far from the Norristru family as soon as we can. Then maybe we try our luck out west, stay away from Dur Follin for a time."

Egil sighed and stood. "If that's what we must do, that's what we'll do. And now I've prayers to say and then sleep to find. I'll note only that if you start acting odd due to the sisters' witchery, I'll kill you quickly. Well enough?"

"Fak you," Nix said with a smile.

Egil chuckled. "In the morn, then."

"In the morn."

Nix sat before the fire, trying to solve the puzzle of his situation, and succeeding only in irritating himself over his inability to do so. At length the eunuch emerged from the carriage, bearing Rusilla as easily as Nix might have carried a child. Her face was turned toward Nix, the vacant eyes on him, her hair a red curtain falling from her head. Seeing her caused Nix's heart to thump. His eye itched, watered, and he wanted to scream at her to leave him alone.

The eunuch placed Rusilla in one of the tents, saw that she was blanketed, then did the same with Merelda. Once he had them ensconced, he tied their tent closed and took station just outside, arms crossed over his huge chest, eyes unblinking and staring at nothing.

Nix wanted very much to face Rusilla again, to look into her eyes, get to the bottom of her game, but the eunuch afforded him no opportunity. The man didn't move and showed no signs of fatigue. He might as well have been carved from stone. Once, Nix rose and made as though to walk in the general direction of the sisters' tent.

Instantly the eunuch had his knife in hand and his vacant gaze fixed directly on Nix. Nix diverted to the supply wagon and took another loaf of flatbread from the sack. He returned to the fire and stared at the flames, his left eye pained.

"Leave me be, woman," he said.

He listened to the wind and his eyelids soon grew heavy. He fell asleep to the crackle of wood and the pounding of his pulse in his skull.

Nix dreamed of an ancient, dilapidated mansion. He stood in a long hallway, where dim light flickered. Paint peeled from cracked plaster walls. The lines of the cracks, the whorls and spirals, called to mind the indecipherable script of a madman. Dread settled on him, a heavy, dire foreboding.

"Hello," he called, his voice small and high-pitched, girlish.

At his utterance the plaster and cracks in the wall wrinkled, shifted, finally coalesced into the outline of a pair of huge eyes. Paint and plaster chips rained to the floor as they opened, bloodshot and terrible. Pupils dilated as they fixed on him, their regard judgmental, terrifying.

He staggered back, reached for a weapon but had none. In fact, he realized to his shock that he was not in his own clothing. He wore a dress, a blue dress like Tesha's, but with a ragged, dirty hem and a torn bodice. For a reason he could not articulate, the attire made him feel vulnerable, and the vulnerability deepened the terror gnawing at his self-control.

He hurried down the hall and the eyes swiveled in their plaster orbits to watch him go. New pairs of eyes formed in the walls as he went, cracking open in the plaster and paint. They were the eyes of men, he knew, judging, planning, plotting. He could not escape them.

Thick wooden doors lined the hall between faded, moth-eaten tapestries. Sounds carried through the doors: a bestial, rhythmic grunting, the pained screams of women. He felt something sticky and warm under his slippers. He looked down and saw bright red blood seeping under the bottom of the doors, soaking the floor, drenching his feet in crimson.

The grunting behind the doors grew more urgent, the screams more pained. He put his hands to his ears, unable to bear more, but he could not escape the terrible sounds. He fled, speeding down the hallway, past an endless processional of doors behind which horrors and bloody violations occurred unchecked.

"Stop it!" he screamed, and banged a fist on one of the doors. "Stop!"

But it didn't stop. The grunts grew faster, harder, the entire floor shook. A woman screamed desperately. He reached for the handle on the door but there was no handle. He put his shoulder into it, once, twice, but it would not budge.

He whirled to glare accusingly back at the eyes in the wall – it was their fault, he somehow knew – but they were gone. Instead, the cracks in the plaster formed words, a sentence.

This already happened. It will happen again.

The grunts and screams stopped. He blinked, breathing hard.

Down the hall he heard wet respiration, deep and steady. He licked his lips and turned slowly on his heel to face the sound. The hallway ended at another door, larger than the others, and this one with a handle.

The door was breathing, stretching and expanding as it respired, a great wooden lung that exhaled the smell of sweat, sex, and terror. He stared at it a long while, stuck to the ground by his bloody slippers and his fright.

The handle on the door started to turn, a slow rotation that caused him nearly to faint.

Panicked, terrified of the hulking form he knew must lurk on the other side of the wooden slab, he ran down the hall and grabbed the handle with both hands, preventing it from turning. Small, fearful sounds escaped his lips as he tried to hold it still.

"Go away!" he shouted. "Leave me alone."

He heard cracking and feared the wood of the door giving way. A titter of laughter sounded in his ears, wispy and otherworldly.

He opened his eyes, his heart a hammer against the cage of his ribs.

The wood of the fire crackled, not the door of his dream. He'd fallen asleep around the fire. Two of the guards lay on the ground near the fire, too, wrapped in their bedrolls. One of the pack horses stirred, whinnied, the sound like laughter.

"Shit," he whispered, and sat up. His head was pounding, his eyes aching. He dabbed at his nose and it came away bloody. Inexplicably, his mouth tasted vaguely of pepper. He spit out the taste and glanced over at the tent that sheltered Rusilla and Merelda. The eunuch remained in his station, as immovable and expressionless as a mountain. A breeze carried down the cut, stirred the flames, Nix's hair.

He absently poked the still-glowing embers with a stick. Sparks and smoke carried off into the air, and the breeze carried them toward the tents, the carriage. He watched them go, but they didn't go, not directly. Floating embers and swirling smoke gathered in a cloud around the window of Rakon's carriage, as if caught there in a tiny cyclone. For a fleeting moment, Nix thought he saw the outline of an enormous winged form just outside the carriage. Too, he thought he heard the faint titter of laughter in the wind, but the sound and the suggested form lasted only a moment before vanishing into nebulous shapelessness. Fatigue and the stress of traveling the Wastes were making him imagine things.

He lay back before the fire, closed his eyes, and soon fell into dreamless sleep.

The sylph hovered invisibly outside Rakon's carriage, its voice a breeze in his ear, smoke from the fire outlining its winged form for a moment. Open tomes and several ancient, yellowed maps of the Wastes lay on the upholstered bench beside Rakon. He'd pored over them constantly in recent days, confirming and reconfirming his thinking, testing his conclusion.

Each of the maps showed different parts of the Wastes, yet each part showed a road not unlike the road they traveled, which was actually not a road at all.

"Lines, angles, shapes," said the sylph, its voice rustling the pages.

Layering the maps one on top of each other, though clumsy, had brought revelation, had allowed Rakon to discern the truth of the Wastes, and, he thought, the location of Abrak-Thyss.

"The lines of the roads are as I've described to you?" he said.

The sylph could see the lines from high above, discern the angles, and note the shape.

"They are as you've surmised," the sylph whispered, the breeze of its voice tickling his ear, stirring his hair.

He replayed the spirit's words in his mind, tested them for ambiguities, saw none that troubled him.

"And the prison of Abrak-Thyss?"

"The winds here say nothing of Abrak-Thyss. His prison is in the earth, and the air knows him not. The winds speak only of a great mirror that covers the earth where a city once stood, not far from the end of the valley you travel even now. The winds whisper of the Vwynn devils whose delves hollow the earth below us. They say the Vwynn do not go to the place of the mirror."

"A mirror," Rakon echoed thoughtfully. "Glass."

Glass made sense. The mirror had to be it.

The sylph stirred and its winds caused the maps to flutter, flipped pages in the open tome. "The Vwynn suspect you are here," the sylph said, and giggled. "They don't hear the wind, but they smell it, smell the sorcery on it. They're all around you, under you, prowling, stalking. The gusts sing of their hunger."

"Silence," Rakon said, but the sylph continued.

"But there is more, master. The breezes from Dur Follin hint that the Norristru pact with Hell is broken. Perhaps your enemies move against you even now. There are sorcerers and witches in Dur Follin gleeful at your fall, even now plotting your demise."

"I said *silence,*" Rakon hissed. "Begone from me, spirit."

The sylph whirled around the carriage, incensed. "Perhaps next time you call for me, Rakon Norristru, the King of the Air will not heed and will not order me to come. Perhaps after that the wind will carry word of your death."

Rakon growled, snatched at the air where he knew the spirit to be but his hand passed through its incorporeal form. He jabbed a finger at empty space.

"And perhaps after I awaken Abrak-Thyss and renew the Pact, when House Thyss of Hell is bound once more to lend its strength to my house, then maybe I shall demand of the King of the Air that he give me you, to imprison in an airless jar with naught for company but your own voice. Forever. Do you think the King of the Air would gainsay me, then, sylph?"

The sylph keened in terror, swirled gently around Rakon. "A zephyr offered in placation, master. I meant no offense, and of course wish you only good fortune on your quest to find and free Abrak-Thyss."

"Leave me now, fickle creature."

"But master, the thought of an airless jar–"

"Think on it elsewhere. Leave me, I said, until I call again!"

Keening, the sylph merged with the wind of the Wastes and was gone.

For a long while, Rakon eyed his maps, the tomes that had led him to the Wastes, to the sole hope for his family. He looked out the window of the carriage, up through the cut and into the sky. Minnear floated against the black vault, nearly full. The thin, waning crescent of Kulven floated above it, a silver scythe. The Thin Veil was almost upon the world.

Hell, too, blinked in the velvet of the night sky, a crimson dot of fire and stone. He glanced at it for only a moment. Hell was no longer his salvation. His salvation lay somewhere in the Wastes.

He studied his maps a final time, folded and rolled them up, and tried not to think of the Vwynn.

CHAPTER TEN

Nix awoke before the dawn, as was his wont when he wasn't otherwise knocked unconscious by a blow to the head. The eunuch still stood his station, and Nix assumed he had not moved through the night.

"Does the man piss in place?" Nix muttered through a dry mouth that tasted peppery. He sat up, prodded the embers to life, and put two logs on the fire to get it going.

The camp stirred as dawn turned the sky gray. Men coughed, spit, pissed, pulled on mail and weapons, yoked horses.

At Rakon's call, the eunuch carried Rusilla and Merelda back to the carriage in turn. Nix did not dare interfere, despite his impulse to do so.

Egil soon emerged from his tent, yawning, the ruff of his hair sticking out in all directions. He offered a brief prayer to his dead god and came to Nix's side.

"You feel all right?" the priest asked. "You look like shite."

Nix made a helpless gesture. "Bad dreams."

Egil turned and looked at the carriage. "The sisters, you think? Or this place?"

"Maybe both," Nix said.

Egil rubbed his palm over his head briskly, as if shaking the eye of Ebenor to wakefulness. "I slept poorly as well. But hopefully we'll not have too much of this. I make us only three days from Afirion."

"Aye."

Egil leaned in close and whispered, "I don't have the stomach to fight the worm today. I still ache from yesterday. I think we just surrender to the compulsion and get the damned horn. Then we get clear."

Egil's choice of the word "surrender" caused Nix to recall his disquieting dream, the screams, the blood, the sense of hopelessness he'd felt, a hopelessness so profound that surrender seemed the only option.

"I dislike surrender," Nix said.

"Aye," Egil agreed with a nod. "But what else can we do?"

To that, Nix said nothing, and he, Egil, and the guards ate on the move as they worked breaking camp, the guards tearing things down as efficiently as they had set them up. Within the hour, they were moving again, following the enspelled road through the cut. The clouds returned and dull, filtered light leaked down from a gray sky. They traveled for leagues through the cut, walled by the blood-colored cliffs, the skeletal trees atop the cliff walls rattling in the wind.

Around midday the driver of the supply wagon spotted something ahead and pulled the horses to a halt.

"What is it?" Baras asked, and Rakon's head emerged from the carriage and repeated the question.

"Something on the side of the road," the driver said, pointing. He was the oldest of the men, his hair going to gray and his body paunchy. "There."

Half the guards readied crossbows, and the others, including Baras and Jyme, drew blades. Nix and Egil came to the front of the wagon train, their own weapons drawn, and saw the thing to which the driver was pointing, a broken form lying just off the side of the road about thirty paces ahead.

"Probably an animal," Baras said, and pointed at his men. "The five of you stay with the wagons. Jyme, you're with me." To Rakon, he said, "My lord, we'll just have a look."

"Be quick," Rakon said.

Egil and Nix fell in beside Baras and Jyme. Nix kept his eyes on the cliffs as they approached, sniffing for an ambush, but none was forthcoming.

"What is that?" Jyme asked as they neared the form.

A body lay on the side of the road, the limbs twisted as if from a fall. Scales the color of sand covered the creature's wiry form, or what remained of its form. Its thin limbs were all sinew and muscle. Each of its five long fingers ended in black claws. The hairless head was a thin oval, vaguely humanlike, and thrown back as if in pain. Fangs filled the overlarge, open mouth. Two vertical slits in the center of its face must have been its nostrils. Many small cuts and bite marks covered the flesh, scores of them. Scavengers had been at the remains. Tatters of dried, leathery skin flapped in the breeze, a drawn curtain revealing ribs and spine.

"It's a demon," Jyme whispered.

Nix could not disagree. He'd never seen anything like it.

"Fell from the top, I'd wager," Egil said, looking up at the valley walls.

Baras looked back at the caravan, at the creature. "Whatever it is, it's dead. We need to keep moving." He waved the wagon and carriage forward.

Eyes lingered on the dead creature's form as they passed. The guards made the protective sign of Orella. Rakon stared at the remains with hooded eyes as his carriage rolled past.

As they traveled, they passed seven more carcasses. All of them were dead many days, perhaps weeks, and appeared broken from a fall. Bites and scratches covered the scaled flesh, and all had been torn open.

The men gave the bodies a wide berth. Twice after passing bodies Baras consulted with Rakon, but he never shared the subject of the conversations with Nix.

The valley seemed neverending and they continued on for hours, walled in by the cliffs, walking an inexplicable thoroughfare littered with the corpses of demons.

The men remained tense and alert, keeping weapons to hand. Nix watched the sky, the tree-fringed top of the cut, the walls, but nothing occurred, and by nightfall the men seemed to have shed much of their nervousness.

"Three more days," Nix said to Egil, as they assisted the guards in setting up camp.

"Hmmph," Egil grunted, hammering tent stakes into the red earth.

"What?" Nix asked.

"Notice the sun?" Egil said.

"That blazing orange circle in the sky? It's called the sun? I hadn't noticed it before."

Egil didn't smile. "I mean did you notice its position."

"We're surrounded by rock walls and it's cloudy. How would I notice its position?"

Egil nodded. "You didn't pay attention. In any event, we're not headed due east anymore."

"What? Shite. What direction are we headed? Are we lost?"

Egil looked Nix in the face. "We're headed northeast. Rakon seem lost to you?"

He didn't. "Maybe he just wants to stick on the road. Keep the wagons and carriage as long as possible before de-yoking the horses."

"Maybe," Egil said.

"You doubt it?"

"I trust nothing about him," the priest said. "I think he aims for something other than a direct route to Afirion's deserts. But why, I can't say. And I think he knows more about those bodies we saw than he's telling. Did you see his face when we passed them?"

Nix considered, and made up his mind. "Then let's see what we can see." He hustled over to Baras's side.

"What is it, Nix?" The guardsman wiped his brow of sweat.

Nix kept his voice low. "Afirion is due east and we're not headed due east. Why?"

Baras's expression twisted up as he tried to find a suitable lie.

"The truth, Baras."

"The Lord Adjunct knows we're not headed due east. He wants to stay on the road."

"Why? We could lose the wagons, divide the supplies between the men and horses, and head east overland."

"I just follow orders, Nix."

Nix looked to the carriage. "He's looking for something in the Wastes, isn't he? What is it?"

If he had an answer, Baras didn't offer it.

"You're in deep water here, yeah?" Nix asked.

"I do what I'm told. You do the same."

Nix rubbed his nose. "That doesn't work well for me as a philosophical matter."

"Make it work," Baras said. "Meals in a half-hour."

With that, he walked away. As always, they started a meager fire, just large enough to heat coffee and warm bodies. Rakon repeated his warning to them to keep the flames low, but he needn't have. The bodies they'd seen on the road had taught all of them caution.

They ate as night came on. Afterward, Baras set

double watches and the men sat near the fire and speculated about the bodies they'd seen. Egil went to his prayers early and Nix lingered near the flames, fearing sleep and dreams. He waited for the eunuch to remove Rusilla and Merelda to their tents, but he never did. The sisters remained in the carriage, as did Rakon. Nix recalled the small vial he'd seen in Rakon's hands when he'd broken into the carriage. At the time he'd assumed it was medicine, but now thought otherwise. He suspected it was a drug, designed to keep the sisters from practicing their witchcraft, or mind-magery, or whatever it was they did. Perhaps that explained why he hadn't had an ache behind his eyes or a head full of foreign thoughts. For that, he was thankful.

Expecting a peaceful sleep, he dozed off near the fire. The dreams came anyway.

Once more, Nix found himself standing in the long hall. Doors lined the hall, hiding horrors. The large, respiring door was directly before him. Again he wore a tattered dress with a torn bodice.

Grunts and screams filled his ears. The handle on the respiring door started to turn and he lunged for it, grabbed the handle. He was sweating and his hands slipped. The door unlatched, opened a crack. He screamed in terror, slammed his shoulder into it to close it, and took the latch in both hands. A terrible force tried to wrench it into a turn.

"No, no!" he said, his voice fearful and high-pitched.

An impact against the other side of the door nearly

dislodged him, but he held on. The door pulsed against him, sickening and warm.

"Go away!" he screamed. "Leave me alone."

More screams from behind the other doors in the hallway, more grunting, a desperate wail. He could smell the coppery stink of fresh blood, imagined it flowing under the doors and into the hall. He was shaking, unnerved, surrounded by horror.

"Let me in!" said a voice from the other side, a woman's voice, intense, insistent. "You must see!"

"I don't want to see!" he screamed. "Leave me alone!"

Another powerful thud against the pulsing door. He leaned against it and held it closed.

"See it this way, then," said the woman's voice, her tone as final as a dirge.

A piercing pain in his groin, as if he'd been stabbed, elicited a prolonged scream and doubled him over. He looked down to see blood pouring from between his legs, soaking his dress, pattering the floor in a flood of crimson.

He shrieked in sickened horror and the sound of his own fear startled him awake.

Wakefulness did not end the shrieking.

He opened his eyes to see a cloud of keening creatures descending toward the campsite like a thunderhead, blotting out moons and stars. It was the flock of creatures they'd seen the day before, dropping on the camp in a cloud of fangs, scales, and beating wings. He could not easily distinguish individual creatures among the multitude.

Men were shouting all around him, horses whinnying. Egil shouted his name. He had time enough only to curse, leap to his feet, and put hand to blade hilt before the creatures were upon him. Chaos followed, a mad churn of sound: men screaming, the creatures shrieking and growling, the beat of wings, the snap of fangs.

Nix ducked low, eschewed his falchion, and put a dagger in each hand. He slashed and stabbed at anything within reach. In rough form, the creatures were about the size and shape of a goose. Leathery skin covered their bodies, and four overlapping membranous wings sprouted from their backs. Their necks ended in sleek heads. Small, red eyes perched over mouths lined with tiny fangs. Their taloned claws looked like those of a raptor. They shrieked, growled, and hissed as they swarmed.

A creature tore at Nix's arm, a claw scratched his hand and cheek, and another creature landed on his back and sank its teeth into his scalp. He shouted with pain, reached back, grabbed it, and threw its fluttering form to the earth. He stomped it to death as he slashed another of the creatures hovering before him and snapping at his face. The fiends were everywhere, shrieking, biting, tearing exposed flesh.

One landed on his legs, talons sinking into flesh, biting at his thigh. Another one appeared, diving for his face, clawed feet and toothy mouth snapping at his eyes and nose. He reeled backward, ducking, stumbling through several more, slashing as he went, severed wings and legs and throats. But for every creature he killed, another took its place, another. Teeth sank into his ear; claws dug into his scalp. He roared and twirled, stabbing and slashing wildly.

Egil did the same five paces from him, the priest's shouts like the bellows of an angry bull. His hammers spun through the air so fast they hummed, pulping the creatures three and four at a swing. All around the campsite, the other guards were shrieking, bleeding. Blood dripped into Nix's eyes from his wounded scalp. Already his arms were tiring. Panic fogged the air along with the screams.

The horses, unyoked from the wagons for the night but tethered to outcroppings of rock, whinnied and stomped, trapped by their tethers. Dozens of the creatures landed on the poor animals and tore at their flesh. The horses bucked, bellowed, pulled at their reins, heads shaking, muscles straining.

"Save the horses!" Baras shouted, and several of his guards ran for the animals through the cloud of creatures. They chopped wildly with their blades as they ran.

One of the guards, separated from the others, went down. Nix ran for him, but more than a dozen of the creatures swarmed him. Teeth snapped before his eyes, sank into his hands, causing him to curse and drop a dagger. He drew another as he recoiled from the creatures, slashing and stabbing those he could reach.

"Help! Get them off!" the downed guard called.

The creatures squawked and swarmed the guard until he was covered in a blanket of their scaled bodies. He dropped his weapon, his arms flailing wildly, desperately, screaming in terror and pain.

Baras and Egil roared and charged toward the fallen man from opposite directions, but before they could get to him, the creatures had sunk their talons into his flesh and clothes and lifted him into the air. He hung limp in their collective grasp, perhaps already dead, arms and legs dangling like a doll's. Egil leaped for him but the man was already out of reach.

Baras cursed and, shielding his head and face, ran to help his men in protecting the horses. Egil fell in with him. The draft animals were panicked, kicking and whinnying, and Baras went down trying to dodge a kick from one of them. Egil grabbed him by the collar and pulled him away, and together with the other guards they beat back a furious attack from scores of the flying creatures.

"Everyone here!" Egil called. "We need to fight together! Nix!"

Nix slashed a creature tearing at his arm, stomped another on the ground, cleared the air before him with a furious series of slashes. The creatures formed a cloud around him, an endless flutter of wings, snapping teeth, and slashing talons. Bleeding and fatigued, Nix made a run for the horses, slashing furiously as he ran. Blood ran into his eyes, blinded him, and he stumbled on rock, fell.

The moment he hit the ground dozens of the creatures landed on him, ripping his clothes and flesh, tearing at his leather jack. One bit the back of his neck, his scalp again, tearing loose a clump of hair. Another bit his ear. He tried to roll over and bring his blades to bear, but before he could he felt the sickening, terrifying feeling of his body being lifted up. Two score of the creatures at least clutched him by his flesh and his clothes and were bearing him into the air. He watched in horror as the ground fell away beneath him. He flashed on an image of himself carried into one of the holes in the earth they'd seen earlier, his body reduced to bones, made part of a mound of the dead. Panic lent him strength. He kicked and squirmed frenetically, desperately.

"Egil! Egil!"

He tried to turn his body, slash with his blade, but only managed to writhe to no effect. A talon tore a furrow in his cheek, narrowly missing his eye. He twisted and squirmed wildly, fueled by fear and adrenaline. He managed to dislodge enough of the creatures that they lost some altitude, but they did not release him. Teeth sank into his legs, his arms. Blood dripped from his wounds, dotted the earth. He started to rise again.

"Shite! Egil!"

He glimpsed Egil a fraction of a second before the priest leaped high for him and tackled him back to earth. Nix felt the squirming, fluttering death throes of several of the creatures crushed between his body and the earth. He rolled to the side and climbed to his feet, swinging his blade at the hissing creatures attacking him from all sides. Egil did the same, his hammers reaping the creatures in twos and threes.

The priest grabbed Nix by the arm and propelled him along toward Baras and the horses, fending off the creatures as best he could with one hammer.

"I'm good," Nix said, shaking his arm free and stabbing a creature with his dagger.

"Maybe put on some weight though, eh?" Egil said, grinning, his face bloody and torn.

"We need to find cover!" Baras shouted, hacking at the creatures attacking him and the horses. The poor draft horses kicked and screamed piteously. Baras and his fellow guards stood in a cluster near the horses, fighting desperately against the swarm that seemed unending.

"There is no damned cover!" Egil shouted, and slammed his hammer through another two scaled bodies.

Rakon's shout from within the carriage cut through the tumult. "Get wood on the fire! Now, Baras! Right now!"

The creatures thronged the carriage too, coating it in their scaly, winged forms, but Rakon had pulled the wood slat windows closed except for a slit, and that appeared to have kept the creatures out.

"Now, Baras!" Rakon said.

Two of the creatures lunged for the slit, got their talons on either side of it, wings fluttering, and tried to pry it open and wriggle through. Their heads darted forward into the opening, teeth gnashing. Rakon cursed and slammed the slat shut on them, pinning their necks there, the creatures shrieking, flapping, and soon limp.

Baras ducked his head and ran for the fire pit. Nix, Egil, and Jyme followed, slashing, grabbing, stomping. The ground was crunchy with dead and wounded creatures, slick with blood. Nix stumbled as he ran, his arms and legs leaden. Before him, Jyme stumbled, fell, and the creatures landed on his back, tearing and biting. Nix stabbed three of them and pulled Jyme to his feet with a grunt. One landed on Nix's arm and bit him hard on his shoulder, but his jack turned it. Jyme ran it through with his blade.

Baras and Egil fought off the creatures as best they could while they tossed logs onto the embers. Egil crushed two with a swing of a log before he threw it on the flames. Sparks rose into the sky. The creatures shrieked in response to the spark shower, cleared away from the rising flames and smoke.

"More wood! They don't like the fire," said Jyme, and moved to throw another log on. Nix grabbed him by the arm.

"You'll smother it!"

In moments the wood Egil and Baras had thrown onto the pit crackled and burned. But still the creatures came on, and Nix, Jyme, and Egil plied their weapons and tried to stay on their feet.

When the flames rose high behind them the door to the carriage flew open and the eunuch lurched out, followed by Rakon. Immediately scores of the creatures attacked them. A dozen of the scaled, toothy creatures flapped around the eunuch, biting and scratching his face and bare arms, but he seemed barely to notice, instead methodically grabbing the creatures one after another and squeezing them in his hands until they burst in a shower of gore and blood.

"Stay near the carriage, eater!" Rakon said to the eunuch, and stumbled toward the fire, hood pulled up, waving his thin blade wildly as he went.

Baras and two of the guards left the fire to meet him, shielding him from the creatures' attacks. Egil, Nix, and Jyme awaited them near the fire, slashing, stabbing, and cursing.

A short break in the attacks gave Nix a moment to look up and assess the swarm. He could barely see the stars through the fog of them. There weren't hundreds – there were thousands, wheeling in a dark cloud above them, diving to attack by the score.

"Keep them off me," Rakon said to them.

"Aye," Baras answered.

While Baras, Egil, Nix, and Jyme did their best to keep the onslaught of creatures at bay, Rakon stood over the fire incanting. The syllables he uttered hurt Nix's ears and seemed to excite the flames, which roared and danced in answer to Rakon's words. In moments the flames swelled to a bonfire and still Rakon incanted, his hands weaving in the air before the flames.

Nix stabbed a creature, slashed another, another. The heat from the fire grew uncomfortable. The creatures squawked and squeaked, withdrew from the growing flames and smoke.

Rakon's cadence grew more rapid, louder, reached a climax. He threw his hands over his head and the fire erupted upward in a searing column that blossomed into a disc of flame, exploding outward in all direction, for a few moments roofing the campsite in fire. Nix turned away, blinking, his eyebrows and hair singed, as a collective shriek went up from the creatures and the stink of charred flesh perfumed the night.

Thuds sounded around them, the bodies of the creatures raining from the sky, scores of them, hundreds, maybe a thousand. Nix looked up and against Minnear's green light saw what was left of the flock fleeing into the distance.

"Gods," Jyme breathed. He put the point of his blade in the ground and leaned on it. Dead creatures lay all around them.

Nix could only nod. The men stared at one another, hands on their knees, gasping, bleeding. Baras cleared his throat, wiped the blood from his face.

"We have to go after Lormel," he said.

Nix presumed he meant the guard who'd been carried off by the creatures. "Baras..."

"He's dead by now," Rakon said, lowering his hood to reveal his own face scratched by a claw. "Or will be before we can get there."

"My lord–"

"He's dead, Baras. There's nothing to be done for him. We have to break camp and get moving."

"Moving?" Baras said. "My lord, the men are wounded, exhausted."

"Truth," Nix added, sagging to the ground.

"And the horses..." Baras continued.

Rakon looked past Baras to the darkness outside the firelight.

"Do as I say, Baras. The Vwynn will be coming. If they didn't see the light from the flames, they'll smell the sorcery. We must hurry or we'll all die." He looked over to the horses. Two were down and bloody. The other two bled from many small wounds, but at least still stood.

"Yoke the two still standing to the carriage. Put the other two down. Divide the supplies from the wagon amongst the men and leave the wagon behind. I have poultices for the wounded men. Quickly now, Baras."

Baras stared for a long moment, then said, "Yes, my lord."

"The bodies we saw on the road," Nix said to Rakon. "Those are the Vwynn?"

Rakon looked up at the moon, at the high walls of the cut that hemmed them in. "Yes. The demons of the Wastes. Debased descendants of the people who once ruled these lands."

Egil took a step toward Rakon, but the thoughts implied by his angry expression triggered the spell-worm. He doubled over with a groan and Rakon sneered.

Nix gave voice to what he assumed to be Egil's thoughts.

"You knew about these Vwynn the whole time and see fit to tell us only now?"

"I'd hoped to avoid them altogether," Rakon said. "Now do as I've said. We must hurry."

"Hurry to where?" Egil said, teeth gritted against nausea. "The Wastes are two days in every direction. If these Vwynn are coming..."

"If they're coming, they'll catch us," Nix said. "This is a decent place to defend. I didn't see wings on those corpses, so they'll have to come at us on the ground. With these walls, they can approach from only two–"

"No," Rakon said.

"We're vulnerable if we get caught in the open," Egil said.

"There's a... refuge ahead, not far out of the cut. The Vwynn will not enter it. If we can reach it, we'll find safety there."

"Safety for how long?" Egil asked.

"And how do you know about this refuge?" Nix asked. "And that the Vwynn won't enter it? Why not mention it before?"

"I know many things about which you are ignorant, Nix Fall, and mentioning all of them to you would occupy all of my days."

"Now *he's* a wit," Nix said to Egil.

"Assist my men in breaking camp," Rakon said. "Then we'll see to the wounded. We leave as soon as it's done."

Rakon returned to his carriage and soon provided Baras with several large pouches of herbal poultice.

Baras mixed it with a small amount of beer, turning it into a lumpy yellow paste flecked with bits of leaves, and the men smeared it on their cuts. All except Egil.

"The only magic I trust comes from your gewgaws," he said to Nix. "And those only half the time."

Scratches and a few oozing bites marred the priest's face, scalp, and arms. He daubed at them with bits of burlap cut from an unused sack. Of course, Nix had seen Egil endure far worse wounds without slowing and without complaint.

"You're sure?" Nix asked.

"Aye."

For his part, Nix was too wounded to be particular about the source of relief. He spread the paste over the many wounds on his arms, his legs, his scalp and face. The paste went on cold but grew warm as it did its work.

After about a sixty count, it lost its warmth. When Nix scraped it off he found that the shallowest of his cuts had vanished, the deepest reduced to pink lines that would heal in a day or two.

"The man knows his craft, I concede," Nix said to Egil.

"Don't get too fond of him," the priest answered. "It'll be awkward when we have to kill him."

Mention of violence against Rakon caused the spellworm to twist up Egil's guts, which he endured with a grimace.

"Fair point," Nix said, and his own violent thoughts triggered nausea and cramps that doubled him over.

There were several hours of night left, so the guards lit torches, Nix pulled forth his crystal eye, and the caravan got underway, traveling the high-walled cut under the lurid, nearly full eye of the Mages' Moon. The night sat heavy on them and they moved in near-silence, the only sound the low rumble of the carriage wheels on the road and the occasional whicker from the horses.

Only when dawn lightened the sky did they breathe easier. Yet still the cut – really a canyon, a long, deep gash in the earth – went on so long Nix feared it would never end, that it would just continue forever, condemning them all to a subterranean existence where sky and wind and sun were forever just out of reach. They watched the sky, the walls, fearing the return of the flying creatures, dreading the appearance of the Vwynn.

When the road at last began to rise, so too did their spirits. The walls of the canyon shrank around them and Nix could see the end of the cut ahead, the road gradually rising to elevate them out of the Hellish pit.

Several of the guards gasped when the group reached the top of the canyon and emerged into the unfiltered light of day. The leagues they'd traversed seemed to have transported them to another world.

Instead of boulders and scree and broken hills, they saw instead monumental ruins. Huge rectangular stone blocks jutted from the red landscape at odd angles. Faded script showed on some, the whorls and twists of the characters mostly lost to time and the weather. Looking too long at the script that had survived made Nix's eyes ache. Everyone stared about in awed silence. Baras made the protective sign of Orella.

"What do you make of them?" Egil asked, nodding at the blocks.

"I don't," Nix said, shaking his head.

"Man-made," Egil said, nodding at a huge stone sticking out of the earth, the bones of a lost civilization.

"Made," Nix agreed. "But I'm not sure it was by men. The size of them..."

In their day, the blocks must have been part of structures larger than anything in Dur Follin, larger than anything Nix had ever seen. He could not imagine the destructive force it must have taken to topple them. The mere passage of time seemed insufficient to the task.

"Norristru has a great interest, it seems," Egil said, nodding at the carriage.

Rakon had opened the carriage's window and stared out at the blocks, his eyes gleaming, his thin lips set in a straight line.

All day they traversed the gigantic architecture, the residuum of a people who constructed wonders and died – shattered domes, megaliths the size of small buildings, and pyramidal blocks, the sharp points of which stabbed at the earth and sky.

"How many do you suppose have seen this?" Egil said.

"Few," Nix said, and thumped the priest on the shoulder. "And now us among them. This is why we do it, yeah?"

"Aye," Egil said. "Though I'd prefer to be doing it of my own accord."

"Seconded."

The carriage set a brisk pace and the ruins grew denser as they traveled. Towering shapes loomed on the horizon ahead. At first Nix mistook them for hills and rock formations, but as they drew closer, he saw they, too, were ruins, great heaps of stone.

"Gods," Egil breathed.

All of the guards slowed in their steps, shared worried glances, and tightened their grips on sword hilts.

"It's all just ruins, men," Baras said, his tone false.

Rakon called out from the carriage. "We need to reach those ruins before nightfall, Baras."

"Is that the refuge you spoke of?" Nix called, but Rakon ignored him.

"You heard him," Baras said. "Leg it."

They picked up the pace, but the day wore on and still the high ruins seemed too distant.

"Faster," Rakon urged them. "We must go faster."

"Easily said by the man riding in the carriage," Nix said, jogging along with the rest. Sweat soaked his jack and shirt. Despite the pace they'd kept, they hadn't covered enough ground. The cloud-shrouded sun sank low in the west. Dread settled on the men. They watched the sky, the ruins around them.

"We press on until we reach the ruins," Baras said.

When night outvied day for rule of the sky, the Vwynn showed themselves.

CHAPTER ELEVEN

Nix caught motion in the dark crannies of the ruins that loomed around them.

"I saw something," Nix said, pointing with his sword at a pile of rectangular blocks that formed a makeshift post and lintel. "There."

"Keep moving," Rakon called. "Do not stop."

Nix spotted more movement, a lithe form dashing through the shadows.

"There!" he said.

"I saw it, too," said Derg.

"Faster!" Rakon shouted. "Everyone, faster!"

"Is it the Vwynn?" Baras asked. "Is it?"

Rakon didn't answer, the driver whipped the reins and the exhausted, wounded draft horses whinnied and picked up their pace. The men followed suit, almost running. There was no way they could keep it up for long.

Nix's eyes darted right and left, following motion, trying to discern the details of the creatures. A small stone fell from atop a megalith, disturbed by the motion of something. He saw more movement on the other side, a lot of it, a mass of forms. Over the sound of his own labored breathing, he heard growls, snarls, a growing chorus of them.

"We should find a defensible spot, Baras!" Egil said, rattling his dice in one hand, holding a hammer in the other. "We're going to get caught in the open!"

"No," Rakon countered from the carriage. "Faster. We must make the ruins."

"My lord has spoken," Baras said, breathing heavily, his mail jingling as he ran. "Move it!"

The sun shot its last, hopeless rays into a sky being overrun by night. As darkness stretched over the land, the Vwynn emerged from the shadows, hundreds of them.

"Here they come!" Nix said.

"Onto the carriage!" Egil ordered. "Now, now!"

"Wait," Baras said. "We should–"

"Go!" Egil said. "Now, Baras, or we're all dead."

The Vwynn charged out of the ruins, seething from all sides, the stonescape vomiting up their muscular, clawed forms.

"Onto the carriage," Baras said, echoing Egil. He bounded onto the driver's bench and took station beside the driver, already cocking his crossbow.

Egil, Nix, Jyme, and the rest of the guards leaped onto the step rail of the carriage and grabbed hold where they could. Rakon leaned halfway out the open window of the carriage and shouted at the driver.

"Go, man! Go!"

The driver shouted at the already straining horses, snapped the reins. The animals laid back their ears, snorted, and ran as best they could. They weren't chargers, and with the weight of the additional men to pull, they moved alarmingly slow.

"Faster!" Baras called, and the driver snapped the reins again and again. The draft horses snorted, lowered their heads, whinnied, pulled.

Behind them, before them, and to their left and right, Vwynn poured out of the night, loping over the ruined terrain on their long legs. They moved with an odd jerky stride, more leap than run, and their clawed feet threw up clods of earth behind them at every stride. Muscles rippled in their thin, scaled frames as they moved. Their claws flexed open and closed as they ran, as if in anticipation of rending flesh.

The carriage wasn't going fast enough. The driver beat at the horses mercilessly and the beasts picked up speed.

"Crossbows!" Baras shouted. "Clear the road!"

"Do not stop for anything!" Rakon ordered the driver.

Baras took aim and fired. His quarrel slammed into the chest of a Vwynn ahead and to the right, sent the creature tumbling head over heels to the earth. The Vwynn's fellows ran over and past him without slowing.

The horses picked up more speed, but not enough. Guards cursed as they tried to load, the bumpy ride making it difficult to lay quarrels into cocked crossbows.

Nix held his falchion in one hand and held onto a rail on the top of the carriage with the other. Beside him, Egil held a hammer in one hand and held on with the other. His dice had vanished back into his pocket.

The guards got their ammunition set and crossbows sang, the bolts sizzling into the moonlit darkness before the wagon. Two Vwynn fell, a third, all of them screaming as they tumbled into the rockscape. The rest closed from all sides, fangs bared, claws flexed, their muscular bodies lurid against the stone.

The road behind them closed like a drawn curtain as the Vwynn coming from either side met up in a churning mass and ran frenziedly after the carriage, which was now careening wildly over the road.

"Don't overturn us!" Nix shouted at the driver, and the older man nodded.

"Don't let them get the horses!" Baras shouted over his shoulder. "Crossbows! Crossbows!"

Jyme, loading his weapon, lost his balance and would have fallen if Nix hadn't grabbed him by the collar and steadied him. He didn't bother with thanks, just loaded his crossbow as fast as the situation allowed.

Vwynn poured forth from the sides, before them, a mob of claws, teeth, and violence. One of them leaped onto the driver's bench, its claws scrabbling on the wood. Baras stabbed it through the midsection with his blade.

"Keep driving!" he shouted to the driver. "Keep driving!"

Blood spurted from the Vwynn's gut and it screamed. Baras kicked it off the carriage, wary of its slashing claws and snapping teeth. Another Vwynn leaped onto the bench from the other side, wrapped arms and legs around the old driver. The guards on the side near the driver cursed, swung their blades at the Vwynn, but it did little good. Baras spun on his seat, reached for the driver, but too late.

A chaotic swirl of limbs, claws, screams, shrieks, and blood ended with the Vwynn toppling over the side and into the road with the driver still in hand. The wagon continued on, the horses whinnying in terror. Baras grabbed the reins and whipped the creatures onward.

Behind them, half a dozen Vwynn fell upon the writhing, screaming driver, devouring him in the road.

Meanwhile another Vwynn closed from the side and leaped at Jyme, Egil, and Nix. Nix impaled it through the chest on his blade and a backhand from Egil's hammer crushed its skull and sprayed gore.

"Shite!" Baras cursed, and Nix saw why.

Perhaps a dozen Vwynn had reached the road ahead of them and now charged directly toward the wagons.

Emotions churned around her, a lightning storm of fear, anger, and dread. Rusilla perceived them only thickly, the drugs her brother had given her attenuating her perception. She fought through the fog, swam up through the roiling emotional ocean, seeking acuity.

She could not focus.

She could discern nothing but the inchoate mass of feeling, a mash of indistinct emotions. No individuation. Her mind drifted and she sank, falling back into somnolent quiescence.

A voice sounded in her mind, roused her from lassitude. Merelda's voice.

Rose!

Mere's mental call was unfocused, a blind flailing in the midst of the emotional churn. Rusilla felt the terror in it.

Rose, where are you? I'm alone.

Mere's fear, the desperate hopelessness of it, brought Rusilla renewed focus. She waded through feelings, seeking the thread of her sister's thoughts, but could not pinpoint them. Instead, she projected soothing thoughts with as much power as she could muster.

I'm here and all is well, Mere. Go back to sleep. All is well.

In truth Rusilla had no idea if all was well, if her plan was working. She was blind, trapped by her brother's drugs in the cage of her own mind. The world outside her mental space was blurry, sensed as if through thick glass.

Her frustration spiked and she felt her body, felt a moment's control over her flesh, just a flash of feeling. She might have clenched her fist, or perhaps just lifted a finger.

She was bouncing, moving fast. There were sounds all around her, shouts, the rattle of carriage wheels.

Feeling her body allowed her renewed mental focus. She snatched at the emotions around her, taking the measure of each until she perceived a familiar thread, an emotional resonance she'd felt before her brother had increased her dosage and drowned her in drugs – Nix Fall.

She held on to Nix's emotional thread, climbed up it and settled into his consciousness.

"Run them down!" Rakon shouted, leaning out the window to see ahead. He sat back and Nix peeked into the carriage through the window.

Rakon had his thin blade drawn, fingers white around the hilt, his expression tense and nervous. The implacable eunuch sat beside him, knife in hand, an empty smile on his slack face. Across from them sat the sisters, their bodies bouncing here and there from the rough ride of the carriage.

Nix glanced ahead. The carriage was bearing down on the Vwynn before them. Nix looked back into the carriage. Rusilla's head was tilted to the side, her body bouncing, but her eyes were fixed on him. A shooting pain rooted in his skull, behind his eye. He winced, looked away, but too late. He tasted pepper, and Rusilla's mental voice penetrated his head, displaced his thoughts with two words uttered with such rage and hate that they nearly caused him to lose his grip on the wagon.

Kill Rakon! she said.

The words bounced around in his brain, drowned out the sound of everything else around him. His hand tightened on the grip of his falchion. He brought it up toward the window. He could jam it through, stab Rakon in the chest.

The violent thoughts against Rakon triggered the spellworm. Nix's stomach cramped. His muscles seized and he held on to the bouncing carriage only because his spasming hand closed over the rail he was holding on to.

Kill him!

A sharp pain started in Nix's chest and radiated toward his left arm. He couldn't breathe. He couldn't hold on.

I am Nix Fall of Dur Follin. Nix Fall...

It was no good. He felt as if he'd been stabbed in the chest. His legs went weak under him and still his hand slowly, incrementally raised his falchion for a killing strike that would surely result in his death. He forced his teeth apart and shouted, spitting as he spoke.

"Stop it! You're killing me!"

Rakon looked at him sharply, at Rusilla. He cursed and fumbled for his bag. He withdrew a metal vial and popped the wax seal with his thumb.

Kill him! Kill him! Kill him!

Rakon leaned across the carriage's interior, roughly took his sister's face in his hand, and dumped the contents of the vial into her mouth, spilling some in the process.

Almost immediately the drumbeat of violence in Nix's head ceased.

Rakon shoved his sister back into her place, glared at Nix, and slid the wood window panel back into place. Nix could hardly breathe.

"You all right?" Egil asked him.

"All right," Nix said.

"Good. Because here we go."

Ahead, a dozen Vwynn loped down the road toward the wagon.

"Hold on!" Baras said, and whipped the reins with one hand while holding his blade in the other. Nix put the episode with Rusilla from his mind and gripped his sword.

The wagon closed on the Vwynn. Ten strides. Five.

Baras pulled the reins slightly to steer the terrified horses into the Vwynn as the groups met. The huge draft animals trampled two of the creatures, who died in a spray of blood and screams. Another leaped high, over the horses, and landed on the roof of the carriage, claws scrabbling for purchase. Egil's hammer and the swords of two other guards bloodied it and sent it careening off the back. The other Vwynn parted around the carriage and leaped at the passengers from the side as they passed.

A Vwynn bounded at Nix, claws outstretched. Nix slashed wildly and his blade opened the creature's shoulder in a spray of blood. It snarled, clawed at him as it fell away to the road. Egil's hammer caught another Vwynn in mid-leap, slammed into its head, and sent it spinning away with a shriek of pain.

The guards on the other side of the wagon chopped

and slashed and screamed. A Vwynn tore one of them off the rail and onto the road. He was swarmed, screaming with pain and fear as claws and teeth ripped flesh.

The guard beside Egil, Derg, lashed out with his blade at a Vwynn that loped beside the wagon, an awkward swing made still more awkward by the fact that his foot slipped as he swung. He lost his balance and the Vwynn coiled and pounced on him. One of the creature's claws sank into the wood of the carriage's top, with which it pulled itself up onto the rail, and the other tore bloody furrows in the man's face. Before Derg could ply his blade, the creature sank its teeth into his shoulder and tried to use its weight to pull him off the carriage.

Egil snatched at Derg's shirt, held him precariously on the hurtling wagon. The Vwynn clambered over Derg and clawed Egil's arm, tried to bite it. The priest endured the attack and held on to Derg, whose one leg was dangling free, hanging in space.

"Nix!"

Nix stabbed at the face of the creature, once, twice, and it lurched back, lost its balance, swayed. Derg shoved at it, but almost dislodged himself in the process. A blow from Egil's hammer to its face finally ended it, sending bits of fangs flying and knocking the creature back onto the road.

"We're clear in front!" Baras said.

Behind them, Vwynn thronged the road. Egil assisted Derg back onto his perch.

"My thanks," Derg said to the priest.

Egil thumped him on the shoulder, eliciting a wince of pain from Derg.

"Two wounded on this side," Nix said.

"We're all right over here," the guard called from the other side.

"My lord?" Baras called over his shoulder into the carriage.

"We're all fine, Baras. Don't stop until we reach the ruins."

"Yes, my lord."

Nix sagged against the carriage, blew out a sigh. "You all right?" he asked Egil.

Egil winced with pain but nodded. "I'm all right."

Derg, however, was not. He did the best he could to stanch the blood flowing from the bite in his shoulder, but he was already pale. Yet the carriage could not risk a stop for fear of another Vwynn attack.

In time they could no longer see the mass of Vwynn behind them. Minnear rose as they rode onward, casting the landscape in sickly, pale green. The ruins thickened, towering, monumental blocks looming out of the darkness, the stone ghosts of a lost world.

It looked as though an entire city had been torn from the ground, jumbled in the air, and cast back to earth in a heap. Tumbles of stone suggested pillars, statuary, monolithic building blocks that dwarfed everything in Dur Follin save the Archbridge and Ool's clock.

"They say Ool had the building secrets of the ancients," Nix said, as they rolled past a bygone age.

"Seeing this," Egil said, grimacing at the pain of one wound or other, "I believe it. What do you say, Derg?"

Derg glanced at him, glassy-eyed, pale, and started to fall back. Jyme and Egil grabbed him simultaneously. Derg's eyes rolled. His head flopped back.

"Stop the carriage, Baras," Nix called. "Now."

"Don't stop," Rakon said.

"Derg needs attention. Stop the damned carriage!"

Baras looked over his shoulder, saw Derg, and pulled the reins. The horses pulled up, sweating, steaming. Egil and Jyme quickly lowered Derg to the road. Baras hopped off the driver's bench and came to his man's side.

"Derg!" Baras said. Everyone gathered around as Baras rolled him over. Rakon looked on from the carriage.

"What is it, man?" Baras asked, tapping Derg's cheeks. "Derg? Derg?"

Derg's eyes rolled and his mouth fell open, moved, but no sound emerged. Flecks of foam rimed his mouth. Nix kneeled beside him, touched Derg's face.

"Is it blood loss?" Baras asked.

"No," Nix said. "He's burning up."

"We cannot stay here," Rakon said from the carriage. "The Vwynn will be coming."

All eyes looked back down the moonlit road. Nix saw no Vwynn.

"Watch the ruins and the road," Baras said to his men. "Stay sharp."

"Check his wounds," Egil said, nodding at Derg. "The bite especial."

Baras hurriedly cut off Derg's tunic and pulled the man's makeshift bandage away from his shoulder wound. Gasps sounded from the men. The ragged, bloody oval of the deep bite wound was surrounded by skin that looked purple and gangrenous.

"The bite's poisoned," Baras said. "Shite! What do we do?"

"Get his mouth open," Nix said, and started rifling through his satchel. He soon found what he sought, a smooth, crimson-colored pebble of enspelled jasper, etched with a rune puissant against poison.

"I said we cannot remain here," Rakon repeated.

"We heard you the first time," Egil snapped.

Nix held the jasper pebble between forefinger and thumb. He'd been given it by a priestess of Orella after he'd performed a service for her church.

"What is that?" Baras asked.

"It should help," Nix said. He spoke a word in the Language of Creation and the jasper glowed with a faint light.

"Is there no end to the contents of that bag?" Jyme asked, and thumped him on the back.

"Oh, there's an end, and it's getting light in there," Nix said.

In truth, he had nothing magical left in it save his the crystal eye. He looked over to Egil, who watched intently. "No comment on gewgaws?"

"Is that the only one you have?" Egil asked.

"Yes," Nix said. "Why?"

Egil ran his hand over Ebenor's eye. "No reason. Go on. Give it to him."

Nix nodded, placed the jasper under Derg's tongue, and pushed his jaw closed over it. The gem flared, the flash lighting Derg's face from the inside out.

"I see movement," one of the guards watching the road behind called out. He crouched and peered off into the darkness.

"Me, too," said another. "There. I think."

"Shite," Baras said. Then to Nix, "Did it work?"

Nix frowned, opened Derg's jaw, looked under his tongue. The jasper was gone, consumed by the magic. "I... think it did."

"You think?" Baras asked.

"Sometimes it's hard to tell..."

"Look at the wound," Egil said, pointing.

At first Nix thought it was a play of the light, but it wasn't. The black and purple skin around the wound faded to pink as they watched.

"And sometimes it's not as hard to tell," Nix said to Baras, and winked.

"Orella be praised," one of the guards said.

"I also accept praises," Nix said, standing.

"Well done," Baras said.

"Agreed," Egil said, gripping Nix by the shoulder. "Now let's get out of here."

Egil slung Derg over his shoulder, mail and all, and they all climbed back onto the carriage. The horses, shaking from being overstrained, nevertheless lowered their ears, threw their heads, and started moving.

Minnear shone fat and gibbous over the landscape. With Kulven now new, the Mages' Moon ruled the sky alone. The mountainous wall of rubble loomed before them, growing taller as they closed the distance, stretching off into the darkness.

The road cut through the wall of stones, the rubble rising high to either side. The walls were thick, more than a hundred paces, and for a time it was as if they walked through a tunnel. No one spoke and the clop of the horses' hooves sounded loud, bouncing off the ancient stone wall. When they emerged from the tunnel of ruins, Nix gasped in awe for the second time that day.

The walls of rubble formed a circle, ringing a circular expanse several acres in diameter. A shimmering sea of dark glass covered the expanse, its smooth finish reflecting the night sky. The vault of night was at their feet.

For a long while no one spoke. Everyone stared at the shimmering, glittering spectacle before them. Jyme broke the spell of silence with a whisper.

"Gods."

"What is this place?" Nix asked.

Rakon threw open the carriage door and stepped onto the rock.

"It's a holy place," Rakon said. "The Vwynn will not come here. That's enough for now. Set camp, Baras. We'll remain here only a short time before continuing to Afirion."

"A word, lord Adjunct," Nix said to Rakon.

Rakon eyed him coolly, nodded. They moved to the side.

"What in the Pits happened back there?" Nix said. "With your sister? With you?"

Rakon's hooded eyes narrowed, the thoughts visibly turning behind them. "Did you… hear her? What did she say?"

"She said to kill you."

Rakon was quiet for a time, then said, "She won't do that again."

"What was that you gave her? Drugs?"

"My sisters are dangerous," Rakon said. "I told you that. You have nothing more to fear. Leave me now. I have work I must see to."

With that, he left Nix. As the guards set up the camp and tended the horses, Rakon walked out onto the glass sea, striding among the stars.

"I think I'd like to do that," Nix said, watching Rakon.

They started a fire, placed Derg near it for warmth, ate a meal of cheese, bread, and dried meat, and washed it down with bitter coffee. Baras toasted the men they'd lost, spoke their names, told Egil and Nix of their lives. Rakon remained on the glass throughout. After they'd eaten and honored the fallen, Nix made up his mind.

"I'm going to go walk on it," Nix said.

"I'll come," Egil said, grunting as he rose.

"Is that… wise?" Baras asked.

"Probably not," Nix said with a smile. "But even so."

He and Egil walked the short distance to the edge of the glass sea, shared a glance, and stepped onto it. Nix's feet tingled and the hairs on his body rose and stood on end.

"It's enspelled," he said.

"I didn't need you to tell me that," Egil said.

They walked gingerly across the glass, treading on stars, noting constellations and planets in reflection. Nix found it surreal.

"Maybe this is what it would be like to travel night's vault," he said.

Egil only grunted.

The glass covered acres. They ranged far on it, though always keeping a good distance between themselves and Rakon. They discovered that other roads like the one they'd traveled cut through the ring of ruins and reached the glass from other directions.

"Like the cardinal points," Egil said. The priest seemed winded.

"Aye. And all leading here. Curious." Nix looked over at his friend. "You all right?"

"I'm all right. Just winded."

"Had enough, then?" Nix asked.

"Aye," Egil said. The priest stumbled and nearly fell as they walked back.

"Mind the smooth surface there," Nix chided with a chuckle.

They returned to the fire, and enjoyed more coffee with Baras, Jyme, and the other guards. The eunuch emerged from the carriage and took station outside its door, arms crossed over his chest.

Rakon remained on the glass, and as the night deepened, the sorcerer's voice carried across the mirror of stars, incanting in the Language of Creation.

Flashes of green light accompanied his spellcasting. The guards seemed untroubled by the sorcery and fell asleep in their tents, while the eunuch stood forebodingly outside the carriage. Egil and Nix sat around the fire while Rakon continued his exploration of the glass sea.

"What do you think he's doing?" Nix asked.

"I don't care," Egil said, worrying at his arm.

"I do," Nix said, and stood. "Let's go see."

Egil considered, sighed, stood, and joined his friend.

They picked their way through the moonlit ruins until they reached one of the highest parts that ringed the glass expanse. Both of them were skilled climbers, and even without gear they reached the peak.

Nix spotted Rakon out on the glass, walking among the reflected moon and stars. The sorcerer incanted a spell, touched a hand to the glass, and thin veins of green light snaked out from his touch and wormed deeply into the translucent surface of the glass before fading out.

"Look like feelers almost," Egil said. He was still breathing heavily.

Rakon rose, moved off twenty paces, and repeated the process. Again jagged lines of sickly green lit up the subsurface of the glass sea.

"He's searching for something," Nix said. "Something under the glass."

"Gods," Egil said. His voice sounded tense.

"I know, it's–"

"Not that," Egil said, putting a hand on Nix's shoulder and turning him around. *"That."*

Behind them, lit eerily in the green light of the Mages' Moon, the ruins-dotted ground outside the ring that bordered the sea of glass crawled with so many Vwynn it looked as if the landscape itself was undulating. They prowled through the ruins, lithe, inhuman forms picking their way through the megaliths, their slit eyes always on the circular border of ruins that encircled the mirror. There were thousands of them, a horde of fangs and teeth and scales.

"Gods," Nix echoed.

"Indeed," Egil said. "Why do they wait, I wonder?"

"Rakon said this was a holy place," Nix said. "Maybe they fear it?"

"They don't seem the religious type."

Nix chuckled. "Neither do you, and yet your head wears the eye of a god."

"A dead god," Egil said.

"Your words, not mine. I'll not blaspheme in this place. That many Vwynn is going to make leaving here a complicated affair."

"Aye. I need to get down, Nix."

"Well enough."

They picked their way back down the mountain of stones, Egil struggling far more than Nix would have expected.

"What's wrong with you?" Nix asked, when they reached the bottom. "Egil?"

He took his friend by the arm and recoiled at the febrile heat he felt.

Egil opened his mouth to speak, but instead sagged to the ground.

"Egil!" Nix said.

The priest's eyes rolled in his head and he sagged. Nix caught him to prevent a hard fall, and lowered the priest's limp weight to the ground.

"Baras!" he called. "Up! Everyone up!"

CHAPTER TWELVE

Nix rolled Egil over onto his back. The priest's eyes were closed, his breathing rapid and shallow. He looked pale. Nix cursed. How had he missed it before? The stumbles, the breathing.

"Are you sick? Wounded? What?"

No answer. He tried to imagine his life without Egil and couldn't, no more than he could imagine it without Mamabird.

Baras, Jyme, and the other guards rushed over, blades drawn.

"What is it?" Baras asked. "Oh, shite."

"What happened?" Jyme asked.

Nix gently tapped his friend's face.

"Egil? Egil?"

Egil's eyelids fluttered open. Glassy eyes fixed on Nix and the priest smiled.

"Bit," the priest said, and tried to lift his left arm. "Like Derg."

"Shite, shite, shite," Nix said, and pushed up the sleeves of Egil's cloak and shirt. His forearm was black, as big around as Nix's calf. The guards gasped.

"Why didn't you say something? Godsdammit, Egil!" The priest must have been bitten by the same Vwynn that bit Derg. "We could've used the jasper on you."

He felt the eyes of Baras and the guards on him but he didn't care. If he'd had to choose between one of them and Egil, it would've been no choice at all.

The big priest raised his right arm and patted Nix on the shoulder, the gesture sloppy, fading. "That peasant needed the coin more than us."

At first Nix did not understand Egil's point, and then he remembered the wagon driver outside of the *Slick Tunnel*, the silver pieces Nix had given him.

Grace, Egil had said. Alms.

"You fakking idiot. You godsdamned idiot. You're not even a real priest!"

Egil smiled, closed his eyes. "Do you think I'll see Gretta and Misa?"

Nix could not bring himself to reply. He sat over his friend, head bowed, mind racing. He had nothing left in his bag of tricks. For once, it'd come up empty. *He'd* come up empty.

"Maybe we should move him to the fire?" Jyme offered.

"The fire won't help, you fakkin' whoreson," Nix spat. But maybe the sorcerer could. "Get Rakon, Baras!"

"What?" Baras asked.

"Rakon!" Nix shouted. "Get over here right now!"

The sorcerer was still out on the glass, but not too far from them.

"Gods, mind your tongue, Nix," Baras whispered.

"Fak that and fak you! Rakon! Get over here! Now!"

"My lord!" Baras shouted. "We need assistance!"

Rakon left off what he'd been doing on the glass and made his way to the gathered men. His face looked drawn, strained. He stared down at Egil.

"He's wounded?" Rakon asked.

"He's poisoned," Nix said. "Same as your man, Derg. I used the enspelled jasper on your man and I don't have another. What can you do?"

Rakon looked taken aback by Nix's directness. "What can I do?"

"Am I unclear? What can you do to help him?"

For a time, Rakon did not answer. Again those turning gears behind his eyes.

"You won't like what I can do."

"Try me."

"There's a price."

"Name it."

"He's nearly gone. For him to live, someone else must die."

"A transference," Nix said. He'd heard of such magic.

"Yes," Rakon said. "A transference. One life for another."

The guards shifted from foot to foot. Jyme cursed softly.

Rakon looked meaningfully back to the campsite, a question in his raised eyebrows.

Nix, too, looked back to the campsite, licked his thin lips.

Rakon put a voice to Nix's thoughts.

"Derg may not live anyway. He's not as strong as the priest. You may have given him the jasper too late. Were he the object of the transference..."

Rakon trailed off, the dark possibility dangling before Nix.

"What are we talking about here?" Baras asked.

Rakon continued. "If you'd have known, if you'd have been asked to choose, you'd have chosen Egil."

"Of course I'd have chosen Egil," Nix said.

But Egil hadn't chosen Egil. That was the rub. The priest had known what he was doing and had made his decision. That's why he'd asked Nix if he had another stone.

Alms. Grace.

Maybe Egil *was* a real priest, after all.

But Nix wasn't. He tried to reconcile what he wanted to do with what he knew he should do.

"Nix..." Baras said, perhaps understanding at last.

"I already told you to shut up, Baras," Nix said. "Just keep your mouth shut. You have nothing to say here."

"These are the choices life forces us to make," Rakon said, though Nix wasn't entirely sure whether he was talking to Nix or to himself. "We do what we must for the ends we desire. It's why I put a spellworm in your guts. It's why you'd kill Derg."

"I won't allow Derg to be murdered for the priest," Baras said.

The other guards nodded, murmured agreement.

"Wait, is that what you're saying, Nix?" Jyme asked.

"You'd do exactly as I command," Rakon said to Baras.

"My lord!" Baras said, appalled.

"I haven't said anything," Nix said. "But you couldn't stop me if I wanted to do it. All of you couldn't stop me."

"It's wrong, Nix," Baras said.

Nix looked up and glared at him. "I know it's wrong! But Egil dying is wrong! I won't have it, Baras! I need another option–"

An idea struck him, a divine bolt of inspiration perhaps. He jumped to his feet and whirled on Rakon.

"You said someone has to die? What about one of those things, one of the Vwynn? You said they were the descendants of the people who lived here once. That means they'll work for the transference, yeah?"

Rakon raised his eyebrows, nodded after a long pause. "Yes. But then–"

"I'll get one," Nix said.

"Get one?" Baras asked. "What do you mean?"

"Fakking follow along, Baras," Nix snapped. "There are thousands of them just beyond these ruins."

"Thousands?" Jyme asked.

"No," Rakon said.

"No?" Nix rose and went nose to nose with the sorcerer. The spellworm roiled his guts. Not even Baras tried to move him away. "I'm going to get one. I'll bring it back and you'll cast your transference."

"You're going to go get one of those things?" Jyme asked, incredulous.

"I forbid it," Rakon said. "You can enter Abn Thuset's tomb alone, retrieve the horn alone. I don't need the priest."

"*I* need him," Nix said.

"Stop him, Baras," Rakon ordered.

Baras made no move toward Nix. "He seems determined, my lord."

"I'll kill him if I have to," Nix said to Rakon. He looked at Baras. "I'll kill you, Baras. No offense."

Jyme put a hand on Baras's shoulder, restraining him. "Not your fight."

"I'm telling you that you cannot leave," Rakon said.

"And I'm telling you to fak yourself. I'm leaving."

With that, Nix turned and walked toward the road. He'd take it back through the mountain of ruins, capture one of the Vwynn from the thousands lurking outside, and bring it back.

"Stop," Rakon said.

Nix's legs felt leaden almost immediately. He lifted one, then another. He tasted bile, felt nausea rising. He fought it, sought the hidey-hole he'd made for himself.

I'm Nix Fall of Dur Follin.

He thought of his days prowling the Heap, and took a step.

I'm Nix Fall of Dur Follin's Warrens.

He thought of Mamabird and took another.

He felt as if he was dragging boulders, but he kept walking. He reached the road. Vomit rushed up his throat and he puked in a spray before him.

"I... will... keep... going."

"My lord," Baras said.

"Shut up, Baras," Rakon snapped. "It'll stop you, Nix."

"It... might... kill... me," Nix said.

He thought of the old man he'd stabbed for bread and took another step. "But... it... damned... well... won't... stop... me!"

"I cannot have it, Nix. My sisters."

"My *brother,*" Nix spat in answer. "Now loosen the compulsion or kill me, sorcerer. If Egil dies, I will not enter the tomb. I promise you that. I'll die first. And then so will your sisters. And even though they want you dead, I know you don't want them dead."

He glared at Rakon, wobbly on his numb legs, his hands slack and heavy at his sides.

The sorcerer stared at him, eyes narrowed. The guards looked on wide-eyed, gazes moving from Rakon to Nix, Nix to Rakon.

"Loosen it!" Nix demanded. "Or everything you've done will go for nothing."

Rakon's thin lips tightened, the gears turning between his snake eyes.

"Let him go," Jyme said. "Gods. He's owed the chance."

Rakon glared at Jyme, then at Nix.

"My lord," Baras said, "if any of us can get one of those things and bring it back, it's him."

Rakon stared at Baras, then at Nix. "Go, then," he said, and the sorcerer's willingness to release him loosened the pressure holding Nix in place. His body recovered immediately from the nausea and pain.

"You're still bound to me, Nix," Rakon said. "This is a just a temporary loosening of the compulsion. You bring one back – alive – and I'll kill it to save your priest."

Nix nodded at Baras and Jyme, turned and started to head off.

"Wait!" Baras called. "I'll help you. Least I can do for… everything."

Nix shook his head. "You'd be in my way, Baras. Nothing personal."

With that, Nix put the hilt of his falchion in one hand and the hilt of his punch dagger in the other and headed off. The ruined tumble of stones bordered the road closely to either side, almost a tunnel cutting through the ruins that circumscribed the sea of glass. He hugged the deeper darkness to one side of the road.

Ahead, the ring of ruins ended, opened onto the wider expanse of stones and rubble that littered the plains beyond. He felt exposed the moment he crept out of the tunnel and into the moonlit ruins. Crouched low, he darted to his right and sheltered behind a megalith. There, he listened.

He heard movement out in the darkness, first from one direction, then from another: the scrabble of a claw over stone, the low growl of a Vwynn, the crunch of weight on the rocks. In his mind's eye, he saw the thousands of Vwynn he and Egil had seen from their perch atop the ruins. Thinking of their numbers accelerated his heart, but he pushed the fear down. He needed only one.

The wind blew from east to west, a steady breeze that whined over the rubble. He put his face into it and prowled the darkness, moving in silence, hugging the jagged hummocks of stone, all eyes and ears. He didn't have long to wait before he encountered the Vwynn.

Movement ahead froze him: a low growl, a curious chuffing. He licked his lips and moved forward in a crouch, hands tight and aching around his blade hilts. Lurking in the shadows of a towering pyramidal stone, he crept toward the sound until he saw the source – two Vwynn, idling at the base of a low hillock of jumbled stones.

He watched the scaled, inhuman demons for a time, fascinated and disgusted. The slits of their nostrils pulsed wetly with each breath and they seemed to communicate in a guttural, clicking tongue. They kept their eyes on the ring of ruins, beyond which was the caravan and the sea of glass.

He circled wide around. He spotted more Vwynn within easy earshot, dozens of them, some in groups of five and six, others perched singly and in pairs atop megaliths, their silhouettes dark and sharp in Minnear's light. All of them eyed the ruins, a demonic congregation of the faithful.

He would have to quick. They'd be upon him fast if they heard anything.

He stalked back to the original pair he'd spotted,

went around to the opposite side of the hillock and belly-crawled up it. When he reached the top and glanced down, he saw that they remained where they'd been. He waited for the wind to put a dark cloud in front of Minnear. When it did and the darkness deepened, he rose, tensed, and leaped down.

He swung his falchion two-handed as he descended, neatly splitting the skull of one of the Vwynn. Blood and brains spattered his hands and it died in silence. The second Vwynn whirled on him, lips pulled back from its teeth in an angry snarl.

Before it could respond further, Nix slashed its knee. His blade's edge knifed through flesh, bit bone, and the Vwynn fell, shrieking. It lashed out with a claw as it went down, clipping Nix's cheek. Blood, warm and sticky, flowed down his face.

He jumped atop the writhing, screaming creature, put a knee on its bony chest, and slammed the hilt of his punch dagger into its face. The blow would have felled an ox but it seemed only to make the Vwynn angrier. Claws tore through his cloak, his leather jack, and bit into flesh.

Spit sprayed from the Vwynn's mouth, the rope of its tongue lashed about, and its fangs dripped poisonous ichor. Nix struck it again, again, again until it finally moaned and went still. He quickly checked his hand and arms to ensure he hadn't caught a poisonous bite. He was clean.

Growls and snarls out in the darkness, the rapid tread of approaching Vwynn.

"Shite."

Adrenaline fueled him. He shoved his falchion in its scabbard, grabbed the Vwynn, slung it over his shoulder in a side-carry, and pelted back through the ruins.

It occurred to him only then that he had no guarantee the ring of ruins would provide him safety. The Vwynn seemed unwilling to breach the ring, but would they respect its border when they saw Nix, realized that he was carrying one of their own? What if seeing him triggered such rage in the creatures that they all breached the ring and pursued him back to camp?

Too late to worry about it. He ran as fast as he could.

A Vwynn bounded atop a megalith to his right, crouched on its haunches for a moment, snarled, and bounded down. Nix pulled one of his throwing daggers from a belt sheath and threw it underhand, on the run. It caught the Vwynn in the leg as the creature came toward him. The Vwynn screamed, lost its footing, and flipped head over heels down the pile of stone. Nix ran past it without slowing, its shrieks of pain chasing him through the ruins. He could hear more of the creatures behind him, to the right and left, the scrape of their claws over stone, their wet chuffing.

"Shite, shite, shite," he muttered.

His legs burned; his lungs ached.

He reached the road, saw the border ring of ruins just ahead. It was twenty paces away, ten.

He stumbled with fatigue. He managed to keep his balance, but the error had cost him. The Vwynn behind him gained, closed on him, their snarls hot in his ear. He prepared to turn, fight, and die.

Crossbow bolts sizzled out of the dark, whistling past his ear. They struck Vwynn flesh with heavy thunks, summoning screams and angry shrieks.

"Run, you damned slubber!" Jyme called.

The hiresword stood on the road, in the pseudo-tunnel, just inside the tall ring of ruins. Baras and two of the other guards stood beside Jyme, all of them now reloading crossbows.

"Keep running!" Baras said, laying a bolt in his weapon.

Another volley from Baras, Jyme, and the guards hissed past. More thunks, more screams.

Nix staggered into their midst. Jyme and Baras caught him up and started retreating down the road under cover of the other guards.

"They're not coming," shouted one of the guards.

The Vwynn outside hissed and snarled in frustration but did not pursue. Instead, they slunk back into the ruins, into the night. Nix set the unconscious Vwynn down for a moment so he could catch his breath.

"My thanks," Nix said to them, gasping for breath.

"I give what I get," Baras said, and thumped him on the back.

"Help me get this thing back to camp," Nix said, nodding at the Vwynn.

Together, they carried the bleeding body of the Vwynn. The guards who'd stayed behind rushed toward them as they came out of the tunnel. Everyone crowded around the naked, scaled figure of the Vwynn.

"How's Egil?" Nix asked one of the guards.

"Alive still," the man answered.

The creature stirred, rolled onto its side. Claws slipped out of the sheath of its fingers and it growled, showing fangs. It remained unconscious, but wouldn't stay that way.

"We need to bind it," Nix said.

"Get rope," Baras said to a young guardsman.

The guardsmen hurried to the wagon and returned with rope for Baras. Nix snatched it from him.

"I know how to knot," Baras said.

"I slipped yours back in Dur Follin, Baras. I'll handle this."

Nix bound the creature at wrist and ankle with a triple hook slip. He tested them, found them satisfactory.

"Help me, Jyme," he said, and the two of them dragged the creature close to the fire, beside Egil. The priest lay flat on his back, pale under his beard, his breathing shallow, his forearm swollen and discolored.

The creature's slit eyes opened, reflected the firelight. Muscles, veins, and sinew surfaced in its hide as it strained against its bonds. The guardsmen backed off a step, expressions nervous, weapons at the ready. The Vwynn's lips peeled back from its teeth and it hissed.

"Rakon," Nix called to the carriage. "We're ready."

The eunuch emerged from the carriage and assisted Rakon out. The sorcerer bore a black bag in his hands, his own satchel of needful things. He said something to the inscrutable eunuch and the huge man took station outside the carriage. Rakon eyed the Vwynn as he approached, his expression unreadable.

"Hold it down so it doesn't move," he ordered. He kneeled and started rifling through his bag.

"Get its legs," Nix said to Jyme, while Nix took position at the creature's head. He held it flat by its bony shoulders, its scaled flesh cool and dry in his hands. The Vwynn twisted its neck to bite at him, hissing and spitting, but could not reach.

"Mind the teeth," Jyme said.

The Vwynn's legs flailed wildly, catching Rakon and causing him to drop a small container he'd been holding. Rakon cursed irritably.

"Just get its legs, Jyme!" Nix said.

The hiresword wrapped up the Vwynn's legs. The creature continued to struggle, squirming, hissing, and snapping its teeth.

"Get a blade to its throat, Baras," Nix said, struggling to hold down the creature. "See if it understands that."

"Aye," Baras said, and put a blade at the Vwynn's throat. The creature did not still at first so Baras pricked it with the blade.

The Vwynn cried out in pain as a line of black blood flowed. After that, the Vwynn went still. The creature's slitted eyes darted wildly here and there, and it respired wetly from the lines of its nostrils.

"Do it, Rakon," Nix said. "Hurry."

Rakon removed two metal bloodletting tubes and a ceramic mortar and pestle from his bag. He jabbed one of the tubes into Egil's arm – the priest did not stir – and collected the blood in the mortar. Rakon then kneeled beside the Vwynn and jabbed the bleeder tube through its scales and into its arm. The Vwynn squealed and squirmed while Rakon collected its black blood.

Rakon moved closer to the fire. Other than Baras and Jyme, who assisted Nix with the Vwynn, the other guards backed off. Nix understood. No man who made his way with sharpened steel felt comfortable around those who made their way with spells.

"How long will this take?" Jyme asked over his shoulder, still holding the Vwynn's legs.

Rakon did not answer. He placed the mortar in the edge of the embers to warm it, kneeled beside the fire, and stirred the mix of blood with a hollow glass rod.

"My bag," he called over his shoulder.

After a pause, one of the guards brought the black bag to him and withdrew.

Rakon removed tubes of powder and small bottles of liquid from the bag, adding a pinch of this, a dash of that.

The mixture in the mortar crackled. Rakon stirred it anew with the rod, intoning a chant under his breath. Soon the mixture emitted a puff of smoke. Rakon nodded, picked up the mortar, and stood.

The Vwynn's eyes fixed on the sorcerer; its chest rose and fell rapidly. A forked tongue licked the ridges of its lips nervously. Small clicking noises sounded from somewhere deep in its throat. Perhaps it had a sense of what was transpiring.

Rakon moved to Egil's side and dipped his fingers into the mortar. They came away covered in a glob of a thick, clear substance.

He rolled it between his palms like clay, thinning it more and more, letting the thin line his movement created spool to the ground at his feet.

"What's he doing?" Jyme asked.

"Hsst," Nix said.

Rakon incanted as he spun and the thin line glistened, twitched. When he'd spun a length of it out, he took the spun end, held it to Egil's nostril, and whispered words of power. The line snaked into Egil's nose and kept going, more and more of it disappearing into the priest's body. Rakon held the other end, still incanting.

The priest's body arched and thin lines appeared on his flesh, like veins but not veins, welts caused by the intrusion of the magical line as it wormed through his body. The process went on for a long thirty-count, and during that time the exposed line that Rakon still held changed from clear to yellow, then from yellow to the deep blue-black of a bruise.

"Is it drawing out the poison?" Jyme whispered.

"I think so," Nix said.

Still incanting softly, Rakon turned from Egil and toward the Vwynn. He continued to work the blob of magical material in his hands until he'd spun it all out, and held the opposite side of the discolored line in his hand.

The creature struggled anew, the blade at its throat no deterrent. Nix grunted with the effort of holding it flat, and Jyme laid his weight on the creature's legs to maintain his hold. Baras moved his blade aside and put a hand on the frantic creature's chest. The Vwynn whined, the sound high-pitched and frighteningly human. Rakon turned to the creature, holding the other end of the line between forefinger and thumb. He kneeled.

"Wait," Nix said.

Rakon halted but did not stop his incantation. He loomed over the Vwynn, an executioner with axe held high.

"Wait?" Jyme said. "Wait what? Do it, man." Then to Rakon, "Do it, my lord."

"No, wait," Nix said. "Wait, godsdammit."

"It's just an animal," Jyme said. "Look at it. It'd kill us if it could."

Nix knew it wasn't just an animal. The transference wouldn't work on an animal. The Vwynn was bestial, savage, but it was a thinking, feeling creature akin to a man. He was murdering it to save Egil.

Nix had killed a helpless creature only once before. Then, he'd been a boy fighting for bread, and had stabbed the granther in the kidney when the old man had been too exhausted to fight back. He regretted it still, and he always would.

And when he helped kill the Vwynn, he'd regret that, too. But he'd do it anyway. For Egil. He stared down at his friend's wan countenance and spoke loud enough for everyone to hear.

"No one ever speaks of this to Egil or I cut out your fakking throat. Rakon's sorcery healed him and that's the whole of the story. You don't know how it worked. It just did. Understood?"

"The priest isn't gonna care about this animal," Jyme said.

"You don't know him," Nix said. "And this is not an animal."

"What?" Jyme asked. "It's not?"

Nix ignored Jyme. "Baras, pry open its mouth with a blade."

Baras stuck his dagger in the creature's mouth, forcing it open, and Nix was uncomfortably reminded of Baras putting his blade against Nix's face to force him to accept the spellworm. The Vwynn flailed but it was too exhausted to resist much.

"Do it," Nix said to Rakon.

The Vwynn made a hopeless, desperate sound as Rakon fed the magical filament into its mouth and the line snaked down its throat. Almost immediately the Vwynn's body arched and it bared its teeth in pain.

The line pulsed, bulbs of black moving along its length, man and Vwynn connected by a cord of magic. Whatever the spell had taken out of Egil was now being pushed into the Vwynn. Rakon stood, holding the filament that bound man and Vwynn. He waited,

waited, and then gave the line a hard jerk. It came free of both bodies in a spray of mucus, squirmed for a moment, then dissipated into nothingness.

The Vwynn seized, arched, exhaled loudly, and went limp.

Egil groaned, rolled over to face the fire, and started to snore.

Baras, Jyme, and Nix let go of the Vwynn's cooling body.

"How could its own poison kill it?" Jyme asked.

"It's not the poison that was transferred," Rakon said, gathering his things. "The poison had already done its work. The spell transferred death's grip on the spirit."

"Gods," Jyme said, standing and backing away from the Vwynn.

Baras cleared his throat, nodded at the Vwynn's body. "Let's get that carcass out of here."

"I'll do it," Nix said, looking at Egil, at the Vwynn. "It's mine to do."

Nix carried the Vwynn's body away from the camp and laid it gently, respectfully among the rocks. He covered it with a few stones, but didn't have the energy to do much more. He walked away without looking back.

Once he returned to the camp, he planted himself around the fire, keeping watch over Egil. Baras and Jyme joined him. None of them spoke. They simply sat, content with the silent presence of the others. Nix feared nightmares should he slumber – perhaps of the sisters' making, or perhaps born of his own deeds – but the trials of the day soon overwhelmed him. He lost the fight and fell into slumber.

CHAPTER THIRTEEN

Nix awoke late, well after dawn. Everyone else remained asleep. He coughed, spit, and heated the kettle of coffee in the fire's embers.

He spotted Rakon near the edge of the sea of glass. The sorcerer had somehow removed a few shards of glass from the edge of the sea and they lay stacked on the ground beside him. Nix walked over and nodded at the shards.

"How'd you manage that?"

Rakon only grunted for answer.

"What were you looking for out on the glass last night?"

Rakon looked at him over his shoulder. "Why do you think I was looking for something?"

Now it was Nix's turn to grunt.

Rakon cleared his throat. "I was looking for something that would help us get through the rest of our journey safely."

"And? Did you find it?"

Rakon gathered up the glass shards. "We'll soon

see. Get me my bag, Nix."

Nix hocked, spit, and chuckled. "I'm not your fakkin' eunuch. Get it yourself. Egil almost died because of you. Him and me are here only because of your compulsion. You and your sisters could all die tomorrow and I'd mourn you not at all. Don't ever forget how it is with us."

Rakon stared at him, a faint smile on his lips. "I don't forget anything."

"Good."

Nix turned to walk away and found himself staring into the enormous chest of the eunuch. The man had walked up behind him as silently as a ghost.

"Speaking of my eunuch," Rakon said.

Nix stared into the face of the bald mound of flesh and sweat. "You're in my way, oaf."

The eunuch just smiled his empty smile and stood his ground. He stank like something two days dead.

"You hear me?"

"Let him pass," Rakon said. "And fetch me my bag from the carriage."

The eunuch stalked off, not so silent this time, and Nix walked back to the fire and filled his coffee cup. Egil soon awoke, sat up, and rubbed the back of his neck.

"What happened?" the priest asked, and looked at his forearm, the bite already healed to a healthy pink. "The bite?"

Nix glanced off in the direction of the ruins, to where he'd placed the sacrificed Vwynn's body. "The sorcerer healed you."

"The sorcerer? How?"

"Sorcery," Nix said. "How else? Coffee?"

"Yeah," Egil said. He looked to Rakon. "I dislike owing that one a favor."

"We owe him nothing. Not a damned thing." Nix handed Egil a cup of coffee. "And listen, no killing yourself without my permission henceforth, yeah?"

"I wasn't killing myself," Egil said, and winced at the bitter taste of the coffee. "But you only had one stone. I knew I could hold off poison longer than Derg. And if I did die, well, I've had many good moments."

"I'm interested in having a few more. Well enough?"

Egil inclined his head. "Well enough."

While the rest ate and broke camp, Rakon retreated off by himself and engaged in some ritual involving the shards he'd taken from the sea of glass. Nix didn't bother watching him. Of late, he'd had quite enough of sorcery.

"Good to see you up," Egil said to Derg, as the young guard helped break camp.

"And you," Derg said with a grin.

When Rakon completed his ritual and returned to the campsite, he held a leather bag. Powder dusted his hands.

"We must move on. Minnear will be full in two days. We have to reach the tomb of Abn Thuset before that."

"Pardon, my lord," Jyme said, "but you didn't see how many of those things are out there. We saw them last night. There are thousands of them."

"They won't trouble us," Rakon said.

"And how's that?" asked Egil.

"The Vwynn fear this place. They smell the magic."

"Which is why they haven't attacked us," Nix said, nodding. "So?"

"So this," Rakon said, holding up the leather bag he held. "This is dust made from the glass of this place. To the Vwynn, it will have the same magical stink as this location."

"You're going to cover us in dust?" Baras asked.

"I trust my armor more than magical dust," said Jyme.

"You'll have to trust both," Rakon said. "We leave within the hour."

"And if it rains?" Egil asked, eyeing the slate that roofed the sky.

"Let's hope it doesn't," Rakon answered. "Maybe you could pray about it, priest."

Egil ignored Rakon's insulting tone. "I think I will."

"Divide up the supplies amongst the men, Baras," Rakon said. "We leave the carriage here. We'll be leaving the road to make straight for Afirion."

"Yes, my lord," Baras said.

After they'd loaded up, Rakon dusted all of them in the magical powder, even the horses. The dust felt slick on the skin, like talc, and it proved resistant to removal. Nix supposed that was a good thing.

They set off, pale ghosts trekking through a dead land. Rakon rode a horse with Rusilla. The eunuch rode with Merelda. The rest of them walked.

They emerged from the ring of ruins with blades and crossbows ready, but the Vwynn did not attack. Nix saw movement in the shadows of the ruins, reptilian eyes glaring out at them from the dark crannies and coves.

"Night will tell the tale," Jyme said nervously.

Throughout the day the Vwynn trailed them, circled at a distance, dozens of them, maybe hundreds, always hugging the shadows. Nix felt the creatures' eyes on him, an itch between his shoulder blades.

The Vwynn called to each other from time to time: growls, howls, clicking, grunts. Nix feared they were arranging an ambush, but the Vwynn did nothing but follow and watch as the group moved through the ruined land, left the road behind, and struck out due east across the forlorn terrain of the Wastes.

At nightfall, Rakon dusted everyone once more. They passed the night without an attack, troubled only by the guttural sounds that carried to them from time to time out of the darkness. Minnear rose, huge in the sky, nearly full, and in that baleful moonlight the Vwynn three times prowled sidelong up to the edge of the camp, their thin forms all scales, muscle, sinew and claws. But they ventured no closer and seemed more puzzled than aggressive.

One by one the men fell asleep. When Nix fell off, dreams came.

He was not standing in the long hallway lined with doors. Instead, he was in a small bedroom behind one of the doors. The room smelled of unwashed bodies and fear. He was sweating, his heart racing. He lay flat on his back in the bed, his hands manacled to the bedpost.

A sense of dread settled on him, sank into his bones. He was nude, terrified, vulnerable. Something awful was about to happen, something unspeakable.

He heard a scuffling from the hall outside the door, the thump of a heavy tread on the floorboards. A shadow darkened the slit of light leaking between the door and the floor.

He screamed, his voice high-pitched, feminine, an echo of the screams he'd heard in the earlier dreams. He struggled against the chains, pulled against them until they cut into his wrists and stained the sheets with his blood.

The handle on the door turned.

He couldn't breathe! He couldn't breathe!

The door opened and a huge form filled the doorway, blotting out the light.

He closed his eyes, screamed and screamed.

He awoke to Egil shaking him. Dawn lightened the sky. Baras, Jyme, Derg, and the other guardsmen were already nearly done breaking camp.

"Nix," the priest said, still shaking him.

"I'm awake," Nix said.

His head felt as if it were filled with cloth. His eyes ached. He'd been crying in his sleep, maybe.

"Gods, you were out," Egil said. "And you look like shite."

"Feel it." He rubbed his head. His eyes went to the

horses, where Rakon and the eunuch were seating Rusilla and Merelda. Egil's bucket head followed his gaze.

"We'll be clear of this soon," the priest said, and helped Nix sit up.

"Maybe." Nix touched his nose and his finger came away with a smear of blood.

Soon they were underway. Throughout the gray day, the ghost of his nightmare haunted him. He felt anxious, frightened, and angry by turns.

"You all right?" Egil asked him, as they trudged along the enspelled road.

"As well as can be," Nix answered. He stared at Rusilla as they walked.

Rakon shared a horse with her, holding her upright as they rode. Her head bounced around and Nix took care not to meet her eyes. Merelda shared a mount with the eunuch, four vacant eyes between the two of them.

Even afoot they made good progress. The terrain smoothed as they traveled eastward, the world healing as they went. Around sunset they cut through a patch of scrub-dusted, scree-covered hills. From atop the low summits, Nix could see Afirion's sands stretched out before them, a sea of beige dunes that stretched as far as he could see. To the north, the failing light of the setting sun glittered feebly off the dark of the Bleak Sea. He could not see the Gogon Ocean to the south but he knew it was there. The guards audibly exhaled, pleased to be leaving the Wastes behind them.

"The Milai Peninsula," Nix said, picturing in his mind the narrow slice of uninhabited land that connected the Demon Wastes in the west to the Afirion Desert in the east. He and Egil had seen it many times, always from the south, while riding the waves of the Gogon Ocean.

"I'll confess to doubting we'd make it," Egil said to him.

"Hate for this to be one of the last things we see," Nix said, wiping sweat from his brow. "Still have the tomb ahead of us. Of course, I don't plan on dying in it. You?"

"I do not."

They descended the hills and broke for a meal while Rakon and Baras consulted a yellowed map in the failing light. Rakon spoke animatedly, pointing northwest, toward a series of cliffs that overlooked the curving shoreline of the Bleak Sea. Sea birds wheeled in the air near the shore. Baras followed his lord's gesture, nodded.

As Baras returned to the rest of the group, Rakon studied the sky, his brow creased in tense worry.

"The tomb of Abn Thuset is in those cliffs," Baras said, pointing.

"Really?" Egil said sarcastically.

"Let us see the map," Nix said.

"Lord Norristru said–"

Nix and Egil walked through Baras toward Rakon. "I'd see that map, sorcerer."

"I'm sorry, my lord," Baras said, trailing them. "They're–"

"It's all right, Baras." Rakon gently unrolled the map and held it for Nix to see. "See for yourself."

Nix and Egil studied the yellowed parchment until their eyes glazed over. The map was ancient, faded almost beyond legibility. In typical Afirion fashion, the image of the terrain had been superimposed over a treatise written in tiny script. Nix recognized the script as Afirion pictoglyphs and some numerals, but he could read only snatches. He noted a repeated pictoglyph for "wizard-king," though the glyph looked somewhat different to him than others he'd seen previously. He focused on the terrain, compared it to what he saw around him and what he knew from experience.

He made out the ocean coastline to the south, but the shore of the body of water that should have been the Bleak Sea was too far north and much too small. There were symbols on the map he took for cities, two of which would have been in the Demon Wastes, one of them about where the sea of glass was located.

"This isn't accurate," Nix said. "Look here. The Bleak Sea is too small."

"It was much smaller then," Rakon said. "Before it... changed."

"Changed?" Egil said. "An entire sea? How old is this map?"

"Quite old," Rakon said, rolling it up carefully.

"How can you be sure the tomb's here, then?" Egil asked. "There's no scale on that map. We could be leagues away. The tomb could be underwater, if it's even the right tomb. I don't intend to abide this fakkin' spellworm forever, sorcerer."

"He does not need to explain himself to you," Baras said, and put his hand on Egil to steer him off. Egil shoved him away.

"Yes, he does," the priest said.

The eunuch rumbled from atop his mount.

Rakon stared into Egil's face. "I've cross-referenced this map with others in my possession, both current and ancient. Those, combined with the text on this map, describe the location of the tomb quite precisely."

"I'd like to see those other maps," Nix said.

"They were too delicate for such rough travel," Rakon said. "But be at ease. The tomb is in those cliffs. We press on a few hours more tonight, resting when we reach the shore of the Bleak Sea. Then you'll recover the horn for me and I'll release you."

"And you'll save your sisters," Nix said.

"Yes," Rakon agreed, licking his thin lips. "I'll save my sisters."

By the time they reached the shore of the Bleak Sea, Minnear had risen over the horizon, full but for the slimmest crescent. Tomorrow it would sit full in the night sky, reigning over the night, since Kulven was new and dark.

They camped in the lee of a scree-covered rise two or three bowshots from the beach. Rakon stared at the moon's cratered face as the guardsmen set up camp.

The air smelled of the sea and the wind carried the rush of the waves to their ears. That night the men sat around the fire mostly in silence. Nix and Egil, too, held their tongues, each alone with his thoughts about the tomb, what they expected to find there.

Nix drank sour beer until his vision blurred.

"You'll need to be clearheaded tomorrow," Egil cautioned him.

"That's why I'm doing it," Nix said.

Only after collecting a fine drunk did he try to fall asleep. Thankfully, the alcohol stupor held at bay any dreams of breathing doors and manacles and impending doom. He woke in the late morning with a hangover, but nevertheless felt better than he had in days. Egil was not in the camp.

"Egil?" he asked Jyme, who was sipping coffee from his tin cup.

Jyme pointed northwest, toward the steep cliffs that walled part of the Bleak Sea in its basin. Nix squinted, his head aching from too much beer. He thought he saw three small figures moving around at the top of the cliff.

"Baras and Rakon are with him," Jyme said.

Nix nodded and geared up. While he did so, he looked over to the tent in which Rusilla and Merelda lay. The eunuch stood before the flap.

"No more plaguing my dreams after tonight, witches," he said softly. "We get this horn and bid you farewell forever."

"You say something?" Jyme asked, his mouth full of bread.

Nix ignored him and jogged up the rise for the cliffs. Sea birds cawed behind him, wheeling in the air near the beach below. Working up a sweat helped him relieve the hangover. He found Rakon consulting the map, Baras standing beside him, and Egil at the cliff's edge, looking out over the sea. Nix stepped up beside his friend. From the high vantage granted by the cliff, Nix could see blue-black water for leagues.

"It should be here," Rakon called to them, his voice irritable and nervous. "It must be here."

"Nothing looks like an entrance to a tomb, though," Baras said.

"The sorcerer seems convinced the tomb is hereabouts," he said to Egil. "Perhaps they imagine there'll be a sign announcing its presence."

Egil smiled. "There is," he said, and nodded down at the surf.

Rocks jutted from the shallow water, all of them ruffed by foam. Sea birds perched on them. Bird shite and the ages stained them.

"The rocks?"

Egil nodded. "The rocks. Watch."

Nix soon saw it. The surf rolled, surging forward to smash the cliffs, then pulling back.

"There," Egil said, pointing as the surf receded.

Nix saw it. A carved stone face staring up at him. The water quickly covered it, only to reveal it again as the surf ebbed. Time and water had eroded the details, but Nix could make out sunken eyes, the nub of a nose, the outline of a mouth formed into an inscrutable smile, and, most importantly of all, the stylized serpent headdress of an Afirion wizard-king.

"Well, well," Nix said. He turned a circle, studied the terrain. He thought about Rakon's map, the fact that the Bleak Sea had once been much smaller. "Has to be the cliff face. This was probably a valley once. What say you?"

"I was thinking the same."

Nix nodded toward Rakon and Baras. "You show them yet?"

Egil shook his head and put his palm on his stomach, as if the spellworm had squirmed. "I haven't. Wanted to get your thoughts first."

"And you wanted Rakon to suffer."

"There was that," Egil said. He put his palm on his stomach. "Though withholding it seems to agitate the damned spellworm."

"Let's get on with it," Nix said. "The sooner we get this horn, the sooner we're free of the compulsion. I want some space between us and this sorcerer and his sisters."

"We could always kill him instead," Egil said, and groaned as the spellworm did its work.

"You really need to tame your thoughts," Nix said with a grin. He turned to Rakon and Baras. "Over here!"

"Did you find something?" Rakon called, his voice eager, hopeful. "What did you find? Speak, man."

Nix let him dangle until they reached him. When the surf receded, he showed them the Afirion face staring up at the sky. Rakon's intake of breath was sharp enough to cut meat.

"It's here," he said.

"In the cliff face, probably," Nix said. "We're going to need rope. We'll hitch it to the horses."

Baras sidled up to the edge of the cliff, leaned over to try to see the cliff face.

"Mind yourself," Egil warned. "You go over the edge, we'll be looking for your body in the surf. That's rough water."

Baras nodded, backed off.

Rakon licked his lips, stared down at the face in the water, appearing, disappearing. His hands fidgeted.

"Go get as much rope as we have, Baras. And bring the horses."

"And whatever torches we have," Nix said. "Now, tell us what this horn looks like."

CHAPTER FOURTEEN

It was late afternoon by the time Nix and Egil had gathered up such supplies as they expected to need, checked and re-checked their own gear and weapons, and taken a hearty meal. Egil prayed. Nix got his mind right.

Rakon paced and fumed throughout.

"We never rush," Nix explained.

"Body, soul, mind, and gear need to be prepared," Egil said.

"Prepare faster," Rakon said. "Minnear rises full tonight."

When they were ready, all but the eunuch and the sisters ascended to the top of the rise. Nix tied a series of step knots in the ropes and harnessed them to the pack horses. Egil took them in hand and pulled. The harnesses held and the horses seemed untroubled.

"Well tied," the priest said, as he tossed the lines over the side of the cliff.

"Of course they are," Nix said. "I tied them, didn't I?"

"You must return with the horn quickly," Rakon said.

"We don't even know for certain that this is the right tomb," Nix said.

"And neither do we know that it holds the horn," Egil added.

"It is and it does," Rakon said. "It must. My guards will accompany you. All but Jyme and Baras."

Nix shook his head. "They'll be in the way." He looked to the guards. "No offense."

They shrugged. None of them looked eager to descend the cliff face on a rope.

"They go with you," Rakon insisted.

"The spellworm already ensures our return," Nix said. "We don't need guards hounding us."

"They go with you, Nix Fall," Rakon said again.

Nix's anger made him think of striking Rakon, which made the spellworm squirm, which made him groan with nausea. Rakon smirked, no doubt surmising the truth.

"Fine," Nix said. He faced the guards, and indicated one of the rope lines. "You and your men use that line and only that line. I don't want one of you slubbers falling on my head."

Derg smirked. "You take care of your work, and we'll take of ours."

"Just like you did when that Vwynn tore open your shoulder and filled you with poison, yeah? You're only standing here because of me."

Derg colored, looked away.

"That line," Nix said, pointing at the rope. "And you'll want to lose your mail, too, unless you fancy heaving another four stone of weight up that rope when we come out. Or maybe you don't intend to come out? You think they'll come out, Egil?"

"Doubtful," said the priest.

Mutters, sheepish glances.

"I'm jesting," Egil said. "Find your balls, men."

Nix continued, "When we get into the caves, you do exactly what we say. Nothing more and nothing less. Your lives will depend on that. Well enough?"

The guards shifted on their feet, hesitated. Derg looked to Baras, but Nix spoke before Baras could offer any words.

"Baras isn't in command once we enter the cave. So I say again: well enough?"

"Yes, well enough," the guards said, and started to remove their mail shirts.

"Fakking slubbers," Nix muttered, and set to evaluating his gear, weapons, and gewgaws a final time. All was in order. Egil checked his hammers, his crowbar, then offered a prayer to the god who existed only on his pate.

For their part, the guards made the symbol of Orella and muttered prayers to Borkan, God of Warriors. Egil and Nix divided the torches between the two of them.

"Ready?" Nix asked.

Egil nodded; the guards nodded.

"Then over we go," Nix said. "Keep those horses still, Baras."

Nix and Egil went deftly over the side, Egil first, Nix following. The wind assaulted them the moment they hung exposed. Below, the surf roared over the rocks.

"Mind the breeze," Nix called to the guards. "And don't look down."

Egil and Nix braced their boots on the cliff face and walked themselves down. The guards followed on the other line, creeping awkwardly over the side and shinnying down the rope, using the knots Nix had tied.

Egil looked up at them and tsked. "Hope they can swim."

Nix looked down – heights did not trouble him – and waited for the surf and foam to pull back and expose the stone face of Abn Thuset.

"Comin' for you," he said with a wink.

While the guards made their slow, diffident climb down the rope, grunting and cursing throughout, Nix and Egil reached the cave mouth. Light from the late-afternoon sun set the large chamber's limestone alight. They swung off the rope and stepped inside.

A thicket of stalactites hung from the ceiling, and stalagmites jutted from the floor. Along the sides they joined into single columns that reached from the rough, irregular floor to the low ceiling. Down the center of the cave, however, the smaller stalagmites and stalactites stretched for one another like hopeless lovers, but didn't touch.

Beyond, the cave stretched back and down at a gentle slope, out of reach of the day's light.

"Goes back a ways," Egil said.

"Aye."

The first of the guards reached the cave mouth. Egil grabbed him by his belt and pulled him inside. He did the same with the others, one after the other. Derg started to walk deeper into the cave but Egil grabbed him by the arm and pulled him to a stop.

"Don't move unless we say," the priest said to them.

Wide-eyed, Derg nodded.

Moving his feet as little as possible, Nix examined the ceiling and floor, looking for man-made seams disguised as cracks. He saw none.

"Don't look much like a tomb," Derg said.

Nix did not bother to explain Afirion burial customs to the youth. Typically, Afirions dug tombs for their royalty in caverns that already existed.

The earth awaited the body of wizard-king thus and so, the inscription usually read.

"The tomb proper will be deeper in," Egil said.

"If it's here," one of the guards said.

"It's here," Egil and Nix said in unison.

"How do you know?" the guard asked.

Nix pointed with the tip of his falchion at a faint discoloration on the ceiling. "That's a soot stain. Very old."

"And note the stalactites and stalagmites," Egil said. "See how they're thinner and shorter in the center of the cave?"

"So?" the guard said.

"So," the priest explained. "The ones in the center are not as old as those on the sides. That's because the original ones in the center of the cave were cleared to allow passage of workers and matériel. Probably that statue in the water was cracked or broken in transit and discarded by lazy workmen. Proved good luck for us."

While the guards digested that, Nix used a matchstick from his bag to fire a torch.

"I lead," he said. "Then Egil, then the rest of you. Don't touch anything."

Nix led them through the thicket of stone, and followed the slope of the cave downward into darkness. The tunnel narrowed to a neck at twenty paces and they advanced in single file. The guards' rapid breathing betrayed their nervousness.

The narrow passageway opened abruptly into a large vaulted chamber of worked stone. The flickering light of Nix's torch illuminated plastered walls and a ceiling covered in pictoglyphs and Afirion script, a riot of colors and imagery. A large metal door stood on the opposite side of the chamber. Nix saw nothing to indicate the name or station of the person buried in the tomb, but that was not unusual. The receiving room was used to prepare the body for eternity. Afterward, the room was typically covered in curses and trapped. It was probably a good thing he couldn't read much Afirion script.

The guards filed in behind Egil, clustering around Nix.

"Gods," one of them said in a hushed tone, eyeing the ancient artwork.

"What does it say?" another asked.

"I can't read much of it," Nix said, "but it's warnings against defiling the tomb, a promise of curses on tomb robbers."

"What kind of curses?" said the youngest of the guards, his voice betraying a slight quaver.

"The kind that makes your balls fall off," Nix said absently, studying floor and ceiling in the light of his torch.

"Or that makes you shite yourself to death," Egil added.

"Gods," said the guard.

"Shite," said another.

"Exactly," Egil said solemnly.

"I need more light," Nix said. He handed Egil his torch and took his magic crystal eye from his satchel. He tapped it with a finger and spoke a word in the Mages' Tongue.

"Wake up," he said, and the eye opened, blinked a few times, and emitted a beam of light. Nix used it to pore over the walls, ceiling, and floor, keeping his feet planted.

"There," he said, indicating the floor before the door.

"I see it," Egil said.

"And there," Nix said, indicating a spot on the ceiling near the wall.

"What? What?" asked a guard.

"Traps," Egil said. "There are always traps."

Derg cleared his throat. "I don't... feel like we need to enter the tomb any farther. Probably just be in the way of these two. You, mates?"

Murmured agreement.

Nix smiled. "Wise," he said.

"Maybe that could stay between us, though?" Derg said.

"Of course," Nix said.

"Ought to spring the traps, then," Egil offered. "Else they'll set them off."

"Right," Nix said.

Nix ventured into the chamber and walked near the metal door opposite them.

"This looks like a door," he said and stepped before it. When he felt the floor give slightly, triggering the counterpoise, he bounded aside. The metal slab fell forward and crashed onto the floor with a ferocious crash.

"But it's a deadfall."

"Shite!"

"Gods!"

"Pits, man!"

On the otherwise blank wall revealed by the door's fall was scrawled a death curse. Nix pointed at it.

"And there's Egil's 'shite yourself to death' curse. Nicely anticipated, priest."

Egil half-bowed.

Nix walked toward the tomb's actual door, its location hidden by the plaster coating the walls.

"The actual door is here."

"Where?" asked Derg.

"Careful," Egil said.

"Aye," Nix said.

"I don't see it," said another guard.

Nix took a chisel from his satchel and chipped away the plaster until it revealed another metal door, flush with the wall and with no handle, the hinges sunk into the stone of the cavern by screws. He examined the screws. Time had rusted them.

"Hinges are soon to give," he said.

A dusting of rust coated the door. Nix rubbed it off as best he could and read the characters engraved on the door.

"Abn Thuset of Afirion, beloved of the people and the gods."

"It's the right tomb, then," Derg said.

Nix took his crowbar from his satchel, got it in the seam between the wall and the unhinged side of the door.

"Mind," Egil cautioned.

Nix nodded, pried at the door, once, twice, a third time before it finally gave. The moment it started to open, he heard the expected sound of falling counterweights. He leaped backward as the hidden pegs holding the block of ceiling stone above the door slid back and let the block fall. The huge block of stone hit the floor with a dull, ponderous thud, and would have crushed anyone standing under it.

"The Afirions liked crushing tomb robbers," Nix said.

The guards looked wide-eyed at the stone, at the now-gaping opening in the ceiling.

"Help me slide it aside," Nix said.

With help from Egil and the guards, he moved the stone aside and opened the door to the tomb. He held the crystal eye high.

A series of carved steps led down into a large oval chamber. Smooth columns of limestone ran floor to ceiling. More artwork adorned the walls. Nix put away his magical eye and struck another torch to match Egil's.

"Stay here and don't move until we come back," Nix said to the guards.

"Aye," said the guards. Nix saw their nervousness. They eyed the ceiling, floor, and walls as if they might fall in on them at any moment.

"If it'll make you feel better, close the door after we're through."

He'd been jesting about the door, but the moment he and Egil stepped down the stairs and into the columned chamber beyond, the door squeaked closed behind them. They, like Abn Thuset, were entombed in stone.

"Timid slubbers," Nix said.

"Look at this," Egil said, holding his torch high and indicating the walls.

Mindful of his steps, Nix moved closer to the walls and held up his torch to view the wall murals.

Placatory to the gods, tomb murals always showed the truth of a wizard-king's life. A false mural risked divine wrath and condemnation to the Nether Void.

The murals began on one end of the chamber and stretched along the wall. They began as they all did, with the birth of the wizard-king and a detailed rendering of the sky on the day of birth. Subsequent murals showed the wizard-king's childhood, education, tutors, parents, siblings, their entire life told in pictoglyphs painted on limestone. The workmanship was excruciatingly detailed and often done in symbolic fashion. Nix had seen enough of them to deduce meanings. He followed them along the wall but stopped, frowning, when he reached the images showing Abn Thuset in adolescence. The images of tutors and other servants looked typical but the clothing…

"He wears a girl's clothing," Nix said. "Look. That's not a wrap. It's a dress."

Egil grunted, his interest in Abn Thuset's life already slaked.

Nix followed the murals along the wall, a spectator to the truth of Abn Thuset's life. Scenes showed the battles fought in the rebellion that put Abn Thuset's father on the Serpentine Throne of Afirion. Nix could hardly believe what he was seeing. He narrated for Egil.

"Her brothers were killed in the rebellion–"

"Her?"

Nix nodded, his finger tracing the images on the walls as he narrated. "Her brothers were killed in the rebellion that put her father on the Serpent Throne. With no male heirs…"

Nix stared at the image a long while. Egil moved beside him.

"What?" Egil asked.

Nix tapped the wall mural that showed Abn Thuset's transformation. "*She* became the male heir."

"How do you mean? She pretended to be a man? I've heard of such things before, though not in Afirion."

"No," Nix said, shaking his head and studying the mural. "She *became* a man."

Egil's face wrinkled in confusion. "What are you saying?"

"I'm saying the Afirions were masters of transmutational magic." He pointed to the key events of the narrative, which occurred during Abn Thuset's youth. A scene showed her and her father in solemn prayer to a jackal-headed god. A subsequent scene showed her father pointing something at her – Nix assumed it to be a wand – and her body haloed in light. Scenes thereafter showed her with the hairstyle and clothing of an Afirion nobleman, not a noblewoman.

"And they used it to make a daughter a son. She *became* a man."

"One of Afirion's greatest wizard-kings wasn't a wizard-king at all?" Egil said. "But a queen?"

"Aye."

"But... the magic wouldn't last, would it?" Egil said. "No magic lasts forever."

"Not forever, no, but it would last a considerable time." He recalled his introductory lessons at the Conclave. "The closer the changed form is to the original form, the longer the transmutation will last."

"And the change from woman to man is slight," Egil said. "Though much in life rides on it."

"The Serpentine Throne rode on it for Abn Thuset."

Had one of her brothers lived and assumed the throne, she would have remained a woman. As such, she'd have been subject to the authority of her brother, who would have married her off to a husband to whom she would then be subject. By making herself a man, she had instead been able to rule and become one of history's great names.

"Think of it," Nix said. "She was born with the mind and talent to rule, but only rose to it because her brothers were killed and Afirion magic could change her form."

"What a waste had events not unfolded so," Egil said.

"A waste indeed," Nix agreed.

Images from her later reign showed her from time to time using the transmutational wand to renew the magic that had made her a man.

To his surprise, Nix felt a kinship to her. She'd lived a lie, her true self buried in her core, visible to no one but the gods. Nix empathized, though his own secret self was trivial compared to hers.

"You're in love again?" Egil said, his voice carrying a smile. "You wear a doltish smile."

"No," Nix said, losing the smile. "Just impressed. And thoughtful. Think about it, Egil. Abn Thuset's talents were rare, but probably not unique. How many other Afirion women lived lives made for them by men but unsuited to their talents and natures? How many women in Dur Follin?"

For some reason he flashed on his dreams, breathing doors, long hallways, screams, and bloody beds.

"Your point's well made," Egil said, "though I question the timing. We're here to rob her tomb. We should be about it."

"I believe I'd turn from this if I could," Nix said, and the spellworm churned his guts for the thought.

"Yet we can't and we both know it," Egil said. "We've robbed tombs of men both good and evil. And now we'll rob this one, though she be admirable. Come on, Nix."

Nix felt an odd sense of sacredness, but not out of respect for the dead. He'd long ago come to regard dead flesh as nothing but decaying matter. Its provenance was, instead, the connection he felt to Abn Thuset. The truth of her life was known to her father, herself, and now Egil and Nix. There was something in that secret shared that demanded reverence.

And yet he'd have to honor her in the breach, for he could not do anything but what he'd come to do. The spellworm would not allow anything else.

"Let's go," he said to Egil, and they continued deeper into the tomb, Nix went through the motions mechanically, picking locks, avoiding a pit trip, dodging another deadfall, avoiding a vicious spring-propelled scything blade designed to sever legs below the knees.

Presently they stood over a smooth-sided circular hole in the floor, as wide in diameter as Egil was tall. Oddly, the scroll of celebratory artwork continued down the walls of the shaft. Nix had never seen anything of the kind before.

Two statues of cast metal flanked the hole, one of the Afirions' jackal-headed god, the other of a hyena-headed goddess. Both had their arms raised, palms out, in a gesture that forbade further desecration.

Nix checked the ceiling, saw the holes in the stone where a block and tackle had been mounted to lower heavy things down the shaft, no doubt including Abn Thuset's body and sarcophagus. The workers and architects would have used rope ladders to get up and down during construction, so there were no handholds.

Nix dropped his torch down the shaft. It hit the floor after falling seven or eight paces and lay there smoking. An opening led to a chamber beyond, though Nix could not see it from the top of the shaft.

"Down is easy," Egil said. "Up's a harder one. Rope in your bag?"

"We used all we had to get down the cliff."

"We could go back and get some," Egil offered.

"You want to do that?"

They looked at each other a long moment, then said at the same time, "No."

Egil put a hand on one of the divine statues, leaned into it, and rocked it a tiny amount on its base. "It was cast hollow. Let's see if we can walk it over, then."

Grunting and sweating, with Egil doing most of the work, they leaned into the statue of the jackal-headed god and walked it toward the shaft. The base of the statue screamed along the floor as it scored the stone. Nix smiled, imagining the guardsmen back in the cave hearing the sound and trying to guess its cause.

They edged the metal deity to the edge of the large shaft and pushed the statue in. It tipped as it fell, catching the outstretched arm on the edge of the pit and snapping it off. The impact caused the base to swing back hard against the shaft wall, the sound of the collision enough to ring Nix's ears, but the statue hit the bottom of the shaft base first, still intact and standing. The top of the god's head was just below the lip of the shaft.

"Down we go," Egil said. He stepped on the god's head, one of many blasphemies the two had committed over the years, and descended. Nix followed him.

The shaft opened into a large, long chamber. Pictoglyphs covered the walls from floor to ceiling, and four alcoves lined the walls to right and left. Ensconced in each were the bodies of armed and armored Afirion royal guardsmen.

The close, still air smelled vaguely charred. An archway opened on the opposite side of the room. The stone carvings on the door's jambs – sand serpents, land lampreys, and toothfish – indicated that it was the entrance to the royal burial chamber.

Nix took out his crystal eye, activated its beam, and studied floor and ceiling with care. He noticed nothing to alarm him and stepped into the chamber. He approached one of the alcoves, blade in hand, and studied the body.

"Mind," Egil cautioned, armed now with a hammer in one hand.

"Always," Nix said.

The guard wore a ceremonial breastplate and once-rich attire, now rotted to ruin. A round shield emblazoned with a serpent and rising sun sat on the floor at his feet, and a khopesh hung from his wide girdle. Nix could have sold the guard's intact weapons to a collector for a year's worth of drink, but he had little interest in it.

Desiccation had thinned the guard's face and the helm he wore sat askew on his head. Empty eye sockets stared out at the bygone centuries, and his lips, peeled back from his teeth, left him leering at eternity. His exposed skin was blackened, blistered. Nix checked his hands and found them the same way.

"He isn't embalmed in the Afirion fashion," Nix said over his shoulder. "He's burned."

"Burned? Alive?"

Nix shrugged. "Couldn't say. But he was dressed and armored *after* being burned."

"Messy work, that," Egil said, walking slowly from alcove to alcove.

Nix checked the bodies of the other guards and found them in the same condition – burned, then dressed, armored, and stationed in the tomb of their wizard-king, or wizard-queen, as it were.

"They're not animating," Egil said. "So let's get this over with, yeah?"

Nix nodded, and together, they walked the long hall, watched by empty sockets, unsettled by the grins of burn-blackened teeth. Nix held his hands before the jambs that led to Abn Thuset's burial chamber. He felt nothing to indicate a ward.

"Not enspelled," he said, so they walked through a few steps.

The vaulted, circular chamber beyond featured the

expected gold-chased sarcophagus in the center. Statues of Abn Thuset in her royal garb stood at the cardinal compass points. In one of the sculptures, a large horn hung from a chain around her neck. In another, she held a thin stick in her left hand, the transmutation wand that had allowed her to live and rule as a wizard-king rather than a wizard-queen. In all cases, the lifelike statues showed her as she really was – robes curved over breasts, around wide hips. Steely eyes looked out from an otherwise soft-featured feminine mien. The eyes reminded Nix of Tesha's.

"The tomb shows the truth of her," Egil said, his deep voice somber.

"Aye."

Between the statues of Abn Thuset, and taller by a head, stood four sculptures of the animal-headed gods and goddesses of the Afirions. All were carved with arms held wide, open to receive Abn Thuset's spirit to their Heaven.

Nix surveyed the room from the doorway but saw nothing to alarm him. He and Egil went to the sarcophagus. Nix held his hand out, just above the sarcophagus, but again felt nothing.

"Also not enspelled," he said.

"She seemed to want to make this easy," Egil said.

"Maybe she wanted someone to know the truth of her," Nix said.

Egil only grunted.

Nix had never felt any qualms about defiling tombs, but he hesitated in reaching for his crowbar.

Abn Thuset was different. Her tomb was her truth. He felt as if he shouldn't defile it. His hesitation caused the spellworm to writhe around his innards. Egil must have read his expression.

"We should open it," Egil said, "though I don't like it either."

"Right," Nix said. "Maybe say a prayer beforehand?"

Egil's eyebrows went up in surprise. "Not sure she'd appreciate it. Not her faith."

Nix thought about how rarely she'd been able to live her life as a woman, how few moments of truth in her life.

"I think it fits," Nix said.

Egil acceded and bowed his head. Nix joined him and Egil intoned a short prayer to the Momentary God. He finished in fitting fashion.

"I pray she lived richly and lingered long in the moments that delighted her."

"Well said," Nix said. "Let's open it."

Egil jammed his crowbar under the lid's seal and pried it open. The smell of embalming spices and the faint whiff of perfume wafted out.

"Even her corpse smells like a woman," Egil said.

"Well done, milady," Nix said with a smile. He hoped she didn't rise. He didn't relish the thought of stabbing her animated corpse.

Grunting, they slid the sarcophagus lid aside to reveal the silk-lined interior of Abn Thuset's resting place.

The expertise of her priests had left her well preserved, though time and alchemy had left her desiccated, her skin cracked and leathery. Once-fine robes of turquoise-colored silk, now falling to rot, adorned her slim frame. Her long dark hair was braided with filaments of gold, and a modest gold tiara crowned her, rather than the full ceremonial head-dress. Turquoise rings adorned her fingers. She lay on a sea of triangular gold coins.

A horn hung from a leather lanyard around her neck. Carved from yellowed bone and chased in silver, the horn matched the image from the statue. Tiny script, written in black ink, covered the horn's entire surface. Nix did not recognize the script.

Near her left hand, but not in it, lay the teak and gold wand of transmutation, the magic stick that had allowed her to lie to history.

"Forgive me, lady," he said. He cut the lanyard with his dagger and lifted the horn from the sarcophagus. The magic it contained caused his fingers to tingle. He quickly joined the two ends of the lanyard with a hitch knot and put it around his neck.

"What about that?" Nix said. He nodded at the teakwood wand. It tempted him, he had to admit.

Egil stared at him across Abn Thuset's body. "I'd just as soon not see another wand in your hands."

"Could prove useful, though. And my satchel's gotten light, what with everyone getting poisoned and whatnot."

"Take it, or not, but be quick. Let's put her back to sleep and get clear."

"Aye," Nix said, and his love of things magical

overcame his reverence for the sanctity of Abn Thuset's tomb. He slipped the wand from the sarcophagus and into his satchel. But they took only the wand and horn. They did not otherwise disturb her rest, and left her with the rest of her grave goods.

Together, they slid the sarcophagus's lid back into place.

"Let's go," Nix said, and they left the burial chamber, under the watchful eyes of Abn Thuset and the gods she'd worshipped.

Neither would say it for fear of tempting the spirits, but Nix knew that he and Egil were both thinking it: they'd never had an easier go in an Afirion tomb.

They hurried through the hall of alcoves, the gazes of the immolated guards seeming to follow them. As they walked through the archway leading out of the hall of alcoves and into the shaft, where now resided the broken-armed statue of a god, Nix heard a soft pop and sizzling sound.

"Uh-oh," he said.

"What?" Egil said, freezing in place, his voice tense. "Uh-oh, what?"

Nix turned and looked back, saw nothing but the alcoves, the guards, the artwork. Then the floor vibrated under their feet and somewhere, stone ground against stone.

"Shite," Egil said. "What's that?"

Nix shook his head, tense, listening, but nothing more happened.

"Some kind of failed ward, maybe. I–"

A fizzle sounded behind them, then a boom that blew heated wind through the chamber and up the shaft. A luminous orange light blossomed in the burial chamber, a light that grew more fulgent and soon revealed its cause: fire crawled along the walls on either side of the chamber in undulating, crackling waves. It swarmed into the alcove chamber, reached the first alcoves on either wall and engulfed the bodies.

Immediately a deep-throated roar of rage and pain came from the dead royal guardsmen, and a flaming specter of their forms, holding a khopesh made of smoke, stepped from the alcoves. The fire raced through the room, devouring the art on the walls, awakening the ancient guards to flame and rage.

"Climb!" Nix said, shoving Egil toward the statue of the broken-armed god. "Climb!"

CHAPTER FIFTEEN

The flames pursued them as they clambered frantically up the metal body of a god. Egil reached the top first, hopped over the lip of the shaft, turned, and pulled Nix up by his shirt. His eyes were wide, orange with reflected fire.

Nix glanced down, saw flames ringing the shaft around the walls in a blazing vortex, rising fast. A sudden blast of superheated air forced both of them to lurch back from the edge. Nix's eyes fell on the artwork in the chamber, and he remembered the odd artwork in the shaft, and it registered with him.

"The ward uses the paintings for fuel! It's going to keep coming! Go, go!"

They scrambled to their feet and pelted off down the corridor, but made it only a dozen strides before blazing light lit the tomb behind them as bright as a noon sun. A chorus of enraged, otherworldly screams rebounded off the walls.

Nix looked back, shielding his eyes and face, to see a cloud of roiling flames pursuing them. And before the inferno went the blazing effigies of the royal guards, flaming spirits, fire in the form of men. They bore blades of smoke and glared through the black holes of their eyes.

"Run!" Nix said, and shoved Egil toward the exit.

They ran as if Hell were at their heels, but the flames gained on them, crawling along the walls beside them, crackling and sizzling. Nix felt his hair singe, found the scalding air hard to breathe. Smoke clouded the hall, made his eyes water, his throat tickle. The howls of the guards were in his ears and he expected their burning touch at any moment, but still he ran, leaping the pits they'd skirted, dodging the pressure plates, running without a care over the weighted stones in the floor.

"Run, damn it!" he shouted, partially to Egil, partially in hopes that Baras's guardsmen would hear them and get out of the tomb. "Run!"

They burst into the columned entry hall. Nix dared a momentary glance back and wished he hadn't. An inferno of smoke and fire swelled behind them, caustic and effulgent. The flaming guardsmen rode the heat, their expressions twisted in rage, their smoking blades held high.

"Keep running!" Nix said, dashing with Egil through the columns, across the length of the hall. Images of Abn Thuset's life and transformation flitted by him as he ran.

Egil was coughing as he ran but Nix dragged the bigger man along by the arm. Ahead, the door that opened into the natural cave was… closed.

"Gods damn them all!" Nix said.

"You *told* them to close it!" Egil said.

"I was jesting! Open the door!" Nix yelled as they ran, hoping the guards would hear him.

The fire raced along the walls, the floor, the columns, turning the entire chamber ablaze, effacing in fire the truth of Abn Thahl's life. The flaming spirits of the guards howled.

"Open the door!" Nix shrieked.

Sweat poured into his eyes, stung the scalded skin of his face and scalp.

Egil roared and picked up his pace. Nix saw right away what the priest intended and lagged a couple strides behind him.

From behind, flaming hands reached for Nix. Something hot scalded the back of his neck, burned his hair.

Egil lowered his shoulder and sprinted full speed up the stairs and into the metal door, his shoulder lowered. He hit it like a battering ram. The slab of metal shrieked as the impact drove the hinge bolts from the masonry. Egil and Nix tumbled into the room, landing on their stomachs atop the dislodged door.

The startled guards stood around them, eyes wide, blades in hand.

"We thought you was something else entire," Derg said. His relief lasted only a moment as he looked back into the columned hall, saw what was flowing up the steps.

Nix was already on his feet, pulling Egil up behind him. "Run for your life, you dumb gits! Run!"

He didn't wait to see if they heeded his words.

Fire, heat, and the roaring guards burst up the stairs and through the door. One of Baras's guards screamed, an agonized, pitiful sound, and the stink of charred flesh chased Nix through the narrow corridor that led back out to the natural cave. Despite the absence of murals, the flames and burning guardsmen chased them still, turning the cave into a furnace.

More screams from behind; more stink. Nix's legs felt numb. He was gasping, his hair singed, his throat raw from smoke and heat. He stumbled, slammed into a stalagmite.

"Keep going!" Egil said, both of them now communicating between exhausted gasps. "We grab the ropes, climb for our lives!"

"Too slow! We have to jump!"

"That water's too shallow!"

"The tide is in by now!"

"If it's not?"

"Then we're fakked!"

Egil muttered prayers to Ebenor as he and Nix drained their final reserves of energy and sprinted the last fifty paces for the cave mouth. But they were too slow and the crawling flames caught them at last. The walls of the cave turned to curtains of fire. The floor under their feet blazed. Nix's boots smoked. His cloak and trousers caught fire. He had breath enough only to scream at the pain.

Egil echoed his pained shriek but both kept running.

The howls of the guards rang in their ears. Swords of

smoke slashed the air beside Nix. Blazing hands grabbed at his cloak, causing him to stumble and threatening to turn his clothing into a conflagration. In the crackle and roar of the flames he thought he heard the distant, mumbled sound of the Afirion tongue.

They reached the cave mouth at a dead run, both of them screaming, both of them aflame, and neither of them so much as slowed. They leaped out into open air, arms flailing, clothes ablaze and trailing smoke, twin comets falling into the watery void of the Bleak Sea below.

The flaming guards pursued them even over the edge. In the few heartbeats it took to plummet down the cliff face, Nix saw the blurry glow of the guards' blazing forms reflected on the surface of the water below, trailing them down.

Nix tensed his body and tried to angle himself slightly, but nothing prepared him for the force of the impact, the sudden cold. He might as well have crashed into a rock wall. The impact rattled his body, made him see sparks, forced the air from his lungs. He sank deep into the dark, quiet water, his body already turning numb from the frigid water.

Around him the water lightened then glowed brightly as the flaming guardian spirits knifed into the sea and floated toward them. Bubbles and steam boiled away from the flaming guards' forms as they descended, the holes of their eyes fixed on Nix.

Nix kicked his legs and recoiled, going deeper, until his back thumped against the rocky bottom. And still the guardians came, diminishing with each stroke as the water claimed more and more of their forms, but performing their vengeful duty even as it destroyed them. They descended closer, closer, and a flaming hand reached for Nix's face… and surrendered entirely to the sea before reaching him. The flaming bodies died out, dissipated with the faint echo of Afirion curses.

Nix's lungs burned. His clothes were soaked, weighing him down. He had no idea how deep he was, though he could perceive the filtered light of dusk. Panicked, he pushed off the bottom with what strength he had left and made for the surface.

Water, unending water. He needed to breathe, and the instinct to gulp air became overwhelming. He was lightheaded, failing.

A hand seized him by the cloak and jerked him to the surface. He broke the waterline into the gray light of twilight, felt cool air on his face, and drew it into his lungs in greedy, heaving gulps.

"Breathe," Egil said, gulping air himself and keeping Nix afloat. "Breathe."

Nix could not speak. He nodded, gasping, coughing. Egil held him by the collar and kept his head above water.

The waves surged them back and forth, driving their wounded, burned bodies into rocks, pushing them toward the cliff. Nix did not have the energy to resist the water's will. He and Egil just fended off the rocks as best they could with their legs and arms.

"Good," Nix said after a time. "I'm good."

"Anyone else get out?" Egil said.

"I don't think so," Nix said.

They called out, hoping to hear a response over the rush and hum of the surf. When they heard nothing, Egil uttered a short prayer to Ebenor, wishing the guards' souls a safe journey into the spheres of the afterlife.

"Let's get out of the water," Egil said. "We'll die of cold."

"Aye," Nix said.

"Got the horn still?"

A moment of panic seized Nix at the thought he might have lost it, but the strap hadn't broken. The horn still hung around his neck. For good measure, he felt for his satchel of magical and mundane paraphernalia, his weapons. He had everything. Except the men he'd come in with. Damn.

Abn Thuset's final ward had gotten some good men, but she hadn't gotten them all. Somewhere under him, he knew, the stone face of the wizard-queen's statue looked up at him with ire.

"You have a lovely home, milady," he said to her.

They fought the waves and their wounds as they tried to make for the distant beach, further exhausting themselves. They swam, floated, and sputtered along the cliff face toward the shoreline. By the time they made it, Nix felt as though he had swum a league. His arms hung dead from his shoulders. He was giddy when he felt a sandy bottom under his feet. He and Egil stood in the chest-high water and waded in, assisted by the rolling surf. Nix's body ached all over. He was burned in places, and he'd wrenched his right leg. He favored it as the water grew shallower, stumbled often.

Beside him, the priest looked slumped, bedraggled, his mustache, beard, and ruff of hair sodden. Burns pinked his face, forearms, and his tattooed scalp.

"Hurt the leg?" Egil asked Nix. "Can you walk?"

"Barely," Nix said, limping on the wounded leg. "Must have twisted it fleeing the flames."

Gulls flew around them, cawed irritably. Shouts sounded from their left, from atop the cliff. Nix saw figures there, and raised a hand to hail them, but they must not have seen him. More shouts from behind the rise that hid the beach from the plains. Sounded like Jyme.

"Here," Nix tried to call, but his raw throat mustered a poor shout. He stripped off his cloak and shirt as he plodded through the surf, wrung them out. Egil did the same. Both of them shivered in the cool air.

"Anything?" Nix said, holding his arms out and turning a circle so Egil could see his back.

"An unimpressive physique and a few burns, but nothing that'll kill you," Egil said, and held out his own arms and turned. "Me?"

Nix eyed the priest's broad back. "How am I supposed to see anything through all that back hair? No wonder you didn't get burned. You've a pelt."

"Fak you."

Nix chuckled. "No wounds that I can see through the thicket, save minor burns. You're good."

"I wouldn't say that," Egil said, and sagged to the sand. Nix did the same. He felt like he could have slept a week. They sat there shivering, too tired to stand. A few gulls approached, eyeing them warily.

More shouts from over the rise. Jyme was getting closer. Startled by Jyme's shouts, the gulls cawed and flew off.

Halfheartedly, Nix said, "Maybe we should kill Rakon now. What do you think?"

The spellworm rewarded his words and thoughts with a bout of nausea. The discomfort felt almost quaint after the pain of fire.

Egil clutched his stomach, grimaced against the pain of the worm. "Tempting, I admit. But I figure he was just aiding his sisters. We all do things to help those we love, right?"

"Right," Nix said, thinking of the Vwynn he'd killed to save Egil.

"We can't kill him just because he's a prick, can we?" Egil asked. "We make that our rule and our blades will be bloody until we're graybeards."

"Plenty of pricks in Ellerth," Nix agreed. "And yet… the sisters he seeks to help are witches."

"And he's a sorcerer," Egil said thoughtfully. He looked up. "Perhaps we should kill him, do the world a service."

The words made Egil groan with pain, the worm vexing him. He punched himself in the stomach.

"It's worth it, you fakkin' worm."

"I think we'd have to kill Baras and Jyme to get to him," Nix said. "I've no stomach for that."

"Baras, maybe," Egil said. "Not Jyme. But what if the Lord Mayor somehow learned we'd killed his Adjunct? We'd never be able to return to Dur Follin."

"I do sort of like it there," Nix said. He sighed. "Well enough. You make fair points. We let him live. I was just trying on a thought, is all. I get irritable when my flesh is nearly consumed in fire. Another time, maybe."

"Another time," Egil agreed.

Jyme's shouts sounded nearer.

"Over here!" Nix called, managing a creditable yell.

Jyme appeared atop the rise that overlooked the beach, his eyes wide, his face wearing an expression of shock.

"Gods, men! There you are! We saw that fire! Hells, the whole hill vibrated!" He shouted up at the cliff. "My lord! Baras! I've found them! They're here! Over here!"

Baras's shout answered from atop the cliff.

"On our way!"

In moments Rakon and Baras were hurrying down the hill, leading the horses.

Jyme hurried toward Egil and Nix, stumbling in the sand as he ran. "Where are the others?"

"It's just us," Nix said.

"Shite," Jyme said. He made the symbol of Orella with his hand.

"Aye," Egil said. "Shite. They were good men."

Nix stood and pulled on his shirt, wincing from various pains. Egil did the same.

"Is that it?" Jyme asked, nodding at the horn Nix had placed on the sand. "The horn?"

Nix had almost forgotten about it. He picked it up and examined it more closely. It felt heavier than it should, given its size and composition. His hands tingled from its enchantment.

"What's all that writing mean?" Jyme asked.

Nix shrugged. "I can't read it."

"How in the Pits do you rob all these tombs if you can't read Afirion?"

Egil shook his head. Nix sighed.

"Jyme, robbing tombs, as you so genteelly put it, involves avoiding traps, crawling through dirt, picking locks, and sometimes, *sometimes*, killing guardians. As a rule, poetry readings are not required. I can read enough, but not this. It's an older dialect, I think."

"I... I only meant..."

"Just shut up, Jyme," Egil said.

Rakon and Baras crested the rise, leaving the horses behind them. Rakon stood his ground atop it. Baras continued toward them.

"Do you have it?" Rakon called. He shifted from foot to foot. "The horn? Do you have it?"

"We have it, you bunghole," Nix muttered.

Jyme chuckled.

"My men?" Baras asked, looking up and down the beach.

Egil shook his head. "They didn't come out."

"Sorry, Baras," Nix said.

"Shite," Baras said.

"Do they have it, Baras?" Rakon called again, his voice tense.

Baras's face flashed irritation, but only for a moment. His eyes fell on the horn Nix held. Over his shoulder, he called, "They have it, my lord."

"Well done! Bring it to me, Baras."

Nix handed the instrument to Baras.

"It damned well better work after all this," Baras said softly, eyeing the horn. "Good men died for it."

"Uh, take anything else out of there?" Jyme asked. "Anything valuable?"

"Our lives," Nix said irritably. "But maybe you meant something else?"

"No offense meant," Jyme said. "Just asking, is all."

"It's forgotten," Nix said with a sigh. "I'm irritable, is all."

"Hurry, Baras," Rakon said, his voice greedy with anticipation. The sorcerer looked to the sky, the setting sun turning it red. "Hurry!"

Baras jogged the horn over to Rakon. Egil, Nix, and Jyme started for the rise. The moment Baras handed the horn to Rakon, Nix felt a sharp pain in his abdomen, as if he'd been stabbed. He doubled over, groaning. Egil did the same.

"What is it?" Jyme asked. "What's wrong?"

Nix tried to speak, but the squirming in his guts allowed him to do nothing but heave. He put his hands on his knees and puked bile, then a long, thick stream of sputum that seemed to go on forever. Beside him, Egil did the same.

"There's something wrong with them," Jyme called to Rakon.

"There's nothing wrong," Rakon said. "They completed their charge and now they're free of the spellworm."

The heaves went on for some time, Egil and Nix purging themselves of Rakon's compulsion. When they were done, twin snakes of greenish-black phlegm lay glistening in the sand.

"That's unpleasant," Egil said, wiping his mouth, kicking sand over the mucus.

"Seconded," Nix said.

"You all right?" Jyme asked. He'd lingered while they'd puked.

"As well as can be," Nix said. "Come on. Time to take our leave, I think."

By the time they reached the camp, Rakon and the eunuch had already laid his sisters on the ground. The horn hung from Rakon's neck and his satchel of needful things from his shoulder. Baras stood at a distance from Rakon, watching with a curious look on his face.

"What is he doing?" Jyme said.

Nix shrugged. "Breaking the curse, maybe? That's what this was all about."

"Was it?" Egil said.

"You have a thought?" Nix asked him.

"Suspicions," the priest answered. "Let's hold here."

"I want to get supplies and get clear," Nix said. "We're done. I'm done."

"Just hold," Egil said.

Baras walked toward Rakon and the eunuch. "My lord, your sisters need to be strapped to the horses for the return journey to Dur Follin. Unless you intend to lift the curse here?"

Rakon did not turn. "We won't be taking the horses, Baras. I cannot spare the time to return on foot. The Thin Veil is near."

"The Thin Veil, my lord? I don't understand."

"Of course you don't," Rakon said. He nodded at the eunuch and the huge man took Baras by the arms and steered him away from Rakon and his sisters. Meanwhile, Rakon rummaged through the pack on the ground until he found what he sought: a wrist-thick candle. He stood it in the sand, uttered the words to a cantrip, and a flame sprung from his finger. He touched it to the candle and thick black smoke rose into the twilight air.

"You've done me a service," Rakon said over his shoulder to Egil and Nix. "I won't soon forget it. Nor will I forget that all of this was necessary to begin with only due to your interference in matters beyond your ken. Tomb robbers and thieves almost brought down the house of my forefathers."

"You blather, man," Nix said. "We had nothing to do with any of this. At least I don't think we did. Did we, Egil?"

Egil didn't answer. He had his eyes on the sorcerer,

his hand on a hammer. Jyme stood with them, lingered at a distance.

"And now those same imbeciles have saved it," Rakon said.

"Imbeciles!" Nix said.

"What's he doing?" Jyme asked in a hiss.

Nix shrugged.

Jyme said, "I thought you learned magic before dropping out of the Conclave?"

"He was expelled," Egil said absently.

Nix pointed an appreciative finger at his friend.

Smoke spiraled from the candle in a thick black line. The smoke smelled of burning flesh, pungent and foul. Rakon looked up to the darkening sky, held his hands aloft, and began to incant.

To Nix, the words Rakon used sounded much like the Language of Creation, but the inflection was off, the pronunciation harsher. Nix knew none of the words, but he didn't have to. He could see the result.

The wind picked up, swirled in tiny vortices around Rakon, sent sand churning into the air, a fog of grit.

"Maybe we should, uh, leave?" Jyme said.

Nix was thinking the same thing, but just as he was about to suggest as much, Rakon's incantation intensified, the candle wick flared, and the candle burned half its length in a flash, sending a column of foul black smoke into the whipping air. Rather than dissipate, the smoke lingered in the swirls, outlining a nebulous, shifting shape. Nix heard a voice in the wind, the words too soft to make out, a high-pitched, otherworldly titter similar to the one he'd heard back in the Wastes when he'd awakened from a dream.

"A sylph," Nix said. "I should've guessed before."

Rakon pointed at the air, where the smoke gathered and hinted at a huge, winged form. "Carry my sisters and me back to the prison, spirit."

The wind whispered in answer, the words audible only to Rakon.

Gusts formed a wall of whirling sand around Rakon, the desert orbiting him and his sisters. Baras pulled his cloak over his face and turned away. Egil, Nix, and Jyme shielded their faces. Only the eunuch, standing just outside the wall of sand, seemed unbothered. Rakon and his sisters sat in the center of the winds, untouched by the swirling sands.

"My lord!" Baras called over the swirl. "What is this? What about the horn, your sisters?"

"The horn will do its work and so will my sisters," Rakon answered. "Goodbye, Baras."

"Are you... leaving us?" Baras asked. "My lord, we'll die out here."

"Then die, Baras. You've done your work, too."

"My lord! I–"

"Enough, Baras!"

The wind picked up and the sylph, invisible now except when grains of sand momentarily defined its form, lifted Rakon and his sisters from the sand. Rakon glared at them as he rose higher into the air.

"Eater!" Rakon called down, and it took a moment for Nix to understand that he was addressing the eunuch. "When Egil and Nix are dead, you're free, the binding undone."

The eunuch grunted, turned, and fixed his vacant eyes on Egil and Nix.

"Really, that seems uncharitable," Nix muttered. "And a eunuch, no less? Not even a creditable assassin. I'm insulted. You hear me, Norristru? I'm insulted!"

Egil made an obscene gesture at Rakon as the sylph bore him and his sisters higher into the air on a blanket of air.

"All that shite I said about not killing him… forget I said any of that. Next time we see him, we kill him."

"Agreed," Nix said, drawing his falchion and hand axe. He considered taking a shot with his sling at Rakon, but the sylph's winds would make it fruitless, like trying to shoot gulls at the Heap.

"He was a bunghole right from the beginning," Jyme said.

"Truth," Egil agreed.

"Did he say you two caused all this?" Jyme asked. "The curse and such?"

"I think he did," Egil said.

"Makes no sense," Nix said. "And anyone who thinks it does, so indicate."

Nothing.

"Are his sisters even cursed?" Jyme asked.

Egil pulled his hammers. "They're witches and he's a sorcerer and the deeds of witches and sorcerers seldom make sense. But we're clear of them now. We kill this eunuch and go home."

The eunuch strode purposefully toward Egil and Nix, his heavy tread leaving depressions in the sand behind him.

"Things always seem to end in blood," Nix said.

"I blame you," Egil added.

"You would."

While they readied themselves, Baras stalked up to the eunuch and grabbed him by the shoulder.

"Stop," the guardsman said. "You're not killing anyone. Jyme! Help me restrain him."

"Why restrain him?" Jyme called. "Just kill him."

The eunuch stopped, but did not turn his head to look at Baras.

"Jyme!" Baras called, still struggling with the eunuch.

Cursing, Jyme hurried down the rise.

"Enjoy," Nix said.

Jyme and Baras tried to take the eunuch by the arms, but the hulking man would have none of it. His eyes still on Egil and Nix, the eunuch started walking, dragging the two guardsmen along with him.

Baras dug in his heels, reached for his blade. "I said stop."

Without breaking stride, the huge man broke an arm free of Baras's grip and loosed a backhand that caught the guardsman flush on the side of the head. Baras went spinning into the sand and lay still.

Jyme loosed his hold and backed off, tried to pull his blade, but it stuck in the scabbard.

"Egil!" Jyme called. "Nix!"

The eunuch lurched toward him and punched him

in the face. The ham fist shattered Jyme's nose and drove him to the sand.

"Strong whoreson, isn't he?" Nix said.

"We'll see," answered Egil, his hands opening and closing on the hilts of his hammers.

The priest closed his eyes in prayer, a momentary imprecation for the Momentary God, then charged. Nix hurried after as fast as his wounded leg allowed. The eunuch, seeing them coming, drew his knife.

Egil closed the distance in ten strides, sidestepped the eunuch's clumsy knife stab, and slammed a hammer into the eunuch's side. Bone crunched but the eunuch did not buckle, did not so much as groan. A punch to the side of the head from the eunuch's off hand staggered Egil.

The priest wobbled, eyes rolling, waved a hammer clumsily, and fell. The eunuch lurched forward and stomped on his head, driving his face into the sand. He straddled the priest, knife held high, and turned toward Nix.

Nix shouted and hurled his hand axe at the eunuch. It hit the huge man in the chest, sank half the depth of its head into his sternum, but the eunuch made no sign he even felt the wound. The hulking man looked down, regarded the axe protruding from his sternum, and pulled it out as if it were a splinter in his thumb. Blood seeped from the hole in his chest.

Nix bounded into blade range, sidestepped a slash from the eunuch's knife, ducked a crosscut from his own axe, now wielded by the eunuch in his other hand, and drove his falchion half its length into the eunuch's gut. Stinking gore spilled into the sand but still the man did not fall.

He dropped Nix's axe, seized Nix by the throat, and lifted him into the air. Nix cursed as he lost his grip on his falchion, leaving it sticking out of the eunuch's guts like a bloody pennon.

"What... are... you?" Nix said, barely able to breathe.

Still wearing the dumb smile and eyeing Nix through vacant eyes, the eunuch stabbed Nix in the gut with his knife.

Nix's leather jack turned the blade enough that it cut only skin, not organs, but it wouldn't turn another. Nix heaved his legs up and kicked the eunuch in the face, once, twice. The man's nose shattered, spraying blood and teeth, but he did not release his grip.

Smiling stupidly, the eunuch reached back for another stab, but before he could drive the blade between Nix's ribs, a roar from the side turned his head – Baras.

Having recovered from the punch, the guardsman bulled headlong into the eunuch, hitting with enough force to push the eunuch sideways a step, causing him to drop Nix to the sand.

The mountainous man, his face ruined, intestines leaking from his stomach, turned to face Baras. But Baras was too fast, too enraged to be stopped, and he drove his sword into the eunuch's chest and out his back. Blood showered the sand, sprayed Nix.

The eunuch's eyes should have widened with pain; he should have fallen to his knees, but he did neither. Never losing his vacant smile and empty gaze, he snatched Baras's wrist with his free hand, pulled him close, and drove his knife into the underside of Baras's jaw, up through his mouth, and into his brain. Wide-eyed, Baras's jaw moved up and down, as if masticating the steel. Blood poured from his mouth.

The eunuch pulled the knife free and Baras crumpled to the sand, dead flesh in a bag of chainmail, leaking crimson from the hole in his jaw. The eunuch dropped the knife, pulled Baras's blade from his own body, and turned to Nix, still smiling.

"Shite," Nix said, climbing to his feet. The blood rushed from his head when he stood and a bout of dizziness caused him to wobble. Adrenaline kept him upright. He pulled the dagger he kept in his boot, another he wore on his belt. He wanted to back away, put some space between himself and the eunuch, but he didn't trust himself to move across the sand and stay upright.

"Come on, whoreson," he said, faking a bravado he didn't feel.

Holding Baras's gory blade in one hand and Nix's hand axe in the other, the eunuch lumbered toward Nix.

Since Nix couldn't easily kill the man, he resolved to disable the eunuch's body somehow, ruin his locomotion, and then cut him to pieces.

The eunuch plodded straight for him. Nix circled

laterally as best he could, trying to keep some space between them and wait for an opening.

Impatient, the eunuch rumbled forward, stabbing at Nix's chest with Baras's sword, but Nix sidestepped the stab and ducked under the eunuch's follow-up slash with the hand axe. He jabbed his punch dagger into the eunuch's knee and the big man stumbled.

"Got you," Nix said, bounding back out of reach.

The eunuch, however, surprised Nix when he half-lurched, half-hopped forward on his good leg and swung a crosscut at Nix's throat. Nix ducked the swing, but in the process his own wounded leg gave out and he fell sprawling to the sand. Panic fueled him. He whirled around just in time to get his dagger crosswise of the eunuch's down stroke with Baras's sword.

The parry sent a shooting pain through Nix's wrist, but he steered the larger blade into the sand and rolled away as fast as he could. He heard the eunuch plodding after him, the crunch of sandals on the sand, and climbed to his feet. His leg nearly buckled on him again. Wincing, he held his ground. He held up his daggers as the eunuch closed.

"These are going into your eyes, slubber. You can't hit what you can't see."

No answer but the dumb smile and an inexorable advance.

As Nix prepared to die fighting, Egil appeared behind the eunuch, teeth bared, his hammer raised, blood streaming from his nose and a cut on his scalp, as if Ebenor's eye were crying tears of blood. The eunuch never turned, fixed as he was on Nix. Holding one of his hammers two-handed, Egil slammed the head of the weapon into the eunuch's skull.

Bone audibly collapsed, brain and shards of skull sprayed Nix in a gory rain. The eunuch stood upright for a moment, the eyes still vacant, the mouth still open in the dumb half-smile, all with Egil's hammer buried halfway in his hollowed-out head.

For a moment, Nix thought not even the priest's blow would fell whatever the eunuch was, but the huge man sagged to his knees, then fell face first into the sand.

And when he hit the sand and the light went out of his eyes, an onslaught of thoughts and memories exploded from the opening in his head.

CHAPTER SIXTEEN

Memories pelted Nix, a storm of thoughts and experiences not his own. The mental onslaught knocked him backward to the sand, left him face up to the twilight sky, screaming in pain at the setting sun. His head pounded, the pressure building in his temples to such a degree that he knew his head would soon explode in a shower of gore to rival that of the eunuch's.

He was distantly aware of Egil's screams echoing his own, the priest writhing in the sand with his hands on either side of his head as if he could hold his skull together with the strength of his arms. Jyme, too, seemed to be screaming.

Nix rolled over, the pain in his head curling him into a fetal position. He pressed his face into the sand and screamed into the granules. He felt as if acid had been poured inside his skull. He could not bear it; *he could not*. Images, memories, and thoughts slammed into him, rooted into his mind as if they were his own. He could not shelter himself from them. He could only writhe, scream, and endure.

Phrases thronged his mind, filling his skull, the words portentous: breeders, House Thyss of Hell, the Pact. They stuck in the forefront of his consciousness, the stars around which everything else orbited.

Of a sudden he knew that House Norristru had pacted with House Thyss of Hell. He knew, too, that to seal the Pact, the Norristru men had sacrificed their seed, cursing themselves to infertility, while the Norristru women had been made to sacrifice their wombs, cursed to annual violation by fiends. They were fertile only to a Thyss-born devil.

A fiend from Hell – it had been Vik-Thyss for the last hundred and eleven years – arrived once every two years on the night of the Thin Veil, when the walls between worlds were weakest, and violated all Norristru women of child-bearing age. Of the resulting offspring, House Thyss claimed those of fiendish appearance and House Norristru retained those who could pass as human. The alliance with Hell brought the Norristru line ever more arcane knowledge, brought them command of spirits who feared Hell's wrath should they disobey.

Nix understood that the Pact had become harder and harder to honor with each generation, as more and more of the offspring proved devilish in appearance and were taken by the Thyss. House Norristru had become less like the house of a noble family and more like a mausoleum, empty rooms filled only with memories and the horrors of the past.

Memories knifed into his brain. Nix was Rusilla, filled with measured hate.

He was lying in his bed, speaking to Rakon, who stood at the door of her chambers.

"The Pact was made by Norristru men, for Norristru men. Yet it's the women who suffer for it."

Against his will, images solidified around the words, mental pictures of diabolic violations of generations of Norristru women. He tried not to see them, tried not to understand the reality of the horror, but the images would not relent. They filled him with disgust. He did not know if they were actual memories or Rusilla's guess at what had occurred, but they were terrible enough make him squirm.

"Not this," he groaned, his mouth full of sand. "Not this."

He lay on his back in a bed, arms chained above him to the bedposts, while the scaled, hulking form of a devil pressed down on him, nearly smothering him. He gritted his teeth against the agonizing pain below his waist, at the dry, reptilian stink of the creature. He wept with shame and fear and pain as the creature drove itself into him again and again.

He was himself, remembering the dreams he'd had in the Wastes. They had come from Rusilla. She had been trying to reach him, show him what awaited her and her sister. But he had resisted and never seen. He recalled the swelling, engorged doors, the blood leaking under the jambs, the horrors occurring on the other side of the wood, the bestial sounds of lust a counterpoint to the desperate screams of pain that they hid.

He could not bear it.

"Stop!" he shouted. "Stop."

He was Rakon.

"Vik-Thyss is dead," the sylph said in its singsong voice. "His death has been in the wind for many days."

His thoughts had swirled. In his mind's eye, he saw the family's power foundering, saw House Norristru losing what wealth it still possessed, its seat on the Merchants' Council. He saw himself losing his position as Adjunct to the Lord Mayor, saw his many enemies emboldened and coming for him. Without the protection of House Thyss of Hell, he would be quickly dead and his house annihilated.

"How?" he asked.

And the sylph had told him.

"An ancient breeze in Afirion had the tale of the devil's death," the sylph said. "Vik-Thyss was slain by Egil Verren of Ebenor and Nix Fall of no god, whose names are known on earth, in the air, and to the knowledgeable in Hell. They killed Vik-Thyss while robbing the tomb of Abn Thahl."

He needed another true scion of House Thyss, no half-breed born of human-devilish blood would do. He'd queried the sylph, and again the sylph had answered – Abrak-Thyss lived, imprisoned somewhere on Ellerth, but the sylph did not know where.

Rakon would find out.

Nix was himself again, and understanding dawned. Rakon had located Abrak-Thyss's prison in the Demon Wastes, at the sea of glass. That is what he had been looking for. And he needed the horn to free him.

Nix screamed again as more memories filled him. He was Rusilla.

She lay in her bed, her mind reaching out through the manse, her thoughts gently poking, prodding, drawing Rakon to her chambers. Her magic worked poorly at a distance, but still she reached, filling the air of the manse with a disincorporated need to see her. She simply wanted Rakon to bump into the idea and respond to it.

He was Rakon.

As he walked the halls of the manse he was possessed of a need to see his sisters, a need he didn't understand.

Nix was himself, and he understood. He understood it all, now.

He was Rusilla.

Her brother stood in the door of her chambers, his smaller form almost invisible behind the hulking form of the memory eater. She sensed his preoccupation and snuck through his mental defenses. Once in, she sifted gently through his recent experiences, touching them as lightly as a ghost, seeing them as if they were her own. She saw his conversation with the sylph, learned the fate of Vik-Thyss.

She'd formulated rough plans on the instant, knowing she'd not get another chance at her brother while he was so distracted. She shoved thoughts into Rakon's mind as rapidly as she could.

When you find Abrak-Thyss's prison, you will need help entering it and freeing him. You should use the same tomb robbers who killed Vik-Thyss in the tomb of Abn Thahl, Egil of Ebenor and Nix Fall of Dur Follin to assist you. What delicious irony. After Abrak-Thyss is freed you can kill them in revenge for what they did. You'll use the memory eater to kill them. The eater will kill them. The eater will kill them. But only they can do it. Only they can do it. And the eater will kill them, the eater must kill them.

She'd buried the idea deep, made it as compelling as she dared, then added another.

You cannot leave Rusilla and Merelda alone in the manse. They must accompany you. You'll drug them. But you must take them with you. It's too dangerous to leave them alone. You'll tell your men they are sick, that you're seeking a cure. But you must take them with you.

But she'd pushed too far, too fast, and Rakon had sensed her mental invasion. He'd flooded his mind with foul arcana and reasserted the integrity of his thoughts. But she'd seen what she needed to see, done what she needed to do.

For the first time in years, she'd dared have hope for herself and Merelda.

Later, she'd entered the mind of the memory eater, enduring the screams of the vanishing eunuch while she shoved memories, thoughts, and images into the vacant spaces of its mind, some her own, some stolen from Rakon. She knew Rakon would drug her and Merelda, making it difficult for her to communicate with anyone. The eater would be the vessel to carry the truth, her living plea to this Egil and Nix. She hoped the memories would go unnoticed by the eater long enough to reach their target.

She'd thought that if Egil and Nix could slay Vik-Thyss,

then surely they could kill her brother and free Rusilla and Merelda. Surely they could.

But only if they were the kind of men who would feel obliged to save them.

And in that, she was taking a risk. She didn't know their hearts, couldn't know, but she had no choice.

A knife stab of pain lanced Nix's head, burning itself into his skull, and it carried a single thought.

Be that kind of man.

He was Rusilla once more.

She lay awake in her bed while Merelda slept, thinking of the frailty of her plans, thinking, too, of what awaited her and her sister if the plan failed and Rakon somehow found and freed Abrak-Thyss.

The hopeless, helpless terror caused Nix to weep. He'd had a taste of it in dreams, but then it had been attenuated. Now he felt it firsthand, what the sisters had endured, and he felt deep pity for them, deep shame for himself.

He'd thought them witches. He'd feared them, thought they'd been trying to hurt him. He wept for his own foolishness.

Abruptly the pain subsided, but the memories remained, images of horror etched into his brain forever. He lifted his head from the sand and vomit rushed up his throat. He puked into the sand.

A word moved through Nix's mind, a foul word, an appalling word irreducible beyond the horror and pain it evoked, the word at the center of everything he'd learned from the memories implanted in the eater's mind.

Rape.

Rusilla had not been trying to manipulate him. She'd been trying to communicate to him the horror of her existence, the debased, painful fate that awaited her and Merelda if they did not free themselves from their brother.

Their brother. Their own brother.

Thinking of Rakon filled him not with his usual sense of smug contempt for fools, but with rage, righteous wrath. His fists balled around the desert sand.

Rakon had enslaved his own sisters, made them whores to Hell.

And for what?

For power.

Nix had never before wanted a man dead as badly as he wanted Rakon dead. Nix had lived in Rusilla's skin, even if only for a moment, and what he'd felt was beyond words.

He thought back on his dreams, wincing over the lustful grunting he'd heard behind the doors of the hallway in the Norristru manse. Through the dreams, Rusilla had made him feel an inkling, a mere inkling, of what she and Merelda had felt, the terror and helpless rage that generations of Norristru women had felt while being made to suffer at the hands of Norristru men and the foul devils of Hell.

He wept anew.

How could a man do that to his sisters? To any woman?

Be that kind of man.

The words echoed in his mind, in their way more compelling than Rakon's spellworm had ever been.

The many lewd glances and lascivious comments that Nix had made to women through the years stared at him accusingly across the gulf of his memory. Tesha. Kiir. He'd always told himself that he was a wit, a flirt, but he could not escape the feeling that his words echoed, however distantly, the kind of thinking that allowed Rakon to justify his sisters' sexual enslavement. He suddenly felt like he weighed four hundred stone. Shame weighed him down.

"Nix?" Egil called.

He sat up and looked around, bleary-eyed, and saw the priest standing over the ruined body of the eunuch. Egil, too, had tears in his eyes. He covered Ebenor's eye with his hand as if doing so would blind him to what he had seen. The priest's voice broke when he spoke.

"What have we done, Nix? Gods, what have we done?"

Nix bowed his head. He had no words.

Be that kind of man.

The priest turned and looked up at the twilight sky, in the direction the sylph had carried Rakon and his sisters. They were no longer visible. The sylph flew as fast as the wind. There was no way they could catch them. Rusilla and Merelda's hopes had died on the Afirion sands. Egil and Nix had failed them.

"I'm upside down here," Egil said, in a voice smaller than Nix had ever heard the priest use. "I didn't see it. I was so, so wrong."

CHAPTER SEVENTEEN

Jyme, prone in the sand to Nix's left, groaned and rolled over to face the sky.

"Gods, what happened? Why do I…? How do I know what I know? Is it real?"

Nix did not bother to explain. He looked over to the eunuch, at the bloody crater in the skull from which the truth had erupted.

"Gods," he said, balling his hands into fists. "Gods."

He stood, pacing the sand on his wounded leg, agitated, periodically returning to the eunuch's corpse and unleashing a frustrated kick into his bulk.

"You're bleeding," Jyme said, pointing at Nix's side.

Nix's shirt was stained where the eunuch's blade had penetrated his leather jack. He waved off the wound with a grunt.

"We have to follow them," he said to Egil. "We have to."

Egil's expression fell. "How? They're gone."

"Follow who?" Jyme asked. "Rakon? Are you both mad?"

Nix whirled on Jyme, the hiresword a convenient target for his displaced ire. "Did you see what we saw when Egil split this... *thing's* head? Did you?"

Jyme colored, looked away. Nix did not relent.

"So you know what awaits them? You'd just let them go? What kind of man are you, Jyme?"

Jyme looked up, shame coloring his cheeks, but his chin stuck out defiantly. "The kind that wants to stay alive. I see things different now, sure. I wish I'd never pawed at that lass back at the *Tunnel* and that's sure. But bad things happen everywhere, all the time. I'm worried about my own skin, you know?"

Nix didn't know.

Be that kind of man.

"They're too far gone anyway," Jyme continued. "You saw how fast that... thing flew. You'd never catch them, not unless you could fly. You got something in that bag of yours?"

Jyme meant his words as a joke, but the words triggered an idea for Nix, a hope, a desperate ploy. He turned to the shoreline. He could not see the surf but he could see the wheeling sea birds. He reached into his bag, touched a wand he'd pocketed in the tomb of Abn Thuset.

"What are you thinking?" Egil asked, reading Nix's expression.

"I'm thinking we *can* fly."

"What are you talking about?" Jyme said.

"I'm talking about flying," Nix repeated, warming to

his idea. He held up the teak and gold wand. "With this. All I need is a living bird. The magic in the wand..."

Egil cut him off, eyeing the wand with distrust. "I thought Abn Thuset used it to change her sex?"

Jyme looked on, hopelessly confused. "What about sex, now?"

Nix ignored him and spoke to Egil. "Yes, but that's a particular use of the wand's general power. It's transmutational magic, Egil."

"Which you learned in your year at the Conclave, before..." Egil held up his hand to forestall Nix's inevitable correction. "... you ceased attending."

"Yes. It'll work, Egil."

The priest looked skeptical, but Nix saw hope in his eyes. He ran his palm over Ebenor's eye. "You're certain?"

Nix pulled the end of his nose. "Fairly certain."

Egil stared at him while the tattooed eye of Ebenor stared hopelessly at the sky. "Fairly certain? That's it?"

Nix looked over at the eunuch, back at Egil. "That's it."

Jyme shook his head and paced a tight circle. "After all we've been through, now you're talking about changing into birds? You are mad. Don't you remember the last wand you used?"

"I remember," Egil said darkly.

"That was a mistake," Nix said. "I missed something. This won't be."

"I can tell you I'm not doing this," Jyme said. "If you two do this, you do it alone. Think me a coward if you want."

Nix never took his eyes from Egil's blood-spattered face. He forced a grin.

"Come on, Egil. Fun's in finding out, right? This is a moment, right?"

Egil sighed, shook his head, obviously torn. He stared at the wand as if daring it to do something other than what Nix claimed.

"Look," Nix said. "We both know what's going to happen to Rusilla and Merelda. Isn't it you who talks about alms and grace?"

"That's not why I hesitate," Egil said.

"Then what is it?"

Egil shook his head. "Never mind. We do it."

Jyme stomped his foot in the sand. "That's just a stick you found in a tomb! Gods, you're fools! What if it… does something awful?"

"When it comes to Nix and his gewgaws, I find it best to anticipate something awful," Egil said. "Then, if it doesn't, I'm pleasantly surprised."

Nix gave him a half-hearted obscene gesture.

"Come on," Jyme said. He looked at the eunuch, at Baras's body, back at Egil and Nix. "Get your heads on right. We find the nearest city, spend whatever gold you took out of that tomb on drinks and women, and forget any of this happened."

"There's no forgetting," Egil said somberly.

"Truth," Nix agreed. The story of House Norristru had been graven into his brain, etched there by horror.

"No, I guess there's not," Jyme said. "Even so, I don't understand you two."

"You're not the first to say that," Nix said. He waved the wand at Jyme. "Last chance, slubber."

For a moment, Nix thought Jyme might reconsider. He stared at the wand a long moment, then said, "I can't."

"Well enough," Nix said. "No shame in it, Jyme. We are who we are."

"How will you get back to Dur Follin alone?" Egil asked him.

Jyme shook his head. He looked around as if he were lost and seeking direction.

"I'm not sure I'll go back. But if I decide to, I'll manage. Find a ship or something. But I ain't riding the magic of some ancient wizard-king."

"Ah, you're no fun," Nix said.

"And it's a wizard-queen, as it turns out," Egil said.

"You two make my head swim," Jyme said.

"Not so difficult a task," Nix said. "Now, we need to get moving."

Jyme seemed to have something to say, so Nix gave him a moment. Finally, the hiresword spit it out.

"Listen, I plan to collect payback on that coin you lifted from me, yeah? If I get back to Dur Follin and the two of you ain't there, well, I'll have to come looking for you."

Nix was almost touched. "I think he loves you, Egil."

"You, maybe," Egil answered.

"Whoresons," Jyme muttered.

Nix smiled sincerely and shook Jyme's hand. "We'll see each other again, Jyme. I haven't lived like a hero, so I have no intention of dying like one. And when we meet again, I'll pay you that coin with interest. Drinks on me, yeah?"

"You have no notion of how rare an offer *that* is," Egil said. "Both on the interest and the drinks." The priest shook Jyme's hand, too. "Apologies again for the jaw and the insults. You're all right, Jyme."

"Done is done," Jyme said, and waved off the apology. "I hope I see both you slubbers soon."

And with that, they parted. While Jyme scavenged supplies and tethered the horses together, Nix and Egil recovered their weapons and hurried toward the shoreline. As they ran, Nix took out his sling, and let it hang loose at his side.

"There's some sense in Jyme's words," Egil said. "I have an ill feeling about this."

"Me, too," Nix admitted. "But you saw what I saw. No one should have to endure that. I couldn't live with myself if I just let it happen."

"Agreed," Egil said. "I wonder though..."

Nix waited, eyebrows raised. Egil continued:

"I'm beginning to wonder how much of what we've been doing since the beginning has been our own thinking, and how much hers."

"Rusilla?"

Egil nodded. "She's been planning from the outset. All of this could be her plan."

"If so, she gets drinks on me and that's sure. And she's no one I'd ever play in chess and expect to win."

"I'm serious."

"I know, but not now, yeah?"

Egil didn't let it go. "She said, 'Be that kind of man,' and here we are, doing just so."

Nix considered that. "But Jyme's not. He heard and saw the same things."

Egil grunted. "A fair point."

"We *are* those kind of men, Egil. But, uh, let's just not tell anybody."

"Aye."

They crested the rise. The surf lapped the shore, the sunset splashing the sea in color. Rocks stuck out of the shallow water here and there. Sea birds stood on one leg on the rocks, raced the incoming surf along the shore, and picked at mollusks in the pools.

Nix took a lead bullet from a pouch on his belt and, with it, loaded the sling. He swung the leather strap loosely as he picked his target.

"Could've used a crossbow and fowling quarrel from the supplies," Egil said.

"Could've," Nix acknowledged, and picked his target. "But I've been shooting rocks at birds since I was a boy."

He wheeled the sling over his head and the humming sound it made caused the nearby birds to take wing. He picked one, thought of his days scrounging the Heap, and let fly. Feathers flew and a black-winged gull spiraled to the shore. It hit the shallow water, fluttered. The surf washed it toward the beach.

Egil and Nix sprinted toward it, the priest easily outrunning Nix. Egil waded into the ankle-deep water and took the still-struggling bird in his huge hands.

"Still alive!" he called, and waded out of the surf.

The priest cupped the bird in his hands and the creature went still. Nix met Egil at the shore, the teak wand in hand.

"So, what? You touch the wand to the bird and…?"

"And it shapes the magic of the transmutation. Then I use it to change us."

Egil stared down at the bird. "I don't understand how magic works."

"In truth, neither do I," Nix admitted, and pronounced a word in the Mages' Tongue before Egil could object. He felt the wand warm in his hand and touched it to the bird. The gold cap on the end of the wand shimmered, the magic powered and shaped. He and Egil shared a glance, the priest released the bird and held out his hand, palm up. Nix touched the wand to him, then did the same to himself.

"Feels odd," Egil said, his speech slurred and indistinct.

Nix watched with horror and wonder as the priest's facial features ran like melted wax, his body, clothing, and weapons dripping in lazy runnels until the core of him collapsed in a viscous heap at Nix's feet.

"Egil," Nix tried to say, but the word came out garbled. His body tingled, then burned. He held his hand before his face and looked with horror on the streams of flesh falling from his fingers. His vision went blurry as his body began to collapse, pooling in a mass on the shore. The burning continued somehow, and even in shapelessness he seemed destined to retain thought and feeling. He perceived a flash, or a popping, and tried to scream but all that emerged was a caw.

A caw.

He stood a few hand spans in height. The water temperature registered only distantly through the skin of his thin legs. His feet, however, felt almost every grain of sand and pebble under them. He twisted his head nearly all the way around to view his body – sleek, feathered, *winged*. He let out an exultant squawk.

He looked at Egil, who had also transformed into a gull. Together, the two squawked, called, and cawed at one another for a few moments of collective, uncommunicative idiocy before leaving off.

Trying to familiarize himself with the new form, Nix extended his wings and walked a few steps along the beach. When he felt comfortable, he beat his wings and jumped into the air. The bird form seemed to know what to do, or perhaps the transmutational magic conveyed some facility to use the new form, but Nix cried with delight as the ground fell away beneath him. He swooped and dove, reveling in the feel of the air under his wings, the wind in his face.

Looking to his right, he saw Egil – or the bird he assumed to be Egil – doing exactly the same. Nix flew to Egil's side, called sharply, and wheeled westward.

Take me back to the prison, Rakon had commanded the sylph. *Back* to the prison.

Nix knew where they were going, where they had to be going. He should've seen it the first time. Rakon had been looking for looking for Abrak-Thyss's prison in the sea of glass. He needed the Horn of Alyyk to open it and free the devil.

And then the devil would violate Rusilla and Merelda.

They soared upward on a warm column of air, and the rolling, tan ocean of Afirion's sands stretched out below. Behind them, many leagues in the distance, his sharp eyes saw a shoreside town, two dozen wood and stacked stone buildings, a few small boats. Jyme would make his way there. Nix hoped he saw the hiresword again someday.

Ahead, the brown outcroppings of the Demon Wastes extended into the desert sands like stone fingers. The outcroppings gave way to the tumble of hills that marked the true border of the Wastes. They flew high over hills, the wind in their faces and under their wings, joyous in flight despite the somber nature of their task.

As soon as they crossed over the hills, the acridity in the air over the Wastes put a scratch in the back of Nix's throat. Waves of heat rose from the surface, as if the world were feverish. The thermals made it easy to soar at speed. He glanced down and the jumbled, ruined terrain reminded him of the skin of a pox patient soon to die – dry, discolored, lined with jagged cracks and bulbous pustules. He tried not to think too much about it.

Using the setting sun as his guide, they flew west until Nix saw below them the enspelled road they'd followed. It stretched through the scarred terrain in a clean, straight line. Height provided perspective and in the distance Nix saw the other roads that joined it, the angles at which they met, the arcs the outer lines described. At first he did not believe what he saw. But it made sense. Four roads had come together at the cardinal points at the sea of glass.

He angled higher to get a better view, scanned the terrain with his sharp eyes, and it only confirmed his initial thought. He cursed in amazement but it came out only as a squawk.

The roads formed a shape, a shape he knew. He could not see the entirety of it, of course, but he could see leagues of it, and it was enough. The implication was clear. The roads were not roads at all. They were the lines of a binding cross, a circle divided into quadrants by perpendicular lines, a tool used to summon, contain, and constrain horrors.

He squawked and cawed at Egil but the priest just made a confused squawk in response. Egil couldn't see it. Nix could see it, but he could hardly believe it.

Almost the entirety of the Demon Wastes was circumscribed by a magic circle, an arcane symbol carved into the face of the world, a circle that delimited an area leagues in diameter.

He tried to imagine the time and power it would have taken to scribe such a symbol, but could not wrap his thoughts around it. He struggled in vain to come up with a compelling reason to scribe it in the first place.

His mind worried at the problem. Was it connected to Rakon's plan somehow? Could the circle be designed to contain the Vwynn? Or perhaps to hold some other horrors that slept under the broken land?

Had the civilization that once ruled the lands have inadvertently awakened something under the earth, scribing the circle as a way to hold it, perhaps while they fled the region? Or had the civilization been trying to *draw* something toward Ellerth? Perhaps to use as a weapon?

He looked skyward, in his mind's eye seeing magical energy reaching up from the circle and into the vault of night, into neighboring planes and dimensions, drawing and pulling creatures and magical esoterica from all over the vault of night. He imagined flaming objects shrieking toward Ellerth, drawn by the power of the symbol carved into the face of the world. He imagined balls of stone and metal and flesh and scales slamming into the surface, leaving the once-fertile plain a ruined waste inhabited by degenerate devils. He imagined slits in reality forming in the air, saw spirits and demons and devils slipping through, summoned by the symbol.

He thought the idea fanciful, but then... he'd seen much. Anything was possible.

He pushed it from his mind and gave it no more thought. He didn't need to know the purposes of the people who'd once ruled here. He knew Rakon's purpose, and that was purpose enough.

They flew on in dour silence, chasing the sun, chasing

the sisters, heading to the center of the binding cross, to the glass sea, where sat the prison of Abrak-Thyss.

Nix stayed as high as he was able, hoping thereby to avoid the swarms of fiendish, bat-like creatures that patrolled the night skies of the Wastes.

They eyed the air ahead, looking for the sylph and its cargo, their speed westward stretching the day's length. Frustratingly, they saw nothing. After a couple hours in the air, Nix felt his body tingle. He knew what it meant. He tried to curse, but the beak allowed only an angry squawk. He angled downward for the earth. The tingling increased and his body started to shift back, the magic unable to maintain such a foreign form for long. Egil followed him down and they alit on the rockscape of the Wastes as their bodies painfully reverted back to their normal form.

"Shite!" Nix shouted.

Egil held out his arms, checking his form, his gear. "What? Change us back. You still have the wand."

"I need to touch the thing into which I change us, Egil. You see any gulls about?"

"Shite," Egil said. He started to say something else but Nix held up his hand.

"Don't! Don't!"

"Damned gewgaws," Egil said with a grin.

"Fak you."

"I jest because this problem is easily solved," Egil said. "We find a flock of those winged things we encountered before. Touch one of those. Change, and continue the pursuit."

"You call that easy? A flock of those nearly killed us all."

"Aye," Egil said. "You have a better idea?"

"No. Let's go find some. Wait..."

"Wait what?"

Nix checked his body, saw that the cut in his stomach was healed, most of his burns. "My wounds seem healed. Reconstituting after the transmutation must help the body heal."

"I take back what I said about your gewgaws," Egil said.

With that, they readied weapons and stalked off. The sun stared at them, red and orange, just hanging on over the horizon. The both knew that nightfall would bring the Thin Veil, and the Thin Veil promised horror.

"The roads here aren't roads," Nix said to Egil, making conversation to distract himself. "They're the lines of a binding cross. I could see it from the air."

Egil stared at him. "So what does that mean?"

Nix made a helpless gesture. "I don't know."

"Bah. Then stop worrying about it. It's ancient. Whatever happened here happened long ago. Ponder it when we next sit at the Altar of Gadd in the *Slick Tunnel*, yeah?"

Nix nodded slowly, letting go of the problem. He appreciated his friend's pragmatism.

"Aye. Let's find a hole and get airborne."

CHAPTER EIGHTEEN

They kept their eyes open for Vwynn, but saw none, saw nothing but the cursed red earth of the Wastes. After about a half-hour, they located a likely hole in the ground. The soft mound around the lip of the hole, bones and bonemeal, was spongy under their boots. Warm air emanated from the aperture, carrying with it a fetid, organic stink. Nix could hear distant rustling, a faint squeaking.

They looked west, where the sun was about to fade under the horizon. Nix held the wand in one hand, his hand axe in the other. Egil had shed his cloak and held it in one hand. The priest looked to Nix.

"We grab the first one we can, before the whole swarm gets clear," Nix said. "We change and we get the Hells clear."

"Aye, that," Egil said. "Try not to get carried off this time."

"I'll do what I can."

The priest cupped a hand to his mouth and shouted down the hole. Squeaks and intense rustling sounded from deeper down in the hole. Nix had the eerie sensation of the entire earth shifting below his feet.

"Ready, now," Nix said, tensing.

They could hear the creatures moving, shrieking, but none emerged from the hole. Egil, holding his cloak at the ready, looked over at Nix with raised eyebrows. Nix shrugged, leaned over the hole. Lots of movement somewhere below, but nothing coming up.

Suddenly the swarm burst from the earth ten paces to their left, a dark cloud of flapping wings, scales, and fanged mouths. A cacophony of their angry shrieks polluted the air. The cloud of the flock turned and wheeled toward them.

"Shite!" Nix said. "There, Egil!"

With nothing else for it, Egil and Nix ran straight toward them. Immediately Nix was swimming in an ocean of wings, shrieks, claws, and teeth. The creatures ripped clothing and flesh, tearing holes in Nix's skin, drawing blood. Nix flailed frenetically at the creatures, threw one to the ground, stomped it, struck another from before his eyes, took another by the throat and held it before him. He drew the wand and spoke a word in the Mages' Tongue. The wand warmed, the golden tip glowed, and he moved to touch the creature he held, but another of the creatures, perhaps drawn by the light, snatched the wand from his hand.

"The wand!" Nix screamed, lunging after the creature. But the weight of the creatures that clung to him proved too much and his leap turned into a stumbling fall. He crushed a few rolling on the rock, but dozens more took their place and tore at any exposed skin. He rose to all fours, trying to spot the one that had taken the wand.

Egil, covered in the creatures and bleeding all over, dove after the winged fiend bearing the wand, his cloak spread wide like a scoop. The priest enveloped the creature, hit the ground in a roll, his body crushing half a dozen of the creatures, and rose, soaked in his blood and theirs. His cloak, looped into a bag, bounced about from the movement of the creature's he'd caught.

"Here, Nix!"

Scores of the creatures swarmed them. Nix climbed to all fours, the creatures tearing at his flesh. He could barely see, so thickly they flew before his face. He stood, flailed through a fog of them.

"Keep talking!"

"Here, over here, here," Egil said.

Nix grunted against the pain, killed the creatures where he could, and kept moving. He took care only to protect his eyes. Egil met him halfway and Nix stuck his hand into the priest's makeshift bag. He felt the wand and pulled it free, taking a bite on the hand from one of the captive creatures. He touched the wand's end to one of them and, without hesitating, touched the glowing end first to Egil then to himself. When his skin started to tingle, the magic taking hold, the swarm of creatures shrieked and fled off, perhaps sensing the unfolding magic.

Bleeding, gasping, the two of them stared at one another as their human forms sloughed away and they transformed into creatures small, scaled, and winged.

Nix's vision was not normal, nor sharp-eyed like the gull's form, but was instead a field of reds, oranges, yellows, blues, and blacks, and it took him a moment to realize that he was "seeing" temperature differences. He adjusted to the new sense as best he could, shrieked at Egil, and took wing to the west. He hoped the magic would last long enough to get them to the sea of glass.

Of course, he wasn't sure what they'd do if they caught up with the sylph. They'd be stuck in the form of the scaled, winged creatures. Nix supposed he could annoy them to death with his shriek.

Anticipating Egil's commentary, he rebuked himself.

Damned gewgaws, he thought.

The sylph bore Rakon and his sisters west, back over the cracked earth of the Wastes, knifing through the sky at speed. Rakon stood in the center of the sylph's swirl, supported by an invisible pillow of air.

Winds howled and gusted all around him, the sylph ecstatic in its joyous, rapid flight. Rakon, too, was exultant. He held the Horn of Alyyk in his hands. Made by Abn Thuset, a note blown from the horn was said to break the strongest of binding wards.

Perhaps Abn Thuset had intended to use it on the great ward of the Wastes, as a way to unleash the Vwynn on Afirion enemies. Perhaps the wizard-king had used it to free the creatures bound in the Wastes from time to time.

In the end, Rakon didn't know and didn't care. He only knew that, if the secret histories he'd read were correct, he could use the horn to free Abrak-Thyss and save his house.

Pressure built in his mind as they neared the center of the Wastes – his sisters' growing fear laying siege to his mental defenses. The drugs he'd given them must have been wearing off. Rusilla and Merelda had proven enormously resistant to his alchemy. Their terror gnawed at the edges of his mind, haunting his consciousness.

They floated beside him, arms and legs limp, their hair and dresses spread out gently on the invisible bed of the sylph's winds. They looked like spirits, archons descending from the Three Heavens.

He regretted the sufferings his sisters must endure, but he knew they would accept them in time, as his mother had. He'd enter into a false marriage with the more fertile of the two, and soon the Norristru line would be renewed, and his position, and that of his house, would be secure for another generation.

The sylph gusted over the Wastes, covering miles in moments. The setting sun reddened the sky to the west. Minnear would rise full soon after sunset. The Veil between worlds would thin to a wafer.

Ruins dotted the landscape below him, the gravestones of the dead civilization that no histories named. Ahead he saw the ring of ruins encircling the sea of glass. It glistened red in the setting sun, an ocean of blood.

Vwynn coated the ring of ruins like flies on a corpse, thousands of them, lurking in what shade they could find among the jagged bones of stone. They must have crept forward to occupy the ruins after the caravan had left. And yet none dared touch the glass. Yet.

They looked up, eyes glittering, and let out a collective snarl as the sylph descended onto the sea of glass. The winds of the sylph faded and Rakon put his feet down on the smooth surface. He felt the pressure of the Vwynn's regard like a physical thing. It was all around him, thick in the air, their anger a weight on his person.

The fear projected by his sisters grew to panic, infected him, sped his heart. The Vwynn, too, seemed to feel it. It, too, was thick in the air. Motion in the dark places in which they sheltered spoke of their agitation: growls, snarls, the scrabble of claw on stone.

"We'll need to leave immediately after freeing Abrak-Thyss," Rakon said to the sylph.

The wind whispered the sylph's agreement.

Rusilla's voice sounded in his head, penetrating his defense, a desperate plea from far off. *Don't... Rakon.*

He turned to look down on Rusilla. Tears leaked from the corners of her wide eyes. Her forefinger lifted, as if she were trying to point at him accusingly.

He kneeled, took her hand in his. "I must. You'll forgive me in time."

She replied with nothing but fear.

"You tried to use those tomb robbers to help you. Did you think I didn't know? They're dead now,

Rusilla, killed by the eater. No one can help you now."

The tears flowed unchecked down his sister's face. Again the raised finger.

He stood, his expression hard. "You lost this chess match, sister. And now you'll do what you were born to do. Both of you."

He took the Horn of Alyyk in his hands and turned away from his sisters. The magic in the horn caused his hands to tingle. He walked toward the location on the glass where his spells had located the prison, his tread loud on the glass.

The Vwynn fell silent. The winds died completely, even the sylph overwhelmed by the moment.

As he walked, Rakon intoned a phrase of awakening in the Language of Creation. In answer, the horn vibrated in his hands.

The Vwynn moaned.

Rakon put the horn to his lips, aimed its bell at the glass surface before him, and blew. Shimmering air poured from the horn in a swirling column, the recoil pushing him back a step. The long, low note emitted into the charged air made his teeth ache. The vibratory energy struck the glass, cracked it, shattered it, and put a furrow in it deep enough for a burial. The impact threw millions of tiny glass shards into the air and they fell in a tinkling, musical rain. Scores fell on Rakon, cutting his hands, his face, his scalp. He cursed, shielded himself as best he could with his cloak.

"Sylph!" Rakon called.

"Yes, master," the sylph said, surmising his command.

The wind swirled around Rakon, formed into dozens of vortices that collected the shards and expelled them away from Rakon.

Rakon ignored the pain of his flesh wounds, ignored the warm blood dripping down his face, braced himself against the recoil, and blew another note. The magic of the horn deepened the gash in the glass. The air around him filled with more shards, filled with his sisters' fear, with the pensive terror and anger of the Vwynn. The sylph protected him from the rain of glass and he blew another note, another, digging deeper into the strata of the dead civilization, putting a deep scar on Ellerth's face. Another note, another shower of shards, and he saw what he sought, what his researches had told him he would find.

A metal cylinder lay revealed at the bottom of the gash. Engraved glyphs covered it entirely, the straight lines of the characters a script Rakon did not recognize. Staring at the characters made his head ache.

Movement in the hills around him, all around him: the Vwynn edging closer. He had to hurry.

His sisters' terror grew incoherent, a cloud of fear polluting the air of the ruins.

He stared at the cylinder, the contents within it the hope of his house. He put the horn to his lips and blew another blast. The energy slammed into the cylinder, sparking, sizzling, a shower of magical pyrotechnics that left Rakon blinking in its wake. When the note subsided and the sparks died, the prison remained sealed, but many of the glyphs were effaced. The horn was warm in his hands. He blew another note, effacing more of the glyphs in a storm of energy, another, and when the echoes of the final blast were nothing more than echoes, the cylinder lay blank.

"Abrak-Thyss," Rakon shouted in Infernal, a dialect of the Language of Creation. "Come forth! Emerge and honor the ancient pact between your house and mine."

The Vwynn watched in pensive silence.

His sisters were reduced to animal terror.

For a long moment nothing happened, but then two dots appeared on the smooth surface of the cylinder. The dots moved, leaving lines in their wake, seams, cracks in an egg that would soon birth a devil. Rakon watched it unfold with terrified fascination.

A deep, bestial roar sounded from within the cylinder, the sound as pregnant with power as had been notes from the horn.

The Vwynn moaned, snarled.

Another growl from within the cylinder quieted them, awed them perhaps. A ferocious blow from within the cylinder buckled it outward. A roar, the pent-up rage of centuries, sounded from within.

The Vwynn snarled, their terror turning to anger, their anger to action. Two or three took a reluctant step forward, breaking the border of the glass.

Rakon's sisters' terror reached a climax, momentarily catching Rakon up in its flow, then diminished altogether. Perhaps they'd fainted.

Another blow widened the cracks in the cylinder.

The capsule rocked back and forth and frenetic snarls filled the air. The Vwynn echoed them.

"Emerge, Abrak-Thyss!" Rakon said.

A final, forceful blow exploded the cylinder outward. Dust and chunks of bent and broken metal flew into the air, crashed against the glass of the ground. A scaled, serpentine arm as thick as a man's leg emerged from the cylinder, gripped one of its edges. Instead of a hand, the arm ended in a fang-filled rictus. Two small black eyes above the mouth blinked in the light of the setting sun. A second hand joined it, a third, a fourth.

The bulk of Abrak-Thyss shifted within the prison that had held him for millennia. He roared, the sound like an avalanche, and heaved his thick, scaled trunk out of the confines of the cylinder.

Whatever spell or decadent beliefs had held the Vwynn at bay fell away the moment Abrak-Thyss emerged. A collective shriek, desperate and hate-filled, announced their advance. They poured wildly down from the ruins and onto the glass, coming from all sides, a savage horde of claws and teeth, loping wildly over the smooth surface, thousands strong. They tumbled and clambered over each other in their haste to reach the freed devil.

Abrak-Thyss answered their howls with a roar of his own. The fanged, lamprey-like arms attached at the broad shoulders stretched and writhed. The devil stood half-again as tall as a man, his muscular, scaled form as broad at the chest as two barrels. Where a head and neck should have been, there was instead a mouth lined with glistening yellow fangs as long as knives. Two more arms, also serpentine and fanged but somewhat smaller than the other two, jutted from the devil's abdomen just below the mouth. They flexed and twisted in sickening jerks, as if already shoveling Vwynn into the fang-lined maw.

"Sylph!" Rakon called.

The devil crouched, his great muscles churning beneath the deep green scales, and leaped out of the furrow the horn had put in the glass. He landed near Rakon, the force of his impact veining the glass with tiny cracks. He roared again, his outer arms whipping around, regarding Rakon, the advancing horde of Vwynn. The gaze of one of the arms stopped when it fixed on the prone forms of his sisters.

"Yes, Abrak-Thyss," Rakon said, sensing the devil's lust. "They are yours, offered in honor of the pact between House Thyss and House Norristru. Your blood requires you to honor that pact."

The devil growled low in answer. Ichor dripped from the lamprey mouths at the end of his arms. One set of eyes darted around, following the movement of the Vwynn as they stormed across the glass. The other set stayed fixed on Rusilla and Merelda.

"Sylph!" Rakon called again.

The winds swirled around man and devil and sisters. The sylph's high-pitched voice rang out of the gusts.

"Master?"

"Remove us from here, and take us back to the manse."

"Yes, master."

The devil whirled on Rakon, the eyes of both arms glaring at him. When he spoke from his central mouth, his voice sounded like the coarse grinding of boulders.

"No. Stay. Kill. Feed."

Rakon held his ground in the shadow of the devil. "No, Abrak-Thyss. I freed you and you must honor the pact sworn by your house." He gestured at the setting sun. "And you must do it tonight, when Minnear is full in the vault. Feed as you will after honoring that obligation."

The devil's arms squirmed in agitation, muscles and scales rippling. The beady eyes looked at the Vwynn, at Rakon's sisters, at Rakon.

"Master?" prompted the sylph.

The seething horde of Vwynn was closer, tumbling toward them, their claws slipping and scrabbling on the glass surface of the crater.

"Those who rule your house will be as unhappy as I should the Pact fail, devil." The mouth in Abrak-Thyss's chest opened wide in a frustrated roar, but the huge shoulders slumped in surrender.

"Do your duty tonight and help me repopulate my house. Then return to Hell, take a mate, and repopulate your own. The Pact will be honored for generations to come."

Rakon took the devil's silence for agreement. "Now, sylph," he said.

The winds picked up, spinning shards of glass, bits

of metal from the capsule, and dust into the air. Rakon, the devil, and his sisters rose up, lifted by the invisible, gusting grip of the air spirit.

As they rose, the Vwynn shrieked and howled in frustration. Abrak-Thyss answered with a frustrated roar of his own. The Vwynn kept coming, bounding over each other, slavering, all teeth and fangs. The sylph struggled to gain altitude, the weight of the devil perhaps challenging even the air spirit's abilities.

"Higher, sylph!" Rakon shouted.

The Vwynn massed below them, leaped up on their powerful legs, their claws slashing the air, teeth snapping in rage. Abrak-Thyss growled, lashed downward with one of his arms and plucked one of the leaping creatures from the air.

The creature wailed, writhed in the devil's grasp, slashed in a maddened frenzy with its claws at the serpentine arm, all to no avail. The devil's arm constricted the creature, shattering bones, and transferred the still-living Vwynn to his other set of arms, which shoveled the Vwynn toward the central mouth in his chest. A single bite cut the creature in half, spraying blood into the sylph's swirling winds. The devil dropped the gory lower half of the Vwynn back into the mass of the Vwynn shrieking below, his great body shaking with mirth while he devoured the upper half.

They flew west, the immense, shifting but always winged form of the sylph outlined in crimson by the blood droplets of the Vwynn.

• • • •

Nix adjusted to the new form quickly. As a gull he flew with graceful, rapid beats of his wings. As a devil, he flew with long, ungainly strokes. He could scarcely see – the dying light of day pained his eyes and made him blink, and everything mostly an indistinct blur of red and orange and yellow – though his sense of smell was keen. The air above the Wastes, redolent with the scent of sulfur and ages long gone, acrid from alkalis, filled the slits of his nostrils. Ahead, he saw the ring of ruins. Vwynn thronged the glass sea, thousands of them, howling in maddened rage. A deep furrow gashed what had been the smooth surface and within it lay the metal fragments of some kind of lozenge-shaped capsule. Empty now, it had blown open from the inside. They circled the area, looking for any sign of Rakon, the sylph, or what Nix assumed to be the freed devil, but saw nothing.

He shrieked in rage.

They were too late. Too godsdamned late.

And he had no idea how much longer the transmutational magic would last.

He plumbed the mnemonic fragments stuck in his mind by Rusilla, searching them for the location of the Norristru manse. It was the only place Rakon could go.

He found it right away, both its location and appearance, half a league to the west of Dur Follin, a series of squat, interconnected towers perched like an unlanced boil on the edge of a steep escarpment called the Shelf.

He shrieked at Egil, beat his wings, and arrowed west, as fast as their new forms allowed. Before long they could no longer outrun the sunset, and the day cast a final, coruscating blaze of red and orange across the sky before fading to night.

At once Nix's vision improved. The landscape below him was blue and black, the occasional holes that led down to the Vwynn's particular Hell glowed orange. Otherwise the Wastes were little more than a void, a lesion on the face of Ellerth. They flew on, their small bodies exhausted.

In time he tasted pepper and felt a familiar ache behind his eyes. It intensified as they flew, finally coalesced into haunting, terrified screams, a woman's screams. He heard them as though at a great distance, and at first he thought them the aftereffect of the storm of memories that had exploded out of the memory eater, but soon realized they weren't memories at all. They were too sharp, too acute, as jagged as the Wastes below. They were Rusilla's or Merelda's, invisible currents of terror that lodged in his mind and scarred his psyche, a trail of fear floating in her wake like psychic breadcrumbs.

He glanced over at Egil, his friend's scaled form knifing through the air, the membranous wings billowing like sails with each beat. The priest's slit, reptilian eyes were somehow still Egil's, and somehow still communicated the priest's pain.

Egil shrieked and Nix echoed it, their own cries sorry echoes of Rusilla and Merelda's. For the moment they could do nothing but endure, follow the fear, and use it to fire their need to catch Rakon and stop him. He pressed on.

Minnear rose, crawling into the sky until the pockmarked disc of its full face dominated the sky near the horizon.

The Thin Veil.

They had little time, but they'd already almost cleared the Wastes.

Ahead and to his left the blue-black of the jagged, broken Wastes gave way to a smooth sea of reds and oranges – the warm, stinking miasmic stretch of the Deadmire. They were close to Dur Follin. Soon he saw dots of red sprinkled on the horizon, the mage lights and watch fires of the city. He shrieked again and Egil answered in kind. To his right, the blue-black serpentine line of the Meander wound across the terrain, vanishing temporarily into the dark blot of the city, only to reappear on the other side to feed the Deadmire, its cool blue consumed by the steamy, organic heat of the swamp's red.

Following the invisible road delimited by the terror of Rusilla and Merelda's mental emanations, they angled northwest. The city soon came into clearer focus, west and east, rich and poor, divided by the thick line of the river. Ool's clock dominated the skyline on the near side of the city, its sharp, smooth surfaces a dark blue in Nix's vision, and the waters of the clock's perpetual cascade – the water's motion which powered the clock's workings – a lighter azure. The arc and towers of the Archbridge soared into the sky.

Seeing the bridge, remembering the huge, smooth blocks they'd seen in the ruins of the Wastes, Nix felt certain the same hands had been at work on both. The bridge had to be left over from the civilization that had died in the Wastes, the sole intact monument to a people who'd been destroyed, or who'd destroyed themselves. Considered that way, the bridge seemed not so much awe-inspiring as melancholy.

They wheeled over the city, high above its cracked and crumbling walls. Street lamps lit the maze of streets here and there, populated by the red blobs of pedestrians and animals. He looked to the Warrens and would have smiled had he been able. The absence of street lamps did nothing to dampen the sea of red that thronged the streets and alleys. People, animals, life. The Heap's decaying organic matter glowed red, yellow, and orange, a mountain of brilliant color. For the first time, he thought the Warrens possessed its own kind of beauty, a warm, stubborn glow of red, orange, and yellow, a beauty that birthed people like Mamabird.

Be that kind of man.

He would.

He was, or so he hoped.

They winged over the Archbridge, with its dozens of shrines and hundreds of faithful, and to the western bank of the Meander. The bridge was the terminus for the ordered spokes of the roads that divided Western Dur Follin into the Temple, City, and Noble Districts. Large manses, expansive plazas, and parks dotted the streetscape. Far fewer people filled the streets.

From up high, Western Dur Follin struck Nix as a lovely museum, a kind of tomb, enjoyable to look at, but devoid of life, absence the beautiful reds and yellows of the east.

As a boy, he'd craved a life across the Meander, amongst the clean streets and manses. Hell, as a man he'd wanted it, which is why he'd suggested to Egil that they buy the *Slick Tunnel*.

But he didn't want it anymore. He wasn't *that* kind of man. He was the kind of man who lived in the filth, heat, and beautiful decay of Eastern Dur Follin. He swooped over and past the wealth.

He realized that Rusilla and Merelda's mental screams had gone quiet. They must have lost consciousness or given up.

Or worse.

The city disappeared behind them, giving way to a patchwork of tilled land and farmsteads, the terrain sloping ever upward as they moved away from the Meander.

Ahead, he saw the steep escarpment traders called the Shelf. More than a long bowshot tall at its highest point, the Shelf served Dur Follin's wealthy as a location for their country homes, away from the hubbub of Dur Follin, a high perch from which they could look down on the city. It stretched a full league, running roughly north to south, and only two passes cut their way through it – the Neck and Zelchir's Fall. Otherwise, it presented only a sheer face of cracked, water-stained limestone.

A tingling ran the length of Nix's body. He recognized it immediately and mentally cursed. The magic of the wand was expiring. He shrieked at Egil, who must have been experiencing the same feeling, and the two of them sped through the night air as fast as their leathery wings would bear them. They needed to at least reach the top of the Shelf. If not, they'd have to leg it to the Neck or Zelchir's Fall to get up the escarpment, and that would add hours. Nix angled upward to get a better view. He'd know the Norristru manse if he saw it: its image was graven in his brain by memories not his own.

And there it was. Below and ahead Nix saw the cold stone walls and four squat towers of the Norristru manse, perched on the edge of the escarpment, as if the entire building were hanging on to the stone to prevent a fall over the edge.

Nix shrieked and started to descend. The tingling he felt sharpened to needle pricks. He had only moments.

The manse was part of a large walled compound that covered acres of gardens, orchards, and outbuildings. Even from a distance Nix could see that the whole of it was ill tended: gardens overgrown, walls crumbling, statuary toppled. Even a portion of the manse's roof had been removed or fallen into ruin. One corner of the upper floor stood exposed to the elements, the roof beams like ribs, the whole overlooking the cliff, the distant lights of Dur Follin.

Motion drew his eye: blobs of red distinct against the cold blue-backs of the cliff face – Rakon, his sisters, the hulking form of the devil. They flew in a swirl of blue winds provided by the sylph.

Nix squawked softly to ensure Egil had also seen. The priest's gaze was locked on them. They beat their wings and closed, moving much faster than the sylph. Perhaps bearing the devil put a strain on even the air spirit.

The hulking form of the devil reminded Nix of his brother, Vik-Thyss, whom Egil and Nix had slain in the tomb of Abn Thahl, thereby triggering everything that came after.

Abrak-Thyss was wider than his sibling, taller, the huge mouth where his neck should be filled with misshapen teeth as long as knives. Like Vik-Thyss, Abrak-Thyss had thick, lamprey-like arms that ended in toothy sphincters, but unlike Vik-Thyss, Abrak-Thyss had four arms: two at the shoulder, and two sprouting out of his chest under his mouth.

In his serpentine stalks the devil clutched the limp, delicate forms of Rusilla and Merelda. They dangled in his grasp, heads and arms thrown back, Rusilla's hair floating free in the sylph's winds like a pool of blood.

Seeing them in the devil's arms recalled to Nix his dreams, the memories he'd inherited from the eater, and kindled his anger to rage. He darted downward as the needle pricks of pain in his body gave way to a burning sensation. Aches flashed in his body here and there. He felt his form loosen as the magic began to dissipate. He shrieked urgency at Egil, both of them tucking in their wings and diving like shot quarrels toward their quarry. Nix had no idea what he would do when he reached them.

The magic of the wand expired during their dive. Nix transformed in mid-air, shedding his scaled form, the magic carving him back into his normal form. Wings gained size, rolled up into arms; Legs lengthened, thickened. Then everything transmogrified at once and he groaned with the pain of being reborn into his own body.

His descent was instantly fouled. He was hurtling toward Rakon and the devil, his heart in his throat, his stomach churning. He flapped his arms as if they were still wings, but that only served to make him cartwheel and tumble helplessly through the air. His field of vision spun wildly, a swirling mix of the night sky, the green moon, the devil, the Norristru manse below. His stomach rushed up into his throat and he could not hold back a shout.

Rakon heard it, for he spun around, looked up and back, eyes wide, and saw Nix plummeting toward him. Nix thought the sorcerer shouted something at the sylph or the devil. The sylph tried to veer right but too late.

Egil and Nix plummeted into the sylph's form and the winds of the creature, like an undulating pillow, absorbed some of their speed, but not enough. They slammed into the devil and Rakon in a tangle of limbs and shouts and chaos.

Nix crashed hard into the devil's back, the impact knocking the air from his lungs, slamming his jaw forcefully on the creature's scaled back, and sending them both tumbling. The devil roared, his arms flailing.

Nix saw sparks, his vision blurred, faded to black, but he deliberately bit down hard on his tongue before he lost consciousness. Warm blood filled his mouth, but the sharpness of the pain brought back his senses.

The sylph keened, the alarmed sound in the wind all around them, and the air bearing them all swirled chaotically, as if the sylph had lost control of its own body. Nix separated from the devil, and the pillow of air below seemed to give way. He was falling, buffeted by ordinary winds, tumbling, shouting, the rapid spins of his descent ruining his perception.

Shouts sounded all around him, mixed with the alarmed high-pitched keening of the sylph. Emptiness all around him. A disorienting, heart-pounding fall. He thought he caught sight of Rusilla and Merelda floating free of the devil's grasp. Perhaps the devil had released them when Nix had crashed into the creature, but he couldn't be sure. At the moment, he couldn't sort up from down, could not fix on any one thing for longer than a heartbeat. Sky, devil, moon, the manse below. Sky, devil, moon, the ground rushing up to meet him.

He tensed in anticipation of impact but it did little to prepare him for it. His legs clipped the edge of the roof of the manse, flipping him head over heels as he fell the remaining distance to the hard floor of the unroofed, exposed room below. He landed on his back and the impact sent spikes of pain through his spine, chest, arms, and legs. Other loud thumps sounded near him, groans, the sound of wood cracking, the devil's snarl. Winds buffeted him, the agitated swirl of the sylph.

"You are safely arrived at the manse, master," the sylph said, its voice like the breeze. "My duty is performed and I go. Pray do not call me again for another decade."

The winds ebbed and all was silent. Nix tried to move his hands, his legs. They protested with pain but they moved. He hadn't heard anything break. The sylph must have slowed the fall enough to let him survive it, at least for the moment. He turned his head to the side and spit the blood he'd earned from biting his tongue.

If Nix had survived, then so had Rakon, and so had the devil.

CHAPTER NINETEEN

Nix had no time to evaluate himself more thoroughly. He lifted himself to all fours, to his knees, blinking, his vision swirling for a moment. He'd landed in the center of a summoning circle, the lead of its lines inlaid into the wood. The nonsense thought struck him that he'd been summoned out of the sky. He would've laughed aloud but his body hurt too much. There were other symbols carved or scribed or inlaid into the wood in other areas of the floor – an elemental circle, a thaumaturgic triangle, a binding diamond. They'd landed in a summoning chamber. Rakon's summoning chamber, which was open to the sky, to the vault of night, to Minnear, which shone full in the velvet of night.

A metal staircase stood in the center of the open room, supported by cracked scaffolds. The stairway – thirteen steps, Nix noted – ended in an elevated platform. There Abrak-Thyss lay, his huge body and serpentine arms flowing over the sides. Ichor dripped from the sphincters that ended his thick arms. The small eyes at the end of the arms were closed.

Nix shook his head to clear it, looked around. Rakon lay across the room, lifting himself off the floor with his hands, his face dazed, bloody, his skullcap askew, hair for the first time mussed. Egil was already on his feet, kneeling over Rusilla and Merelda, who lay near one another on the floor. The priest turned them over, put his ear to their mouth.

"Egil?" Nix called.

"They're alive," Egil answered, relief in his tone. "And untouched by the fiend, near as I can tell."

Rusilla groaned; her forefinger curled.

"And stirring!" Egil said. "Their eyes are open, Nix!"

"Get away from them!" Rakon said, his voice a hiss.

Egil rose slowly, turned to look at the sorcerer. His heavy brows darkened, vowing violence.

Nix, too, rose. He wobbled, swayed, but stayed upright.

"Kill them both, Abrak-Thyss," Rakon said. He coughed, spit blood. "Then honor the Pact."

"Your devil is dead, sorcerer," Nix said, and drew his falchion. "There'll be no rapes in this house tonight. Just an execution."

Rakon chuckled, the sound broken and wet.

Wood creaked and cracked above Nix. He looked up, saw the eyes at the end of the devil's arms open, staring at him with menace.

"Shite," he whispered.

Rakon laughed louder.

"Egil…" Nix said.

"I see it," the priest answered. He put hafts in his hands, fixed his eyes on the devil. "Just something else I need to kill, then."

Behind the priest, the lone door that led back into the house flew open and a bent crone in the faded garb of a noblewoman tumbled through. Her gray hair stuck out from her head in wild tufts. Her crazed eyes, one of them marred to a half-open droop by a scar, took in the devil, Rakon, Rusilla and Merelda, Egil and Nix.

"Rakon!" she shrieked.

"Back inside, Mother," the sorcerer snapped.

But she didn't go back inside. She charged Egil, her thin hands bent like claws, a snarl revealing rotted teeth. Egil caught her up in his grasp while she clawed bloody furrows into his face. He lifted her from her feet and set her down firmly on the ground near the door.

"Sit, grandma!" Egil said, and stuck the head of his hammer in her face. "Do *not* move."

She snarled at him, hissed like a serpent, but stayed put as if planted there.

Above Nix, the wood platform at the top of the infernally numbered stairs cracked as the devil shifted his bulk, twisted and stood. His arms flailed, muscles rippled under the scaled form, and the mouth in his chest opened in a roar of triumph.

Nix backed off, treading on arcana, and the devil coiled himself and leaped from the top of the platform. His huge misshapen form landed with a thud that shook the floor.

Dry, reptilian stink filled Nix's nostrils. One of the devil's larger arms snaked sidewise to eye Egil, who stood over Rusilla and Merelda. The other jutted forward and eyed Nix, the mouth open and dripping ichor. The two smaller arms flexed and bent near the devil's mouth, a reflexive motion like those of an insect's mandibles.

Nix eyed the partially engorged member dangling between the trunks of the creature's legs.

"Been a while for you, yeah? Gonna be a bit of a wait yet, fakker."

The devil tensed and roared, his exhalation the stink of a charnel house. The eyes in both arms fixed on Nix and it charged, his tread shaking the floor.

While backpedaling, Nix drew and threw his throwing daggers at the brute's torso, but the creature's hide turned them as well as plate armor. Nix pulled his hand axe as the creature lurched toward him. An arm lashed at him, toothy maw snapping, but he ducked under it, hacked at the arm with his axe. The axe's edge rang off the devil's hide, sending a shock up Nix's arm. He lunged forward and stabbed with his falchion but it, too, bounced off the creature's hide. He lurched backward as the devil tried to stomp him with one of the tree trunks of his legs. The impact vibrated the floor, caused Nix to stumble. The devil lumbered after him, his huge bulk pushing him back toward the edge of the room, which overlooked a fall down the escarpment.

Egil roared and charged from the side, hammers held high. The devil whirled to face him, so Nix planted his feet and hurled his axe at the creature's mouth but missed. He cursed and took his falchion in both hands for better leverage.

Egil sidestepped a crushing blow of one of the devil's arms, spun, and smashed both hammers down simultaneously on the appendage. Scales gave way with a wet crunch and the devil shrieked with pain. His wounded arm spasmed with agony. Egil whirled to parry a blow from the other arm but too slow. The thick serpent of the creature's arm hit Egil squarely in the chest and sent him flying backward across the room. He landed on his back near Rusilla and Merelda.

"Shite," Nix said, and a backhand lash from the devil's arm snatched at him, caught him by the wrist, and jerked him toward the creature's chest maw. Panicked, Nix twisted and pulled, nearly dislocating his shoulder, but finally pulling himself free. The fanged mouth from the other arm lunged for him. He dodged it but the move sent him careening backward off balance. The devil plodded after him, an arm swinging crosswise for his head. Nix managed an overhand, two-handed strike with his falchion, chopped with all his strength. He grinned when he felt the blade bite into flesh. Black blood spurted from the squirming arm. The devil howled in rage, withdrew the arm, but advanced on him, his bulk inexorably driving him backward, his arms a nest of toothy snakes, snapping and biting.

Nix retreated, waving his blade defensively, as a sphincter of teeth snapped closed a finger's width from his nose. He grabbed a dagger from his belt and flicked it underhand at the devil, but the creature's scales turned its point. He was running out of both options and room to maneuver.

"Egil!" he shouted. "Get up!"

Nix stumbled back from a swing of the devil's arm, but was too off balance to dodge the backswing. It hit him squarely in the back, drove the air from his lungs, and sent him careening into a wall, abrading his face. He ducked as one of the fanged sphincters lunged at his face and instead took a bite of the wall, removing a divot of plaster and wood. Nix spun into a crosscut, hoping to disembowel the devil, but his boots clung to the floor, slowing his movement. The devil lurched backward, arms waving menacingly.

Nix cursed. He must have stepped in something sticky. He tried to maneuver, found his feet even more fixed to the floor.

"What in the Pits!"

He tried to dodge a swing of the devil's arm, but his stride, clutched by the floor, slowed him and the blow caught him in the abdomen, doubled him over, and sent him flying across the floor.

Coughing, gasping, he clambered to his feet. His boots stuck to the floor again, more strongly this time. He put his weight on one foot to lift the other and the first sank ankle deep into the floor. He cursed, tried to pull his boot free but no use. He might as well have been standing in hardening quicklime.

"Egil!"

The devil roared as it turned to face him. Nix looked over to see Rakon lying on his belly, one hand caressing the floor, the other cupping his mouth, as if he were uttering secrets to the wood, and Nix supposed he was.

"Egil!" Nix said. "I'm stuck! The sorcerer! Egil!"

The priest sat up, his eyes bleary. He took in the situation at a glance.

The devil lumbered for Nix, hissing, great mouth snapping, his arms a swarm of toothy snakes. The enspelled wood held Nix fast, his boots sunk into the floor almost to the ankle.

"Egil!"

Nix took his falchion in two hands, readied himself.

The priest hurled his hammers in rapid succession. One flew for Rakon with fearsome velocity, flipping head over haft, and slammed into the sorcerer's unprotected side. Whatever whispers Rakon had been making to the floor ended with broken ribs and a howl of pain. He curled up, gasping, coughing blood.

The priest's second hammer hummed as it flew at Abrak-Thyss, striking the devil in the chest, in his open mouth, turning his roar into a shriek of pain as the weapon shattered a tooth. The enraged, pained devil bit the haft in two and spit head and handle to the floor, but the blow had done its work, halting the creature's charge at Nix.

Nix pulled at his boots with his hands but even with Rakon disabled he could not get them free. His stream of expletives would have shamed a crew of seamen.

Egil pulled his crowbar and held it in both hands, eyeing the devil.

"This worked well on your sibling, darkspawn. Let's take its measure on you."

The devil charged Egil and the priest answered in kind.

Unable to dislodge his boots from the melted stone, Nix slit his boot laces with the dagger he kept in his boot and pulled his bare feet free. He looked up in time to see one of the devil's serpentine arms catch Egil on the run and send him spinning and cursing to the ground. Another arm darted in, serpentlike, the fanged mouth at its end biting for Egil's face, but the priest caught the arm in the vise of his grip and stopped it a few fingers' width from his face. The mouth snapped open and closed, dripping spit in its hungry lust for flesh.

Teeth gritted, arm shaking, Egil used his free hand to slam the claw end of his crowbar into the creature's arm. The crowbar bit deep into the devil's hide, drawing a spurt of blood and a squeal of pain. The devil reflexively pulled back his arm, and the sudden motion jerked Egil, off balance and staggering, toward the creature.

Seizing the opportunity, one of the smaller mandible arms caught Egil about the waist and lifted him bodily toward the fang-lined, cavernous mouth in the creature's chest. The priest squirmed in the devil's grasp, legs kicking, curses flying, as the devil drew him toward a mouth that could bite him in half.

Nix charged barefoot across the roof, falchion held in a two-handed grip, shouting oaths.

Egil's roar answered the devil's hungry growl and when he was close enough, Egil slammed the crowbar he still clutched into the devil's teeth. The blow shattered another tooth and fragments of it flew in all directions. The devil shrieked with agony, spasmed with pain, and reflexively hurled Egil across the rooftop. The priest hit the wall near the door, near the old woman, and sagged to the ground once more.

The devil whirled to face Nix, arms coiled for a strike, but Nix did not slow. He parried a swing of the devil's arm, rode the momentum of the parry into a spin, leaped over a swing from the other arm, and slashed downward at the creature's shoulder. His blade rang off the scales, and he bounded backward. A fanged mouth snapped at his ear. He ducked as the mouth bit again and the teeth collected a tithe of his hair rather than his flesh. He unleashed a twisting backhand swing of his falchion and the blade cut into the devil's arm. Teeth snapped all around him as he spun, slashed, twisted, and leaped. He loosed a furious onslaught of slashes and stabs, his blade mostly bouncing off the devil's hide, but occasionally opening a scratch. The devil's arms swarmed around him, the fanged mouths snapping in the air, snatching at his clothes. He tried to lead the creature toward the edge of the floor that overlooked the Shelf, hoping to somehow trick the devil into falling over the side, but the devil did not come near when Nix retreated to the edge.

Egil stirred, one leg bending at the knee. Rakon, too, was trying to rise, still coughing and spitting blood. The devil cared nothing for either. He roared and lumbered at Nix.

Nix darted to the side, slashing defensively with his blade. He stumbled over the lead line of a thaumaturgic triangle and went down. He whirled to see the twin mouths on the end of the devil's arms streaking toward his face. He rolled to his side but too slow. One of the mouths closed on his arm, the sphincter of fangs twisting as it clamped down.

Blinding pain summoned a shout of agony from Nix. Blood poured from the wound, the devil's arm pulsing grotesquely as it nursed fluid from his arm. Nix slashed down with his falchion to dislodge the bite, once, twice, and the creature released his arm in a spray of blood.

He staggered backward, bleeding profusely, already weakening. The devil did not relent. His arms flailed for him, his mouths snarled and snapped, as he moved toward Nix on the thick cylinders of his legs.

Nix's eyes fell to the floor and a desperate stratagem occurred to him. He acted before he'd thought it through. He circled wide to draw the devil toward the binding circle inlaid into the wood. The moment the devil stepped within it, Nix dove forward on his belly, touched the activating glyph on the circle, and shouted a word in the Language of Creation.

Instantly the circle flared and a translucent green sphere of power encapsulated the devil: another prison for Abrak-Thyss, albeit a temporary one.

Realizing what had happened, the creature roared with frustration.

Nix scrabbled backward, bleeding, breathing hard, while the devil flailed his arms and railed his anger against his binding. Where he struck the sphere, sparks of energy flew. Nix knew the circle would not hold for long. He didn't know the proper incantation to use the glyph properly, and even if he did he doubted it could have held Abrak-Thyss for long.

"Stay there," he said to the creature, but couldn't even muster a grin.

Still bleeding from his shoulder, he turned around to find Rakon standing and Egil on all fours, coughing. The sorcerer eyed the bound devil, Nix, then Egil. Fear entered his expression and he ran for the half-open door. He staggered as he went, favoring his side, and Nix thought he'd make it, but Egil saw him, roared, scrambled to his feet, and proved the faster. The priest tackled Rakon right before the door and they went down in a scrum of arms and legs. The sorcerer was no match for Egil's strength and size, and almost instantly the priest was astride him, his huge fists slamming into Rakon's head and face again and again.

Rakon shrieked, wailed as blood sprayed, bone crunched, and teeth flew. The sorcerer held his hands up, feebly trying to grab Egil's thick arms or deflect the priest's furious onslaught, but to no avail. The old woman near the door looked on, a dazed look in her eyes, her hand to her mouth in shock.

"Egil!" Nix called, and stumbled toward him, trying to stanch the blood leaking from his shoulder.

But the priest either did not hear him or did not acknowledge him.

"Your own sisters!" Egil said, and hammered Rakon's face again, again. "Your own sisters! We saw it, you fakking monster! We saw it!"

The devil shrieked in rage, the binding circle sizzling as he tried to break free.

"Your own sisters!" Egil said again, repeating the phrase with every punch, the words a vengeful incantation.

Rakon went limp under him and still Egil did not stop. The priest would beat Rakon to death if Nix did not stop him.

"Your own sisters!"

Nix staggered to his friend's side, caught his right hand by the wrist.

Egil whirled on him, tears in his eyes, left hand cocked.

"You can't beat it out of you by beating him!" Nix said.

The priest stared at him, blinking, pain in his eyes.

"You can't, Egil," Nix said, more softly. "We saw it. We *felt* it, at least in part. It'll never be out."

Egil lowered his fists, looked over at the old woman. There were tears in her eyes, too. Egil slouched, started to weep.

Rakon groaned, his face a broken, bloody mess.

Behind them, the devil raged in his prison.

They didn't have much time.

"I have an idea," Nix said, staring at Rakon.

Egil looked up, his bushy brows raised in a question.

Nix glanced over at the old woman, who was trembling against the wall. "Get her for me, Egil."

"Nix..."

"I'm not going to hurt her. You know me better than that." He nodded at Rakon. "I'm going to hurt *him*. Get me Rusilla, if you'd prefer."

The devil's attack on the binding circle grew frenetic, his rage-filled slams against the magic causing it to spark and flare.

"Hurry," Nix said.

While Egil gathered Rusilla, Nix tore a strip of his clothing and did his best to tie off his shoulder wound. Egil laid Rusilla down gently on the floor near Nix. Her eyes were open and she stared into Nix's face.

"I'm touching only your hand," Nix said to her, not sure if she could hear him.

He took her hand in his, removed the transmutation wand from his satchel, and activated it with a word in the Mages' Tongue. Once more the gold cap glowed and the wand warmed in his hand.

"What are you doing?" Egil asked.

"Watch," he said, and touched it to Rusilla.

"I still don't see..." the priest said.

Nix then touched the wand to Rakon. "Let him experience what he intended for them."

Rakon's eyes snapped open as the magic poured into him. As the transformation began, his eyes widened and his mouth opened in a silent scream.

The sorcerer's facial features softened. His body lost height, gained hips, his waist narrowed, his chest swelled with breasts. In moments the magic had turned him from sorcerer to sorceress.

"What have you done to me?" Rakon said, his now high-pitched voice slurred. The transformation had healed some of his wounds. His face was bruised, red in places, but not the ruin Egil had left it moments before.

"You wanted to honor your damnable Pact, whoreson," Nix said, and jerked him to his feet. "So you will."

Accompanied by Egil, he dragged Rakon toward the devil, who still flailed and raged frenetically against his binding. Rakon seemed dazed, not quite understanding what Nix intended.

"Do you understand me, beast?" Nix said to Abrak-Thyss.

"The Pact demands a Norristru woman of child-bearing age."

Nix pulled Rakon toward the binding and shook him.

"I've brought you one."

The devil stopped struggling. The eyes at the end of his arms fixed on Nix. The slits in his abdomen, his nostrils, flared wetly as he inhaled Rakon's scent.

"What?" Rakon said, finally understanding, his voice high-pitched and feminine.

"Let's have our own pact, devil," Nix said, and shook Rakon again. "This one is yours. But the others are left alone. Do we have agreement?"

Rakon struggled against Nix's hold. Nix shook him like a rag doll. Rakon's fear seemed to excite the devil, to judge from the further engorgement of his member.

"I think he likes you," Nix said to Rakon. "I'm sure he'll be a gentle lover."

"No," Rakon said, swallowing, going limp in Nix's grasp. "You can't do this. You can't."

Nix pulled him around and stared into his – her – face.

"This is what you would have done to your sisters! This is the fear they felt. Worse than fear awaited them. I've seen it, Norristru. I've seen it! And now worse than fear awaits you. You've earned it."

"Don't do this," Rakon pleaded. Tears fell from his eyes.

"It's done!" Nix said, the anger in his words spraying Rakon with spit. "And you did it!"

Nix nodded at Egil and the priest withdrew, picked up Rusilla and Merelda, and carried them to the far side of the room. Egil recovered his hammers, his crowbar, and stood at the ready.

Nix turned to Abrak-Thyss, holding Rakon like an offering. "Devil, what say you?"

The devil growled, a low, predatory sound that reminded Nix of a cat's purr.

Without warning, the energy sphere around the binding circle winked out. Rakon screamed, sagged.

Nix shoved the sorcerer toward the devil and backed away fast toward Egil.

He drew his blade but needn't have worried. The devil grabbed Rakon around the waist with one of his serpentine arms. Rakon flailed, his small fists beating at the devil's grip, his screams high-pitched and fearful.

"Honor the deal, devil," Nix said, backing up until he bumped into Egil.

The devil did not even glance at them. Carrying Rakon, who screamed helplessly, the devil strode for the open door that led into the manse.

The old woman abased herself before the devil as he approached.

"Scion of the Thyss, welcome."

The devil neither paused nor acknowledged her. His girth barely fit through the doorway, but he squeezed through and inside, Rakon still screaming plaintively.

Nix knew where the devil was taking Rakon: to the hall of doors he'd seen in his dreams, a place of horror.

"It's worst the first time," the old woman called after Rakon. "It's easier after that. Take heart."

Rakon's screams were desperate. Nix endured them only by reminding himself of the generations of women who'd uttered similar screams as a result of the scheming of Rakon and his sires.

Egil shifted on his feet. "I don't know if that was the right thing to do."

Nix stared at the open door, the darkness beyond. "I don't know either. But death seemed... too neat an end for him. We both saw what'd been done here. If it was the wrong thing to do, it was my wrong thing."

"No," Egil said thoughtfully. "I'm with you. If it was wrong, then it's our wrong and we both own it."

"Well enough."

"We should go," Egil said.

"Aye."

Nix kneeled and looked into Rusilla's pale face, her intense green eyes. Her hands spasmed, probably some aftereffect of the drug her brother had been giving her.

"Can you hear me?" he asked her. "Do you know what I just did? Was it the right thing?"

They stared at one another a long while.

"The drugs, Nix," Egil said. "She can't answer."

Then her lips moved. She made no sound and he wasn't sure if the movement was intentional. He stared at her, willing her to mouth again what he thought he'd seen. She did and he read her lips.

Applause, Nix.

For a moment, he could think of nothing to say, then he stood and said, "I've been waiting for those."

Nix and Egil bound their wounds as best they could. They'd need to see a priestess of Orella when they returned to Dur Follin, maybe visit the Low Bazaar to procure a healing elixir or ten. But before leaving, they approached the old woman, Rusilla and Merelda's mother. She remained by the door, and at their approach hid her face behind the wall of her wrinkled, veiny hands. She rocked back and forth, muttering to herself.

"Is she... lost?" Nix asked.

"I think maybe," Egil said sadly.

"It's worse the first time," she muttered repeatedly. "Always worse the first time."

"Grandma..." Nix said.

She looked up between the gaps in her fingers. "Don't hurt me. Don't hurt an old woman."

At first Nix felt a surge of scorn, but it gave way to pity when he thought of Mamabird, thought of the pulsing doors of his dreams, the blood and screams, and what the poor woman must have endured in her youth.

"We won't hurt you, grandma."

"Of course we won't," Egil said. "You've been hurt enough."

She looked up at them, uncomprehending.

Nix kneeled to look into her face. "We're going to Dur Follin and we're taking Rusilla and Merelda. They can make their own lives there, free of... all this. You can come with us, if you wish."

She stared at him as if she didn't understand. Perhaps she didn't. Nix and Egil had destroyed the foundation of her world, as depraved and terrible as it had been.

"Do you hear me, grandma?"

Finally, she said, "This is my home. My son lives here with me. I can't leave. The Pact must be honored."

Nix did not bother to tell her that she no longer had a son, that the Pact was among the most depraved things Nix had ever seen. He looked up at Egil, who shrugged. Nix went to put his hand on the old woman's shoulder but she recoiled and he kept his touch to himself.

"You needn't ever be hurt by man or devil again," he said to her. "Pact or no Pact. Do you understand? Never again."

She looked past him, through him. "We are Norristru and we will honor the Pact. Rakon will honor it, preserve the line. House Thyss will be satisfied. We can rebuild our wealth..."

She went on like that for a time and Nix finally stood, shaking his head. She was what Norristru men had made her. Nix could not unmake her with his words; they had no such magic.

It was time to leave.

Bearing Rusilla and Merelda in their arms, they walked into and out of the Norristru manse. Nix was pleased to get out of the pain-haunted halls. They pretended not to hear Rakon's screams that carried through the cracked plaster on the walls.

The moment they stepped out under open sky, under Minnear's ghostly light, Nix swore.

"What is it?" Egil asked, turning, his free hand on a hammer haft.

Nix looked down at his feet. "I'm fakking barefoot."

Egil chuckled. Nix waited while the priest circled the grounds for a stable. He returned presently with saddled horses. They mounted the horses, Egil with Merelda, Nix with Rusilla. Nix felt awkward with his body pressed against Rusilla's, the smell of her hair in his nose. He reminded himself of recent events and banished all thoughts from his mind but the purest.

They spoke little as they rode away from the manse, heading for Zelchir's Fall, and from there, back to Dur Follin. After an hour of riding, the sisters could speak clearly, though their bodies were still mostly paralyzed by the drugs.

"Will the city be safe for you two?" Nix asked them.

"It's a big city," Merelda said. Her voice was lilting, musical. The sound of it made Nix smile.

"The Lord Mayor will be free of my brother's spells for the first time in years," Rusilla said. "When he realizes my brother had enspelled him..."

"Rakon will never enter Dur Follin again," Merelda said. "Oh, Rose! We're free."

"We are, Mere. At last."

"You will help us get situated when we arrive in the city," Rusilla said to Nix.

Nix chuckled, looked to Egil. "She gives orders like a noblewoman. And this time with her lips instead of her mind."

"Speaking of," Egil said, "how much of this did you plan from the beginning?"

"As much as I could," Rusilla answered.

"And how much of what we did was you and not us?" Egil asked her.

She looked off to the side and smiled, a secretive look. She was striking in profile, a strong jaw and regal nose. "Does it matter?"

"It matters," Nix said.

"Why?" she asked softly.

It mattered because he wanted to *be* that kind of man, not be made to *behave like* that kind of man. It mattered because he wanted to believe that the difference between him and Rakon Norristru was a gulf of moral sense, not opportunity and circumstances.

"It just does."

"Aye," Egil answered.

Rusilla was silent a long time. Minnear had vanished from the sky. Finally she said, "I don't know how much was me and how much was you. You have to answer that for yourself."

ACKNOWLEDGMENTS

To Marco and Lee, for believing in the book. To Leiber, Howard, Brackett, and Moorcock, for inspiring the book.

MEET EASIE DAMASCO...

KEEP YOUR HAND ON YOUR COIN PURSE, JUST IN CASE...

We are Angry Robot.

Web **angryrobotbooks.com**

... SF, F, WTF.

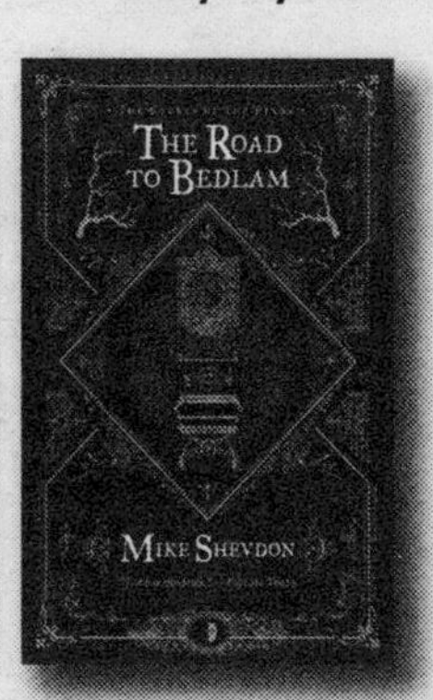

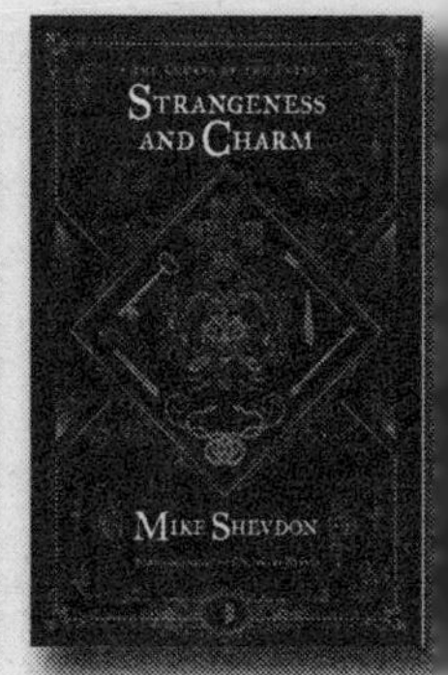

***Twitter* @angryrobotbooks**

WHO NEEDS FOOD?

Own the complete Angry Robot catalog

DAN ABNETT
- ☐ Embedded
- ☐ Triumff: Her Majesty's Hero

GUY ADAMS
- ☐ The World House
- ☐ Restoration

JO ANDERTON
- ☐ Debris
- ☐ Suited

LAUREN BEUKES
- ☐ Moxyland
- ☐ Zoo City

THOMAS BLACKTHORNE
- ☐ Edge
- ☐ Point

MAURICE BROADDUS
- ☐ King Maker
- ☐ King's Justice
- ☐ King's War

ADAM CHRISTOPHER
- ☐ Empire State

PETER CROWTHER
- ☐ Darkness Falling

ALIETTE DE BODARD
- ☐ Obsidian & Blood

MATT FORBECK
- ☐ Amortals
- ☐ Carpathia
- ☐ Vegas Knights

JUSTIN GUSTAINIS
- ☐ Hard Spell
- ☐ Evil Dark

GUY HALEY
- ☐ Reality 36
- ☐ Omega Point

COLIN HARVEY
- ☐ Damage Time
- ☐ Winter Song

CHRIS F HOLM
- ☐ Dead Harvest

MATTHEW HUGHES
- ☐ The Damned Busters
- ☐ Costume Not Included

Westminster Public Library
3705 W. 112th Ave.
Westminster, CO 80031
www.westminsterlibrary.org

TRENT JAMIESON
- ☐ Roil
- ☐ Night's Engines

K W JETER
- ☐ Infernal Devices
- ☐ Morlock Night

J ROBERT KING
- ☐ Angel of Death
- ☐ Death's Disciples

ANNE LYLE
- ☐ The Alchemist of Souls

GARY McMAHON
- ☐ Pretty Little Dead Things
- ☐ Dead Bad Things

ANDY REMIC
- ☐ The Clockwork Vampire Chronicles

CHRIS ROBERSON
- ☐ Book of Secrets

MIKE SHEVDON
- ☐ Sixty-One Nails
- ☐ The Road to Bedlam
- ☐ Strangeness & Charm

DAVID TALLERMAN
- ☐ Giant Thief

GAV THORPE
- ☐ The Crown of the Blood
- ☐ The Crown of the Conqueror

LAVIE TIDHAR
- ☐ The Bookman
- ☐ Camera Obscura
- ☐ The Great Game

TIM WAGGONER
- ☐ The Nekropolis Archives

KAARON WARREN
- ☐ Mistification
- ☐ Slights
- ☐ Walking the Tree

CHUCK WENDIG
- ☐ Blackbirds

IAN WHATES
- ☐ City of Dreams & Nightmare
- ☐ City of Hope & Despair
- ☐ City of Light & Shadow